SET LIST

After reading *Camp Redemption* and *Sweetwater Blues*, I became a serious fan of Raymond Atkins's writings. With his latest novel, *Set List*, I may have just become his *biggest* fan. The novel and its main character are more than a little identifiable to me personally. Blanchard Shankles is a sixty-year-old, life-long guitar player who has played in bands for over forty-five years. Now the rough life of a rock and roll musician is catching up with him, landing him in the hospital with serious heart problems and forcing him to look closer than ever into the deepest recesses of his own life. Atkins titles each chapter after a rock song, usually the songs that most of us players of that same age have performed countless times, from "Free Bird" to "Crazy Mama," "Lucky Man," and "Heart of Glass." The conversations and nostalgic memories discussed by Blanchard, and his songwriting partner John Covey, ignite a fire within those of us who recall the music with love and happiness. One side note that I found absolutely cool was Atkins including actual, complete lyrics of many songs penned by Shankles and Covey. *Set List* is an honest, well-written novel for anyone who longs for the days of Grand Funk Railroad, Black Sabbath, or the James Gang—a story of life, love, mortality, and music—a true rock and roll dream.

—Michael Buffalo Smith, author of *From Macon to Jacksonville*

Ray Atkins's *Set List* took me back to the times my cousin and I were running wild on the beach, popping in bars for a few sets, then making it on down the road. Maybe on some of those nights we were the girls who characters like Bad Boy Blanchard had singled out to sing "Brown Eyed Girl" or "Black Magic Woman" to. The thing is—the songs, the night, the moment—it all screamed "we are young and we shall live forever." And later when we realized, as Blanchard does, that may not be so true, the sound of the music always brings us back to possessing a time when life held no stop light. *Set List* is also a story of true friendship—the kind of bond the Celts called a soul friend. Someone who runs with you through all the back alleys and days of your life and knows you better than you know yourself. Atkins perfectly captures that friendship with Blanchard and Covey. Readers will make fast and furious friends with the *Set List* characters, follow them right out to the bus, and eagerly ride along to catch one last show.

—River Jordan, author of *The Messenger of Magnolia Street*

America boasts many authors who can make us feel at home in Buckingham Palace, the Taj Mahal, and various mansions of the rich and famous. There are far fewer artists who have the same flair for making us feel comfortable in unfamiliar yet commonplace happenings and walks of life. In the later decades of the twentieth century, full-time employment as a musician was no longer just for churches, orchestras, and music teachers; clubs and restaurants in all major cities supported live music, creating a large number of "blue collar" musicians who had no trouble finding work despite any lack of formal training. *Set List* takes the reader into that vibrant and colorful era we assumed would never end yet became extinct before our eyes. For those born too late, it's a glimpse of history. To those of us who lived it, *Set List* is a nostalgic reminder of all we lost. There is no present-day miracle as wonderful as playing real music on a real stage for real money: I feel incredibly sad for all the coming generations of musicians who will never know this experience. Thank you, Raymond Atkins, for remembering those days and their accompanying sound track. As my hair greys, my fingers wither, and my mind is present less and less, it's great to know that this book will be there to take me back…

—Elaine Drennon Little, author of *A Southern Place*

Raymond Atkins is a chameleon. This time he is an aging rocker with a heart broken by life and lifestyle, but that's not why you read this or any of his books. You read Raymond Atkins to laugh, to marvel at description and insight, to see yourself in each of the characters he swears are fictional, and to understand yourself and your fellow man a little better. This time, however, he's taking his readers back, back, back to long summer nights of little sleep with the hum of a box fan wedged in a window while the dim glow of the green light on a Pioneer stereo receiver plays the soundtrack of youth pressed forever on vinyl. That he can take us back there, is but one of his gifts.

—Shari Smith, author of *I Am a Town*
and publisher/creator at Working Title Farm

Other books by Raymond L. Atkins

The Front Porch Prophet

Sorrow Wood

Camp Redemption

Sweetwater Blues

South of the Etowah

Set List

SET LIST

A Novel

Raymond L. Atkins

MERCER UNIVERSITY PRESS | *Macon, Georgia*
2018

MUP/ H953

Published by Mercer University Press
1501 Mercer University Drive
Macon, Georgia 31207

9 8 7 6 5 4 3 2 1

Books published by Mercer University Press are printed on acid-free
paper that meets the requirements of the American National Standard for
Information Sciences—Permanence of Paper for Printed Library
Materials.

Printed and bound in Canada.

This book is set in Adobe Caslon and American Typewriter

ISBN   978-0-88146-666-9
eBook   978-0-88146-667-6
Cataloging-in-Publication Data is available from the Library of
Congress

If you believe in magic, come along with me
We'll dance until morning 'til there's just you and me
And maybe, if the music is right
I'll meet you tomorrow, sort of late at night
And we'll go dancing, baby, then you'll see
How the magic's in the music and the music's in me
—John Sebastian

A long long time ago
I can still remember how
That music used to make me smile
And I knew if I had my chance
That I could make those people dance
And maybe they'd be happy for a while
—Don McLean

My gift is my song, and this one's for you
—Elton John, Bernie Taupin

Thanks and appreciation to my lovely wife, Marsha, who once again did not throw me out when I decided to write another book. Thanks to Mercer University Press for the continued support of my efforts, and to my editor, Kelley Land. Thanks to my great friend Dwight Cassity, for setting the words to music. Thanks to all the music makers who have provided the songs that comprise the set lists of our lives. And finally, special thanks to Bill Anderson, Greg Strayhorn, Danny Coots, Devann Jackson, and Randy Barkley, longhaired wild boys who stood with me under the lights back when the world was new.

Contents

SET LIST

Prologue

Blanchard Shankles stood on the makeshift stage with his timeworn 12-string guitar. Blanchard's band, Skyye, was playing a street dance to celebrate the arrival of summer, and Friday night revelers thronged the area in front of the stage. Behind him on a riser nailed together from old pallets, Ford Man Cooper tightened the head on his snare drum. He tapped, and twisted, and tapped some more until he had the tone just so. To Blanchard's left, Jimbo Tant gently strummed his Gibson as he searched for the sour note he had heard during the previous song. He frowned and plucked at the A string, then turned the tuning key to make a slight adjustment. To Blanchard's right, facing the rest of the band rather than the audience, Tucker McFry stood behind his keyboards and took a small sip of beer. John Covey, the bassist, also stood to the right of Blanchard, and a bit behind him. His back was to the crowd, and he was talking to Simpson Taggart, Skyye's roadie. Chicken Raines, the band's lead singer, stood at the mic center stage, next to Blanchard. He was in his Robert Palmer phase and stood shirtless, bantering with the crowd between songs.

It was the first Friday night in May, and the air was warm and humid in the Georgia twilight, but not yet hot and nasty, which was how it would be in another month or so. Blanchard glanced at the set list taped to the side of Covey's amp and saw that the next song up was "Hotel California" by the Eagles. He turned and nodded to Simpson at the control panel, and the stage illumination dimmed. The amplifier lights shone red and green in the darkness like miniature Christmas decorations. Blanchard kicked off with the intro, and as the crowd realized what was being played, cheers arose from among them. Blanchard stretched the haunting first notes of the song into three repetitions rather than the usual two before Ford Man fell in with the first distinctive drum beats and Chicken began to sing: *On a dark desert highway, cool wind in my hair....* As Blanchard played, he watched the crowd as he always did. He enjoyed seeing the faces of the people who came to hear him and the rest of the boys play. It was a fine evening—if not in the world at large then at least in the Georgia foothills.

Blanchard spotted her at the lead break, right when Jimbo Tant cut loose on the Gibson. She was dancing slowly, off by herself, moving in time with the rhythms of her inner music, the songs in her head that were hers alone, never to be transcribed or sung by others, never to be shared with a sweaty crowd on a Friday night. She looked thirty-ish, and she was pretty in a tired and melancholy way. She bent down to pick something up, and Blanchard saw that she was actually dancing with a hula-hoop. There were three little girls gathered about her who each bore hula-hoops of their own and more than just a passing resemblance to the woman. Blanchard guessed that she was their mama, and that she had brought them out for a night under the stars. As he watched, she slid the hoop up to her midriff and started it spinning once again. The hoop worked its lazy way down from her waist, to her hips, to her thighs, and finally to her knees before dropping once again to the cracked asphalt.

She bent to retrieve it, and one of the girls leaned in close and spoke to her. The woman nodded, and the three little ones dropped their hoops in unison and ran with excited abandon toward the refreshment stand that had been set up for the event. The woman tracked them to their destination, and once they were safely there, she started her hoop again. She closed her eyes, and a slight, sad smile was on her lips. Blanchard wondered where she was. Physically, of course, she was dancing with her little girls on the warm street in front of the old Sequoyah depot, taking a pleasant break from a world of trouble and bother. But Blanchard could tell that in her head she was traveling to other places. The music was taking her on a passage to younger, better times, perhaps, days without unsatisfying jobs, constant bills, demanding husbands, and the never-ending worry of children, days when all things were possible and her life was a bare page before her, waiting for the pen strokes as she wrote each chapter with the benefit of hindsight. Or maybe she was meandering among the unexplored dreams still forming out on the misty horizon, gently touching and examining the gravid possibilities of worlds that were not yet reality, but could be with a small measure of luck, a great deal of courage, and the iron will just to take a deep breath and leap.

Blanchard watched her as he played. Her hula-hoop had spiraled once more to earth, and her little girls had come straight back to their mama, bearing stale popcorn, watery sno-cones, and melted candy bars, all courtesy of the Sequoyah Indians Band Boosters. She smiled fondly as she kissed the smallest one, patted the middle one on top of the head, and spoke to the oldest, perhaps thanking her for her excellent supervision of the short excursion for treats, and for doing such a fine job taking care of her sisters. Then she picked up her hoop and began again. Blanchard smiled even as he added his voice to the chorus: *Plenty of room at the Hotel California....* Tonight, she was the one. Tonight, he played for her.

"Heart of Glass"
Blondie
Sunday: First Day

Blanchard Shankles sat in the hospital room and stared out the window at the cars as they went about their automotive business. They were just one smudged and brittle pane of glass away from him, out in the land of the healthy and the free, but it seemed as if they were in another reality altogether, an alternate dimension in which there were no wars, famines, or chest pains to plague mankind in general and guitar players in particular. Blanchard was an aging musician, a large, rough-looking man crashing hard toward sixty who had been playing rock and roll for the past forty-five years. His current band was called Murphy's Law, the latest and most likely final iteration of a group of musicians who had first come together in Sequoyah, Georgia, way back in 1970, when he and John Covey had gathered their friends and formed a group known as Skyye.

It was late afternoon. The orange sun was already slowly dipping below the tops of the trees that held back the horizon, and it would soon be dark. Blanchard was not normally covetous, but he envied the random motorists, if for no other reason than because they were out *there*. He, on the other hand, was in *here*, and that was the crux of the problem. He knew it was foolish to be jealous of strangers' freedoms, and unfair, but there was no avoiding the fact that he was. If he were out there with them, in a '69 Mustang, maybe, or a vintage GTO, he would aim the front fender toward the setting sun, turn up the radio until the speakers rattled in distress, drop that baby in gear, and follow the twilight all the way to the Pacific Ocean. Once there he would slam on the brakes and lock the car down at the land's end, sliding up sideways until the tires met the gray-green sea. Then he would get out and stand in the surf, bare toes clenching the sand as he breathed in the salt air and embraced the night.

"Lucky bastards," he said to the cars in the road below, but they did not hear his words.

Blanchard realized that each and every person in those vehicles might be dealing with calamities perhaps even worse than his own, troubles that would make his present difficulties seem petty, but foolishness was a hobby of his. It made the time pass, he was quite good at it, and he saw no reason to change, particularly at this uncertain stage of his life. As it was, he was trying hard to not dwell upon his predicament at all, which was a bit like the old saw about avoiding thoughts of pink elephants. The more he tried to think about anything besides his aching, stuttering heart, the harder the pink elephants stomped on it and made the damn thing hurt even more.

"Kill me or leave me alone," he growled at his latest twinge. As if to remind him that he was not in charge, an additional sharp pain burst across his chest like blue chain lightning on a scorched summer's day.

He was actually supposed to be in the hospital bed several feet across the room, keeping calm and not dying, rather than sitting by the window watching strangers motoring the roads, but if there was a chance that he was about to kick the big bucket anyway, and that did seem to be one possible outcome of his current situation, then he was going to do it sitting up, and both his misbehaving heart and his unsympathetic cardiologist could get over it. It was his life while it lasted, and he would live it as he wished, just as he always had. Part of his intransigence stemmed from the fact that it had always bothered him to be in a prone position during the daylight hours. While engaging in his occupation as a guitar player in a bar band, he worked primarily at night, but even so, he slept very little during the day. He liked to claim that he had been raised by wolves, but they had been wolves who believed that a person should be up and about his or her business while the sun shone. They had instilled this obsession into their son, along with a few other trifling quirks, and old habits, like old rockers, tend to die hard.

Now his parents were long gone and mostly forgotten, two wasted people—one sad and crazy, the other a scoundrel on his good days and as malevolent as a demon on his bad—who had left nothing behind but a clutch of wretched memories, two cheap headstones, and Blanchard and his sister, plus Blanchard's peculiar, rowdy ways.

His other reason for sitting in the chair rather than lying in the bed was simply that he was stubborn—Shankles stubborn, some would say—and did not like to be told what to do. This condition was just as hereditary as his narrow and fragile coronary arteries, and he could not do much about either. He felt sure that one or the other would eventually do him in, and the smart money was on the proposition that it might turn out to be a combination of both, and that it would happen sooner rather than later, given recent developments.

So he had waited for everyone in attendance to his ailment to leave the hospital room—the unpleasant nurse who had relieved him of his hidden second pack of cigarettes, the agreeable nurse who had fluffed his pillow and patted his cheek, the lady from the dining hall with the bad news about the lack of supper tonight and of breakfast in the morning, and the woebegone members of his band, six sad companions, each more uncomfortable than the last to see Blanchard humbled and brought low—and then he had wiggled his way under and around the tubes and wires connecting him to the world of modern medicine and moved slowly from the uncomfortable bed to the equally uncomfortable recliner by the window. It was the principle of the thing.

The effort had cost him a hard stab of jaw pain, a clamber of angina that drew itself across his pectorals like a nicked and rusty blade, and a breathless moment when his heart danced wildly under his breastbone like Fred Astaire on bad speed. At that point he had thought that he might have pushed his luck one too many times, and that his mortal coil had begun to shuffle, but finally he completed the task he had set for himself and managed the six slow paces from where he had arbitrarily been placed to where he arbitrarily wanted to be. He declared a silent victory for free will and the luxury of choice even as he acknowledged that he had, once again, nearly killed himself in the process of exercising it.

"That was...really...stupid," he said, breathless, to no one at all as he achieved his goal. His heart skipped a beat, faltered, and then caught back up as if agreeing with the sentiment.

Covey would fuss when he returned from the coffee machine and found Blanchard sitting, of course, but Covey fussed about most things, so why should today be any different? Anyway, Blanchard had always found it much easier when misbehaving to say he was sorry after the fact than to obtain permission before. Covey was already a touch angry at him for driving himself to his own cardiac emergency, so Blanchard knew he was in for a small portion of grief no matter what he did. Covey was the bass player in Murphy's Law. He and Blanchard had been a team for many long years, playing music, traveling the country, and writing songs while searching for their big break and the elusive success that always seemed just one tune ahead of them. They knew each other like they knew the calluses on their own fingertips, had no secret that the other did not know, and had both pretty much given up as a useless endeavor ever changing the other's ways.

"You should have called me," Covey had said early that morning when he arrived at Blanchard's side in the ER. "I would have brought you down here." Blanchard had received this information while flat on his back on a rolling bed in a curtained cubicle, wired to a monitor, plumbed to an IV bag, and cuffed to an automatic blood pressure machine. He was wearing a faded blue hospital gown and his dingo boots. His thinning hair was bound in a loose ponytail. It was brown and sported a few casual streaks of gray, as if it were considering changing colors but had not yet fully committed to the enterprise. His bony white legs were extra pale under the flickering fluorescent lighting, especially in contrast to the scuffed black leather of his footwear, and they looked pitiful, as if they had been very sick, and thus their owner had brought them in for treatment. There was no hair at all on them below the knee and very little above, a condition that had earned Blanchard the occasional nickname of Velvet Leg.

"I was closer to here than I was to you when my heart started acting up," Blanchard said in defense of his actions. This was an untruth, but Covey did not necessarily need to hear the unvarnished version, and Blanchard was in no mood to tell it.

Murphy's Law had played three sets the night before at a road bar called Grumpy's near Gallatin, Tennessee. It had been a Saturday night crowd, raucous almost to the point of unruly, but there had been no trouble aside from a drunken heckle or two. After the show, the rest of the band had adjourned to their rooms at the Day's Inn, but Blanchard always had a hard time winding down after playing a

8

date and had been visiting an after-hours club he knew not too far from Grumpy's. He was sipping bourbon, smoking a Marlboro 100, and minding his own business while looking with fondness and a linger of sadness at a woman who reminded him of his deceased wife when his heart let him know, firmly, that it wished for some medical attention. Blanchard had driven himself and his aching heart to his motel room—three doors up from his bass player's accommodations—where he had then pretended for a couple of hours that what was happening wasn't actually happening. It was only after this unsuccessful attempt to will his heart to behave as it ought that he decided to seek a second opinion and drove to the closest hospital.

"I was having a drink and a smoke when all of a sudden it felt like someone hit me in the chest with a baseball bat," Blanchard told Covey when they met at the ER. He was not prone to idle hyperbole, and this observation was not an example of such. He had, in fact, once been whacked across the chest with a baseball bat—wooden, not aluminum—while earnestly trying to put distance between himself and two raucous bikers who had taken a dislike to him on general principle during a bar fight in Baton Rouge, so he knew what he was talking about. "Once I could stand up and get my breath, I figured it would be quicker to just drive straight here. So I did."

Covey shook his head. "You drove yourself to your own heart attack in a worn-out tour bus."

It was true that the bus, like Blanchard, had seen better days. Blanchard and Covey had bought it third- or maybe fourth-hand from an RV wholesaler named Tex who claimed that it had once belonged to Charlie Daniels, and that "The Devil Went Down to Georgia" had been written right there in the back seat of the venerable coach. They both liked that song but doubted this pedigree, even though Tex had sworn to it with his hand resting upon a pocket-sized Bible he carried, apparently for just such contingencies, but it was a pretty good bus nonetheless, tires notwithstanding, provided they remembered to feed its oil addiction and only use the cranky onboard privy in cases of dire emergency.

"It takes a real man to do something like that," Blanchard had replied absently, wishing that Covey would just let it be. He was breathing slowly, watching the monitor while trying to manually lower his blood pressure and hopefully minimize the random jolts emanating from his tender heart.

"It takes a dumb ass to do that," Covey said. "What are you, twelve? You don't screw around with your heart! Every time I start to think you have finally outgrown being a dumb ass, you go and do something that only a dumb ass would do. Then I have to reset the clock and start over. When you manage to kill yourself one of these days, I'm going to replace you with Simpson Taggart. It will serve you right."

Simpson had been their roadie since the band's earliest days. They had never actually needed a road crew, even if it only employed one person, but Simpson had grown up with them and had always wanted to play with the band. There was a problem with that particular dream, however, in that he had a tin ear, two left hands, no rhythm, and couldn't catch a tune in a washtub full of glue. But since neither Blanchard nor Covey had it in them to dash Simpson's dreams, and in light of the fact that Covey was married to Simpson's sister and wished to keep peace in the family, they had always brought him along on the road and somehow managed to pay him. Over time he had evolved into a pretty fair sound man, a passably competent roadie, and he really enjoyed driving the bus on top of all that, so they kept him on.

"Simpson knows three songs, and he only knows one of them good enough to play in front of a crowd." Blanchard coughed, and it made his diseased heart hurt like frozen anguish. "He can't be me. Some nights even *I* have a hard time being me. I'm almost a legend." Covey rolled his eyes. "If I do die, you may have to hire two guys to replace me." It seemed strange to Blanchard to be speaking of life after his departure from it, but Covey had brought it up, and he had been bantering with him for so many years that he supposed he could do it on automatic.

"Anyone can manage to sound halfway decent if they have a strong bass player backing them up, Velvet Leg."

"I hate that name. Why does Clapton get a cool nickname like Slow Hand, but I get Velvet Leg?"

"He got to pick first. Velvet Leg was all that was left."

"Bite me."

"Anyway, if you're a dead legend, it won't matter anymore. And if you kill yourself, I swear I'll do it. I'll put Simpson up on stage, hand him your Strat, and let him jam."

Blanchard was particular about his guitars. He had three—a beat-up Les Paul Gibson, a ragged Fender Stratocaster, and a flat top 12-string Ovation with a small hole worn through the body—and he didn't like for anyone even to touch them, never mind play them.

"The crowd will love him," Covey continued, warming to his theme. "Promoting him up from the ranks like that will give hope to roadies everywhere. We could even let him play without his pants on, like Flea does sometimes." He was referring to the bass player for the Red Hot Chili Peppers, who had been named, apparently, after his mama's favorite biting parasite and who occasionally liked to let it all hang out when performing.

"I see how you are now," Blanchard said. "I gave you the best years of my life, carried you along for the ride all this time like a bad case of the clap, and this is how you thank me." He coughed again, and his heart skipped like a yard sale LP and fluttered like a drunken butterfly before it finally found a rhythm it could manage. "I've seen Simpson with his pants off, by the way. You better tell that boy to keep his britches on and his hands off my guitars. His legs look worse than mine do."

"Not even close," Covey said, gesturing at his lead guitar player's current attire. "His velvet leg is not nearly as sleek as yours. Have you started shaving those things? When you get a chance, by the way, that gown is supposed to tie in the back." It was a terrible sight, but Covey supposed he had seen worse. "Why didn't you at least call an ambulance when you started having trouble? You might have died driving here."

"I might have died in an ambulance, too," Blanchard pointed out.

"Well, then, you could have wrecked the bus, driving it like that, and the rest of us would have had to walk home. It's a long way on foot over Monteagle Mountain."

"A little exercise would do all of you boys some good," Blanchard said. "Every one of you is getting a little paunchy. Anyway, I was at

Eddie's. You know it's not the kind of place where it's okay to call 911."

Covey nodded. He did know. Eddie was generally only about a half step, if that, ahead of trouble with the law, and he would be slow to forgive anyone who intentionally summoned the authorities to his establishment, regardless of the need.

"And I didn't have my phone with me anyhow," Blanchard continued. This was no surprise. He was a relative failure as a citizen of the new millennium and could not manage most days to stay connected to the world at large, although to be truly honest, he didn't have much interest in the concept and didn't try very hard. His view on the subject of telecommunication ran to the supposition that if someone really needed to speak with him, they could just come find him. It wasn't that hard to do.

"Dumb ass," Covey repeated yet again. He seemed to be developing a definite fondness for the phrase. It rolled smoothly across his tongue like good Scotch.

"Hand me a smoke," Blanchard said. "I'm about to die for a cig. They took mine away from me when I checked into this joint." He reached out his hand and waited for a lit one to appear, as if by magic.

"I heard they started with the one hanging from your lip when you walked in," Covey said, shaking his head. "Did you really stroll into the emergency room smoking a cigarette and then grind it out on the floor?"

"What was I supposed to do? They told me to get rid of it, but there wasn't an ashtray in sight! You know I smoke when I'm nervous, so I lit one before I came in to kind of take my mind off my heart. You'd have thought I had walked in with a gun in my hand! They got real huffy, real quick, and me standing there sick. It's no secret how bad I react to huffy." It was true. Blanchard had always hated huffiness, and he tended to dig right in whenever he encountered it. It was one of life's ironies that he generally responded to huffy with huffier bordering on huffiest. He became that which he detested, but he did not realize that about himself, or at least wouldn't admit it.

"They got huffy because you can't smoke in here. It's a hospital! You were probably leaned up against a NO SMOKING sign while you lit up." This was just a guess on Covey's part, but since he had seen Blanchard do just that before, it wouldn't have been out of character.

"What better place is there to smoke than in a hospital?" Blanchard asked. "I'm already hooked up to the machines, and there's doctors and nurses everywhere, and all kinds of serious medicine. If I die, all they have to do is jump me off. You could probably get Simpson to do it. He has to jump start the bus all the time."

Covey had a momentary vision of Simpson Taggart leaning over Blanchard, clamping the jumper cables to his nipples, then leaning back and hollering, "Okay, try it now!" He shook his head to try to clear the mental picture, but it wouldn't quite go away. "No smokes," he repeated as he gestured at their surroundings. "They have sick people in here, including you, and all kinds of stuff that will explode. Even if they allowed it, I wouldn't give you one. So put your mind on something else."

"You smoke!" Blanchard said. The unfairness of the no-smoking rule was heavy upon him, like a ballast stone. Knowing Covey as he did, he realized he would lose this struggle, but sometimes the battle was the point.

"Yep. As a matter of fact, I'm going to step outside in a bit and have one. But I don't have heart trouble, so maybe it won't kill me on the spot when I do. You, on the other hand, do have heart trouble, and it might. It won't hurt you to hold off for a day or two, at least until they get you straightened out. A little fresh air in those lungs might do you some good."

"Fresh air is overrated. Have some respect for a dying man!" Blanchard tended to talk with the aid of his hands, and he tried to point to himself to punctuate his sentiment and almost pulled out his IV needle. "That hurt. See what you made me do?" A spot of blood appeared in his IV tube right behind the needle. It shone bright red against the backdrop of his pale arm. "You ought to slip me a puff or two because you made me hurt myself."

"Blanchard, you're sick! No smokes. No drinks. No sex. No drugs. No anything. Just lay there and be quiet. Rest. Do what the doctor tells you. Think good thoughts. Take a nap."

"Just one drag? I won't even inhale it much."

Covey shook his head. He had made his decision and would not be swayed, no matter how cruelly his guitar player begged. "Knock it off," he said. "Asking for a cigarette while you're flat on your back in the hospital with chest pains, surrounded by sick people? How crazy is that, even for you? You always do this. You have to get right up in life's face, poke it in the eye, and dare it to do something about it if it has the guts. And if anyone should know that life absolutely has the guts, it's you. Don't tempt fate, or it'll take you down."

"I think God hates me," Blanchard said in a petulant tone. "I ask for a smoke, and I get a lecture." He looked up at the ceiling of his cubicle.

"God?" Covey asked, smiling. "Really? You want to bring God into this? You think He has a pack of smokes tucked in his shirt pocket, and maybe He'll bum you one? He ain't studying on you at all, even if you do have a death wish."

"Oh, no," Blanchard said, shaking his head. "I forgot it's Sunday. You always get religious on Sunday. It's one of your most annoying habits." He shifted, rubbed his chest, and shifted again. "Well, that and knocking on wood before we start every show. Nice talk with the death wish, by the way. Real upbeat stuff. Thanks for being there for me, buddy. Keep it up and you'll have me out of here in no time, fit as a bluegrass fiddler."

"Hanging around with you for most of my life has brought me to Jesus for my own protection," Covey replied. "It's kind of like a spiritual flak jacket I wear so that when the lightning bolt hits you, I won't end up as collateral damage, taken out by the shrapnel."

"The lightning bolt has hit," Blanchard said. "You're safe."

"Your heart trouble is nothing personal on His part, you know. He doesn't have it out for you. You are not on the Big Radar. He's not going to kill you, or cure you, for that matter, but you're going to end up killing yourself if you don't start taking this whole thing a little more seriously."

"What's that the Bible says about sparrows?" Blanchard asked. His eyes ached, and he closed them. He wished he had a warm washcloth. And a cigarette. And maybe a half pint of Four Roses. And a joint of black Jamaican. And a sweet woman with a fondness in her heart for him and him alone to help administer these treatments, and to stroke his hair and tell him softly that everything was going to be all right.

"The Bible? Really? You—Blanchard Shankles—are using the Bible to make a point?" Covey really wasn't expecting that and was momentarily taken aback. "Have you ever even read it?"

"I have. Every word of it, which is more than I can say for you, I bet. You should know this one. It's easy. Sunday school stuff." He looked at Covey with raised eyebrows.

"Let me think. Something about how one can't fall to the ground without Him knowing about it? Is that how it goes?" Covey had no issues with some of the more reasonable parts of the Bible, but he was no scholar on the subject and could not quote chapter and verse.

"There you go," Blanchard said, his case apparently made for him by Saint Luke, Apostle of Christ. "If that's true, then God knows just exactly what's going on this morning. He knows who I am, and where I am, and why I'm here, and He hasn't done a thing about any of it." His head really hurt, a deep ache that pounded behind his eyes and throbbed down into his neck like a pile driver. If it didn't ease up soon, he might throw up.

"How do you know He didn't keep you from dying until you got here?" Covey asked. "Maybe the battery on the bus was dead, but He let it crank up anyway. Or maybe He jabbed you in the heart in the first place, just to get your attention because you're kind of stubborn." Blanchard looked at him with an odd expression, as if he had not thought of that. "Anyway, it's funny how you can use the Bible to prove a point when it suits you while ignoring it the rest of the time." It was true. The lead guitar player for Murphy's Law was prone to play the devil's advocate when the mood was on him, which was most of the time he was awake and sometimes when he was not. He didn't care which side of an argument he was on, usually, just as long as he was solidly engaged in the debate.

In his heart of hearts, the one without any arterial blockages at all, Blanchard knew that what Covey had said was true and that he did occasionally tempt fate, but he believed in a personal relationship with the Almighty that included accountability for all involved. Thus he, Blanchard, had lived a relatively good life, all things considered. He hadn't been perfect by any stretch, but he had been as good a man as he knew how to be and had always tried to be a better one than he was. Doing both had been difficult for him, and he wanted credit for the attempt. He had been nice to widows, orphans, and puppies, and as a reward for doing the right things most of the time and living like a decent human ought, he felt that not being brought down by heart trouble while minding his own business was a reasonable expectation, especially considering the many disgustingly healthy rat bastards he knew who were out there running with the wind at their backs, wild and free like antelope on the Serengeti. In his worldview it was just that simple. He had scratched God's ethereal back, in a manner of speaking, even up there at that spot between the shoulder blades where it was hard to reach. And now he had an itch under his sternum that needed some attention. As explained in the Golden Rule, it was a quid pro quo situation.

"I really don't like having a bad heart," Blanchard said, steering the subject away from sparrows, omniscience, and the supposedly benign neglect of the cosmos, and instead navigating toward a much smaller issue. "It cuts into my drinking and smoking time, which is important to me. Plus, I've been thinking about trying to find another wife lately, and this heart business might get in the way."

"You've had a wife. And you have a girlfriend."

"She doesn't like me all that much. I think I might want a better one."

"I understand."

"So if I find a new girl and she marries me, how am I going to keep her happy if I can't perform my husbandly duties without falling over dead?"

"That could be a problem," Covey admitted. "At least for her."

"I don't want to give my new wife a complex," Blanchard said. He could see how accidentally killing a man while making love to him could really put a girl off sex.

Blanchard had been married just once over the years; the marriage had ended badly, and he had never had the heart to try it again. He liked women, but he had only ever loved one. It was Covey's opinion that the core issue was that his friend was just not the remarrying kind, and that he should quit while he was behind, but he kept this point of view to himself lest his lead guitar player feel compelled to marry a random stranger right there in the emergency room, perhaps the woman in the adjacent cubicle wearing the compression bandage, as a rebuttal to Covey's judgment that it was a bad idea.

"I know you don't like having a bad heart," Covey said. "I wouldn't like it, either. I really do get it, but pretending you don't have it is not going to make it go away. You've been trying that, and it's not working. None of us is getting any younger, you know, and you're not exempt from the clock ticking any more than I am. Did you at least have your nitro tablets with you last night?" Blanchard had been prone to angina for the past couple of years and had taken to carrying a small bottle of nitroglycerine tablets as a preventative measure, or at least to occasionally having the prescription refilled when he remembered to.

"I think I left them with my phone," he admitted. In addition to being a failure as a citizen of the new millennium, Blanchard was a disappointment as a cardiac patient as well, and had never actually managed to be in possession of his medicine when the chest pains came to call. It was as if his pills knew when trouble was coming and went and hid, lest they be called upon to render assistance. Whenever his heart took a notion to act up, the pills were always in his other pants, or out on the bus, or at the pharmacy waiting to be picked up, or sitting on the dresser back in the motel room right next to his cell phone. Whenever that happened, and it had been happening with greater frequency as time passed, he would dutifully stub out the Marlboro 100 he was smoking, take a deep, cleansing breath and let it out slowly, and administer a medicinal taste or two of bourbon if he had it, which he usually did. Generally, when treated with this homeopathic remedy, his ticker would settle down and try to behave for a while. But not this time. This time it had been cranky and wanted special attention. It had been abused and ignored long enough, and it had caught an ugly mood as a result of this neglect.

"You have to start doing better than you have been," Covey repeated. "If I lose you, I'm out of a job. I'm too old to break in another guitar player. It took me this long to get you up to speed. I don't have another forty-five years to spend on your replacement."

The curtain had whisked open at that point. A harried-looking nurse entered the cubicle, smiled distractedly as she busied about her patient, and advised Blanchard that it was time to go for a visit with the cardiologist, his heart catheter, and the likelihood of bad news.

"I'm feeling a whole lot better," Blanchard lied hopefully to the nurse as she pulled off his boots and placed them carefully in a plastic bag in the corner. She slipped a pair of blue ankle socks onto his feet and rearranged his gown so that it covered most of what it was meant to. Then she draped him with a thin blanket that managed to cover the rest.

"That is very good news!" the nurse said. She unclipped the leads from the heart monitor, removed the blood pressure cuff, and unplugged his IV. Then she raised the rails on his bed and stepped on the pedal to disengage the brake. "We still have to do the test, though. Just to rule out trouble."

"She means she knows you're lying, and you still look like death on a biscuit," Covey said as he gently patted Blanchard on the shoulder. "Except for the little socks. Those are nice. You should wear some of those all the time. You've been looking a little puffy lately, and they really slim your ankles. Do what the doctor says, and we'll have you back in heels in no time."

"You remember a little while ago when I told you to bite me?" Blanchard asked.

"Uh huh."

"I meant that."

Covey reached out and clasped his friend's hand for a moment as the nurse rolled him from his cubicle in the emergency room toward the coronary catheter lab. "If I don't come back," Blanchard continued, "do not let Simpson Taggart play my guitars. He can cook on my grill, but hands off the Strat." Covey nodded. He hadn't even needed to be told.

"CORRIE"
(Blanchard Shankles/John Covey)

Took a left at the church and a right at the shack
Sped a half a mile down past the railroad track
Drove the old dirt road to the back valley quarry
Dove the far deep end with my sweet girl Corrie

I wrote the first page of my life's love story
In over my head with my sweet girl Corrie

Water cool and green as her emerald eyes
On a summer's day hot as her firm brown thighs
I wasn't sure then what I thought I might find
But I prayed and I hoped I could make her mine

I wrote the first page of my life's love story
In over my head with my sweet girl Corrie

Her smile as bright as the heart of the moon
Her embrace as warm as the Ides of June
Her hair as soft as the summer breeze
Her eyes as deep as the bottomless seas

I wrote the first page of my life's love story
In over my head with my sweet girl Corrie

Days turned to years and my hair to gray
But I'll never forget that lazy fine day
When a kiss became two and two turned ten
And I knew she was mine right there and then

I wrote the first page of my life's love story
In over my head with my sweet girl Corrie

Took a left at the church and a right at the shack
Sped a half a mile down past the railroad track
Drove the old dirt road to the back valley quarry
Dove the far deep end with my sweet girl Corrie

I wrote the first page of my life's love story
In over my head with my sweet girl Corrie

"Crazy Mama"
J. J. Cale
-1969-

Long before Blanchard Shankles ever even thought about having a bad heart, his mother, Edna, went completely insane. She had been flirting with the idea for years and had conducted a few scouting expeditions into the darkness at various times during her adult life, but those had been brief two- or three-day dalliances with the Lords of Madness and nothing to get into a twist about. But when her scalawag of a husband, Benton, plopped her down in Sequoyah, Georgia, in 1967 and left her and her two children to mostly fend for themselves while he spent his spare time pursuing loose women, hard liquor, and the broken promises of lost youth, she discarded all pretense of normalcy and became, as her spouse poetically phrased it at every opportunity, "as crazy as a sack full of shithouse rats," which was to say, crazy indeed. From the time she stepped off the edge until the day Benton died, he used her insanity as an excuse for his tomfoolery, although in point of fact, his roguishness had been one of if not *the* main precipitating factor in her final decline, rather than a result of it. That was Blanchard's opinion, at least, and it was up near the top of the extensive list of reasons he disliked the man with an intensity not often seen between father and son. Subsequent to his mother's fall into the lower, darker realms of her mind, he hated his father even more.

In his later years, after he had reached adulthood and acquired perspective, or at least a better vocabulary, Blanchard came to the realization that an unrealistic ideal had finally carried his mother away, which did not lessen his father's culpability in the least. When she had married, at eighteen to the first man who asked her, she had done so with the understanding that this was what she was supposed to do, that it was her purpose in life. In the natural order of things, it was why she was here. She was expected to marry a man, have his children, keep his house, and in all ways be a good and loving wife to that husband of hers. She had been led to believe that this was the path to fulfillment, her road to the unimaginable and intangible joys of womanhood.

Unfortunately, by the time she discovered that she had been sold a shoddy bill of goods and was not a good fit for this lifestyle, she was in too deep to recover. The boat had sailed and she could not swim, so there was no way back to shore. She had been shanghaied into a life of domesticity for which she was not even remotely suited. A better avenue by far would have been to move to the city, buy a cat or two, and work in the public library or become an old maid schoolteacher. These were the two primary occupations open to unmarried women back in the 1950s, and she would have excelled at either. But in life as in skydiving, there are no do-overs. When after a few years of marriage, the cerebral dissonance that was the fabric of her existence became unbearable, her only escape lay within, so that is where she went.

Her final descent into bedlam happened literally overnight. When her two children—Blanchard, fourteen, and his older sister, Geneva, sixteen—went to bed that fateful evening, their mother was playing solitaire with a dog-eared deck that contained forty-nine cards, chain-smoking Raleigh cigarettes, and singing along with the songs on her transistor radio. This was not unusual behavior and was a fair representation of how she spent a great deal of her time. The two youngsters had grown used to looking after themselves and each other over the years and thought very little about their mother's parallel existence to their own. She occupied the same house that they did, but not the same world, and this existential dichotomy gave them no cognitive pause; it was just the way things were. Water was wet, winter was cold, and something about their mama just wasn't quite right.

When they awakened that next morning, however, the mother who had casually ignored both of them for their entire lives was gone, and in her place was something quite different. They learned quickly that day that newer is not always better, and that the devil one knew was generally preferable to the unknown. The fresh addition to the family vaguely resembled her predecessor physically, but the similarities seemed to end there. Edna 2.0 had arrived, and she had done a bit of redecorating to celebrate the unveiling while her progeny was sleeping.

The floor and walls of the kitchen were patterned with mystic script and colorful drawings. These were done in a combination of paint, ink, pencil, crayon, and what seemed to be blood. Many of the drawings were violent, some exceedingly so, and most were sexually graphic if not outright pornographic in their crudity. The focal point in the kitchen that morning was a crucified rabbit nailed to the wall over the stove. The room had an inhuman feel to it, as if an entity from another dimension had spent the shank of the night preparing the chamber for an evil rite. In addition to the kitchen's altered state, Edna's own appearance had changed as well. She had chopped off all the hair from the right side of her head, and in its place was a single malevolent eye drawn with an indelible laundry marker. Additionally, she had outlined her eyes with bright red lipstick and resembled nothing so much as a demonic raccoon. She was barefoot and topless, and she had smeared her breasts with a light blue substance that may have been latex paint. As her children entered the kitchen for breakfast, she greeted them.

"What you do not know I cannot tell you," she said in a singsong voice. "But someday you will understand." She nodded as if to reassure herself of this promise of enlightenment, then shook her head as if to disagree with it at the same time. Then she spat into her right hand and smacked herself on the bottom, as if sealing a bargain. Blanchard swallowed loudly, his mind a blank.

"Mama, what's wrong with you?" Geneva asked. She took a prudent step back the way she had come. Blanchard just stood there and stared at his mother, doubting her previous statement about the eventual certainty of clarification. In a word, he was freaked. This new reality was not to his liking, and he might also have retreated, but he seemed unable to move. His feet, like a brace of unlucky hares, felt like they were nailed to the floor.

"Your mama has gone as crazy as a sack full of shithouse rats," Benton Shankles said from his place at the kitchen table. Both Blanchard and Geneva startled at his words, not realizing that he had been there all along. It was the first of the many times that they would hear him speak this phrase. He spoke calmly in his dry, laconic voice, as if reporting that the toast had burned, or that they were out of milk for the coffee and would have to drink it black that morning.

By this point in their marriage, Edna had ridden the crazy train on more than one occasion, but it seemed that this time she might actually be the engineer, riding up in the locomotive, hat pulled down low, holding the throttle wide open with one hand and laying down on the horns with the other. "I swear to God I'm going to marry a normal woman next time," Benton continued. "You just watch and see if I don't." Edna's head whipped around, and she cast a truly malicious gaze at her husband, one imbued with such hatred and power that he could not quite meet its fierce intensity and lowered his eyes just a bit.

"Your time has already been written in the book," she said as she pointed a shaking finger at him. Blanchard could see that it had been bitten repeatedly and was bleeding. Maybe the crucified rabbit had inflicted the wounds—Blanchard had always been a champion of the underdog, and despite himself he hoped it had gotten in a bite or two before she nailed it to the wall. Or maybe she had bitten it herself. Who knew? Then she hissed like a cat, spat at her spouse, and sat down on the floor. Benton shook his head and sipped his coffee. His apparent complacency was one of the most surreal aspects of the scene in the kitchen, which was saying plenty.

"God damn," he said. He sounded disgusted and more than a little put out, as if his wife's implosion were quite the inconvenience for the family in general and him in particular. He turned to his daughter and spoke. "Geneva, I don't have time for this. I've got to go to work. You stay home from school today and watch your crazy mama. You need to try to keep her hemmed up. If you let her get out of the house, we'll never catch her. She's liable to get in the road and get run over. I'd hate to get sued 'cause my old lady don't have sense enough to stay out from in front of cars." He arose from his seat at the kitchen table and continued speaking as he moved the back door. "Maybe she'll snap out of this while I'm gone. If she's not better in a day or two, we'll take her to see Doc Miller. Maybe he can give her some pills or shock her or something."

"Uh-uh," Geneva replied. "Not me. I don't want to stay with her." She looked at her mother there on the floor, then at the rabbit, and started to cry. Edna stared at her daughter and laughed, but the sound was without mirth or joy and sounded as if she might be strangling on the rigid strands of reality. Geneva backed an additional step and bumped into the wall. Edna reached into the waistband of her pants and pulled out a red crayon. She licked the end of it and began to augment a drawing on the floor. It seemed to be a rendering of a crucifix with wicked thorns sketched in at all four Stations of the Cross, and with an erect penis protruding from the base. The original drawing was black, and now Edna was adding accents of red until both the cross and the phallus began to appear as if they were bleeding the wretched sins of humanity. She sang as she colored, apparently content. Geneva looked fearfully from the artwork to her brother, then slowly back, as if she wished to look at anything else but could not control where her eyes rested.

"Juicy Brucie Braaa-dley. WBZ. Radio 103. Boston...." Edna sang this ditty over and over. He was her favorite DJ from her favorite all-night radio station, and it seemed that his legend had become a part of her new reality on the far side of the looking glass, where the air was hazy with dark magic and the rules of the normal world did not apply.

"I'll stay with her," Blanchard said to Geneva. He didn't want to either, but Geneva was obviously scared to death, his mother needed his help, or at least someone to keep an eye on her movements, and he hated school anyway and usually only made it all the way there about half the time, if truth be told. "You go ahead to school." Geneva nodded, gratitude etched upon her face, and she backed her way along the wall until she found the doorway to the hall, through which she exited without looking back.

"Lock all the doors," Benton said, nodding toward his wife as he stood by the back door. "If she tries to kill you or something, whack her with a frying pan and make her behave. I'll be home late." He left without further comment, and when he showed up three days later, hung over, with a cut above his left eye and his right hand in a thick bandage, Blanchard supposed it did indeed count as being home late.

The Shankles family settled into a new routine that revolved around their matriarch, Crazy Edna, and the bizarre activities with which she filled her long, strange days and endless, surreal nights. It became clear fairly early that she was not a flight risk, and with the exception of her inclination to nail the occasional rodent, bird, or small reptile to the wall, it didn't seem that she was actually a danger to herself or others. So Edna continued to redecorate the house one room at a time, and once every square inch of wall, ceiling, and floor had been added to the archive, she began to annotate all of the books and magazines in the home, one page at a time, enhancing them with symbols, drawings, runes, and commentary, until each was more bizarre, sacrilegious, and repugnant than the last.

Geneva kept up with her newfound habit of staying as far away from her mother as she could, which was probably for the best since Edna seemed to have developed a dislike for her daughter and snapped at her, literally, if she passed too close. Blanchard went back to attending school about half the time and staying home the rest. When not occupied tending to his mother, who needed little physical care, Blanchard spent his time in his room, lost in the notes and chords that he coaxed from his pawnshop guitar. When occupied in this manner, he left the world of trouble and was transported to a better place, one that was certainly an improvement over his current reality. As for the patriarch of the clan, Benton continued his quest to forget his troubles by bathing them in the attentions of a succession of sad and lonely women, notches on his belt who undoubtedly hoped that he would eventually turn out to be a better man than he seemed at first impression to be.

Two weeks into his mother's new way of life, Blanchard determined that someone ought to try to get her some medical assistance, and since Benton didn't seem inclined and Geneva refused to get within five feet of her, it fell to him to take her to see the town's aged physician, Doc Miller. She was his mother, after all, and he loved her and felt sorry for her, and she needed help. Blanchard was not yet old enough to drive but sometimes did anyway, and in fact he was part owner, along with his two friends, John Covey and Chicken Raines, of a 1958 MG convertible. Each of the partners had contributed $25 toward the total purchase price of $75 for the roadster, and each got to drive it every third week plus anytime they had a date with a girl. This romantic happenstance had yet to occur for any member of the trio, but they all knew it was simply a matter of time until it did, and figured it was a good idea to plan ahead when it came to matters of the heart so as to avoid being unprepared. Since none of the owners had yet seen their sixteenth birthday, or had even seen the approach of such out on the far horizon, they thought it best that the car not become general knowledge, so it was kept hidden under a tarp in the abandoned barn at the back of Chicken's father's pasture. And even though it wasn't his week to drive the two-seater, Blanchard declared a medical emergency and borrowed the MG from the barn, loaded Edna into it, and took her to see Doc Miller.

"Are we going home?" Edna asked as they drove down the back valley road to town. It was narrow and roughly paved, and the town end of the thoroughfare sported a sign that proclaimed it to be a dead end, which Blanchard had always found to be prophetic and appropriate, both before his mama had chosen to sail the lost sea and especially after.

"No, Mama. We're going to see Doc Miller."

"I am become death, the destroyer of worlds," she observed. She had been a voracious reader once upon a time, and the occasional famous line of dialogue or unique quotation still found its way into her speech. She closed her eyes while the wind blew through her half head of hair. The baleful eye drawn on her scalp watched the fence posts whisk by.

"That's what we want to talk to him about," Blanchard replied.

When they arrived at the doctor's office, Blanchard corralled his mother into the waiting room, explained the need for the visit, and then accompanied Edna to the exam room at Doc's request just in case his assistance was required. Doc began a cursory examination, but before he got very far it became apparent that his patient was not in the mood to be examined. When he shined a light into her eyes, she hissed at him and spat on the floor. When he bumped her knee with his little rubber mallet, she snatched it away and stuck it into the brassiere her son had insisted she wear for the occasion. When he attempted to listen to her heart, she grabbed the business end of the stethoscope as if it were a microphone and shared her thoughts with her physician.

"I never put out on the first date, old man, but for you I might make an exception." She said this in an exaggerated voice reminiscent of Mae West, looked at him with a lascivious expression, and began to unbutton her shirt.

"Mama, stop!" Blanchard said. She complied and instead began to sing about Juicy Brucie Braaa-dley, radio personality extraordinaire at WBZ, Radio 103, Boston.

"I never heard her say a bad word in her life until two weeks ago," Blanchard told Doc Miller. "Now she talks worse than Leroy Summers." Leroy, a Sequoyah legend, had spent thirty years in the Navy and twenty-one of those in the Pacific Fleet, and his language was colorful. Blanchard went on to present all his mother's other symptoms: the bizarre artwork and strange writings, the animal cruelty and ritual sacrifice, the sexual and religious behaviors, and the dearth of sleep.

"I'm not a psychiatrist," Doc said finally, "and that is what she needs. Your mama's in trouble, and she needs to be in a hospital. She seems to have had a complete psychotic break. Do you have any idea what brought it on?" He scribbled a note as he awaited Blanchard's response.

"She married Daddy," Blanchard replied. It was the truth as far as he was concerned. Doc Miller nodded, as if he could well understand how being espoused to Benton Shankles might drive a person right on over the proverbial line between here and yonder. He made an appointment for Edna with a psychiatrist in Rome and prescribed her some anti-anxiety medication to take in the meantime.

"This won't help her psychosis," Doc told Blanchard, "but it might calm her down a little."

Edna had discovered the replica of a skeleton that Doc kept in his office and was giving its skull a close inspection. Doc and Blanchard watched as she leaned in to where an ear would have been had the skeleton possessed one. As she began to whisper, Doc looked at Blanchard and raised an eyebrow. "Give her two, three times a day," he said, handing over the prescription. "If nothing else, maybe they'll make her sleep."

As Blanchard discovered one black eye and one bitten finger later, Edna would not take the pills because she believed them to be poisoned, but, as it turned out, they were quite beneficial for Geneva and her newfound collage of fears, so the prescription was not wasted. Unfortunately, the appointment with the psychiatrist was not kept because Benton would not spend the money or the time to have his wife seen about. Blanchard would have taken her anyway, but he wasn't sure that the MG would make it as far as Rome, and the last thing he needed was a long walk back to Sequoyah with his demented mother in tow, singing about Juicy Brucie Braaa-dley while her son tried to thumb a ride. So Edna set about her exciting new career as the crazy woman in town without benefit of modern medicine, her children looked after themselves the best they could just as they always had, and Benton continued to build bad karma at an alarming rate, even for him.

About six months after Edna's initial descent into the abyss, Benton took some bad advice from a loading dock coworker who knew absolutely nothing whatsoever about the subject they were discussing, and he brought home a priest to perform an exorcism on his wife.

"You know we're not Catholic, right?" Blanchard asked.

"Always with that smart mouth," Benton replied.

Edna wasn't demon-possessed, at least not that anyone could ever prove, but Benton had hopes of obtaining a second opinion on this matter and a quick blessing, just to be on the safe side. Blanchard and Geneva sat there with gritted teeth and crossed fingers as the padre mumbled a couple of prayers and shuffled a few beads, and the object of his attentions crouched quietly through the ritual and watched him with something akin to interest in her eyes, much like a soaring eagle might be interested in a squirrel. Blanchard hoped she wouldn't go too nuts on him, either because he was a man of the cloth or because he looked to be on the far end of seventy, but recent history was not on his side in this matter, and he knew how events would unfold. She had removed her shirt by that time, but that was such a common occurrence that the Shankles children hardly even noticed it anymore, and if the padre did, he courteously didn't comment upon the development. Just when Blanchard began to relax, the cleric took out a vial of holy water, and in two swift and confident motions, he splashed the sign of the cross on Edna. Blanchard could have told him it was a bad idea, but he had not been consulted. The father must have gotten carried away by the whole business and thought he was in *The Exorcist* or something, but hitting her with that holy water, or with any water for that matter, was the wrong thing to do.

"Uh-oh," Blanchard said, and then all hell broke loose. "Duck!" he said to Geneva.

Since slipping off the deep end, Edna Shankles had hated to get wet worse than a cat, and she took her dousing with poor humor. She screamed and leapt at the man with her long fingernails drawn. Blanchard moved quickly after swallowing down his initial surprise, but by the time he pulled his mother off the priest, she had broken the bottle of holy water over his head and cut one of his hands and both of his arms with a piece of the vial, and she was starting to choke him with the chain from his own crucifix. He looked confused and afraid, as if maybe they hadn't covered this particular situation in sufficient detail back at seminary. Benton grabbed up the priest and hustled him out while Blanchard settled Edna down. He dragged her by one of her legs over to a mirror, and once he got her situated in front of it, she ceased kicking and screaming and began to gaze at herself. She thought reflective glass held magic, and she would stare into mirrors and blank television screens for hours and sometimes days. So no, she wasn't possessed. She was just regular old crazy, which is like being possessed minus the religion and, in her case, the blouse. Of course, she was also pretty mean on top of that, and the two made for a bad combination.

"It must be hard to be a priest when crazy people are in the room," Geneva said after all the excitement had passed. She had taken another of her mother's poisoned anxiety pills and was more or less in control of her emotions. The tablets tended to make her contemplative, and prone to want to explore the bigger picture. Blanchard was tempted to hit her up for a tablet, but he had some pretty good pot up in his room that he figured would take the edge off the day, so he chose to wait for that.

"That's why they get paid the big bucks, I guess," Blanchard said. He thought it was fairly likely that it was hard to be a priest when sane people were in the room as well. All that celibacy seemed off-putting to him. He was still celibate himself, in a manner of speaking, but that was not by choice nor due to lack of effort on his part, and he intended to rectify the situation as soon as any viable opportunity presented itself.

"I don't think they do," Geneva noted. "Make the big bucks, that is. I think they have to be poor. I think that's one of the rules."

"Whatever," Blanchard replied. Poor and horny seemed a bad way to live, and to run a religion for that matter. "I can't believe he brought a priest here," he said. "He must be as crazy as she is! He knows how she is about religious stuff. It was bound to set her off. There's no telling what we'll find nailed to the wall in the morning."

"Well, at least we won't see him for a few days now," Geneva noted. "He'll stay gone, and she'll calm down and go back to drawing and coloring." Edna was working on the windows in the house by that time, and when the sun caught some of her renderings in a certain way, it was easy to believe that she really was in touch with mystical beings in enchanted lands. When the evening light streamed in through the windows, it looked as if the entire living room had become a cathedral for the deranged.

"Suits me. I hope he never comes back. I can't blame Mama. If I was married to him, I'd go nuts too." He shook his head. "This is all on him, you know. Crazy runs in her family, and she can't help that. But he's the one that brought it out." Edna's mother had taken to her bed with a bad case of nerves at the age of forty, just after having and then losing her third child. She spent most of the rest of her life indisposed, only arising briefly during her fifty-third year to cut her husband's throat in his sleep before hanging herself with her wedding gown in the front hallway, where Edna discovered her several hours later.

"If crazy really does run in the family, what's going to happen to us?" Geneva asked.

"Take a look," Blanchard said, pointing at the walls, the ceiling, the floors, and Edna. Their mother was peeking behind the mirror now, as if to stage a flanking maneuver and catch the mirror-dwellers by surprise. "We're doomed. You might as well shave your head, slip off your bra, and go for it. The line forms right over there. Give me a few minutes, and I'll find you something to nail to the wall."

"I think I'll take another pill," Geneva said, making for the kitchen.

"Take two," her brother advised.

That night, Blanchard was asleep in his bed, fast-forwarding through a particularly vivid version of a nightmare he had been having ever since Edna had flipped completely out, an ominous dream about running down a black hallway covered in glowing red neon signs and sigils, chasing after a bear while being pursued by a lion. The bear was not a cute, roly-poly bear, and the lion was not noble in the least. This bear had two heads, red eyes, and was about nine feet tall. This lion was what a lion would look like if its mother had left a waterfront bar one night after doing tequila shots with a drunken sociopathic dragon and then had an illicit union with said dragon behind the dumpster in the alley out back. In the dream, Blanchard was as afraid of catching the bear as he was of being caught by the lion. Neither outcome seemed desirable or wise, but both were inevitable according to the rules of the dream.

He once shared this nightmare with a counselor at his school who was attempting to get to the roots of why Blanchard would not regularly attend his classes. The answer to that question was, simply, that Blanchard did not want to go, but since the counseling sessions kept him out of class, he gladly went along with them and intended to stretch them out for as long as he could. That counselor had told Blanchard that his unresolved trust issues with family members were manifesting themselves in acute and unreasonable fears of the unknown. Ironically, that all sounded about right to Blanchard, but none of it actually pertained to his truancy.

"How much do they pay you?" he had asked the counselor as a matter of curiosity, but before she could answer, their time was up. Blanchard had intended to pursue the inquiry the next time the two met, because it seemed like a pretty sweet job and he was going to have to do something with his life if music didn't work out, but he missed that next scheduled appointment due to being home in his room at the time trying to learn the introduction to "Stairway to Heaven."

The night after Edna's failed exorcism, Blanchard awoke suddenly from his usual nightmare into a nightmare of a different sort. His eyes snapped open, and Edna was standing over his bed, staring down at him with a smile that looked like it had been splashed onto her face by someone who didn't know what a smile should look like but had tried to paint one anyway. Her eyes seemed impossibly back-lit, as if the moonbeams streaming in through the bedroom window were somehow burning through the back of her skull and lighting her up inside. Her breasts were painted with red eyes above and leering mouths below her nipples, which were doing double duty as perky pink noses that evening. She was holding a black stone statuette in both hands, a family heirloom that she always said was the likeness of an ancient Nubian princess whose name she could not recall. Blanchard wasn't certain if that was true, but he did know that the thing weighed about ten pounds, and she was clutching it high above her head with her arms fully extended, looking as if she were about to commence mayhem.

"Ahhh!" he exclaimed. He threw up his arms, rolled off the far side of the bed, and scuttled across the room and into the far corner like a crab at low tide scrambling for safety. She stood where she was, between him and the door, as if she had not seen him. Then she made a noise unlike any that Blanchard had ever heard, even from her, sort of a part scream, part wail, and part he didn't know what. It rumbled up slowly, gaining momentum as it rose, like an earthquake reverberating from deep inside, originating beyond the ragged edges of her soul where the light never shone. It sounded like the echo of pure, uncut malevolence, raw hatred on the return leg of a long, cruel trip to perdition.

Blanchard didn't know what she said, because the language wasn't of that time and place in the world, but how she spoke told him all that he needed to hear. If evil had a sound, this was that sound. It froze him in the corner and drew his breath. Then she swung the princess at the exact spot where his head had recently lain. It landed with a whump, which made Blanchard flinch. He wondered what it would have felt like if his head had received the blow. He wondered if he would have awakened with the impact, or if he would have simply died on the spot from the trauma. Then, slowly, she raised the statue high and swung it again. And then she did it again. And again. He sat curled up in the corner of his room and watched as she thoroughly and without mercy killed his pillow with the Nubian princess. Blanchard didn't know if she had come to murder his pillow, or if she had been after him, or if she was just employing an old Nubian housekeeping method to polish the princess, but whatever the reason for her visit, he didn't disturb her as she went about her business. Over time it had become quite difficult to avoid crazy in the Shankles family, but stupid was another matter altogether, and as long as her attentions were directed elsewhere from him, he had no intention of interrupting her in any way. She went at that pillow for nearly two hours. If the sun hadn't finally come up, she might be whaling away still. She never rested, or broke a sweat, or altered her pace, and she made no sound except for a quiet little grunt of satisfaction every time the Nubian princess made contact with the pillowcase. Then, when the pale dawn—yellow like a wolf's eye—began to seep into Blanchard's room, she ceased her efforts and casually dropped the sculpture to the floor. It landed with a solid thump. Only then did she turn toward her son.

"Practice makes perfect," she said before blowing him a kiss. He nodded, although he had no idea what she meant. Then she casually strolled from the room like she had been in there straightening up, perhaps, or pulling down the covers. Blanchard sat in his corner for some time, mulling the events of the night while shivering as if cold. He took slow, deep breaths while he wondered what he was going to do now. In a short life defined by oddity and dread, the evening's events had raised the bar. His mama was crazy beyond description, crazier than anyone had ever been or ever would be. Of this he was certain. When the shakes left him, he arose, pulled on a pair of jeans, and slowly crawled out of his bedroom window. He was stiff from crouching in the corner. After smoking a couple of slow cigarettes while sitting on the porch roof, he felt a little better. He climbed back in and looked at what remained of his pillow. Then he put on a shirt and went downstairs.

"Mama tried to kill me last night," Blanchard told Geneva at breakfast. Even as he said it, he marveled at what passed for table conversation at the Shankles residence. He described the entire surreal experience to his sister from start to finish, stopping a few times during the narrative when he seemed unable to catch his breath. They were alone at the table. Edna was in the bathroom, gazing into the mirror over the sink and talking in unknown tongues to whatever she saw in there, and Benton was elsewhere that morning, gazing into the eyes of the hostess from the lounge at the Holiday Inn while whispering trite nothings to her.

"Jam the back of a chair under your doorknob," Geneva advised around a mouthful of Cheerios after he told her the tale. "I know it sounds nuts, but that's what I do every night. Sometimes the doorknob rattles, but she can't get in that way. After she tries a few times, she'll give up." She read the back of the cereal box as she shared this household tip.

"That's a good idea," Blanchard noted. He found it strange that he and his sister were sharing strategies for avoiding being bludgeoned by their mother, and he found it stranger still that there was a need for the information exchange, and he found it strangest of all that his sister had relayed the tip sounding as unconcerned as if she were relating a snack recipe she had found on the Cheerios box.

"I saw it in an old movie," Geneva said. "They just shoved it right up under there good and tight. I thought it was corny then, like, you know, who would ever do that? But now I think it's brilliant. Whoever wrote that movie must have had a mama as crazy as ours." She whispered the word "crazy" as she always did, as if it were the dirtiest of words, not fit for the ears of decent company in the clear light of day.

"Has Mama ever tried to kill you?" Blanchard asked. It seemed an obvious question. Who knew? Maybe it was a Shankles family tradition to kill the children while they slept, and as such, he shouldn't take it too personally. Maybe Edna and Benton had produced several offspring, and he and Geneva were the only two left. He reached for the cereal box and poured himself a bowl even though he wasn't particularly hungry. He was still a bit off-kilter, but he was starting to shake off his unease.

"Not with the Nubian princess," Geneva replied enigmatically. She went back to reading the Cheerios box as she munched and didn't seem much inclined to chat further on the subject. Upon reflection, he supposed that the topic was a bit dense for breakfast conversation, anyway.

"Well," he said finally. "I guess that makes me her favorite."

"Lucky you. If she kills you, I want your room."

He nodded. It was a reasonable request.

"NOW THAT YOU'RE GONE"
(Blanchard Shankles/John Covey)

Now that you're gone, time don't tick
Ham don't bone and salt don't lick
Sun don't rise and moon don't set
Coffee don't cup and blade don't whet

Since you left babe, broom don't sweep
Lips don't whisper and eyes don't weep
Fire don't burn and grass don't grow
Rain don't fall and wind don't blow

Out on my own, pipe don't smoke
Dog don't fight and joint don't toke
Song don't sing and train don't roll
Air don't breathe and bridge don't toll

Without you girl, water don't wine
Years don't march and numbers don't line
Bible don't thump and drum don't beat
Feet don't dance and hot don't heat

From now until forever, hill don't side
Book don't read and seek don't hide
Phone don't call and letter don't write
Hand don't hold and wrong don't right

For the rest of my time, sorrow don't heal
Money don't spend and heart don't feel
Hammer don't nail and bride don't groom
Apple don't blossom and love don't bloom

For the rest of my time, sorrow don't heal
Money don't spend and heart don't feel
Hammer don't nail and bride don't groom
Apple don't blossom and love don't bloom

"Lucky Man"
Emerson, Lake, and Palmer
-Sunday: First Day-

Blanchard had first become acquainted with the cantankerous nature of his aging ticker while playing at a club known as Giz Moe's in Staunton, Virginia. It was a New Year's Eve night, and they were playing to a room full of happy merrymakers, a rock and roll kind of crowd with not a mean drunk in the bunch, which was a rarity both at Giz Moe's and in the greater Staunton vicinity, and thus it made for a magical evening. The last song before the first break started with Ford Man Cooper's familiar drum roll that signaled the beginning of the much-abbreviated Murphy's Law version of the Allman Brothers's famous "Mountain Jam." The crowd approved loudly, and for the next eight minutes, first one, then another of the band members did his level best to bring a worthy rendition of that Southern classic to the fine folks of Staunton.

Toward the end of the song, just as Blanchard was winding down his guitar solo, he had been hit with a pain in the center of his chest so severe that he thought he had been shot. He involuntarily dropped to his knees, slid a few feet from the momentum of the fall, leaned forward until his head touched the stage, and then fought to control his panic as he tried to snatch a ragged breath. The agony held on for a few seconds, pounding his sternum like an iron fist decked with brass knuckles, letting him know just how bad it could get. Then the misery peaked, after which it departed as quickly as it had arrived, almost as if it had changed its mind about killing him at this particular juncture but might be back at any time. The pain scrabbled up his neck and out his left ear like an escaped convict followed by a pack of bloodhounds. Blanchard bent there, gasping, and it was only after a moment or two of desperate breathing that he dared to raise himself back to a kneeling position. When he did, he realized that he was still playing the Strat, out of habit, apparently, and that the partygoers seemed to approve of his fancy showmanship and wanted more of the same.

He managed to finish the song, the set, and the show before allowing himself to be driven to the hospital where, after a stress test and a heart catheter, it was confirmed that his angina was caused by a substantial blockage in one of his coronary arteries. In truth, the stress test had gone awry quite early in the procedure when, a mere ten seconds after Blanchard began walking on the treadmill, the doctor hit the emergency stop, quickly escorted his patient to a nearby chair, sat him gently down, and slipped a nitroglycerine tablet under his tongue before dragging the crash cart close by where it would be handy should the need arise, as it appeared it might.

"How'd I do, Doc?" Blanchard had asked as a wave of hotness from the tablet washed over him and the first of many subsequent nitro headaches began to form behind his eyes. Admittedly the signs seemed to be pointing toward him having done poorly, but he wanted to hear the official version from the guy in the white lab coat rather than making a layman's uninformed guess.

"Don't talk," the young resident had advised as he summoned the on-call cardiologist. "Keep still and take slow, deep breaths." Blanchard had been released two days later day with a stent, which was a tiny sleeve inserted into his coronary artery to keep it open for business, a bottle of nitroglycerine tablets for chest pain, and an admonition to see his own doctor as soon as he got off the bus back in Georgia. He was to avoid all forms of sex, drugs, and rock and roll—plus coffee and cigarettes—until he did.

"You need to start taking better care of yourself if you want to live to be old," Covey had said to him after that episode. It was the first of many times that Covey would say these words to Blanchard. They rode the bus south toward Georgia, fourteen hours away. Simpson was driving, and Jimbo Tant was strumming the introduction to "Sweet City Woman" on a banjo he had picked up in Staunton. The rest of the boys were sleeping away as much of the long ride home as they could. Staunton was to be a watershed in Blanchard's life, a before-and-after moment that crystallized all that came before as the good old days and illuminated all that came after as something quite different, but it was too soon for him to realize this.

"I've heard that getting old is not all it's cracked up to be," Blanchard had said. He gazed at the valley of the Shenandoah as the old bus clocked the miles.

"That may be true, but I'm guessing it beats *not* getting old."

"Like I got a reliable diagnosis on New Year's Day in the emergency room in Staunton, Virginia, anyway," Blanchard replied. He was in an argumentative mood. "I bet that first guy wasn't even a doctor. He didn't look old enough to be. They probably decided to let all the good help be off on New Year's and just made do with the new people and the screw-ups for the holiday. He could have been anybody. Maybe he was the guy who swept up. I saw a movie about that once. A man pretended he was a doctor, and a pilot too, I think, and they didn't even catch him. He was just a young guy, but no one figured it out. He was operating on people and flying planes and everything! They paid him for it, too. That boy was making good money. He got away with it for years."

"I'm pretty sure your cardiologist was a real doctor," Covey noted. "He ballooned your artery and put in a stent. He must have known a little something about doctoring, because he had a wire up in your heart, and you're not dead."

"Well, that's what he said he did, anyway. All I saw were some fuzzy pictures on a computer screen. Every time I tried to take a look at where the real action was, someone told me to be still. There's no telling what I was looking at. And even if he did do what he said he did, he could have just gotten lucky. I may be the only person he ever worked on who lived."

"So now you're complaining about being alive?"

"I'm just saying. Do you know what every graduating class of doctors has in common?"

"What?"

"Every class has someone who finished dead last, that's what. I bet my guy was fresh out of medical school, he finished right smack down at the bottom of his class, and I was his first time."

But apparently, even though the Virginia ER doctor didn't look like he had been practicing all that long, the New Year's diagnosis in Staunton had been on the mark, and now, two years later, Blanchard was sitting in a hard recliner chair in a hospital room in another city, watching cars while waiting to confer with yet another heart doctor. All of the morning's excitements were behind him, and all of the afternoon's worries had settled in to torment him. He took deep breaths and tried to manage his various pains as well as his anxiety. His skin hurt in seven separate spots where the EKG leads from the emergency room had been ripped off, bringing large patches of hair with them. His groin throbbed where the coronary catheter had been inserted into his femoral artery before being driven north to inspect his ailing pump. Both arms hurt where two separate IVs had been stabbed in and taped off. The right one ached much, much worse than the left, a phenomenon most likely explainable by the fact that he had sensible veins that tended to dodge sharp needles at every opportunity, making him what was known in medical circles as a "hard stick." Additionally, his offhand remark to the phlebotomist after her first several attempts to find one of these nomadic blood vessels may have inadvertently added to her subsequent failures and to his current level of discomfort.

"I didn't know they let blind people take blood," he had said between clenched teeth, believing that his trauma could not get any worse than the current bloodletting, an assumption that turned out to have been gravely in error. By the time she left the room several additional errant sticks later, he believed that perhaps she had actually been blind, after all, and that maybe he owed her an apology for his insensitive remark. He vowed to himself that if he lived through his present travail he would seek her out, apologize, and perhaps buy her a small token of his esteem such as a seeing-eye dog, a cane, or a pair of dark glasses.

In addition to his other pains, his shoulder hurt where the PICC line had been threaded into and through his veins until it nestled right up next to his heart like a sleeping kitten, and it felt like he had been kicked in the stomach by an entire gang of burly, drunken bikers at the injection site of the blood thinner. He felt tingly and hot all over, sweaty and cold at the same time, which was an aftereffect of the dye they had run through his heart as they mapped out his circulatory woes. On top of all that, he had the worst headache he had ever known thanks to the nitroglycerin drip, but he had to admit that it was preferable to the constant angina he had been experiencing earlier in the day. He was depressed, and he was hungry, and he was angry, but he didn't know exactly where to direct this anger. He wanted a cigarette and a taste of bourbon, and he wanted to go home, or at the very least to the Day's Inn. He was also just a little bit afraid that he might be about to cross the wide river for that joyous reunion with his parents, his grandparents, and all other manner of departed folk. It wasn't that Blanchard didn't want to see some of them again, but the honest truth was that he hadn't liked most of them all that much when they were alive, and he was in no great hurry to see the rest. They were dead, after all, and not going anywhere. Thus time was not an issue, and he had been hoping that he would be allowed to make the journey later rather than sooner.

The door to his room opened with almost no sound, and in stepped Covey with his cardboard cup of coffee. He wore blue jeans as he always did, an untucked work shirt that had never known an iron's caress, and a ball cap worn bill-to-the-front emblazoned with the single word, NO. He glanced at the empty bed where he had recently left his guitar player resting, then over at Blanchard sunk in the recliner, looking like a hermit. He frowned, took a sip from his cup, and frowned even harder as the foul brew assailed his taste buds. He set his coffee on the nightstand by the bed, reached up to remove his cap, and rubbed his close-cropped hair with his free hand as he considered his words. Then he replaced his hat and spoke.

"I was gone twenty minutes," he said in a conversational tone. "Just twenty short minutes. One third of an hour. I walked down to the break room, got eighty-five cents for a dollar from the change machine, bought a cup of brown water advertised as coffee, and walked straight back here." He picked up his cup and sat on the straight chair opposite the bed. He looked at Blanchard with tired eyes; it had been a late night, and he had been summoned to the hospital early. "Didn't go to the bathroom," he continued, as if talking to himself. "Didn't go to the waiting room for a magazine. Didn't even step outside for a quick smoke because you can't have one right now and I'm a nice guy and didn't want you to smell it on me and get all whiney. Just there and back. It probably wasn't even twenty minutes. It may have only been fifteen." He took another sip of the watery coffee and grimaced. "You're supposed to be in the bed," he observed, finally getting to the point of his soliloquy. "Why are you up?"

"No coffee for me?" Blanchard asked. He had a habit of answering a different question than the one asked, especially when he had no good answer for the original query. He rubbed at two or three newly bald spots on his chest. "It wouldn't kill them to buy a razor around this joint," he noted. "They could even put it on my bill. I'd pay it." He pointed first to one and then the other of his hairy arms and the IVs taped to them. "How long would it take to shave a guy where they are going to stick stuff on him? That right there is going to hurt like hell when they rip the tape off. Unless I'm dead, that is. Then it won't hurt much at all."

Covey was not in the mood to be deflected by talk of death, razors, or tape. He continued his line of inquiry concerning the issue of the chair versus the bed, and the location of Blanchard in relation to the two.

"I heard the nurse tell you that you were supposed to be flat on your back for at least two hours. She said three would be even better. She told you that if you moved too much, you might blow out your plug. I'm not even sure what it means to blow out a plug, but it sounded pretty bad to me, and if you do blow it out, I'm not picking it up and putting it back in. It can stay out. Wherever it lands, that's where it'll be." He took another sip of his coffee and shook his head. "I did you a favor on the coffee, by the way. I really don't think your heart is going to kill you today, but this coffee might." He stepped to the sink in the alcove by the door and poured out the rest. "I just hope it doesn't damage the plumbing." He looked at Blanchard. "All of a sudden I'm not feeling so good myself. Maybe I'll get in the bed." Blanchard nodded to indicate that it was available. If Covey wanted it, he was welcome.

"The plug is what they call the little jobbie they used to stop up the hole they made in my artery to run the catheter through," he said. He gently patted the area to the right of his groin. "It's kind of like when they plug a tire at the gas station. The last time I had a heart cath, up there in Staunton, that guy went in through my arm. There's an artery up there they can use, too. Either that, or he really didn't know what he was doing. That one didn't hurt near as much as this one did, but they plugged it when they got through, just like now." Blanchard sighed and shifted in his chair. "I guess I drew a leg man this time, and you can't be choosy. That's Tennessee for you. You get what you get up here. I'm a leg man myself, come to think of it, so I shouldn't complain. Anyway, to answer your question, I don't know what a plug looks like, but I know what it feels like. It feels like I got hit in the nuts with a football. When they made the hole down there, I thought I'd peed myself because it felt all warm and wet. I was sort of embarrassed. But that was blood, not pee. I mean, it was going everywhere. I think there was so much that it kind of surprised them. And if my plug blows out, I'll bleed to death right here in the room unless you are Johnny-on-the-spot hitting that call button over there. Maybe wadding up a towel and putting pressure right here wouldn't hurt, either." He pointed to the money spot. "Now you're a plug expert, just like me." Blanchard related all of this information as if he were discussing someone else's plug, arteries, and nuts. "Remember all you have been told, my son." He held up his hand as if blessing his companion.

"Bleeding to death sounds real unpleasant and kind of permanent," Covey observed. "Maybe you should have stayed put in the bed when they told you to." It seemed a reasonable course of action to Covey, and not too much to ask of a grown man, given the severity of the possible unintended circumstances.

"I wanted to look out the window." Blanchard turned his face to the pane, emphasizing his point. "I like to watch the traffic." The sun had disappeared, and there was an orange glow behind the clouds as if they were aflame. Blanchard had always liked this time of the day. He hoped it wasn't his last sunset, but if it was, it was a pretty one.

"They have this new thing up here in Tennessee called television," Covey noted. "It's kind of like looking out the window, except you do it from your perfectly good hospital bed so you don't run the risk of blowing out your plug and bleeding to death in front of your bass player. You should try it sometime. I think you might like it."

"They have cowboy hats up here too, but that doesn't mean I'm going to wear one." Cowboy hats were a pet peeve of Blanchard's. He believed that cowboys and cowgirls should wear them as protection from the blazing sun while on the lonesome trail, but he had little patience for them as fashion statements. Every time he spotted a cowboy hat without an attendant cow in the vicinity, he discretely rolled his eyes and muttered *yee haw* in a voice just loud enough to be overheard. "Anyway, there wasn't anything good on to watch. Just game shows and the news, plus some medical shows that I couldn't deal with, including one that showed what there's no way in hell I'm going to let them do to me tomorrow."

"Well, there you go. Now that I know you couldn't find anything to watch, risking a horrible death makes perfect sense. What was I thinking?"

"I thought it was a good idea at the time, too, but I have to admit that now I'm not so sure. This chair is like sitting on a sack of rocks. I have sat on curbs in parking lots that were softer than this thing. If I felt better and knew who bought it, I'd hunt them down and kick their ass. I bet it's some pretty boy big shot who plays squash or polo or some other rich boy sport who doesn't have to sit on a chair like this when he gets sick. I bet when *that* guy gets sick, they have a La-Z-Boy for him to sit in, with magic fingers and a cup holder, and I bet his TV has more than ten bad channels on it. They probably have a special hospital just for him and the rest of the swells, something real nice over in the good part of town." Blanchard had winded himself, and he stopped to take a few slow breaths. Then he finished his thought. "After I kicked his ass, I'd kick his boss's ass too, for hiring him. Then I think I might get back into the bed." He looked a bit pale. Planning a full session of Tennessee retribution had worn him out.

"Let's talk about something else," Covey suggested. They had dwelled upon medical issues, ass kicking, and pretty boy furniture-buyers enough for the time being. "You look pretty rough. Do you want me to help you get back into bed?"

Blanchard shook his head. "Not yet," he said. "But maybe soon. Or maybe not. I haven't decided to stay."

"In the chair?"

"In the hospital."

"You're staying. You're sick."

They were silent for a moment, and then Blanchard settled on a new topic of conversation, one more to his liking. "Can you remem-

44

ber our very first set list?" He smiled a wistful, sad smile as he asked. He was looking at the wall opposite his seat, but instead of seeing a painted-over crack in the plaster, he was seeing forty-five years into the past, back when he was hale, hearty, unplugged, and free to come and go as he pleased.

"What? From Skyye?" The question surprised Covey.

"Yeah, you know, the very first songs we played together. After we gathered up the boys and decided to be a band. And you gave us that stupid name. Do you remember the songs?"

"What brought that on?"

"What do you think brought it on?" Blanchard wasn't much of one to reminisce, but today was an unusual day. "I'm thinking about the good old days, I guess. Back when we were young boys, back when we were going to burn this old world to the ground and roast hot dogs over the coals at the end of time. We were going to love all the women, and smoke all the dope, and never have bad hearts or thin hair. Those were fine times. I miss all of it. I want to do it all again."

"Skyye was a cool name," Covey said.

Blanchard sighed. "S-k-y would have been a perfectly good name. S-k-y-y-e had too many letters. You didn't spell it right." He smiled. Pulling Covey's chain always cheered him up, and he needed cheering on this bleak day.

"If I've told you once, I've told you fifty times; the extra y and e were artistic. They made us stand out from the crowd. But they were good days for sure. That was a long time ago. Let me think." He removed his hat, held his palm to his forehead, and tapped his fingers on the top of his skull, a lifelong habit when he was trying to recall facts buried deep, as if he could jog the errant memories loose and coax them to the surface for retrieval.

"Start with Creedence," Blanchard said. "I heard one of their songs on the way to the hospital this morning. They were the best group in the world for a couple of years. Every song they did was a winner. We played 'Proud Mary.'"

"Oh yeah. Everybody played Creedence Clearwater Revival back then. Good tunes, and easy to learn. We did 'Born on the Bayou' too." Covey was a list maker. He slipped his ubiquitous notebook from his jeans pocket and a pencil stub from his shirt pocket and began to jot the titles as they were named.

"Don't forget 'Long as I Can See the Light,'" Blanchard said.

"I loved that song. Still do. Casual and bluesy, and the sax was just right. We should put it back in the lineup one of these days."

"Can't. Chicken sold his sax. He needed a transmission for his car." Chicken Raines had been the lead singer in the group since the very beginning. He was a good singer, but his real talent lay in the fact that he could play almost any instrument, given a bit of time to practice. His given name was Barry, but his father had been known as Rooster ever since he was old enough to crow, so when the elder Raines had a son, the poultry theme crossed the generational boundary like a chicken crossing the road.

"Too bad. I really liked that tune. Maybe we could find him another one in a pawnshop or someone's attic. Didn't we do 'Have You Ever Seen the Rain'? I remember playing it."

"Uh-uh. Not at first. We picked that up later, after we started playing clubs and bars."

"You're right. You're right. I remember now. Is that all the Creedence?"

Covey wrote as he talked. "Who's next? Steppenwolf?"

"John Kay was the man," Blanchard said. "He always looked like he was about to rob a store. Whenever I thought about being a rock star back then, I thought about him. Did I ever tell you about the time I saw him play at the Blue Sky Drive-In in Lafayette, Georgia? He was still playing under the name of Steppenwolf before all that legal business about the name of the band got started. It was maybe around 1980 or so, but I didn't recognize any of those guys who were with him that night. They played like he might have hired them down at the Salvation Army on the way into town and taught them a few quick chords right before the show, but he was still way cool. It was a good show just because he was in it. I loved his voice. He always sounded like he gargled with Drano right before he came onstage. We played 'Born to be Wild,' 'Magic Carpet Ride,' and 'The Pusher.'"

"'The Pusher' was the first song I learned on the bass." It had been, in fact, the band's very first complete song. "I didn't even have a bass yet. Played it on the top two strings of an old Silvertone solid body I borrowed from someone." Covey tried to remember his benefactor's name, but the years had erased the memory like chalk from a blackboard.

"You borrowed it from me," Blanchard observed. "Played through my amp, too. You sort of sucked at bass playing for a while there. We didn't know if you were going to make it or not."

"I got better," Covey replied. He had indeed been a slow starter, but he had turned into a quick study. He also had a pickup truck—which made equipment transport much less risky than tying amplifiers, even small ones, and drums to the tops of cars—and he had a job, which meant he could afford the payments on the Earth amp and the Fender jazz bass he eventually bought.

"You did for a fact. Oh man, do you remember the trouble we got into playing 'The Pusher' at the school talent show?" Blanchard smiled as the memory returned to him like a bad dream with a happy ending.

"Do I remember? I won't ever forget that night! It was our debut. We practiced for months for that gig. I thought Old Man Jefferson was going to die on the spot when Chicken sang *God damn the pusher* right there in school." Clark Jefferson had been the principal at Sequoyah High School during the late sixties and early seventies, and he had not taken it well when long-haired, boisterous representatives of those turbulent times—his own students, no less, country boys who had undoubtedly been raised better by their sainted mamas and grannies—had climbed up onto his stage in his auditorium, plugged their infernal noise machines into his electricity, and let fly. Or at least, they had let fly for about a minute and a half, which was how long it had taken Mr. Jefferson to get from his seat at the back of the auditorium all the way backstage to the electrical panel that housed the circuit breakers, which he then flipped off with outraged authority before declaring to the student body that talent was no longer allowed at his school, and that talent shows were permanently banned. He would have made the trip in shorter order, but he was a rotund man who took a while to get up to speed.

"Three days," Blanchard said, shaking his head slowly. "He suspended us for three days for playing an anti-drug song! Made us all go talk to a preacher before he let us come back. We were performing a public service. I had just gotten myself re-enrolled so I could play in the talent show, and he threw me back out again for playing in the talent show. It was the first time I ever got busted for my music." He chuckled. "I always thought it was pretty cool that we got fired from our very first show. I want that in my biography one of these days."

"It was the first time, but not the last time," Covey noted philosophically. The music business was a tough racket, and only the strong survived it. "If I write the story of the band someday, I promise I'll put it in there."

"Thanks. Remember 'Whiter Shade of Pale'? The ultimate slow dance. Procol Harum was the best."

Covey nodded. "If your girlfriend wouldn't hug you close and maybe give you a little kiss during that song," he said, "she was just stringing you along until she found a better deal." Carlos Santana crossed his mind and jogged his memory. "How about 'Black Magic Woman,' 'Evil Ways,' and 'Everything's Coming Our Way'?"

"I love those old Santana songs," Blanchard said. "'Everything's Coming Our Way' was my favorite out of all of theirs. Tucker always thought he was hot when he played that organ solo in the middle."

"He did have it down pat," Covey noted. "Once he finally bought a Leslie, he sounded just like the record."

"Yeah, he did," Blanchard agreed. "We could have played 'Samba Pa Ti,' too, but I couldn't get the lead run down. I could hit the notes, but it just wasn't a smooth sound. It sounded like Simpson was trying to play the song." He shook his head, still disgusted with his early failure after all that time.

"You just needed a better guitar and amp than you had. You nailed it later. It was a tough riff."

Blanchard nodded. "Three Dog Night?" he asked.

"They were our bread and butter," Covey remembered. "Our go-to band. 'Easy to Be Hard.' 'Joy to the World.' 'Never Been to Spain.' 'Eli's Coming.' I don't think they ever had a bad song."

"Remember 'In-A-Gadda-Da-Vida'?" Blanchard asked. "I don't care what anyone says. Iron Butterfly invented Heavy Metal."

"Back in the day, if you couldn't do fifteen minutes of 'In-A-Gadda-Da-Vida,' you couldn't call yourself a band. Ford Man loved to play his drum solo. He could beat on those drums all night long. I used to love how he would close his eyes while he played that solo. He never looked at the drum set. Once I saw him break a stick in the middle of it. He flipped the broken stick over his shoulder, grabbed a spare, and never missed a beat. And he still had his eyes closed, all up into the song, grooving with the sound."

"'Badge' and 'White Room,'" Blanchard said.

"We should have played more Cream songs."

"Back then I couldn't do it," Blanchard said. "Clapton is so good, he's hard to play, especially when you're playing a pawnshop Douglas guitar with one dead pickup plugged into an old Kustom amp with a cracked speaker."

"You did have a nice raw sound back then," Covey said.

"Real raw."

"And our Doors tunes: 'Riders on the Storm,' 'Love Her Madly,' and 'Light My Fire.'"

"Sometimes I think about how awesome they would have been if Morrison hadn't killed himself. That boy had it made, but he didn't know a sweet deal when he saw one. He had it all and just couldn't be satisfied." Blanchard shook his head. "Stupid." He didn't obsess about it, but sometimes Blanchard found himself angry at the late greats of rock and roll: Jimi Hendrix, Jim Morrison, Janis Joplin, a few others. He wasn't mad at them for what they'd had, but rather for what they'd thrown away.

"They say he drove the Doors' tour bus to his own heart attack over there in Paris," Covey pointed out. "They found him with a Marlboro 100 still burning on his lower lip."

"Liar."

"Don't kill the messenger. I'm just telling you what I heard."

"'Vehicle,'" Blanchard said. "Who did that one originally? I can't recall."

"The Ides of March. I don't remember anything else they did. I know that's the only one we ever played. And Wilson Pickett's 'Don't Let the Green Grass Fool You.' I was a hot boy on that one."

"Yeah, yeah, yeah," Blanchard said. "You were so great that we all wanted to sleep with you. Grand Funk Railroad. 'Heartbreaker' and 'Inside Looking Out.' Man, those boys could play. Mark Farner never got the credit he deserved."

"'Corrie' was in our first set list," Covey said. "We played it during the encore. It was the first time we ever played one of our own songs."

"I was scared the first time we played it for a crowd," Blanchard admitted. "I thought they'd trash us, but everyone seemed to like it. Of course, they were mostly drunk or high, but it was still a good song."

Covey nodded. It was one of his favorites of the many songs he and Blanchard had written together over the years, perhaps because it had been the first. He supposed that first songs about first loves tend to linger.

"We played 'I'm Eighteen' by Alice Cooper," Covey said.

"Good song."

"Don't forget Jimi Hendrix. 'Purple Haze' and 'Hey Joe.'"

"Do you remember that time I did the fire sacrifice up on stage just like Hendrix did at Monterey?" Blanchard asked.

"I remember the time your amp caught fire and almost burned down the high school gym over in Sand Valley before we got it put out. Is that what you're talking about?"

"I like the way I remember it better. Whatever happened, I looked cool putting it out."

"You did," Covey agreed. Even Hendrix would have not looked any cooler putting out an electrical fire in a gymnasium. It had been a defining moment in Skyye's early history. "Do you remember my favorite song?"

"'The Weight.' It was the only song we let you sing back then." Covey was not a natural vocalist, but for some reason he could sing a fair version of the iconic Band tune.

"I remember your favorite too," Covey said. "It was 'Iron Man' by Black Sabbath. I guess it kind of fits you. It takes a real iron man to drive to his own heart attack."

"I told you, the doctor this morning said I didn't have a heart attack. I just almost did. And anyway, driving to a heart attack is no big deal. Anyone can do that. Walking away from one? Now, that takes an iron man."

"WOMAN OF STONE"
(Blanchard Shankles/John Covey)

Been too long cryin' just wastin' my time
Been too long tryin' to hammer this rhyme
Been diggin' for silver in a copper mine
Been foolin' myself that everything's fine

Been drivin' sixty-six in a thirty-five zone
Been lookin' for lovin' from a woman of stone

Been climbin' toward the stars when I oughta lay low
Been swimmin' upstream when I oughta just flow
Been poundin' that door when there's no one home
Been needin' some roots but I'm bound to roam

Been drivin' sixty-six in a thirty-five zone
Been lookin' for lovin' from a woman of stone

Been headin' due east on a northbound train
Been hopin' for the sun while I'm drownin' in rain
Been thinkin' of a reason to climb out of this rack
Been swearin' it's the season to take my life back

Been drivin' sixty-six in a thirty-five zone
Been lookin' for lovin' from a woman of stone

Been eight long days since she flagged that 'Hound
Been eight long nights since I went to ground
Been a week and a day and some hours and a bit
Been as long as I can stand so I might as well sit

Been drivin' sixty-six in a thirty-five zone
Been lookin' for lovin' from a woman of stone
Been drivin' sixty-six in a thirty-five zone
Been lookin' for lovin' from a woman of stone

"19th Nervous Breakdown"
The Rolling Stones
-1970-

After the incident with Edna and the Nubian princess, life settled back into a semblance of what passed for normal at the Shankles home. Blanchard came to understand that it was quite common for psychotics to alter their speech patterns and tonal qualities as they slipped in and out of touch with reality. And he realized that any attempts Edna made on his life were not entirely her fault and that, therefore, she should be absolved from blame. But even these realizations did not detract from the fact that having a schizophrenic parent was a mighty weird experience. On the suck scale, he gave it a nine. The only higher possible rating was a ten, which he would have been awarded posthumously if she had managed to connect with the Nubian princess. It wasn't just the demonic sounds she made or her lack of affect, as if creatures from elsewhere were channeling through her, speaking with her tongue and lips. It was the immediacy of the transformation when she went truly bonkers as well, the random trip from bad to worse that she embarked upon frequently and without prior warning. Blanchard never quite saw it coming. One minute, she would be relatively fine for her, maybe singing her enduring tribute to Juicy Brucie Braaa-dley and the Boss Sounds from Boss Town while coloring a mirror or nailing a hapless starling to a Bible, and then, without warning, the evil humors would descend, she would slip into the unexplored reaches of the nether realms, and something quite dark and evil would escape into the world of light, bringing with it all the wretched legions of hell.

A year or so after Edna's midnight excursion with the Nubian princess to her son's bedroom, Geneva's cats went missing. She was a cat person, which wasn't her fault, and she fed and kept three on the porch. Blanchard had taken his sister's advice and equipped his room with a straight chair that he used nightly to secure his door, so Edna had never again tried to kill him in his sleep, although the doorknob did rattle from time to time, just to keep him on his toes. The cats, however, were not privy to the chair trick, and they had no doors to secure, anyway, no stout barriers between them and calamity. Geneva was quite upset at their absence.

"All of my cats are gone," she said. She seemed to have been crying, but her eyes had a softness to them that spoke of a firm dose of Edna's poisoned anxiety medicine. "I haven't seen them since the day before yesterday."

"Good," Blanchard replied. Unlike Geneva, he was not a cat person, probably due to unresolved trust issues with family members that were manifesting themselves in acute and unreasonable fears of the unknown. Or maybe it was the smell.

"I'm not kidding. I think something's happened to them. I asked Mama about them, but she just hissed at me." Geneva grimaced involuntarily. "Kind of like a cat, as a matter of fact."

"Something about you just pisses her off, I guess." Blanchard was trying to pick out "Blackbird" on his guitar and really didn't want to be bothered with Geneva, her missing cats, or his crazy mother right then. Cats tended to roam. It was in their nature. They would be back, or they wouldn't. His mama was insane. It was in her nature. Nothing was going to change it.

"Says the guy who almost had his skull caved in by the Nubian princess," Geneva replied. Blanchard nodded. She had made a good point.

"Something about me just pisses her off, too," Blanchard concluded. "We're peas in a pod, me and you. Maybe she never wanted children." Or cats, apparently.

"Maybe not. I want you to help me look for my cats." She sounded distressed.

"Are any of them nailed to the walls?" It was an indelicate question, but he had not been into the kitchen that morning—the perennial favorite place for ritual sacrifice—and given family history and some of Edna's less savory behaviors, it had to be asked.

"No. That's the first place I checked." Geneva shuddered. "I hate going in there, but I looked. Thank goodness they weren't there. She hasn't nailed anything up in quite a while. I was hoping she had gotten over that." The little sacrifices were a shock every time one was discovered. More than any other behavior, these mini-crucifixions set the Shankles family apart from the decent and god-fearing world of the sane.

"Maybe she has, but I wouldn't count on it," Blanchard said. "I hid the hammer and threw out all the nails." He made one more run at the Beatles tune, but Lennon and McCartney had used another one of those crazy chords that no one knew, and he just couldn't figure it out, so he gave up for the time being.

Because he was a good brother and in light of the fact that it gave him an excellent excuse to stay home from school, Blanchard spent the following day looking for the cats. He searched the barn and the outbuildings. He crawled up under the porch with a flashlight in one hand and a stick in the other, in case he rousted sleeping snakes instead of malingering cats. He walked the quarter mile of the fence line as far as the county road that led to the chert pit behind the house before cutting diagonally across the field to scout along the other fence. He checked the ditches along the roads bordering the property to rule out mishaps with automobile tires. He searched the length and breadth of the place, but he found no sign of Geneva's missing pets.

And then, around dusk, as he was about to abandon the search, Blanchard discovered what could only be described as an altar, and not the good, velvet-draped kind normally reserved for churches. It was actually an old slab of mountain granite, gray and weathered, partially buried along the northwest border of the Shankles acreage. For 100 years or more it had served as the cover over a deep, dry well, and it still topped that hole, but now it was in a new incarnation as well. It had become a small reliquary littered with the remnants of strange rites: feathers, chalk drawings, driftwood, smooth stones, the remains of a small fire, tufts of fur, a cat food can, and what could only be dried blood. The centerpiece of the display featured three little cat skulls, gleaming white, smiling obscenely in the fading light. A homemade wooden cross was driven upside down into the clay at the head of the slab. The realization that Edna had found something new to do with her free time began to creep over Blanchard. It was warm outside, but he shivered, and as the light of day waned, he found that he wanted nothing so much as to be well away from the site before the sun was snuffed by the horizon and the restless night spirits of the world began to wander the dark landscape in search of prey.

"Holy hell," he said, but in a whisper, lest he stir up forces best left asleep.

After he returned home, he sat with Geneva on the porch. "Mama has taken up a hobby," he said, wondering how best to present his findings.

"Did you find my cats?"

"I did," Blanchard said. Then, because there was really no way to sugarcoat any of it, he described his grisly find to his sister. He spoke in hushed tones, as if he were telling a secret that no one else must share. Edna was inside the house, sitting and staring at her reflection in the toaster, assumedly gaining its confidence. Blanchard looked over his shoulder a couple of times as he told his tale, just to verify that she was not slowly working her way up behind him with a can of tuna in one hand, a length of rope in the other, and a straight razor gripped firmly in her teeth.

"My poor cats," Geneva said. She was crying. "My poor babies." She was quiet for a time. Then she looked at Blanchard. "Do you think they suffered?"

Blanchard figured that they had almost certainly gone out the hard way, but Geneva didn't need to know that. "No. She killed them, but I don't think she hurt them." This was an amazingly stupid statement, one that made no sense at all, but it seemed to be what Geneva needed to hear.

"Are you sure?"

"I'm sure."

They were quiet for a while, each with thoughts enough to spare that they kept to themselves. Then, Geneva spoke again.

"She's getting worse, isn't she?"

Blanchard nodded. His mother was long past being as crazy as just one sack full of shithouse rats. She was at least as crazy as two sacks full and might even be pushing toward three.

"Funny how you didn't think she was getting worse when she tried to cave my head in with the Nubian princess," he noted, but not unkindly. If he hadn't been a light sleeper and fleet of foot when he awoke, he might be out there with the remains of Geneva's felines right now, his white bones shining in the pale moonlight, his freed spirit cat-dancing among the bright stars.

"That was different and you know it." She wiped a tear and sniffed.

"Ah," Blanchard said. The difference was lost on him, but he let it pass since his sister was grieving.

"We need to have her committed," Geneva concluded. Blanchard agreed that it did seem like the thing to do. He was fairly used to the bizarre by that stage of his life, but he couldn't get those little cat skulls out of his mind. Perhaps it was because he had known their names: Pepper, Taco, and Jezebel. Once the dead are named, they linger.

"I think she needs to be put away, too," he said. "But we can't just load her up in the MG and go do it. The old man has to be the one to do it. He's her husband. We're just her kids. And he won't." The subject had been breached on more than one occasion, usually right after another shithouse rat or two hopped into the sack, but Benton had always refused even to discuss the idea. With him, it appeared to be an issue of pride.

"I won't be known as the husband of the town lunatic," he had said the last time his children brought up the topic for family debate, right after Edna burned down the tool shed in an earnest but failed attempt to oust the extended family of demons that she believed had taken up residence there, along with the field mice and a couple of unsuspecting snakes. When Benton made this pronouncement, Blanchard's head had snapped around as if he had been backhanded.

"How about being known as the sorry son-of-a-bitch who won't get his wife some help?" he asked. "You like the sound of that better?"

Geneva gasped, and Benton's eyes bugged out like he was being choked. This was one of Blanchard's early before-and-after moments, the exact point in time when he realized that he was no longer afraid of his father. Benton was a hitter, and as such he had laid into his son a fair amount over the years. But he hadn't done so lately, and Blanchard was determined that those days were now past. If his old man wanted some, he was welcome to come get it.

"What did you say to me?" Benton asked, although he had heard just fine. "Boy, that mouth is going to get you into trouble one of these days," he said ominously.

"I'm free right now, if that day is today." Blanchard's hands slowly became fists. He was ready, he was willing, and he believed he was able. He had hated his father for a long time, and he was ready to lock horns. Benton looked at his son, now two inches taller and fifty pounds heavier than his sire, and decided that perhaps the day of reckoning had not yet arrived.

"You just watch that mouth," Benton said.

"Pussy," Blanchard had replied to his father's retreating back. Benton had stopped then, and almost turned around, but then he had continued on his way.

Now, sitting on the porch at the impromptu wake for Geneva's deceased cats, Blanchard and his sister wrestled with their conundrum. Edna was slipping ever deeper into insanity and needed treatment for her own sake, and there was no denying the fact that it was becoming more and more dangerous just to have her around. But they were at a loss as to what to do without their father's aid. Finally, they decided it would be best to sleep on it, and to talk again in the morning. It was a certainty that something had to change, and that they couldn't continue along as they were. Perhaps the answer would reveal itself while they slept, if they didn't pester it too much.

It is not always possible to determine when fate has taken an interest in the affairs of mortals, but sometimes this mystical power leaves a trail of crumbs that, in retrospect, cannot be missed, and when that happens, all those involved can rest assured that whatever happened was, in fact, supposed to happen. Thus, even though it was a Friday night—which had always been a prime time for Benton to tend to his flock of unparticular women who really ought to have thought it over and held out for a better deal—on this particular Friday, he decided to sleep at home. And Edna—who generally hibernated for a few days after committing a particularly outrageous act such as killing and skinning a trio of cats—instead wandered the Shankles house like a demented bindlestiff, rattling doorknobs, whispering to mirrors, and searching for that which she could not name but would know if and when she found it. And the Nubian princess—

Edna's past companion, accomplice, and silent witness, which had been hidden so well by Blanchard that even he couldn't find it again—somehow managed to reveal its whereabouts in the darkness, while Edna's ostensibly sane children slept a fitful slumber with chairs jammed under their respective doorknobs and one eye open, and while the world hurtled recklessly headlong through the dark and pitiless void on its journey from nowhere much to nowhere else.

Blanchard arose early the next morning, as was his habit, and climbed out onto the porch roof to smoke a cigarette, watch the sunrise, and contemplate the wonder of the day before him. Sometimes when he sat out there and watched the new day begin, he was able for the briefest of moments to forget the strange parameters of his world, and on those mornings, he almost felt normal. This morning, however, he could not bring it off. Something was bothering him, although for the life of him, he could not identify what it was. Maybe it was the cats. So he finished his smoke, climbed back into his room, and dressed. Then he unchaired his door and stepped out to meet the day. When he came down from his room, he saw Edna sitting in the hall by the front door. She was naked save for her left shoe, which was on her right foot and untied. She was spattered with what could be nothing else but blood. Her old friend, the Nubian princess, now red instead of the usual sedate black, sat proud beside her on the floor, a harbinger of change and an icon to carnage.

"Oh, no," Blanchard said. He had been conditioned to fear the worst, a reflex easy to develop in a house devoted to insanity, and he did so now. He stood frozen in his tracks a moment as the scene by the front door tried to arrange itself into meaning, but finally he gave up on the attempt and let his natural instincts take over. His first thought was for Geneva, and he ran back upstairs to check on her, but her door was still secured from within, locked and jammed, so he figured she must be safe.

"Who's there?" she hollered from the other side of the door.

"It's me," Blanchard responded. "Stay put! Don't come out until I come get you!"

"Why?"

"Just do what I say!" Blanchard hurried back downstairs and looked at his mother. She met his eyes and smiled. "What did you do, Mama?" he asked her quietly. "What did you do?"

"My name is John Landecker, and Records truly is my middle name," Edna said with an air of satisfaction. Cold dread descended upon Blanchard like a November Chicago fog. Crazy Edna had forsaken her favorite DJ—Juicy Brucie Braaa-dley—for a young upstart from a Midwest station. The fat was in the fire now, and all bets were off. He hated to, but he knew what he must do. He took a deep breath and slowly advanced the few steps down the hall to the room where Benton slept. Later in his life he would say that it seemed to take hours to walk that short hallway. His feet did not want to move, as if he were trudging through a mire and they were being sucked down. He arrived at the closed door and reached to grasp the doorknob. It was sticky, which surprised him but perhaps shouldn't have. He snatched his hand back and looked at the blood now on his fingers. He held his breath as he gripped the knob again, turned it, and pushed open the door. Then he looked within, although by that point it was a redundant gesture, because he already knew what he would see.

There on the bed lay what appeared to be a headless body, one that, had it borne a head and been standing, would have been similar in height to the former Benton Shankles. Blanchard took a step into the darkened room and turned on the light. He saw that the body was not actually without a head, after all. A pulpy mess on the pillow looked like it might have been a head at one time, before it had been whacked repeatedly for an hour or two by the Nubian princess. Blood was spattered on the floor, on the bedclothes, and on the wall behind the bed. There was even blood on the ceiling. Benton lay flat on his back with his arms at his sides, and Blanchard supposed that he had never seen it coming, which was a mercy he really didn't deserve but had received nonetheless, a final gift from the gods of anarchy.

"Damn," Blanchard said. There was not much else to say, so he said it again. Then he turned off the light, left the room, and gently closed the door. As he walked to the kitchen, he noted that the soles of his shoes were sticky, and that he was leaving footprints as he made his way. Once he arrived in the kitchen, he washed his hands for a good long while. Then he took a deep breath and called the police. After the call, he walked back to the front door, leaned against it, and slid down beside his mother. He looked at her as if seeing her for the first time, looked at her as if she had been a total stranger to him until that very moment. She looked frail and vulnerable, evil and deadly.

"It was a practice run," he said, speaking his thoughts as they entered his consciousness because the silence was too loud to bear. "That night in my room with the princess was a rehearsal. You've been working a plan." He was verbally putting together the pieces of this outlandish puzzle and didn't anticipate or need an answer, but he received one in spite of his expectations.

"Practice makes perfect," Edna observed as she scratched her knee. This was the second time he had heard his mother utter the phrase.

"Are you really crazy, Mama?" Blanchard asked. He had no doubts on that score. He knew that she was hopelessly and utterly insane, that hers was a malady beyond reclamation or repair. But he wanted to hear her thoughts on the subject. He wanted her view.

"As a sack full of shithouse rats." She rubbed her forehead with the back of her hand, and blood smeared.

"Did you have to kill him?"

"You can't always get what you want," Edna noted. She picked up the Nubian princess and flicked a bit of matter from it, examined it closely with one eye closed, then flicked a bit more. She offered the statuette to Blanchard, who declined, so she placed it back on the floor. She turned the statue so that the princess appeared to be keeping watch on Benton's bedroom. "But sometimes you get what you need."

"I guess maybe you do," her son answered. He patted her knee, and together they awaited the arrival of the authorities.

"WHO ARE YOU NOW?"
(Blanchard Shankles/John Covey)

Pose me a riddle, sing a blue tune
Dance a slow step in a rainy, sad June
Ask the wrong question again and again
Who are you now, who were you then?

Tell me a story, cry one sweet tear
Stare down tomorrow without any fear
Take a last breath and count down from ten
Who are you now, who were you then?

Sketch a gray likeness, stay on the page
Make no bold promise, swallow the rage
Crouch still and fierce like a wolf in her den
Who are you now, who were you then?

Sing a raw note, then sing one more
Watch for the signs and nail shut the door
Pray for salvation but save the amen
Who are you now, who were you then?

Try for a lifetime or at least for a year
Nothing but nothing to keep us both here
Speak like a poet and take up the pen
Who are you now, who were you then?

Wander and ponder the dusty bare floor
Cash it all in and walk through the door
Get past the why and bury the when
Who are you now, who were you then?

Days turn to sorrow, nights to regret
Years carve the memories we ought to forget
Ask the wrong question again and again
Who are you now, who were you then?

Pose me a riddle, sing a blue tune
Dance a slow step in a rainy, sad June
Ask the wrong question again and again
Who are you now, who were you then?

"(Don't Fear) The Reaper"
Blue Oyster Cult
-Sunday: First Day-

Sitting in the Tennessee hospital room waiting for the heart doctor, Blanchard and Covey fell into a silence that lasted until the sun set. Covey was reading a pamphlet about heart surgery that seemed way too upbeat for what it was describing, as if it were trying to convince potential patients to undergo the procedure as a recreational activity, like a trip to Panama City Beach, perhaps, or a crawl down Bourbon Street. Blanchard was again watching cars. Now they had their lights on, and pairs of headlights whisked past his window over and over like little twin moons, while the red and orange stars of taillights jaunted by in the opposite direction. The boulevard he looked down upon was broad and filled with a creamy glow from the streetlights overhead. Blanchard could make out a flashing P...A...W...N sign and another that promised to serve its patrons the coldest beer in town. This combination of advertisements made him want to go pawn some slightly used medical equipment and buy himself a cold beer, and maybe one for Covey if he behaved himself.

Traffic lights blinked green, yellow, and red according to their whims. Above the Best Western motel three blocks down, the moon seemed to be nested on a pillow of clouds as if it had stopped there for the night after a long day of travel. Heat lightning flickered, shorting out against the velvet sky like a thousand electric capillaries. A scruffy man Blanchard took for homeless pushed a shopping cart from trashcan to trashcan, inspecting the detritus of the day and selecting small treasures to place in his buggy. Even though the scene unfolding before him was as plain as white bread and as normal as the sun rising and the rain falling from the sky, it all made Blanchard gloomy. He felt apart now, isolated and singled out, like a rogue steer that had been cut from the herd and penned for slaughter. He was no longer of the normal world and might never be again.

Then the door opened and in walked an individual wearing blue surgical scrubs and black athletic shoes. He was compact, nearly bald, and wore wire-rimmed glasses that served to magnify the crow's-feet accenting his blue eyes. Blanchard guessed him to be in his early sixties, but he was a poor judge of ages, and the man could be older or younger. The newcomer looked at the chart he carried, frowned as he quickly scanned the first page, and then frowned harder still as he held the chart closer and took a longer look. Then he turned his attention to Blanchard, presenting him with an earnest approximation of a reassuring smile. Covey stood and made as if to leave, but Blanchard motioned for him to sit back down.

"Stay where you are," he said. "Sit and help me make sense of all this. We have decisions to make." Covey nodded and resumed his seat.

"Hello, Mr. Shankles," the man said as he stepped over and shook Blanchard's hand. "I'm Dr. Forrester, a cardiothoracic surgeon. Your cardiologist asked me to come talk with you about your heart trouble." Blanchard noticed the doctor's gray stubble and tired eyes. He figured that the surgeon had started the day early and had put in some long hours since. In that respect, he and Blanchard were alike.

"He told me you would be coming by to see me," Blanchard said. "He was pretty excited right after he did the heart cath this morning. I think I made his whole day." The doctor had, in fact, muttered a medical term that had sounded remarkably similar to *oh, hell* upon his discovery that his patient's heart apparently had no blood whatsoever coursing through it.

"I imagine he was. I'm a bit excited myself, and not in a good way. If no one has told you yet, you are a medical miracle, one in a million. You have a 100 percent blockage of the LAD artery. We don't see too many of those on live patients." He flipped the front page of Blanchard's chart and began to read the next.

"That's what I hear," Blanchard said. "I guess they don't call it the widow maker for nothing." He had learned that term during his first heart procedure back in Staunton, when it had been explained to him that blockages such as his had produced an uncounted multitude of widows over the ages and more than just a scattering of widowers as well. He had also learned that LAD stood for left anterior descending, that it was the main blood supply to the front of the heart, and that it had an annoying tendency to stop up, intelligent design notwithstanding.

After his most recent heart procedure earlier that morning, Blanchard had further discovered that restenosis was the term used to describe the process whereby a previously unclogged coronary artery—such as the one he had departed Staunton with—became reclogged for no particularly good reason other than it had a bad attitude and could. His was apparently prone to do just that, and a 100 percent blockage of said LAD artery meant that he was well and truly screwed and really ought to be dead. Every time he had a heart cath, Blanchard learned something new. If his luck held and he didn't die first, he might one day be the smartest person in the band, at least when it came to matters of the heart.

"Yes. The widow maker. Dr. Western told me you strolled into the ER like you were looking to buy the place. I have to tell you that most people don't walk anywhere with a blockage such as this. Most people don't survive a 100 percent blockage of the LAD at all. When you hear about people dropping dead from a heart attack, this is the vessel that drops them. You shouldn't even be sitting up, never mind driving yourself to the hospital and walking in the door." He shook his head. "You obviously have extensive collateral circulation." Blanchard knew this one, too. When the body grows new blood vessels around a blockage in an artery, the resulting blood flow is called collateral circulation. It was one of his strengths, seemingly, along with rugged handsomeness, good finger dexterity, and a knack for rudimentary math. It was the reason he was still alive. "That and perhaps more than your share of good old-fashioned luck are why you're still here." The doctor once again shook his head in amazement.

"My LAD and I haven't been seeing eye to eye for a while now," Blanchard told Dr. Forrester. "Bad hearts run in my family. Every Shankles who ever died had heart trouble. Except my daddy. He died of head trouble."

"Bad hearts tend to do that. Run in families, I mean. I operated on a woman a couple of weeks ago. She was pretty young to be having a quadruple bypass, but that's what it was. In the waiting room after the surgery I met her mother and her grandfather. They were both ex-patients of mine. Both quadruples as well." He was now scanning the third page of the medical chart in his hands. "Do you smoke?" he asked.

"Sometimes I smoke a pipe," Blanchard said. Occasional lapses in candor also ran in the Shankles family, which was to say that most of them lied like car salesmen at the end of the month.

"Tell him the truth," Covey said from his perch on the side chair. "He's here trying to save your life. Maybe you ought to help him with that and let him know what he's dealing with."

"I smoke from time to time," Blanchard said as he glared at Covey. He was having second thoughts about asking his bass player to stay for the consultation.

"He smokes two packs of Marlboro 100s a day," Covey corrected. "Sometimes he tears the filter off so he can get a really good hit. The only time he's not smoking is when he's asleep—and even that doesn't always stop him—or somewhere he can't, like in here. He would sell me and you both into bondage for one right now."

"Doc, let me introduce you to my friend," Blanchard said. "This is John Covey. Anything you need to know about me, just ask him." Covey and Dr. Forrester nodded at one another.

"Well, the cigarettes aren't helping your heart, and neither is your cholesterol level, which is very high, but I'm not here to preach at you. I'm here to fix you, and we'll let your own doctor do the preaching. We can treat the cholesterol with medication, and you already know what you need to do about the Marlboro 100s. They will kill you if you don't put them down."

Blanchard knew. He had done mostly whatever he wanted to do for his entire life, but apparently the piper was a union man and now wanted to be paid. He had been smoking since he was ten, when he had sneaked his very first cigarette from his mama's pack of Raleighs and smoked it all the way to the filter while hiding on the roof outside his bedroom window. He had enjoyed every puff of that first smoke and each and every one of the uncounted cigarettes that came after it. His mother had been a chain smoker back during the time when women did not necessarily cease their bad habits while they were pregnant, and Blanchard had always figured that he was born addicted to nicotine, and to bourbon, for that matter. And he had a weakness for amphetamines, come to think of it, but that was a story for another time. Now it seemed that his bad behaviors had finally caught up with him. His impunity was revoked. It looked like it might be time to toe the line.

"This is the second time it has clogged up," Blanchard said, steering the doctor away from speculation about his patient's culpability *vis a vis* his current medical emergency. "I had an 80 percent blockage the last time. I got it fixed up in Staunton two years ago." As if to punctuate his statement, a sharp pain clawed his sternum and a spasm shot down his left arm like an electric current. He rubbed his shoulder absentmindedly.

"Angioplasty and stents are effective a great deal of the time," Dr. Forrester said, "but sometimes coronary arteries are stubborn. I'm afraid you've got one of those." Blanchard nodded. Stubbornness ran in his family, too, so his coronary artery had come by its obstinacy honestly. The doctor continued. "We need to do a single coronary bypass and just circumvent the problem. The remainder of your arteries look fine. We'll do it tomorrow. The good news is that since it is a single bypass, we can probably use your mammary artery and not have to take a graft from your leg. That will shorten your recovery time, and since we'll be using a live vessel, there's a good chance that you'll never have trouble with your heart again. Sometimes leg grafts have to be replaced again ten years or so down the line, but it is very rare to have to go back in to tune up a mammary artery. Especially if you lay off the Marlboros."

Blanchard swallowed. His thoughts were whirling, and he willed them to focus. When he had arrived at the hospital that morning, he was hoping for another quick patch, and that perhaps this time the repair would hold. When the talk of bypass surgery began earlier in the day, his overriding thought was that he needed to get out of there.

"Can't we try another stent?" He believed in asking when he didn't know, and he really didn't want to be cracked open like a Maine lobster on a banquet table sometime after the sun rose tomorrow.

"That's a good question. We could if not for the fact that your artery is completely closed up. That rules out angioplasty. We could try a rotablator procedure, but the problem there is that a patient who exhibits a tendency toward restenosis once is likely to have the same issue again."

"What's a rotablator?" Blanchard asked. It sounded serious.

"It's sort of like a little drill. The cardiologist runs it in there at the end of a catheter and drills out the blockage in the artery."

"You put a drill in someone's heart?"

"Well, it's a very small drill. But again, the option is not a good one for patients who have exhibited restenosis."

"He's saying if you're prone to stopping up, you'll just stop back up," Covey added helpfully.

"My ears are fine," Blanchard said to Covey. "It's my heart that sucks." He turned back to Dr. Forrester. "Is there any other choice?" he asked. "Maybe some pills or something? The more I think about surgery, the less I like the whole idea." What really bothered him was the part where they stopped the heart to fix the problem. He didn't know the medical definition of death, but to his layman's way of thinking, a heart that was not beating could certainly be considered a reasonable candidate. It was counterintuitive to him, somehow, that they were going to kill him in order to save his life. It seemed a sketchy plan at best, resembling something that Simpson Taggart might come up with, like letting the bus run out of fuel to see if the gas gauge was working properly.

"It is a major surgery," the doctor replied. "There's no getting around that. We put you to sleep, cool you way down, stop your heart, and bypass the blockage. But you're an excellent candidate. Heart surgeons fight over cases such as yours." Blanchard wondered if Dr. Forrester had whipped several other surgeons before coming to see him. Maybe there had been a cage match in the doctor's lounge earlier in the day, winner take all, and Dr. Forrester had climbed out victorious only after dispatching all the other members of the hospital's surgical staff, perhaps enhancing his reputation by finishing with a flying drop kick or a dive from the corner turnbuckle. He didn't look that tough, admittedly, but it was always the small guys you had to watch. They were a gritty bunch. "You don't have any other medical conditions," the doctor continued. "Your blood pressure is good, you didn't actually have a heart attack—which is absolutely beyond amazing—you're relatively young, and we only have to bypass one artery. We might even bypass you off pump. It should be no more than four hours start to finish. You'll do fine. It ought to be a piece of cake."

Blanchard nodded. It all sounded swell, just a stroll through the park on a summer's eve, and he didn't want anything to do with any of it, cake notwithstanding. "I'm not much on having any kind of surgery," he insisted.

"That's true," Covey said. "He's kind of a sissy about it. You should hear him take on."

"I think I just want to go home," Blanchard said.

"You can't just go home," Covey said. "Tell him, Dr. Forrester."

"Hush, Covey," Blanchard said. "I'm trying to talk to the man. This is the thing, Doc. The thought of getting put to sleep really nuts me up. They gave me ether one time when I was a kid, and it was bad. It felt like they were choking me to death, and I threw up for days after. I've never forgotten it, and I don't want to go through that again. So if I just unplug all of this stuff, get up, and go home, what do you think will happen to me? Do you think I'll live?" Blanchard's great-uncle had coexisted with a bad heart back during the days before bypass surgery was even an option, and he had lived to be almost eighty. He even drank a small shot of bourbon every evening on his doctor's orders. Right now, eighty with a steady supply of whiskey looked good to Blanchard. It wasn't ninety-five immediately after one last debauch, mind, but neither was it fifty-nine, on the table in an operating room in middle Tennessee, with blood spurting everywhere, alarms sounding, and nurses and doctors wringing their hands while wailing in anguish if not utter despair. Eighty would do. Dr. Forrester looked at his patient a moment with compassion before answering the unexpected question as honestly as he was able.

"Well, first off, we don't use ether anymore. We have much better ways to put patients to sleep now. And the good news is, simply, that your blockage can't get any worse. 100 percent is 100 percent. That's as bad as it gets. Over time you might even develop additional collateral circulation around it, and you could live for quite a while. The bad news is that you could run out of luck and die on the way to the parking lot. There's no way of telling what might happen. The thing is, you should have already had a heart attack. A bad one. I don't know why you didn't have one while you were walking into the hospital, or even while you were getting into that chair. So it's hard to say with certainty what might happen if you leave. If you go home, though, you would always be just one exertion away from maybe having the big one. You would have to be mindful of that fact all the time. As one example, work would be your enemy. What do you do for a living?"

"I'm a musician. I play in a rock and roll band."

"I don't go out all that much, but from what I've seen, that seems like a strenuous line of work. Lots of late hours, lots of secondary smoke, lots of standing, jumping, that kind of thing. I think if you don't have the surgery, you might have to find another occupation or get used to the idea of an early retirement and lots of porch time. You would need to avoid hills and stairs. Driving would be dangerous for you and everyone else on the road. Sex would be out of the question. You would have to sleep a great deal and rest several times during the day. An exciting football game on television might kill you. Changing a flat tire *would* kill you. You would have to settle into an extremely calm and sedentary lifestyle, and you don't look like the sort of person who would be happy with that. I have done hundreds of these procedures, and you really need to let me fix this for you. I am very confident that I can put you back right. Then you can live a normal life."

Blanchard was quiet for a moment, considering the doctor's words. He wasn't much of a football fan, and he had just bought a set of tires for his car, so those particular examples had fallen on deaf ears. But he liked sex just as much as the next person, and he lived in a two-story house and slept in an upstairs bedroom, so he supposed there was really no choice. He sighed and looked at the doctor.

"Doc, have you ever heard 'Mississippi Queen' by Mountain?"

"No, I don't think I have."

"It's a great song with a fine lead run, one of the best I've ever heard, and when I play it, I play it like I wrote it. I never miss a note. At least, I never did until one night at an American Legion club somewhere in…Covey, where were we?"

"We were in West Virginia," Covey said. "I don't remember the name of the town. It wasn't much of a town, but the club was packed and the people were nice, even after you screwed up the song."

Blanchard nodded and continued with his anecdote. "Right. Somewhere in West Virginia. Anyway, I had woman troubles at the time, which is not that uncommon, but these were worse than usual, and they were on my mind while I was playing 'Mississippi Queen.' Before I knew it, I was off-key and three bars behind the rest of the band, just totally crashing and burning on one of the best songs ever written. Seriously, I have been playing that song since I was eighteen years old, and I never, ever miss a note. But I did that night. I messed it up." He looked at the doctor. "So if you have a fight with your wife tonight or if your car breaks down in the morning, or even if you're just feeling kind of off, I want a rain check. I don't want you worried about anything while you're up to your elbows in my chest. You have to be at the top of your game if we're going to do this. I believe you when you say you're good. I know good when I see it—it's in the eyes—and you look like you might know what you're doing, but even the best can screw up."

"Fair enough," Dr. Forrester said. He smiled at the oddity of the conversation.

"And no students. They can watch if they have to, but that's all they can do. Hands off the guitar player! I don't want some kid with good intentions and a case of the colic killing me."

"The A team only," Dr. Forrester agreed, nodding.

"You have any kids?" Blanchard asked.

"I do. I have two."

"Well, if I make it through tomorrow, I'll play at both of their weddings. For free. Except for 'Danny's Song.' I don't do 'Danny's Song,' even if you paid me. Anything else they want, I probably know, but if I don't, I'll learn it."

"You'll make it through," Dr. Forrester said. "My kids are both married, but I'll come listen to you play the next time you're in town. You can play 'Mississippi Queen' for me."

"Okay, then." Blanchard held out his hand, and they shook. "I'll see you tomorrow." The doctor nodded at Blanchard and Covey, then left the room.

"You were kind of hard on the students," Covey said. "They have to learn sometime. So did you."

"They don't have to learn on me," Blanchard responded. "And when I was learning to play 'Ramblin' Man,' I didn't kill the song or either one of the Allman brothers in the process."

"You didn't kill it," Covey agreed, "but I remember you hurt it pretty bad."

"I really hope that smart-ass thing you've got going on runs its course soon."

"You want me to lie to you?"

"Yes!"

"You're a grown man and all," Covey said, changing the subject, "and sometimes you even act like one, but don't you think it's kind of a bad idea to risk ticking off the guy who's going to be cutting you open?"

"What did I say?"

"You offered him a bribe if he didn't kill you."

"He's not mad. He seemed like a good guy, and I was just sharing my concerns with him. Plus, I was putting a human face on my heart. Now I'm not just a statistic to him. I'm a guy he's talked to. If it all goes wrong tomorrow, he'll try a little harder to bring me back because now he knows me."

"Knowing you could actually work against you."

"There's that smart-ass thing again."

"Sorry. But you did kind of audition him."

"Maybe a little. Just asking some questions. You wait. When it comes time one of these days for someone to saw you open, you'll have questions too!" Blanchard was quiet for a moment, then he spoke again. "He's in for a treat with 'Mississippi Queen.' I remember the first time I heard that song. I wanted to marry Leslie West and have his kids. Sometimes I wish I had never heard it, just so I could hear it for the first time again." He sighed. "So many good days and good times gone." Covey sighed too, but for a different reason.

"Well, this whole thing sucks. I hate it for you. I was really hoping they could do something else besides heart surgery."

"It sucks in stereo," Blanchard agreed. "I don't want to do it."

"I know you don't. Who would? But you heard the man. You have to let him fix you."

"I don't have to do anything except pay taxes and die." He fell silent again as he reflected upon all that he had heard. Then he looked at Covey. "I'll tell you one thing. We all have to kick off sometime, but I sure don't want to die tomorrow. If you help me get unhooked and dressed, we'll get out of here." To punctuate this radical notion, he ripped the cuff from his arm and let it fall to the floor. On cue, it began humming as it tried to inflate.

"You're not going to die. Unless you leave. I guarantee you *that* will kill you."

"I'll lean on your shoulder."

"No you won't. Forget it. I'm not helping you kill yourself. I'll sit here with you the whole time, I'll give you blood if you need it, and I'll drive you home after. But I won't help you kill yourself. You need to get fixed."

"Some friend."

"Are you kidding me? I'm the best friend you ever had. Nobody else would have put up with you all these years. Now, just relax. This is a routine deal nowadays. Jimbo's daddy had one of these operations a few years back, and he was eighty-seven. You're going to be fine."

"Jimbo's daddy is dead." Blanchard had been a pallbearer.

"He's dead as a hammer and planted in the ground with an azalea on top of him, but he didn't die during heart surgery. He slipped in the bathtub and cracked his head. So my advice is to have the surgery and be careful in the shower. I know it's hard for you, but don't do something stupid. You can't pretend this isn't happening."

"Stupid stuff is all I know how to do. It's my life's work."

"And you do a good job. But right now I need for you to reach down deep. Try something new. Restrain yourself." Covey stepped to the recliner and picked up the cuff. It had stopped inflating and was now just humming, as if it were confused at the lack of an arm within and the absence of blood pressure to measure. Blanchard stuck out his arm, and Covey replaced the cuff.

"Too tight?" he asked.

"It's okay," Blanchard replied. A thought occurred to him. "Well, on the bright side, after he fixes me up, I can smoke for fifty more years. That will put me at somewhere around 110 years old before I have to quit." This was a definite positive for Blanchard, and for his bandmates as well. The lead player for Murphy's Law was prone to fussiness whenever he tried to quit smoking, so much so that, by the second or third day, he was likely to find anonymous packs of Marlboro 100s left in strategic locations by band members who thought that some people needed to smoke in the interest of the common good.

"I didn't hear the man say anything like that."

"You have to learn to read between the lines. I've been smoking for fifty years, and now I have this little problem. Once he fixes it, it will be like starting over again. We'll reset the clock, and I can smoke for fifty more years. Maybe longer if I start taking an aspirin every day. With any luck at all, I'll die of something else when I'm 109. If I start smoking lights, I might make it even longer!"

"Keep that good thought, and maybe your luck will hold."

"If I tell you something, will it stay between us?" Blanchard had lowered his voice.

"It will if you want it to. You know I don't talk out of school. To this day, has anyone ever heard about Gloria Roades?" Gloria Roades had been Blanchard's first great love, but the physical aspect of the affair had been brief—somewhere around nine seconds, if Gloria could be believed—and both lovers had subsequently sought solace elsewhere. "All bass players know how to keep secrets. Aside from superior talent and extreme good looks, it's why we're the backbone of the band."

"I'm serious. I need to talk about something, but it's kind of embarrassing."

"More embarrassing than Gloria Roades?"

"Covey…"

"Sorry. Just fooling around. You know you can trust me. Whatever it is, get it off your chest."

Blanchard cleared his throat. "Ever since I got sick in Staunton, I've had a—what do you call it—a premonition about dying from heart surgery. I dream about it almost every night. It's like I'm watching from overhead as they work on me. Every time I have that dream, it all goes wrong when they try to restart my heart after the surgery. No matter what they do, it won't go back to beating. They shock it, and nothing happens. They give it shots, and it still won't beat. They massage it, and it just lays there. Finally they give up, and the doctor looks at the clock and calls the time of death. It's always 4:47. I don't know if that's a.m. or p.m., but I guess that doesn't really matter. I'm floating up above everyone, up near the ceiling, hollering at them to please don't stop, to give it one more try, that I'm still with them, but they don't hear me and stop anyway. It's pretty creepy when they pull that sheet over my face. And then one of the nurses writes my name on this paper tag and ties it to my big toe. Then they roll me out of there into an elevator. All this time I'm still floating right along, hollering at them. We ride the elevator down to the basement, me and an orderly and dead me. The morgue's down there. It's really cold, and I can see my breath. Well, floating me can. Dead me's not breathing. Then they move my body onto one of those pull-out drawer things like you see in morgues on TV. Then, with me still hollering that I'm not dead, they slam it shut. That's when I always wake up." He looked at Covey. "Crazy, right?"

"It sounds pretty creepy," Covey agreed. "I reckon I'd try to wake up earlier if I could." It sounded insane, in point of fact, but Covey didn't want to be hasty in his judgments.

"Wow," Blanchard said. "Wake up earlier? Now there's a great idea. Why didn't I think of that? You think I don't try? But I can't. It's like I'm paralyzed." He swallowed. "That dream is why I think I might die with this heart business. It seems real, like I'm watching an actual film of someone else die. It's even in color. I almost never remember dreams. Well, I didn't used to, anyway. But I remember this one. I want to look away or leave the operating room, but I can't do it. I have to float there and watch." Blanchard took a shaky breath.

"It's just a dream," Covey said. "It doesn't mean anything. Dreams are just your brain finding something to do with itself while you're asleep. Don't pay any attention to it. It's like all those times you dreamed about having a three-way with Ann and Nancy Wilson. It was just a dream. It never really happened."

"Not yet it hasn't," Blanchard corrected. "Now that Heart isn't touring as much, there is still time. You had to bring up the Wilson girls? Are you *trying* to kill me?"

"At least I didn't mention Stevie Nicks."

"Bastard."

75

"Or Linda Ronstadt."

"Rat bastard."

"Anyway, I was just trying to cheer you up. Sorry. I wasn't thinking. But if you ever do get your chance with the Wilson sisters, or Stevie, or even Linda, don't you think you might have a better time if you go ahead and have your heart fixed? I'm sure they would, with you not dying halfway through and all."

"Maybe," Blanchard said grudgingly. He took a deep breath while he rubbed at a twinge in his neck. "So you won't help me leave?"

"No."

Blanchard held Covey's gaze for several moments. "If I die tomorrow," he said finally and with great deliberation, "I want to be cremated."

"I told you. You're not going to die tomorrow."

"Yeah, yeah, yeah. Blah, blah, blah. What do you know? Are you a doctor? Believe me, not dying suits me all the way down to the ground. But I might, and if I do, I want you to burn me. Douse me with gas, light me up, and roast hot dogs over me. Good hot dogs, too. Not those cheap red things that your mama used to make for us. Break out the marshmallows and invite the rest of the boys and their families. But first let the people here take out anything they need for other folks. Not my heart, I guess, since it's kind of messed up. But maybe my liver and kidneys and such." Covey wasn't sure that it would be such a good idea to transplant Blanchard's liver into anyone else, either, but he held his tongue due to the generosity of the gesture. "But don't let them take my eyes," Blanchard continued. "I want to keep my eyes."

"Why them?"

"I don't know. I just do."

"Maybe you better write all of this down," Covey said. "We're not kin, and I don't know if they'll take my word for it." He handed his pad and pencil to Blanchard. "You write it down and sign it, and I'll witness it. That ought to do the trick." Blanchard flipped to a clean page and wrote out his wishes in detail. He signed and dated the paper and handed it back to Covey, who witnessed the signature with his own. Then Covey closed the pad and placed it into his shirt pocket. He patted the slight bulge and looked at his friend. "Just in case," he said. "But I promise you're going to be all right, Blanchard. I know it in my heart. If I thought different, I'd load you up and get you out of here right now. I swear I would."

Blanchard nodded, as if he had known this all along. "Do you know why I want to be cremated?" he asked. "Why I don't want to be put into the ground?"

"Besides the fact that you won't be dead? No. Why?"

"They have discovered somewhere in Germany that dead people are not decomposing. They dig them up, and when they do, the bodies look just like they did when they put them in the ground. I read an article about it. When they found the first one, they thought it was a one-shot deal, some kind of fluke or gag or something, but now they claim they have found dozens of them all over the country."

"Why have they dug up dozens of dead German people?" Covey asked.

"Who knows?" Blanchard replied. He wasn't much acquainted with German culture, but digging up dead folks to check on their condition seemed an odd enterprise at best. His personal philosophy tended toward out of sight, out of mind, and along those lines, he believed that the deceased should remain wherever they were put, undisturbed until the end of days, at which time Jesus could do with them as He wished. "Maybe it's some kind of German tradition, like wearing those hats with feathers or having tubas in bands. Anyway, some of these people have been down in their graves for a long time, forty or fifty years or more, and when the box gets dug up and opened, they're still people. They're not skeletons or dust or mummies, like you'd expect them to be. They shrink a little bit, kind of like they're tightening up, and then they just stop. It's like they're asleep or something." He shivered at the thought. "They're just hanging out down there in their caskets. That is seriously weird, and it's why I don't intend to be buried. I don't want to be laying in my casket for all of eternity, staring at the inside of the lid, looking the way I look now, only a little shorter. It's just too creepy." He shivered again.

"Did the article say why this was happening?" Almost against his will, Covey was hooked. He wanted more details about the well-preserved Bavarians. The surreal beckoned, and he was drawn in. He could see the dead just lying there in their lederhosen, their waxy, tight, dimpled knees on display, the buckles on their suspenders a bit tarnished, perhaps, but proud.

"It said they think people are exposed to so many preservatives during their lives now that they become preserved even before the undertaker gets hold of them. We eat chemicals in our food, drink them in our water, breathe them in our air, and wear them in our clothes. Over time, all of that stuff gets into our cells and just stays there. The article said we can't metabolize it, so it's like we're being slowly embalmed from the inside out our whole lives. You know what? I bet if we dug up some Americans, we'd find the same thing happening here." He sounded excited for just a moment, and Covey was glad there were no shovels handy.

"Are you sure you're not making this up?" he asked. Blanchard sometimes had a strained relationship with the truth, and he had a long history of telling tall tales to his bass player, and Covey had yet to hear a good reason for exhuming a flatbed truck full of Germans.

"I swear on *Houses of the Holy* that it's all true. The magazine is probably still on the bus somewhere. You can read about it yourself." Blanchard seemed piqued, as if truth were his middle name and his character had been impugned.

"Settle down. I believe you. I just don't understand you, and you still haven't told me why they're digging up dead Germans."

"Because they can?"

"Let's change the subject."

"But I have death on my mind."

"I noticed, and that's a bad thing to have on your mind today."

"Hey, I may *be* dead tomorrow, and my best buddy in the world won't help me escape. I want to talk about it today, while I still can."

"Here's a new topic. Have you heard from Vanny lately?" Vanny was Blanchard's on-again, off-again love interest, currently off. Her given name was Vanessa Renea Hartbarger, but just plain Vanny was easier on the tongue. In addition to being the estranged girlfriend of the lead guitar player for Murphy's Law, she was a bit of a pistol, which was actually nothing more than the female equivalent of Blanchard's status as a rounder. They had been quite a pair once upon a time, a match made on the periphery of the south side of hell, out past the sulfur pits and the blood swamps where the rent was cheap and the view was hazy.

"I'd rather talk about dying and not decaying than talk about her," Blanchard said. "It's more pleasant." He and Vanny had been a happy couple for approximately one year. When asked, after the first of many breakups, why they had gone their separate ways, Blanchard had stated that it was a case of irreconcilable differences. "She thinks I'm a no-talent loser, and everyone knows I have plenty of talent." This difference of opinion notwithstanding, they had never made those final steps toward complete separation, and they always eventually made up again. Covey wondered sometimes if there was yet hope for the couple. He doubted it, but he hoped for a permanent reconciliation for them anyway. Stranger things had happened during the long history of mankind, and he liked for people to be happy. Blanchard had been mostly alone since his wife died, and alone was not a good state.

"I told you I'm not going to talk about dead Germans anymore," Covey said. "Or dead Americans either. But I can try to get in touch with Vanny if you want her to know what's going on. I think she would appreciate it. She might want to be here."

"She would absolutely love this." Blanchard gestured at their surroundings. "That girl would have me nailed in a box not decomposing in Germany before you could holler Code Blue."

"I said no more dead Germans," Covey said. "So is that a yes or a no?"

"That's a no. If I kick off tomorrow, she can read about it in the newspapers." Blanchard looked at Covey with hard eyes. "I mean it now, Covey. Tell Anna that I don't want Vanny up here." Anna was Covey's wife and Vanny's good friend. "Not that she'd come, anyway."

Covey nodded, but not because he agreed with Blanchard's wishes. He had in fact talked to Anna earlier that day, right after Blanchard's heart cath, and although they had not discussed whether she should or shouldn't share the information with Vanny, he was pretty sure that by now she had done just that. He thought it best to keep this information to himself, given the sad state of Blanchard's coronary artery.

"How about your sister?" he asked instead. "I can try to track her down and get word to her. Do you want Geneva to know about your trouble?"

Blanchard shook his head even more emphatically than he had with Vanny. "Are you kidding? The last thing I need is for my crazy sister to be here. If you get in touch with her, me and you are going to have to go round and round. Do you really want to get whipped by a guy with a bad heart? Word gets out about things like that, and bass players are supposed to be tough. It could ruin your career."

"I thought you liked Geneva," Covey said.

"I like her just fine, and I love her too. But she always wants to rehash old memories and talk about the good old days. In my family, there were no good old days. We were two wolf cubs raised at the dump during the big tire fire and chemical spill. We're like survivors from one of those concentration camps they had back during World War Two. We lived through it, and somehow we stumbled out the front gate on our own two legs when it was over, but there are no sweet memories to talk about. Not even one. Every single day was worse than the one before, and that's not even counting those times when something extra special happened. Edna tried to kill me, my sister packed up and took off as soon as she could find someplace to go, and you know what happened to my father, the prick. I don't want to remember any of it, because time hasn't made it better. It still sucks after all these years, and I've spent most of my life trying to forget every minute of it. It's not working, you understand, but I keep trying. What I don't need is Geneva here warming it all up when I'm in no condition to run from her." He held up his hands, as if to ward off the memories lest they engulf him like a bull tsunami wave. "So have mercy. No Geneva. Please."

"Fair enough. I just felt like I had to ask. You're the one with the bad heart, so you get to pick. No sister, and no Vanny. But when Geneva finds out anyway, and you know she will, she's going to be mad."

Blanchard shrugged. He had seen Geneva in an annoyed state many times and had no wish to repeat the experience, but he could live with it if he had to. "She'll get over it. I'll talk to her after it's all over, if I live. I'll just tell her you were supposed to call her, but you forgot. She'll go for that." Blanchard had been kidding when he said it, but he actually kind of liked this idea now that it was out in the open. It had simplicity, believability, and a built-in bad guy.

"Uh-uh," Covey said, shaking his head. "If you think I'm diving up under the bus for you, you're crazy. I will narc you out in a New York minute." He liked Geneva, but he had no more desire to stand on her bad side than Blanchard did.

"Some friend," Blanchard said. "I ask for one little favor, and what do I get? With guys like you having my back, I'll be better off dead."

"That's not true."

"You know what I hate?" This was an odd segue, but Covey was willing to listen if his friend might need to air some regrets, even though Blanchard's one and only tattoo—a bold statement scribed in Gregorian script on the back of his right shoulder that indicated that its owner had NO REGERTS—seemed to imply that he was good to go on all fronts, with the probable exception of his decision to hire a talented but fairly illiterate tattoo artist one night after a show in Gadsden, Alabama.

"What's that?" Covey asked.

"Sunglasses."

"Sunglasses?"

"I just hate people who wear sunglasses." He looked off as he spoke.

"Okay, I'll bite," Covey said. "What is wrong with wearing sunglasses?" He occasionally wore a pair himself but had not realized until now that it was a character flaw. He hoped the band would survive his foible.

"Only two kinds of people wear them, and both kinds drive me nuts. People who are trying to look cool wear sunglasses, and people who are trying to look tough wear sunglasses. Vanny wore them to look cool *and* tough. She was a double-dipper."

"Well, it worked. She does look cool, and she looks kind of tough, too, in a sexy sort of way."

"That's beside the point. And quit talking about my girlfriend like that."

"Sorry," Covey said. "I hate to break it to you while you're laid up, but those are not the only reasons people wear sunglasses. Most people I know who wear them really swear by the fact that they keep the sun out of their eyes. It's almost like they were designed to do that. As a matter of fact, that's why I wear them when I drive the bus." Covey had a thought. "That's why *you* wear them when you drive the bus, too! You were wearing a pair the other day on the way up here!"

Blanchard thought about this a moment. "Okay, three kinds of people wear sunglasses," he said. "But mostly it's people who want to look cool or tough."

"What about people who don't want to be recognized? Lots of movie stars do that. Don't you ever look at *People* magazine? Just about everyone in it wears sunglasses. Even their kids do, sometimes. If we ever hit it big, I bet we'll all be wearing them every time we head into a Waffle House or a Shoney's."

Blanchard glared at Covey. "I'm not much of a reader," he growled. "I must have missed that issue. Okay, *four* kinds of people wear sunglasses. And if we ever hit it big, we're jumping up a notch to Denny's and IHOP."

"Ford Man wears them at the beach so he can check out the women in their bathing suits without his wife catching him." Ford Man's wife was a staunch member of the Church of Christ of Pentecostal Holiness, and as such, she wasn't particularly interested in her husband seeing even *her* in a bathing suit, never mind random strangers. In her estimation, once the children had gotten themselves born, there was no further need for sexual attraction of any sort, and good husbands understood these things and had the decency to find themselves hobbies. "That's five kinds of people who wear them," Covey concluded. He was having a big time, and wondered if he could make it all the way to ten.

"For someone who's supposed to be keeping me calm and relaxed," Blanchard said, "you're doing a bad job. It's a good thing you're not a nurse. They would fire you and dog march you out the front door, and you'd end up panhandling down by the interstate." He began to rub his temples. "My headache's getting worse, I need to take a leak, and I don't want to talk about sunglasses anymore. Or dead people. Or my sister. Or Vanny. Help me to the can, and then help me get back into the bed." Covey assisted Blanchard as he stood.

Blanchard's free hand drifted to his chest. "Just standing up made it hurt. I hate this."

"I know you do. Let's go real slow." Covey, Blanchard, and the IV pole all shuffled toward the bathroom.

"That's it. If I can't even pee on my own, I reckon there's nothing else for it. I need to let him cut me."

"That's about the smartest thing you've said all afternoon," Covey said. "But I thought you'd already decided."

"I was lying. I was going to wait until you took a nap and then steal your clothes and escape. But if that doctor shows up wearing sunglasses, the deal is off. I mean it."

"He didn't look like a shades kind of guy to me, but as soon as we get you into bed, I'll make sure the nurse puts that on your chart."

"SCHLITZ MALT LIQUOR AND A SWISHER SWEET"
(Blanchard Shankles/John Covey)

Don't mess with me boy, or I'll whip your ass
'Cause guys like you ain't got no class
I'll strap you down tight in that old hot seat
And have a Schlitz Malt Liquor and a Swisher Sweet

They say you're tough, but I'll go you one better
She wants to be mine and I think you best let her
I'll write my name with your ass on this asphalt street
And have a Schlitz Malt Liquor and a Swisher Sweet

If there's one thing I hate more than pretty, it's rich
You're both, and that gives me a case of the itch
I need to scratch it, then rest, then repeat
With a Schlitz Malt Liquor and a Swisher Sweet

I don't really know you but I dislike you just fine
So take my advice and head straight for the pines
I'm gonna count to ten, and you need to use those feet
While I have a Schlitz Malt Liquor and a Swisher Sweet

Bring your brother and a lunch 'cause it'll take all day
And you'll need some help so let him stay
You think you're cool but I'll turn up the heat
With a Schlitz Malt Liquor and a Swisher Sweet

Don't mess with me boy, or I'll whip your ass
'Cause guys like you ain't got no class
I'll strap you down tight in that old hot seat
And have a Schlitz Malt Liquor and a Swisher Sweet

"Young Americans"
David Bowie
-1971-

After they became semi-orphans, Blanchard and Geneva soon realized that they had actually been cast adrift long before the physical
removal of their parents—one to the state hospital for the criminally
insane down at Milledgeville and the other to a little plot of ground
behind Mt. Zion Baptist Church—and that the absence of Edna and
Benton had little negative impact on their day-to-day lives. They
pooled the small sums they earned at their after-school jobs and aug-
mented these funds when necessary by dipping into the sock full of
cash they found in Benton's underwear drawer, tucked next to a nearly empty box of condoms and a loaded .38 pistol. They looked after
themselves, lived frugally, paid only the power bill due to their good
fortune to be piped to well water, and made it a habit to throw away
all other mail delivered to the house and never answer the phone or
the door. They both expected that, since they were still minors, representatives from the state would eventually come calling to see about
their welfare, evil social workers with supposedly good intentions
whose actions would inevitably lead to unintended complications and
unwanted consequences. Still, they were in no hurry to facilitate this
happenstance, so they hunkered down and tried their best to look
normal.

"We're both under eighteen," Blanchard said when they discussed their status as personas non grata. "They're bound to come
screw with us; it's only a matter of time. I don't know why they haven't been out already. Maybe there's a backlog." Perhaps there were
young people all over the state with dead fathers in the ground and
crazy mamas in the nuthouse just waiting for their turns to be rescued
and recycled. "They might even try to put us in a foster home."
Blanchard had no love for that idea. He had been less than impressed
with his *real* parents, and he didn't want to have to break in another

set now. At this low point in his life, he wasn't even sure that the whole concept of parenthood was valid. If his personal experience was any indication, it was a fairly sketchy proposition all the way around, and it could be about time to rethink the parental model in its entirety and come up with something more workable. Or perhaps the whole situation was his fault, his and Geneva's, and responsibility could be laid right at their four feet. Possibly they were lousy at training parents, and better children would have done a better job.

"Maybe they won't," Geneva said. She had just swallowed one of Edna's poison nerve pills and was willing to view life as a glass half full, at least for the next three to four hours. "Try to help us, I mean. They've left us alone so far." It had been about two months since Edna had shined up the Nubian princess on Benton's unsuspecting head. The first week after the incident was filled with state and local officials of all descriptions, wandering, poking, asking, and collecting, but once Edna was in custody and Benton was under the dirt, things had gotten quiet rather quickly. "I'll be eighteen in less than a year, and you look that old now. Maybe they've forgotten about us. Maybe they'll just leave us alone."

"That would suit me, but you can't count on things just working out. What if they don't?" Blanchard, too, hoped they had somehow slipped through the cracks, but his life experiences to date had not led him toward general expectations of pleasant outcomes, and he did not look for one now. He had acquired the habit of anticipating the worst, and if for some reason it did not then occur, he would take the unexpected gift while fully expecting that bad luck would double up on him next time and really wipe him out. He did not yet know the name of the phenomenon commonly known as Murphy's Law, but he believed in it nonetheless with all of his heart. It was his credo and his code.

"Well, I don't know about you, but I didn't survive the two worst parents in the history of the world just to end up in an orphanage or a foster home," Geneva said. She frowned as she crossed her arms. "If they come for us, they're going to have to catch me. I'm running away." It sounded like a fair plan to Blanchard, although it surprised him that Geneva had voiced it. He knew he could do it, and if it came down to it, he would be gone in a blink and eventually forgotten. He had considered running more than once even before Benton rode the midnight train, and it wouldn't take much to put him on the road now. But Geneva was a rule-abider and didn't seem to be the running-away type. He wondered if she would carry through if worse came to worst. He wondered if he should take her with him if he went.

"Where would you go?" he asked.

"Away from *here* is about all I've got so far."

"You'll need to hammer that out a bit before you start packing," Blanchard advised. It was a sketchy plan, for sure.

"Maybe I'll go to Chattanooga and get a job and an apartment. Maybe I'll go farther than that. What about you? What will you do?"

Blanchard hadn't really given a short-term strategy that much thought. The recent bizarre occurrences in his family had planted him firmly in the here and now. He saw no need for plans because they were so easily broken. He wanted to worry about today, and maybe give a little thought to tomorrow, but that was it. Next week might get lost and never even show up. Why cast the net of expectation any further than a day or two into the future when there was a Nubian princess waiting out there somewhere for everyone, silently watching, biding her time, scheming and hoping for the random, critical misstep? But to humor Geneva, he squatted down and leaned against the house, lit a cigarette, and mulled his options. After a good long while, he spoke.

"I think I'll go ahead and quit school, get a real job if I can find one, and try to hang on here. If they come looking for me, I'll hit the woods for a few days." He had hidden out from Benton plenty of times over the years, especially when his father was in a mood, and he knew of several good spots that were custom made for laying low while waiting for trouble to pass by or fade away. One place in particular was close, and it was stocked with cans of peanuts and Coke for emergencies, waiting for him should the need for flight arise.

"That's not a very good plan," Geneva said.

"It's as good as yours."

"You shouldn't quit school. What kind of life will you have if you don't finish school?"

"Better than if I stay in, at least for now. I want to be a guitar player. That's all I've ever wanted to do. I don't need schooling for that. All I need is time to play and a place to do it. I'm not like you, Geneva. You're smart, and you like going to classes and learning things. Me, I hate every single day I'm in school worse than the last. School sucks so bad I can barely stand it. Stupid teachers all the time telling me what to do, making me learn a bunch of stuff that I don't even need to know, and stupid jocks all the time screwing with me because of my hair or my friends. I hate those guys. Plus, I've stayed out so much already that they'll never let me pass into another grade. It's all over for me. I might as well call it quits and get on with my life. I'll probably get drafted anyway as soon as I turn eighteen. Plane geometry and English composition won't do me much good while I'm being shot at in some rice paddy. Besides, the cash in that sock won't last us forever. If you want to keep eating while you finish high school, one of us needs to be making some food money." Blanchard tended to put off decisions until they could no longer be avoided, and then to make them quickly when the time came. So now he was decided. He would quit school, go to work, and support his big sister until she finished school. After that, they would see.

As for the traumatic circumstances leading up to their current existence in limbo, they had only discussed them once before locking them away, hidden and forgotten, like an unlucky pauper in an unmarked county grave. On that occasion, Blanchard had just returned from the surreal excursion to the county jail, during which he had ridden in the back of the police car with Edna because everyone else in her vicinity that day had been afraid to get in there with her. It had taken the sheriff, two deputies, and Blanchard—one person per limb with the largest two relegated to the legs—about fifteen minutes to transport one crazy little woman thirty feet from the house to the car, and even then each had bruises, scratches, and bites to show for their trouble. Once the car door slammed, she sat there looking through the glass with murder in her eyes and handcuffs on her wrists. Occasionally a growl crawled up from deep down in her gut where her hatred was brewed and bottled, and escaped past gritted teeth into the world of goodness and light.

"I should have brought a straightjacket," the sheriff said to no one in particular. "Nobody told me we were dealing with a nutcase." He noticed Blanchard standing there. "Sorry," he said. "I didn't see you."

"Don't worry about it."

"Son, someone needs to ride in the back with her. It's the law. We can't leave her back there alone." He was a big man currently dabbing at a bloody nose with a damp dishtowel provided by Geneva. He was one of the two unfortunates who had drawn leg duty, and Edna had gotten in a lucky kick.

"Uh-uh," Blanchard said, shaking his head. "You don't know her like I do. She is truly pissed. I've never seen her this mad. You get paid, and you've got the gun. You get back there with her."

The sheriff looked pained yet, at the same time, sympathetic. He had a couple of children at home about the same ages as the two Shankles children. He would hate for either of them to have to go through this with their mama. "You're her kinfolk," he said gently. "She might take it better if you do it." As if to punctuate his remark, Edna smashed her forehead against the side glass. A star formed in the window, and blood began to flow. It trickled down the bridge of her nose and dripped slowly from the tip, reminding Blanchard of a melting icicle. When it caught her attention, she dipped a finger in it and began to draw a pentagram on the glass.

"She just beat one of her kinfolk to death in there with a statue," Blanchard said, pointing at the house, just to remind the lawman of the reason for their little get-together that morning. "I don't know that being related means a whole lot to her right now. It might even be worse than not being related to her." He looked at his mother then, the woman who had given him life, handcuffed in the backseat of the patrol car, feral, angry, afraid, bleeding, hopelessly insane, and utterly alone there at the jagged fringe of the strange world in which she lived. "Damn," he said, looking at the sheriff, who nodded in agreement with the sentiment. Blanchard was trapped. He knew he had no real choice. He didn't want to ride in the back with her, but Geneva certainly wasn't an option, and there was no one else who would suffice. He walked to the other side of the car, snatched open the door, and hopped into the lion's den.

Four hours later, he was back at the Shankles home—which he had heard referred to as the murder scene all morning—dropped off by a deputy who had spent the entire trip back shaking his head and offering up ten or twelve different versions of the same basic observation, which was that he had seen a whole lot of shit in his time as a law enforcement officer, but he hadn't ever seen any shit like *that* shit before. Blanchard could only nod. He knew where the man was coming from. He hadn't ever seen any shit like that, either, and he had been living at shit central his entire life. As the patrol car drove away, Blanchard stepped onto the porch. He was shaking, and wretchedly tired. He had a black eye, his cheek was scratched, and there were pieces of rolled-up cotton gauze packed tightly in each nostril. Geneva was waiting for him, rocking in one of the porch rockers. She looked as if she had cried herself raw, rested briefly, and then cried some more.

"You look terrible," she said. Her hands were folded in her lap, and her thumbs twiddled of their own volition. She could have been praying, perhaps nervous about the outcome of the entreaty in light of the circumstances. Given the events of the day so far, Blanchard supposed she had good reason for her anxiety. If he were God, he wouldn't have anything to do with the Shankles family.

"You too." Blanchard sat in the rocker next to hers and picked up her rhythm. They rocked in tandem for a while, just two terrible-looking Shankles children trying mightily not to think. Then Geneva broke the silence.

"How did it go?" she asked.

Blanchard shook his head. "How did it go? Now there's a question. I can't believe how bad the whole thing sucked. First off, Mama beat on me like a bad dog all the way to the jail. Called me everything but her only son on top of that. Her mean streak and her crazy streak joined forces, and she nearly killed me. I truly thought I was going to die. Finally, I got her on my lap, wrapped my arms and legs around her, and just held on." He pointed to his face. "That's when she slammed her head back and broke my nose." He found a spot on his lips that wasn't too swollen and lit a cigarette. "Bless her heart," he added quietly, administering Southern absolution. "Our poor mama is one insane woman."

90

They sat in silence for a long while. Then he looked at his sister and spoke again. "She really is as crazy as a sack full of shithouse rats, you know. That may be the only true thing our father ever said." Geneva nodded. The veracity of Benton's diagnosis could not be denied. They continued to rock, awkwardly numb there in the company of each other and in the relative quiet of the lull after the storm had passed. Whatever came next couldn't be any worse that what had gone before. Or so they hoped.

It had been a long and hectic day, fraught with the cruel, uncaring wiles of existence, and the silence on the porch was therapeutic for both of them. Blanchard looked out across the narrow valley. He watched a car snake its way up Lookout Mountain. From this distance, it seemed to be crawling in slow motion, and he couldn't tell what the make and model was. He wondered who was driving, and if he knew them. The phone rang. Geneva startled at the sound, and his heart skipped a beat, but they both ignored the other nine rings. In a few minutes it began to ring again, but again they paid it no mind. There was no one in the vast and pitiless world with whom either of them wished to speak. Anyone on the other end of that ring would surely be the bearer of bad tidings of one sort or another, but as long as they didn't answer, they were safe from harm. Finally, Geneva broke the stillness.

"Blanchard, what are we going to do now?"

"I don't know." He was fresh out of ideas. In truth, he had been acting on instinct and adrenaline for quite some time.

"Why do you think she killed him?" Her voice was almost a whisper, as if the words were too terrible to be spoken aloud.

"Who knows? Because the voices told her to? Because it was Friday? Because she could? Because she's as crazy as a sack full of shithouse rats and he was a bad man?" He shook his head. "That last one has my vote." There was no telling why Edna did anything, and there really never had been. She had not shared the rules of her world with her children, so they had always been unable to get a good handle on what drove her. Perhaps where she existed there were no rules, and her mind was a collection of haphazard impulses that fired at random intervals, like an engine that has jumped time. She had always been an unexplainable part of their lives, a constant and fixed

91

point of chaos. Trying to understand her was like trying to fathom the west wind. It couldn't be done, and it was a waste of life and effort even to try.

"I guess that's it," she said. "The crazy part, I mean." She turned towards her brother. "I never thought she would do something like this, though. Even that time she came into your room, she didn't hurt you."

"I think I just got lucky then. I think she would have killed me deader than hell if I hadn't woken up when I did. Not because it was me, though. Because I was in the way of something she wanted to do. I saw it in her eyes. It wasn't even her in there. It was something else."

"She scared me sometimes," Geneva continued. "Who am I kidding? She scared me all the time. But I never really thought she was dangerous. Until now."

"She was kind of rough on small animals and holy men," Blanchard reminded her.

"Yeah. Priests and cats."

"Don't forget rabbits and birds."

"I won't forget any of it. It was all so strange and creepy. You know, I didn't look at Daddy before they took him away. I didn't want to see what she had done to him. But I heard the coroner talking to one of the deputies. He said there wasn't much left of his head. They kept looking for a hammer before they figured out she used the princess." She shuddered.

"It was pretty rough," Blanchard replied. "She really messed him up. I wish I hadn't seen it, but I had to go in there to find out what happened. It was one of those things you wish you could un-see." He grimaced. "It was kind of hard to tell where he stopped and his pillow began. It looked like she ran over his head with a tractor. We'll be wanting to go with a closed casket for sure."

They were quiet for another spell. Then, Geneva again broke the silence.

"Are they going to do an autopsy?"

Blanchard shrugged. He hadn't gotten too far past the fact of the killing itself, so the mechanics of what happened next were coming to him slowly, like a tortoise dragging itself across a busy road, hoping to avoid tires. "You got me. You don't have to be a doctor to see what killed him. I mean, he has no head. But maybe they have to do an autopsy anyway because of how it happened. I heard them talking about it down at the jail, but I don't know if they will. I guess we'll hear about it if they decide to do one. To be honest, I'd sort of rather we just get him in the ground as quick as we can and forget about him. Out of sight, out of mind, out of our hair for good." Benton had a brother that Blanchard and Geneva had never met and had no idea how to contact, and no other relatives that they knew of. Unless some of his girlfriends came to pay their respects, it would be a sparsely attended funeral.

"I heard one of the deputies say that Mama beat Daddy to death with a nigger statue. That was such an ugly thing to say! For some reason I felt it was important to tell him it was a Nubian princess, and he looked at me like I was the crazy one, not Edna."

"Crazy runs in the family," Blanchard reminded her. "It passes from mother to daughter in a straight line, so even if she was screwing around on the old man back in her younger days, and I truly hope she did—just because—you got the crazy gene. It could be trying to sneak up on you right now. You've got to try to hold it off if you can."

"Shut up."

"Sorry. I know the guy you're talking about. He's a real piece of work. Lazy, too. Or scared. Don't know which. Probably a little of both. We couldn't get him to take an arm or a leg. He just stood there like a possum eating garbage beside the road while the rest of us loaded her up. You probably confused him. I bet he didn't know what Nubian meant."

"Mama would have hated him calling it something else besides what it was. She was crazy, but she was precise."

Blanchard nodded. Edna had always been smart, and the correctness of things had always mattered to her.

"We should have put that guy in the backseat with Mama and the Nubian princess. By the time they got to Rome, she would have taught him some manners. He would have known exactly what had killed our old man, and he would have a broken nose instead of me." Every time Blanchard said *nose*, the word arrived sounding like *doze*. He hoped this was a temporary condition, and that it would pass once the gauze rolls were removed.

"She would have killed him," Geneva said with certainty.

"He would have been a well-informed dead guy, though." That was the important part.

"I don't know how to feel," Geneva said. "Our father is dead, and our mother killed him. I bet in the entire history of the world, nothing like this has ever happened to anyone else. I bet we're the first."

"Lucky us," Blanchard observed blandly. "That's some of that Shankles luck for you. She didn't just kill him. She really, really killed him. She killed him, and then she killed him some more."

Geneva nodded. It was an undeniable truth. Benton Shankles had indeed been excessively killed. "I guess I mostly feel weird," she said. "And scared, and kind of sick to my stomach. But the strangest thing is that I don't feel very sad about any of it. If anything, I feel sort of relieved. I've been afraid that something really bad was going to happen for as long as I can remember. I don't remember ever not feeling that way. I didn't know what it was, but I knew it was going to be awful, like with my cats, but worse, like the cats were just a warm-up. It was a cloud hanging over our lives. It was just hiding out there, waiting for the right time to happen. Now it has happened, and it was even more terrible than I thought it would be, but it's over now. It's done, and at least I don't have to be afraid anymore." She sighed. "What little sadness I feel is for Mama. It's more like pity, really. I'll never forget seeing her in the back of that police car, drawing one of her pictures on the window with her own blood. She seemed so alone." She wiped at a tear that streaked her cheek.

"That's why I agreed to ride with her back there. I really didn't want to, but she's our mama, and she was all alone."

"As for Daddy," Geneva continued, "except for it being gory, I really don't care. I told you I didn't look because his head was messed up, but the truth is, I don't think I would have looked anyway." Blanchard knew what his sister meant. Benton wasn't the kind of person people missed once he was gone. If anything, they wondered why he had hung around so long, why he hadn't left sooner. "I was sorrier for my cats than I am for Daddy," Geneva admitted. "That doesn't seem right, but there it is."

"That's two of us," he replied, rubbing a spot over his ear where Edna had clipped him with the handcuffs. He supposed he would

94

have two black eyes before morning instead of the solitary shiner he currently sported, all courtesy of the impromptu nose job his mother had delivered. "Good riddance, I say." A thought crossed his mind. "Maybe we should talk to the counselor at school about all of it. She'd love this."

Geneva smiled a strained smile. She, too, had had a couple of sessions with the counselor. "I bet we've got unresolved trust issues with family members which are manifesting themselves in acute and unreasonable fears of the unknown," she said in a monotone.

"If we didn't before, I bet we do now," Blanchard said.

"And if we still don't, we're missing the best chance we'll ever have."

"Well, don't worry about how you feel about the old man. You feel like you feel. I hated him, and he knew it. He went to wherever he is now knowing it. He drove Mama all the way crazy, and he didn't care about anybody in the wide world except himself. I suppose I didn't actually want him dead, but I've wanted him gone for a long time. I always sort of thought he would just wander away one day, that he'd go off with one of his women or maybe someone would shoot him, and we would never see him again. I was good with that and hoping he'd get on with it. But he didn't get the chance. Mama beat him to it. Anyway, he brought this whole thing on himself. Think about it! How long have we been telling him to get her some help? If he had done what he should have done all along and gotten her seen about, maybe he'd be alive right now and she'd be in a nicer place than the county jail."

"I don't get that part," Geneva said. "Why did they have to put her in jail? Anyone can look at her and tell she's not responsible for anything she does. They should have just taken her straight to the hospital."

Blanchard nodded in agreement, then shrugged. "You're right. I think it was a terrible thing to have to do, and I'll never forget that ride to Rome. But according to the sheriff, this is the way the law says it has to be done. They have to treat her like any other criminal until it has been officially determined that she's nuts."

"What happens to Mama next?"

"As soon as they can, probably today if they can scratch up a judge and a psychiatrist, they'll bring her to court, have a hearing, and try to determine her state of mind. And as soon as she jumps up on the bench and bites the judge's ear off or shows him her boobs, they'll send her on down to the state hospital where she belongs. In the meantime, they've got her restrained so she can't hurt herself or anyone else. You should have seen them putting her into that straightjacket! I was sort of rooting for her. I guarantee you that a couple of those deputies will be calling in sick tomorrow, and none of them are getting laid tonight for sure. She beat the living hell out of every one of them. I was going to hang around to try to help calm her down because it seemed like the thing to do. But they told me it would be better if I didn't, and they didn't have to tell me twice, because I really didn't want any more of that, anyway. I'd had enough by then and was ready to get out of there, so I hitched a ride back here."

"I feel bad saying this," Geneva said, "but I'm happy she's gone too. It was just too hard living with her. I was tired all the time."

"I think it's safe to say she's gone for good. Even though she couldn't help it, they'll never let her out after this. I just hope they let her have a radio once they get her settled in. Her life will be a misery if she doesn't get to listen to her music and her DJs." Blanchard sighed. "Anyway, we can both quit sleeping with a chair shoved up under the doorknob."

"Yeah. That's a relief." Geneva's stomach rumbled, and she reached in a pocket for a pair of peppermint candies. She handed one to her brother, unwrapped the other, and placed it on her tongue. He tucked his peppermint between his cheek and gum. "Now all we have to worry about is getting Daddy buried," she said.

"Why did we get him for a father, anyway? Was Edna blind? Burying is too good for him. I say we just leave him at the morgue. Why should we waste what little money we've got putting him away?"

"He had a burial policy. It will be enough to take care of him."

"Once they get tired of tripping over him, they'll figure out something to do with him. They can drag him outside and toss him in the dumpster for all I care! He can spend eternity at the landfill with the rats and the possums."

"We need to bury him, Blanchard. It's something we have to do. If we don't do the right thing, we'll be almost as bad as he was. We'll be on the road to Shankles sorry."

Back before she had gone all the way as crazy as a sack full of shithouse rats, back during that golden time when there was only one rat or perhaps two in the sack, maybe mixed in with a mole and a chipmunk, Edna had from time to time offered a comment concerning some of her husband's least endearing traits and escapades. On those occasions, she would note that Benton was a sorry specimen of a man. She would subsequently point out that there was sorry, and then there was lowdown sorry, and *then* there was Shankles sorry, and that Benton Shankles was the sorriest of those, the crown prince of a long line of low men.

"I vote no," Blanchard said. "I say we roll him into a ditch. Better yet, let's put him out in the field on Mama's altar. Let the coyotes have him. I hear them up in the woods some nights. Those boys are hungry. Maybe I didn't fall too far from the tree, but I say let the varmints have him for lunch. Maybe I am Shankles sorry already, but that's how I feel."

"Let me bury him, then. It's the decent thing to do. We need some decent around here. There hasn't been that much of it."

Blanchard knew his sister was right, but he didn't like it. "Burying him is decent, and so are you, but he wasn't. You reap what you sow."

"We need to put him down right."

Geneva was firm, and Blanchard knew when he was beaten. "It's your choice. I don't want to fuss with you over what to do with him. He's not worth fighting over." Perhaps the novelty of decency within the Shankles clan would become a habit. Maybe the final incarnation of Shankles sorry had breathed its last, and the trait would now pass into genetic oblivion, like a vestigial tail. Perhaps Blanchard would escape the curse that had haunted his line since the days of the cave dwellers. "You know what I hope?"

"What do you hope?"

"I hope Mama screwed around on him and that our real father was someone else entirely. Maybe Mama was kind of frisky back in the day and we each have a different father."

"That would suit me. Maybe they're rich men, you know, really cool dads who will come and take care of us."

"Your dad could buy you some fancy cats."

"Yours could get you a new guitar."

"Yours could send you off to college."

"Yours could buy you a new Mustang."

"Nah," Blanchard said, thinking about it. "We're not that lucky. We have to face it. We struck all the way out when it came to parents, and then we tripped and broke an ankle on the way back to the dugout. Our parents are the town crazy lady and a guy with no head, and she's the better parent of the two by far."

"So what happens now?" Geneva asked.

"Now? It's nothing but good times and gravy for us from here on out."

"GEORGIA THREE-WAY"
(Blanchard Shankles/John Covey)

Each time I try to find somebody new
I turn 'round and run right into you
Get over me, boy, I can hear you say
Don't waste your love in a Georgia three-way

Goodbye to love, hello to sorrow
I'll be sad today and sadder tomorrow
The pale sunshine has faded away
And left me, you, and tears in a Georgia three-way

Look left or look right, the view's all the same
I shoulder the burden and carry the blame
On my knees but don't know how to pray
Talkin' to shadows in this Georgia three-way

Been ten years now just writin' this song
And I try to forget you, but it feels just plain wrong
Lovin' any other woman this side of the clay
And drownin' my pain in a Georgia three-way

Two lovers breathing, then one in the ground
The wind whispers softly, the sky casts a frown
The crush of the memories causes me to sway
As I wait for redemption in this Georgia three-way

Running the Chevy on I-59
Fishing the cooler for the Boone's Farm wine
My eyes met yours, then it all went gray
Now I'm chained to the past in this Georgia three-way

I should'a gone with you but I had to stay
And I'll never feel as fine as I did that day
What's done is done and it's time to pay
Lonely year after year in a Georgia three-way

Get over me, boy, I can hear you say
Don't waste your love in a Georgia three-way

"Green-eyed Lady"
Sugarloaf
-Tuesday: Third Day-

Blanchard knew he was dreaming. There was a certain symmetry to his somnambulant hours that was often missing in his waking moments, so most of his dreams were in the third person, and in them he watched from above, like a hawk scouting the rugged countryside for an unsuspecting rabbit, perhaps, or a tasty squirrel. But this time he was a participant, the main character in a drama that played out while he slept. He was in a flat-bottomed wooden boat floating down a dawdling green river. The planks of the vessel were as weathered as an abandoned barn, ridged and grainy, and a puddle of water sloshed in the bottom. The three wide seats in the boat seemed to indicate that it been designed to accommodate a number of people, perhaps eight or ten. But he was alone, and he felt isolated. Even though he had no idea who the other occupants might have been, he wondered where they had gone and why they had left him behind. He missed them, in fact, even though they had never met. As a general rule, he hated watercraft of any description and avoided them at all costs. He was a poor swimmer from a family of the same, and water deep enough to float a boat was not something he sought out. But despite that fact, he didn't seem to mind this dinghy or the river upon which it nodded. He felt strangely safe despite his usual fears. It seemed natural for him to be there, even normal, and he had no qualms about his nautical adventure.

It was high summer, hot as a coal-fired brick oven south of the gnat line, and both riverbanks were blanketed with thick vegetation: magnolia, wisteria, honeysuckle, hackberry, bamboo, trumpet vine, poison oak, and kudzu. Turtles bobbed lazily on the river's surface, watching him warily as he glided by them. An owl flew in front of him and came to rest in a hackberry tree on the far bank. It sat and regarded him with unblinking eyes. A heron stood in the shallows, patiently waiting for an unsuspecting crappie to swim nearby. There was a ripple as a river cat swam close to the surface, and a flash as it harvested an unwary springtail.

There was a guitar in the boat beside Blanchard, its neck propped on his seat, a Rickenbacker Model 325 in mint condition. It was a magnificent instrument, one that he had always wanted to own but could never afford. He picked it up and struck an E chord, and the crisp, rich sound swelled across the water, building as it traveled, and when it echoed back to him, he could hear each individual element of the chord, an arpeggio both satisfying and profound. There was no amplifier in the boat, but apparently none was needed. As the reverberation reached him, his hair blew gently even though the air was still. Almost as if the note had been a cue, fog as thick as loose cotton began to drift and roll down from the sky, and as it descended, it planted itself on the surface of the river and gathered around the boat like a blanket. He stood, surprised as he did so that the boat was as steady as if it were on dry land. A familiar urge took him then, the need to make music, and he began to play the intro riff to "Smoke on the Water." The song had always been one of his favorites, clean with no cheap frills, and it seemed appropriate to the moment, and to the dream.

The boat bumped into a snag, wobbled a bit, turned in the current, and floated around a shallow bend. Blanchard stopped playing and gently placed the guitar on the seat. There ahead in the cool mist he could just make out what appeared to be a dock jutting into the waterway, or perhaps it was a bridge, since it spanned the river from bank to bank. The deck of the structure stood well above the surface of the water, and Blanchard in his boat thought that he might well pass beneath. The unguided boat slowly rotated as the river drew it along, and every time the dock came back into view, it was closer and more distinct. Blanchard began to make out details, and he saw that the dock was not a dock or a bridge at all; it was a stage. There were amplifiers placed here and there, and roadies with flashlights were walking to and fro between them, making adjustments, running cables and cords, and placing guitars in their proper stands. Spotlights and footlights began to come online, bathing the stage in a blaze of brightness and multiple colors before settling into a subtle blue glow. The roadies finished their setup and faded behind the amps, out of sight but within reach if needed, and seven individuals walked onto the stage and began to strap on their guitars. Blanchard experienced excitement, and the expectation of something extraordinary. As he floated closer, the fog began to thin, and there on the stage stood a collection of people he had never met, but whom he knew as surely as he knew Covey and the rest of the boys in his own band.

"Oh hell no," he said, shaking his head. He laughed like a young boy at Christmas time, one who had been good all year and knew that the big payoff was imminent. It couldn't be happening, but it was, right before his unbelieving eyes.

Jimi Hendrix stood there in a comfortable slouch, his afro nearly invisible in the rising mist, waif-thin and smiling with his Stratocaster slung upside down and backwards. Next to him leaned Duane Allman, lanky and relaxed, tuning his Les Paul Gibson, a lit cigarette stuck under the G string where it met the tuning key, like a smoldering flag. Next in line stood Stevie Ray Vaughn, wearing his distinctive black hat decked with silver medallions, the soul patch nestled beneath his lower lip pointing like an arrow down to where the action was. He was quietly chording Number One, warming it up before he put it through its paces. Stevie Ray looked up and saw Blanchard floating his way, and he nodded as if they were old friends meeting after a long parting. At that moment, George Harrison, the quiet one, walked over from the back of the stage where he had been making a final adjustment to his amp. His Epiphone Casino was slung up high on his chest, and he rested his arms on it while he waited for the show to begin. In front of the rest, closest to Blanchard, Robert Johnson sat in a cane-bottomed bentwood chair with his Kalamazoo flat top guitar on his knees and his old slouch hat perched jauntily on top of his head. A Picayune cigarette dangled from his lips. As he began to tune, he tilted his head to the soundboard of the Kalamazoo so he could hear the notes. Just behind him, B.B. King stood in profile in a coat and tie, dressed to the nines, gold rings on each of his fingers, tuning a Fender Telecaster selected from a harem of guitars all named Lucille. The group was rounded out by Bo Diddley, standing off to one side with his homemade cigar-box guitar hung around his neck, humming a tune while cleaning his black-rimmed eyeglasses with a do-rag that had been handed to him by a random roadie.

"Hey!" Blanchard shouted as the boat bumped into a piling jutting up from the river and came to a halt about ten feet from the stage. "Down here! Help me up! Throw me a rope or something! I want to be up there with you. I want to play." It was uncharacteristic of Blanchard to crash a party, but this was an exception. He wanted to share the stage with his heroes, if only in a dream. He had spent a good portion of his life trying to sound like them, and he thought he would not have a chance like this again. One by one, the group on the stage looked down at Blanchard in his boat.

"Nah, man. You don't want up here," Robert Johnson said. "We all dead. Dead is no good place for a livin' man to be." There were nods all around. Johnson smiled sadly, leaned back in his chair, and crossed his leg. "It's nice enough, but a man needs a little bit of raw from time to time. That's where the music comes from." Blanchard noticed that the great blues player's shoes were scuffed and needed a shine. Johnson lit another Picayune from the first and let it ride his lower lip as he went back to tuning the Kalamazoo.

"I do want up there!" Blanchard shouted. The boat had begun to move again with the current. He grabbed for the piling, but it was already out of reach, as if it rather than he had moved. "Give me a hand. Just one song! Let me show you what I can do."

"He wants up here, and we all want back in the boat," George Harrison said to Duane Allman.

Allman smiled ruefully at the irony of the moment. "He needs to be careful what he wishes for," he replied. "That old clock ticks fast enough as it is."

"Let me show you what I can do!" Blanchard urged again.

"You do fine, man," B.B. King said to Blanchard. "You know your way up and down the neck real good. You sort of remind me of me, back when I was a young buck." He chuckled and slowly shook his head. "Man, now that was a long time ago. Good days, though. Fine days."

"Your time will come," Jimi Hendrix said, sounding a little sad. "It always does. Sometimes later, sometimes sooner. But your day's not here yet. You can't get out of the boat until that day. Even if you jump, you just land back in the boat." He paused a moment, perhaps to see if Blanchard intended to make the futile leap of faith. When he did not, Hendrix continued. "That's the ticket. Stay put, keep at it, and one of these days you might get lucky."

"I'm not a very lucky guy," Blanchard said. "Never have been."

"Neither was I," Hendrix noted. "What little luck I had, I ran right through."

"Luck, schmuck," said Bo Diddley. "You boys are wastin' your breath talkin' about luck. You make your own luck every day."

"But I want to be famous. I want to play with you guys."

"Famous is not all it's cracked up to be," Allman said. "The money's nice, and the women are sweet, but sometimes the rest of it's not so good." His mouth barely moved as he spoke, and his mirror shades caught a light that was not there. He took a drink from an open quart of Jack Daniel's and sucked in a breath, then handed the bottle to Stevie Ray, who swallowed a small sip and shook his head as the bourbon burned its way down nice and slow.

"It ain't what you think it is," Johnson agreed.

"Just let the music be enough, mate," Harrison said quietly. "Make people happy with your songs. The rest is just trouble, and sometimes sadness."

"And stay off of helicopters," Stevie Ray said. He had begun replacing the A string on Number One. "Always ride the bus."

"Do you boys remember this one?" Bo Diddley asked as he fished a pick from his pocket and grabbed the opening notes of Howlin' Wolf's "Back Door Man." There were smiles and nods and a couple of oh yeahs from the group on the stage. One by one, they joined in and began to jam on the old standard, each bringing a lick or a chord variation as they fell in step. Blanchard knew it too, and when the musicians came to the end of a bar, he added the Rickenbacker's full tone to the ensemble. The boat slowly drifted under the stage, but Blanchard kept playing. He was a good guitar player, but today he was playing better than he ever had before. He was one with the song and with the legends on that stage. Arcs of electric blue snapped from his fingertips as he worked the fretboard. When he floated out from under the stage on the downstream side, he noted that the men had stopped playing and were watching him as he stretched the strings, listening to him as he made that song his own, if only for the moment, and only in a crazy dream.

"Boy's got some licks," Johnson said, tapping in time with the music on the back of the Kalamazoo. The Picayune had gone out and hung from his lip, lifeless, cold, and forgotten.

"He's gonna make it if something don't happen," Stevie Ray said. There were several nods of agreement around the stage. "Course, something always happens." More nods and several rueful smiles at the inevitability of fate from a group that collectively knew all there was to know about its careless attentions.

"Every time," Bo Diddley said. "Every single time."

"I swear that boy reminds me of me," King said with a nod. "He's fast and sweet like a hummingbird."

"He stretching them strings," Bo Diddley noted with approval. "And he's got some good combos."

"Nice," Allman said. "Listen to him chime that note."

"The dude's got some skill," Hendrix agreed. "For a right-handed white boy, I mean." He smiled at his small joke, but the rest of the boys onstage had heard it before.

Blanchard swelled with pride at these comments and was going to keep playing for his heroes, but between one note and the next, his guitar faded away, leaving him to play the air. He looked back upriver and saw that the fog was descending again, quickly, and that soon the stage and all it contained would be gone from sight. He sat and placed his hands on the seat, but when he tried to move them again, they were tied tightly to a pair of anchors, and he could not budge them. The fog came down like a curtain and enfolded him, and he could no longer see anything but nothingness. His head began to hurt, and an ache started in his chest that soon became overwhelming in its intensity. The boat floated around another bend in the river, and as it passed close to the bank, a snake dropped from a tree branch into the boat. He hated snakes and killed them when he could, but he was paralyzed and powerless to protect himself from this one. It slithered up his leg to his torso and from there to his face. It looked him in the eye and held his gaze for several long moments, and then it forced itself into his mouth and down his throat.

He noted that his feet were wet, and when he looked down, he saw that the boat was filling quickly with water. This dream was getting out of hand, and Blanchard wished for it to end. The water rose steadily, and soon it was up to his knees, and then to his waist. He was sinking, and he knew that he could not save himself. His hands, still restrained, were now completely underwater. The boat began to tilt, and events seemed to kick into high gear even as time began to slow. He was up to his chest in cool, green water, and a large catfish that resembled Simpson Taggart nibbled at the top buttons of his shirt. Then, before even a moment had passed, the river lapped at his chin. He was still riding the boat, and it was still moving down the river with the current, but now it was almost completely submerged. Finally, he was entirely under the surface. He wasn't panicked, because somehow the snake was breathing for him, which was both weird—considering how he felt about snakes—and calming at the same time. He continued sinking, and he knew that there would be no bottom to this river, and that he would descend for eternity into a gentle, dark abyss, all the while looking for a spit of sand to rest upon, or a rock on which he could lay down his burdens. His last thought before the darkness fell was that he hoped Covey would remember to feed his tree-walking coonhound, Scrounge. He was a good dog, and Blanchard would miss him. Then he was gone, and in his place was nonexistence.

Blanchard awoke from his dream, and his first impression was that he really, really hurt. He had never been dragged behind a car down a gravel road, but if he had, he imagined that he might feel about like he did right now. Every inch of skin on his torso tingled as if it were sunburned, and there was a throbbing ache down the center of his chest that felt as if he had pulled a muscle, been run over by a truck, and then pulled that same muscle again before being run over by a larger truck. He had the sensation of being trussed like a roasting hen on a Sunday afternoon, and he could feel the pull of each individual staple along his chest incision as it helped hold him together. Additionally, there were two separate sharp pains that seemed to come from under his ribs on each side and just below his breastbone. Each produced a sensation reminiscent of a ruptured appendix, which Blanchard had weathered once upon a time back in the days when he had a twinkle in his eye, a spring in his step, and a fully functioning heart in his chest. His PICC line burned from its insertion point around his clavicle all the way to his heart. Both arms thudded from the various IVs jabbed in and taped off. He had an epic, throbbing headache, the worst heartburn he had ever known, his throat was as raw as the north wind, and his urethra was greatly offended by the catheter it currently hosted. And if all of this were not enough, his heart still hurt, and that really ticked him off, because the whole point of the exercise had been to make that stop, and not to just piss it off. It was why they had cracked him open in the first place. He was both nauseous and hungry, a very unpleasant feeling, and his hands were tied to the bed. He couldn't recall ever having felt this bad. It occurred to him that if he had been blown apart with dynamite and put back together with barbed wire and duct tape, he couldn't have felt worse than he did right now.

"Just kill me," Blanchard croaked quietly. He coughed, and he thought for a moment that his ribs were going to burst from his chest. Then he turned his head, and once his eyes focused, he was able to see Vanny sitting right there at his bedside. She was reading her favorite periodical, *National Geographic*, and she held a teddy bear in her lap. She was a woman who generally traveled light, but Blanchard had never seen her without an issue of the magazine somewhere nearby. It was an obsession with her. The bear, however, was something new. He was intrigued by the bear.

In point of fact, he had not laid eyes on her in a year or so, with or without a copy of *National Geographic*, but time had treated her gently. She was one of those people who didn't seem to age all that much, and she looked about the same as she always had. She was slim and short, with long black hair that she wore in a ponytail. She said the streak of gray running through it was a memento of her time with Blanchard. Her legs were crossed, and her right leg swung up and down in its lifelong habit of constant movement, as if it were spring loaded and just waiting for its moment to launch into the sky. She wore a red flannel shirt with cuffed sleeves, faded jeans, and white tennis shoes. She also had the greenest eyes Blanchard had ever seen, kind eyes when they were in the mood and hard eyes when they weren't, but he couldn't see them at present because of the sunglasses she was wearing.

"Damn," Blanchard said, but there was no rancor in his voice. He was too tired to be mean, and he hurt too much to make the effort even if he had been inclined to. It had taken most of what he had just to speak, and a wave of misery washed over him. He had to rest a moment before he spoke again, and when he did, his speech was fractured and hoarse. "I died and went to hell. I knew that was going to happen!" No other explanation would fit the facts.

"No, you lived," Vanny replied, looking up from her magazine, her voice the same soft Carolina drawl that he remembered. "Don't be so glum. There's still time to mend your ways, but you won't."

He nodded at her statement that his inevitable trip to the inferno was probably unavoidable, a forgone conclusion from the beginning of time, a done deal from the word go. Still, he was glad in a miserable, nauseous sort of way that the journey was still in his future rather than his past. Blanchard beheld Vanny in silence for a few moments before gathering the strength to speak.

"I feel so bad. Did something go wrong?"

"No. According to the doctor, you did just fine. He seemed pretty happy with you."

Blanchard considered this news for a while. Then he nodded and thought of responding to her, but instead he drifted into a dreamless sleep. When he awoke, he was surprised to see Vanny sitting next to him, holding what seemed to be a teddy bear.

"Vanny!" he croaked. "Why are you here?" He had forgotten their earlier reunion.

"It's good to see you too, baby," she replied. "You always were such a sweet talker. It is one of your strong points."

Blanchard took a shallow breath, which seemed to be the only kind he was capable of at present. Then the last words he would have expected issued seemingly of their own volition from his parched mouth. "It's good to see you," he said. He was surprised at the gratitude he felt at that moment. He found that he was near tears, and he was not comfortable having that level of emotion with anyone. Perhaps it was the trauma of the surgery making him weepy, or maybe it was a side effect from one of his medications, of which there had been more than a few. Or maybe he was just glad to be alive, and to be sharing that moment.

"It's good to see you too," Vanny replied. She reached and patted his hand. Her touch felt cool to Blanchard.

"Don't get me wrong," he squawked. "I'm not fussing. But why are you here? This is a long way from South Carolina." His voice didn't seem to want to work properly and kept cutting out on him like a bad microphone. His throat felt like hot asphalt. "I thought you broke up with me."

"Well, technically, we sort of broke up with each other," Vanny said. "But I heard you were sick, and I thought you might need some help and want some company. Nobody needs to be alone in the hospital. Not even ex-boyfriends who have sometimes misbehaved." Vanny gave him a slight smile. "And by misbehaved I mean acted like a rat most of the time."

"I know what you meant," Blanchard said ruefully, willing to concede the point. "Remind me to kill Covey next time I see him, though. The man just can't keep his bass-playing mouth shut." Blanchard closed his eyes briefly as an upwelling of queasiness passed through him, followed by a wave of fatigue so profound that it took from him what little breath he could manage. He thought he might pass out for a moment, but he breathed slowly and deeply until the feeling passed. He tended toward the dramatic when he vomited, a full-body reflex that was unpleasant even in the best of times, and these were not the best of times. The last thing he wanted to do on this day was throw up. He thought it might break him in half. He could just see his staples popping as he split open like a busted zipper, ricocheting off the walls and ceiling as his surprised innards tumbled onto the bed.

"Covey really can't keep secrets very well," Vanny agreed. "I can usually read him like a book, especially when it comes to your secrets. But don't fret. He didn't tell me about your heart trouble. He tried to keep it from me. I saw him downstairs just a little while ago, and he denied that you were even sick. He said you were here for a flu shot."

"A flu shot? That's what he came up with?" It was true that Covey had always been an exceptionally bad liar. Blanchard considered this trait to be one of his friend's greatest weaknesses.

"He means well, and he always tries to keep your secrets. The hold you have over that man is something to see."

"I have pictures of him doing bad things with some groupies in West Memphis, Arkansas. If Covey doesn't do what I tell him to, I will narc him out to Anna. Speaking of Anna, if he didn't tell you about my heart, it must've been her. So I'm guessing that Covey told Anna, and she told you, and everybody was swearing everyone else to secrecy the whole time, and now the whole world knows where I am and why. Remind me to kill Anna when I get out of here. I didn't want any fuss." Covey was quite fond of Anna and would take it hard when Blanchard did her in, but it had to be done, and perhaps he would get over it in time. Examples had to be made, and rules had to be enforced, or anarchy would reign.

"Don't kill Anna, either. She means well too, and she loves you enough to tell me to come see about you. She's also been taking care of Scrounge for you. Anyway, heart surgery rates a little bit of fussing, don't you think? It's a pretty big deal."

Blanchard tried to raise an arm to his head to scratch at an itch and realized again that he was restrained. He frowned in frustration. "Why are my hands tied up? I already feel like sixteen pounds of hammered death, and now I want to scratch my head and can't even do that. If you've got me tied down for sex, I'm really not in the mood today. Maybe next year. Or the year after, for sure."

"Too bad," Vanny said in a deadpan tone. "You look so hot with those drainage tubes coming out of your shaved chest and all those needles stuck in you. It makes it hard for a girl to keep her hands to herself. Oh baby, I want to have you right now." She reached over and pulled open the Velcro restraints around his wrists. "Sorry about you being tied up. You kept trying to pull out your wires and tubes while you were asleep, so they had to tie you down so you didn't hurt yourself. They told me I could let you loose once you woke up if you promised to behave. So behave." She smiled. The concept of Blanchard Shankles behaving was amusing to her. "One of the nurses from CCU told me you kept trying to pull out your ventilator tube last night. That sounds like you. Maximum trouble all the time. Such a stubborn, stubborn man." She offered the stuffed bear to Blanchard. "This is for you. From one of the nurses."

"Just what I've always wanted!" He took the bear and inspected it, then dropped it to the bed. "A stuffed bear. Yay. They could have given me one with pants. A bear without pants isn't decent."

"The nurse said it's for you to hold tightly to your chest when you have to cough."

"Are you kidding me? I need some serious drugs, and they give me a teddy bear. They could have at least given me a stuffed wolf, or maybe a lion. Is there another hospital in town?" Just then an irresistible urge to cough overcame Blanchard, and as he began to hack, it felt for all the world as if he would cough up his insides. He grabbed his bear close and held on tightly as his lungs expressed outrage at their recent treatment. He coughed himself insensible before the interlude passed, and once it was over, he found himself in the fetal position, facing Vanny, spooning with the bear while trying to hide his tears.

"Ouch," he whispered.

"That's why you need the bear," Vanny said.

"At least take this stupid tee shirt off him," Blanchard said. The bear was wearing a white pullover with a pink heart right in front. On the heart, Dr. Forrester had drawn a simple diagram of the work he had performed. "If I'm going to sleep with a bear, it's going to be a naked bear."

Vanny took the bear and removed the shirt. Then she handed it back. "I think it's cute."

"Real cute. You were talking about me being tied down. I dreamed about that! Jesus, what a dream that was! At first, I was having this great guitar dream. Hendrix and Stevie Ray and all the greats were playing, and I was right there with them, jamming with some of the finest guitar players of all time. Then they disappeared, and my hands were anchored down, and the next thing I knew, a snake slithered down my throat and started breathing for me. I guess that was the tube I was feeling." He touched his throat as he remembered his dream.

"Yuck. Snake dreams."

"Tell me about it. I hate a snake worse than anything." Blanchard had been known to drive the bus off the road into a ditch to chase a snake. "And I really hate a snake in my dreams. It's hard to run over one when you're asleep." A thought occurred to him. "Hey, wait a minute. You said I'm stubborn. I'm not all that stubborn."

"Are you kidding? You're not just stubborn. You're Shankles stubborn."

"I'm not stubborn. I just hate being sick."

"I know you do."

There was an awkward silence then that lasted for nearly a minute. After a year apart, he and Vanny had run out of conversation. Talking had never been their strong point to begin with, and they were definitely out of practice. Finally, when the weight of the silent room seemed destined to crush them both, Blanchard spoke. "Thanks for coming," he said. "I didn't think I'd want to see you, especially while I was sick. I didn't want you to see me this way. That's why I told Covey not to tell you about my troubles. I'm not used to being helpless. But I'm glad you came."

"You know what they say," she said as she stood. She began to straighten up around the room. Her nervous energy was at its height in stressful situations, and this reunion with Blanchard on his sickbed was certainly that.

"What do they say?" He had closed his eyes again and was considering the wisdom of taking a long nap. About eight weeks ought to do it.

"Men. You can't live with them, most times it's against the law to just shoot them, and you can't let them go through heart surgery alone or else they'll get pitiful."

"I don't get pitiful."

"No baby. Of course you don't." She patted him gently on the head.

"I don't think I've ever heard that saying before." His eyes were still closed. "It's pretty specific. Is that a South Carolina thing, or maybe something they taught you at school?"

"I never got to go to school. We were poor, and I was homeschooled."

"I was sort of homeschooled myself. Homeschooled is usually the best. Except for math...." He dozed for a moment, then startled awake. "But I'm glad you came," he repeated, not remembering that he had already told her. "I promise I'll behave if you stick around for a while."

"I'll believe that one when I see it," she said. "Don't make any promises you can't keep. Behaving has never exactly been your strong suit, and I don't expect that you'll take to it here in your old age."

"Old dog and new tricks?"

"Old dog and new tricks."

"I guess you're right," Blanchard said. "I don't like new things." He closed his eyes for a moment.

Vanny reached behind her chair and fetched his flat top guitar. "Look what I brought you," she said. "I thought it might help you recover."

Blanchard saw his old Ovation and smiled. It was one of the oldest friends he had, and one of the few that had never let him down. "Give her to me," he said. Vanny passed him the guitar and raised the head of his bed so he could sit a little more comfortably. She grabbed the forgotten bear as it tried to fall to the floor, or perhaps to leap for safety.

Blanchard reached for an E chord on the Ovation's fret board, but his fingers had minds of their own and would not go where commanded. "Great," he said absently. "They went in to fix my heart, and instead they screwed up my fret hand. I bet they let some students at me." He shook his head. "I knew this was going to happen. I told him no students! He promised me we were cool on that. I swear, Vanny, you just can't trust people. I thought me and the doctor had a deal, but it looks like he went ahead and had a bad day anyway. Find me a lawyer. I'm going to sue."

"I'm sure it's temporary. You've only been awake a little while. It'll all come back in a day or two."

"When I get through with these people, I'll own this place. Blanchard Shankles Medical Center. How's that sound to you?" He tried for a B flat with no luck. "Bastards," he said.

"Velvet Leg Memorial Hospital has a better ring to it. You could specialize in hair removal. The ladies will love it."

"Don't call me Velvet Leg." He tried for an A minor and missed with two of his fingers. "That's one of the first chords I ever learned. Even Scrounge can reach an A minor, and he doesn't have fingers!" The dog couldn't actually make an A minor, but Blanchard was building a legal case and could not be troubled by facts.

"Give it time. I'll all be back."

"Well, if it doesn't, I want you to kill me, make it look like medical malpractice, and then get a lawyer like we just talked about. The one I want is the guy on Channel Nine who stands under the money shower in a superhero outfit while the insurance company people cry and look scared. Do you know the guy I'm talking about?" Vanny nodded, and Blanchard continued. "He seems like he knows what he's doing, and who couldn't use a money shower? When you get through with these people, I want that doctor who did this to me to be the guy waxing the floors. Are you getting this?" After his diatribe, Blanchard found himself panting.

"Kill you and take a money shower. Got it. Make the doctor regret the day he was born. Check. Change the name of the hospital. Not a problem. Are you hurting?"

"Bad. I wish they'd come give me some drugs." He dropped his hands to his side and let the guitar rest in his lap. He was defeated at present, and didn't have the heart to try for any more basic chords. Maybe later, when he was once again in control of hand movement. He looked at Vanny. "Did you tell me you talked to the doctor?"

"He was in this morning before you woke up," Vanny said. "I talked to him for a little while. He seemed like a nice man. He said you did fine, and that you'd be up and around in a few days. Maybe you can let him have a better job than waxing the floors. How about driving an ambulance?"

"We'll see. He wasn't wearing sunglasses, was he?"

"Well, no."

"And you're sure something didn't go wrong? Maybe he was lying to you. My heart still hurts, and now I can't play the guitar. They were supposed to fix the heart thing. It was kind of the whole point of me being here. And I don't know what is going on with my fingers, but I don't like it." Admittedly, what he felt in his chest was more of a deep ache than the sharp stab he had checked in with, but still, it was the principle of the thing. He didn't know how much all of this was going to cost, but he figured it wasn't going to be cheap, and he wanted value for his money. He wanted to feel like a young boy when he left the hospital, with no pains of any consequence anywhere in his body. At the very least, he wanted to not feel like the engineer at a high-speed locomotive accident, pinned under the wreckage of a smoking diesel engine at the bottom of a blind curve in a mountain pass, which was how he felt at present.

"I think hurting for a few days is kind of a thing with this surgery," Vanny said. "They can't do what they had to do without you being sore. The best thing for you to do is sleep through it. As least for today."

Blanchard began to cough again. Vanny grabbed the guitar from where it lay and handed him the bear. He curled up and held on tight. After the coughing fit passed, Blanchard lay there for a few moments, panting raggedly, exhausted and miserable. Finally, he spoke. "The nose," he said softly, with effort.

"What?"

"The nose," he repeated.

"Does your nose hurt?" She began to reach for a tissue.

"Uh-uh. The bear's nose." He uncurled, and when he did she saw that the bear's snout had been pointed inward—aimed dead center into Blanchard's chest incision—when he had grabbed and held. "Why would they put something pointy and hard on a cuddle bear, something that could jam into a scar?" Blanchard asked philosophically, about three words at a time in his breathless state. "I think these people are trying to kill me. Make sure you add that to the list you're making for the lawyer. We'll go after the teddy bear company, too." He began to cough again but remembered to flip the bear before grabbing. After the spell ceased, he rested a moment.

"I think it's time for some pain medication," Vanny said.

"Oh, yeah. It's been time."

"Maybe they can give you something for the coughing, too. I'm calling the nurse."

"Give them a few minutes. They'll be in. If we bother them, it'll make them mad, and then I'll die in here in agony."

"They don't mind it if you call them. That's why they gave us a buzzer."

"Geneva says they hate it." His sister had been a nurse for the past thirty-five years or so, and most of what Blanchard knew about medical matters had come from her in bits and pieces over time. She was a good nurse, apparently, and Blanchard took on faith her assertion that the last thing she wanted to deal with when herding a floor full of patients was someone who spent all their free time on the buzzer.

"Maybe just Geneva hates it."

"She hates it big time. Of course, she hates most everything, so this is nothing special. But she says they all do, and that nothing will slow a nurse down quicker than laying on that buzzer. My nurse will be in with something when the orders say she can come in. If I'm asleep, wake me up. I want to be sure everyone understands that this is not a Tylenol situation. I want the good stuff, and plenty of it, and soon."

"Okay, then. That's the way we'll play it. Hug your bear and try to take a nap."

"Better to be safe than sorry," Blanchard said. He nodded and drifted off. When he did, Vanny waited a few moments to be sure he was fully asleep. Then she reached for the call button and gave it a squeeze.

"IT'S NOT MY FAULT"
(Blanchard Shankles/John Covey)

No memories here now, no trinkets to keep
No lump in the throat, no remembrance to reap
You left me with troubles and no way to solve 'em
It's not my fault, but it's damn sure my problem

No blood from a stone or wail from the pain
No ease from my heartache or break from the strain
I float on the air like a bloom with no stem
It was never my fault, but it's damn sure my problem

It's our best day so far, you said with a grin
On the morning you left and I uncorked the gin
I don't know my crime but I've still been condemned
It can't be my fault, but it's damn sure my problem

I survive each day and scrounge like a crow
What becomes of me now I guess I don't know
You left me alone like you had never been
It could be my fault, and it's damn sure my problem

My time has worn ragged, my soul has grown thin.
The thoughts in my head are mostly a sin
Wreckage and ruin and chaos and mayhem
I guess it's my fault, and it's damn sure my problem

Days morph to months and love blends to tears
I remember the days when my heart knew no fears
I mined for a diamond but came up with no gem
It was always my fault, and always my problem

No memories here now, no trinkets to keep
No lump in the throat, no remembrance to reap
You left me with troubles and no way to solve 'em
It's not my fault, but it's damn sure my problem

"Third Rate Romance"
The Amazing Rhythm Aces
-2006-

Blanchard first met Vanny when the band stopped at her place of employment while on the way back from a club date at The Triple-H, a mean-dog night spot out in the middle of nowhere about fifteen miles southeast of Spartanburg, South Carolina. At that time in the band's career, they had determined that playing country and western music might be more lucrative than what had come to be termed classic rock, which was just another name for all the tunes they had learned long years ago when the songs were new, so they had assimilated some country songs and were playing the redneck circuit under the name Sawmill Gravy. The experiment was a relative failure, however, and the engagement at The Triple-H was one of their last in the country genre before they decided to change their name to Murphy's Law and get back to musical basics.

The issue had not been with country music per se, which was easy to play and which they all sort of liked except for Ford Man, who thought that the bar for percussion in the genre was set mighty low. The problem lay more in the direction of country music fans and their proclivity to want to dust it up once they got a few beers under their belts come a Friday or Saturday night. The band was unsure as to the reasons the members of this particular demographic always wanted to fight, but they did—man, woman, and, occasionally, child. Maybe they had bad jobs or unsympathetic spouses, or maybe they had been fed gunpowder as children to make them mean, or maybe something about other country music fans really pissed them off. Whatever the causes, these constant interruptions were hard on the collective nerves of Sawmill Gravy and sometimes on the equipment as well. A couple of these donnybrooks had even led to police intervention, which had in turn led to arrests and club closures, and once to deferment of payment when the club owner of a place called Little Lucy's near

Boone, North Carolina, had both hands broken by an angry and inebriated patron and as a result could not write checks for an extended period.

Little Lucy himself was a former long-haul trucker who stood about 6'1" and weighed around 305 pounds with his shoes off, and his main concern with having both hands broken was that he had been blindsided so early in the melee that he'd missed the chance to participate to the extent he generally liked. The drunken rascal who broke those unlucky hands had been arrested for assault with a deadly weapon, in this case the microwave from behind the bar, and as he was dragged away he railed about the unfairness of a world in which a lead guitar player in a bar band could get away with making moves on a guy's girl during a beer break, but when said guy accidentally broke someone's hands while defending said girl's honor, he was the one who had to go to jail.

On the day that Blanchard met Vanny, the band was rolling along in the bus on their way back from the scrub pine and ugly red clay south of Spartanburg. The high point of the trip so far happened when a truck pulling a lowboy trailer with a forty-foot steeple strapped to it horizontally passed them on the interstate. It was an occurrence unlikely enough to engage their momentary interest.

"I thought they built those things in place," Blanchard said.

"I think folks started buying them from the steeple factory around 1750," Covey replied. He had no idea if this was a true fact or not, but speculating about steeples and how they became such was something to do on a long bus ride.

"No kidding?" Simpson asked.

"I think it was one of Benjamin Franklin's early business ventures," Covey continued. "That man was into a little bit of everything back in the day."

"He was a guitar player, too," Blanchard added.

"Don't forget that whole electricity thing," Tucker McFry added.

"It was an electric guitar," Blanchard said.

"Les Paul invented the electric guitar, not Ben Franklin," said Jimbo Cox.

"I never knew all that," Simpson said, shaking his head in wonder.

"Go back to sleep, Simpson," Ford Man advised. "It's getting deep in here."

A few miles down the road, they caught up with the steeple due to a triple blowout on the left side of the lowboy trailer. As the bus topped a rise, they saw the rig ahead on the right shoulder. The steeple was leaning a bit, as if it had considered jumping for safety at some point during the worst of the blowout but had instead elected to just hold on and pray.

"That's a bad sign," said Ford Man.

"If I was the church, I'd send it back," said Simpson.

"You just can't get reliable steeples these days," Blanchard added.

It was a Sunday afternoon, and steeple speculation aside, everyone on the bus had been mostly quiet. There had not been a fight at The Triple H the night before, but the crowd had been cheap, small, and troublesome, and the band's payday was a disappointment. Covey was driving, Blanchard was navigating while nursing a pint of Ancient Age bourbon whiskey, and the rest of the boys were halfheartedly playing hearts in the back.

"Take the next exit," Blanchard said, pointing ahead.

"Why do you want to get off?" Covey asked. "We don't need fuel." They were only three hours away from home, and Covey was ready to be there. If he ever quit playing music, it would be because of the interminable bus trips home. Without the distraction of an upcoming show to look forward to, the journey back to Georgia was just another long and boring ride.

"I want to buy a Bible."

"What?"

"Is your hearing going? That's a bad thing to happen to a bass player. You need to quit standing so close to your amp. I said I want to buy a Bible."

"Right now?"

"We are not guaranteed tomorrow."

"What brought this on?"

"Tell me you saw the sign back there!"

"I wasn't paying attention. What sign are you talking about?"

"There was a billboard back there advertising the Bible Outlet Store. I need a Bible that comes from an outlet store."

"If you need some spiritual guidance, there's a Bible here on the bus somewhere. Ask Ford Man if he has it." Ford Man liked to read the Scriptures on a long bus ride. The graceful language found in the chapters of the King James Bible calmed his ragged nerves. Two or three verses would put him right to sleep.

"Ford Man's Bible is a regular Bible. I need an outlet Bible." Blanchard took another sip of the bourbon and offered a taste to Covey, who declined.

"Okay, I'll bite. Why do you need a Bible from an outlet store?"

"Outlet stores sell seconds, right? Stuff that has something wrong with it. How cool would it be to have a Bible that was a factory second? Maybe it would say something like, 'Thou shalt covet thy neighbor's wife.' It would be like permission to slip in through the back window! Big permission, right from the source. My neighbor is pretty hot, but she's a religious girl, and I've never been able to talk her into giving it up. She practically lives down at the church. I think she has keys to the place. If I could show her a Bible verse that commanded her to give me a little taste, she might go for it!"

"You want to stop at the outlet store in hopes of finding a Bible that will let you get into Flora North's pants?" Covey wanted to be sure he had captured the gestalt of the moment.

"Not just that, although I wouldn't mind dancing the love tango with her, if you know what I mean." Covey knew exactly what he meant, as did the rest of the band. Inside Flora North's pants was a destination Blanchard often discussed on long bus rides. He was mildly obsessed with that particular place. Blanchard continued explaining his biblical rationale to Covey. "But this is not just about Flora North's sweet parts. What if you ran up on some guy who was such bad news that there was nothing else for it but to do him in?"

"So far I've been able to avoid that," Covey noted, although he had to admit to himself that an insistent urge to clean up the more stagnant portions of the gene pool had occasionally descended upon him in the presence of certain individuals, and that, if pressed, he could provide a short list of names, addresses, and suggested methods of dispatch as well as a detailed analysis from a societal perspective as to why these actions might be deemed advantageous to the continuance of the race.

"I'm just saying what if. So let's say you had to cave someone's head in for their own good and for the good of humanity. I can think of four guys right now who qualify. Maybe even five, although I heard someone's already beat me to it on the last one. Anyway, suppose you took care of a little business. And then, after you had sent whoever home to Jesus, what if you could produce a Bible at your trial that said, 'Thou shalt kill'? Think about it! You wouldn't even need a lawyer to get you off! They'd have to let you go! Man, just think of all the cool stuff that might be in one of those Bibles."

"I believe I'd go ahead and get a lawyer," Covey said, "just to be safe. Anyway, don't you think that maybe if anything is wrong with the Bibles, it's something like a loose cover or a messed-up binding? Or maybe there are just some missing pages, or some of them are in there upside down. It could even be that there's nothing wrong with them at all. Maybe they just print a lot of extra copies and sell them in outlet stores to guys like you who think they're getting a deal. Anna says they do that all the time with clothes. When she was a young girl she worked at the sock factory over in Ft. Payne, and every Tuesday was seconds day. Same socks, same bags, but they stuck on a red label that said seconds." Anna had been a poor girl when she had married her equally poor bass player many years ago, but her dowry of socks had lasted all this time and would continue to keep the Covey family's feet warm and dry for many more anniversaries to come.

"Come on! Slow down. I want to check it out. It won't take long." Blanchard was very excited about the possibility of typographically endorsed sin.

"You're killing me," Covey said, but he put on the turn signal and checked his side mirror before taking a detour up the exit ramp to the Bible Outlet Store. Blanchard was a tenacious man, and Covey knew if he didn't stop, he would wish he had for the remainder of the journey home and probably for several weeks after. Plus, he had to pee, and maybe the place had a bathroom, or at least a substantial bush around the side.

When they pulled up outside the Bible Outlet Store, no one on the bus was much impressed, including Simpson, who had a low threshold for fascination and was generally overwhelmed by just about everything. They parked on an un-level gravel lot that sported a multitude of potholes, cigarette butts, secondhand condoms, and empty beer cans outside a yellow and red prefabricated sheet metal building that looked as if it would be happier housing a selection of fireworks, and perhaps once had. There were window air conditioners mounted high every ten feet or in the bright yellow walls. They hummed and rattled and dripped steady streams of water to the sidewalk underneath. Rusty expanded-metal gratings were screwed over the windows, either to keep random heathens away from the Bibles or to keep disgruntled employees inside, selling them. Across the face of the building was a sign sporting five-foot-tall plastic letters that proclaimed the name and perhaps the mission of the establishment: the Bible Outlet S ore. The "t," apparently, had fallen off at some point in the past and was leaned against the building like a crooked cross. The only other vehicle in the parking lot was a brown 1980 Ford Granada.

"I thought the Lord was doing a little better than this," Covey said, shaking his head. "I hope that's not His car." If it turned out that the Almighty drove a brown 1980 Granada mounted with four black wall snow tires and sporting a faded beige vinyl top with several rips in it that had been poorly repaired with gray duct tape, the members of Sawmill Gravy would have to examine in greater detail their many previously held assumptions about the opulent nature of the afterlife and the desirability of going there.

"I'm going to take the old lady to church when we get home," Chicken Raines vowed, sounding embarrassed for all of humanity. "We're both going to put some money in the plate." Jimbo Tant fished a twenty-spot from his billfold and handed it to Chicken.

"Put that in for me," he said. Chicken nodded.

"Now, just think about it a minute," Blanchard said. "There can't be much markup in defective Bibles. It's a volume business, and they have to keep their overhead low."

"It looks pretty low," Covey said.

"Maybe all the profits go to charity," Simpson Taggart offered, trying to put a positive spin on a situation he sensed was somehow awry.

"The recession has hit everyone pretty hard," said Jimbo Tant.

"I hope they have a snack bar," said Tucker McFry. Tucker had been rail thin his entire life and hungry since the moment he had been conceived. There was a Cheeto stuck to his shirt, and when he noticed it, he plucked it from the fabric and put it out of its orange misery.

"You all need to be careful," said Ford Man. "I'm serious. All the time you're making jokes, the Big Man up there is writin' every bit of it down. Come Judgment Day, He'll read it all back to you."

"I wish He wouldn't," Covey said. "But I guess He knows His own mind."

Covey opened the door to the bus, and Sawmill Gravy disembarked and headed in for their first experience with outlet Bibles. Good roadie that he was, Simpson Taggart held open the front door of the store as they entered one after the other, like a line of disciples searching for a slightly flawed version of ultimate truth. The first thing Covey noticed once he was inside was that it was oppressively hot in there. The South Carolina sun beating down on square yard after square yard of sheet metal was overwhelming the air conditioners, and it felt like they were standing in an oven. Blanchard, too, had become aware of the heat index.

"I guess they keep it hot as hell in here as a sales technique," he said. "You know. Buy a Bible, avoid being this hot for eternity."

"Good salesmanship," Chicken said, nodding at the cleverness of the ploy. "I may buy two." He wiped at the sweat that was already beading on his brow. Chicken was a sweater, and this affliction had grown more insistent over the years. He was often on his third shirt by the end of a show. In the days long past before he had sprouted his little belly, he had often just played without.

The next thing Covey noticed was Bibles, which he supposed was appropriate, given the nature of the establishment. There were thousands upon thousands of them. There were Bibles on shelves and Bibles in stacks. There were Bibles in boxes and Bibles in crates. There were Bibles spread out on tables and Bibles piled up on the concrete floor. There were big Bibles and little ones. There were white Bibles, black Bibles, and all colors in between. There were fancy Bibles and plain ones. There were foreign Bibles and good old American ones. There were old Bibles and new ones. There were Bibles in braille, Bibles on tape, and Bibles on CD.

"That's a lot of Bibles," Blanchard said. He was impressed. The sheer weight of the Lord's word lay on him like a steel plate over a sinkhole.

"Boy howdy," said Simpson.

"Welcome to the Bible Outlet Sore," a husky female voice said. "Can I help you boys?" They looked about them in momentary confusion, seeking the source of the disembodied voice. Simpson looked up, perhaps wondering if the words had come from a higher realm. Then a green-eyed, compact woman with a ponytail of long black hair and sunglasses pushed to the top of her head stepped out from behind a stack of Bibles that featured what may have been the most gruesome crucifixion scene any of them had ever seen, all blood and spikes and tendons and anguish and abject misery. Her name tag said she was Vanny, and the tattoo on her right arm indicated that she was Born To Lose. Blanchard already liked her.

"Bible Outlet Sore?" Covey asked.

"You read the sign," Vanny said, pointing in the general direction of the parking lot. "And now you've seen the place. I think Bible Outlet Sore fits it pretty well, don't you? If the boss ever puts that 't' back up, which isn't likely since he's lazy even when he isn't dying of cancer, I'll probably take it back down in the name of truth in advertising."

"We want a Bible," Blanchard said, getting right to the point. Even though he was on a mission to secure the typos of the Almighty, he couldn't help noticing how appealing his salesperson looked. He liked the way her eyes sparkled, and the way her slight overbite caused her to nibble her lower lip. He knew the signs. He was smitten.

"Sorry. Fresh out." She smiled. Then she looked over her shoulder. "Wait a minute! We might have a few left for our special customers."

"How do you get to be a special customer?" Chicken asked.

"Walk in the door, basically," Vanny replied. "That's special enough for me."

"Do you have any Bibles that are misprinted?" Blanchard asked. Covey wandered toward the back of the place in search of the john, and the rest of the boys disbursed and began to browse the sacred store.

"Sorry. These are all just regular Bibles. Nothing's wrong with any of them. Except for this one here." She held up a copy of the Bible with the lurid cover. "If I was Jesus, I'd make it really hard on whoever drew this picture. The artist could at least expect some boils in bad places, or maybe a leg to fall off or to have a mild heart attack. It's pain porn. I mean, just look at the poor man! I think the two-dollar word is gratuitous. This is gratuitous violence! It's just nasty. But you'd be surprised at how many of these things we sell. Some folks just can't get enough of that kind of stuff." She shivered as she placed the volume back on top of the stack just as Ford Man Cooper came back up with a pair of basic black Bibles and a look of dismay.

"Jesus died for us," he offered in defense of the fierce rendering of the crucifixion. "He shed His blood that we might live!"

"Not now, Ford Man," Blanchard sighed. Ford Man Cooper was a fine musician and a lifelong friend, but he was prone to testifying at inconvenient times. Like now, while Blanchard was trying to make a little time with the Bible salesperson.

Vanny shrugged, and nodded at Ford Man in agreement. "That's how the story goes," she said. "He died to save us. And I believe that He did. It was a noble thing. But what He did has not been that uncommon throughout history."

"What are you talking about?" Ford Man asked. "He gave up His life for us."

"I'm not arguing with you. I believe He did just that. But so have lots of other people."

"What are you talking about?" Ford Man asked again. He was not used to philosophical conversations having as their subject matter the Blood of the Lamb, and the intellectual exercise was causing his head to ache and his voice to crack.

"Tell me, do you have any kids?" Vanny asked.

It was Ford Man's turn to nod. "I have two." He held up the pair of black Bibles. "That's who these are for."

"It's nice of you to get them a gift. Would you die to save them? Or your wife? Or maybe your grandchildren?"

"Of course I would."

"Of course you would! Most everyone in the world would give their lives for their children. People have always given their lives for loved ones. Anyone who wouldn't do that is just plain sorry. There are some sorry people out there, but most folks are pretty decent. But here's something to consider. Throughout Christian history, all the people who ever sacrificed their lives for someone or something worth dying for had to be content with having faith that they were going to a better place. But Jesus knew. For Him, it was a no-risk deal."

Ford Man was quiet as he considered the implications of her scenario. Then he shook his head as if to free himself of the lure of this heresy and held up his two Bibles again. "I'll just wait over by the cash register," he said as he headed toward the counter.

"Poor Ford Man," Blanchard said. "He's a true believer, and sometimes it's hard on him when he looks too close."

"Me too," Vanny said. "I'm a true believer. I believe almost every word of it. The whole nine yards. Well, except maybe that Revelations business. That stuff's just crazy. And I believe it even though I can see all the flaws in the story, all the little details that don't quite add up." She pointed at the grisly Bible. "But that picture is just wrong."

She looked at Blanchard as if expecting rebuttal, but he too thought the picture was a bit rough and offered no disagreement. He did, however, have a question. "If you don't think that dying for mankind was something special, which is what Jesus was supposed to have done, then why do you believe in Christianity? It all hinges on that one thing." Blanchard was curious for his own sake. He someday hoped to hear a rationale so compelling that he, too, might become a true believer. He envied those people he knew who were, such as Ford Man. They seemed more content with the world than he was.

"I didn't say it wasn't special. Sacrifice is always special. What I was trying to get across to your friend was that it isn't uncommon. Many people would do exactly what Jesus did under those circumstances. Especially if they knew—not just crossed their fingers and hoped like the rest of us, but actually *knew*—that heaven was waiting for them."

"Ford Man would tell you that he knows," Blanchard said, nodding at his bandmate.

"If he truly does, then he's a lucky man. Me? I don't know. I hope. I believe because I want to believe, I guess. I want there to be

128

something besides a hole in the ground and nothingness forever." When he remained silent, she continued. "You know, this is not the first time someone's asked me about misprinted Bibles. One of you boys looking to slip up behind the preacher's wife with the good book in hand?" Blanchard grinned and lowered his eyes. He was caught. Vanny was the most unusual Bible salesperson he had ever met. The fact that she was the only Bible salesperson he had ever met did not diminish her appeal in the least. "It has happened, you know," she continued.

"What has happened?"

"Misprinted Bibles. Back in the 1600s there was a famous misprinted Bible in England. They call it the Sinner's Bible. The king's printer left out the word *not* from the Seventh Commandment when he was setting up his press. Then he printed a stack of Bibles. The king got really mad when he read, 'Thou shalt commit adultery.' He fired his printer and had the Bibles rounded up and burned, but he didn't get them all, and a few are still around today."

"I'm guessing you don't have one of those."

"Well, they're worth about a jillion dollars apiece these days, so no." She looked around her. "We don't carry jillion-dollar Bibles here at the Sore."

"That printer was lucky all the king did was fire him," Blanchard said. "I bet he was a fast runner. The king probably planned to burn him along with the Bibles."

"He probably got roughed up a little bit while they were getting to the bottom of things, for sure," Vanny said. "Thumbscrews and such. Kings could sort of do whatever they wanted to back then. It came with the job. I don't know much about kings. Maybe they still can."

"What kind of Bible salesman are you, anyway?" Blanchard asked. The unusual story about the Sinner's Bible and Vanny's easy manner in telling it elicited in Blanchard a strong desire to know this woman, and to spend time with her.

"Unwilling," she replied.

"What's that mean?"

"I haven't been in Bible sales all that long, and I may be the worst Bible salesperson who ever lived. Bible selling was sort of forced on me. I didn't have much of a choice."

"How did that happen?" Blanchard had been forced into many courses of action in his life, things he'd had to do in spite of his wishes to the contrary, but he couldn't imagine a set of circumstances that would bring about involuntary Bible sales.

"Well, this used to be an adult bookstore. It was called the Love Sack."

"The Love Sack?"

"I know. Bad name for a porn store, right? Believe me, I've heard all of the jokes. It was really called the Love Shack, but the 'h' fell off."

"You guys need better glue."

"We need something, for sure. Anyway, back when I was selling porn, the place was really hopping. It made money hand over fist, and the merchandise pretty much sold itself."

"Porn will do that," Blanchard agreed.

"All I had to do all day long was ring up smut and pretend not to recognize people I knew from church."

"The perfect job!"

"Mostly. I had to put up with a creep from time to time, but I keep a loaded nine millimeter behind the counter, and whenever someone started talking about wanting to go on a date or see me take my shirt off, I would level it between their eyes and explain to them that I was not part of the merchandise."

"That would make me start behaving," Blanchard said.

"It seems to work pretty well, except for that one guy who wanted me to go ahead and shoot him while he masturbated and watched me pee."

"I didn't even know that was a thing," Blanchard admitted, grimacing.

"I don't think it is. I think he might have invented it right here on the spot."

"Lucky you."

"Comes from clean living, I guess."

"Did you shoot him?"

"Look down." Blanchard did as he was told and saw two holes in the floor, one on each side of his right foot. "I put one in the floor right next to his shoe and told him he had about five seconds to get out of here. He made it in three."

"I bet he did. It was nice of you to give him a warning shot."

"I'm a pretty bad shot. I was aiming for his foot and missed."

"How did the other hole get there?"

"The same guy came back after we became the Bible Outlet Sore. He had grown a beard, and he was wearing sunglasses and trying to look like someone else, but I recognized him as soon as he walked in the door."

"He made a real impression on you, huh?"

"Some things you don't forget. This time he wanted me to read Genesis to him while he masturbated and watched me pee."

"Why Genesis?"

"I didn't ask. Maybe all of that begetting made him horny."

"I am noticing a theme here," Blanchard said. "You know you're going to have to put a slug into this guy one of these days, right? Maybe in the leg, maybe a little higher up. I don't see any way around it." When there was an unpleasant task at hand, sometimes it was best to just get it over with.

"I know. I know."

"Finish your story about becoming a Bible salesman."

"Right," Vanny continued. "The guy who owned the place back when it was the Love Sack still owns it now. He owns that truck stop across the highway, too, and a bunch of crummy rental houses all over the county. He got himself a serious dose of cancer a couple of years back. One of those crazy kinds that no one's ever heard of that almost always kills you. And for a while it looked like he was going to die. Lost all kinds of weight and looked like a living skeleton. But then he had a remission. His cancer just went away. Really had the doctors scratching their heads. Once he thought he had it beat, he went and dedicated his life to the Lord as a kind of thank-you gesture. After he did that, he cleaned out all the naked women DVDs and sex toys and brought in Jesus, Mary, and Joseph, and I was pretty much drafted into becoming the only full-time Bible salesperson in the state."

"You could have quit."

"There's not that much to do around here. Jobs are pretty scarce unless you don't mind working in a rug mill. And I do. Been there, done that, rather starve. So Bibles it is." She paused a moment. "The sex stuff sold much better than Bibles, but I guess that's just the way things are. Folks have their eyes on the hereafter, but their minds are in the gutter. It's human nature. We're hard-wired for sex, so what do we do? We make it a sin to do what we're evolved to do. It's kind of crazy. I may be going back to my former trade soon, though. I have high hopes, at least. The boss's cancer is back. He's pretty upset about it, but not as upset as the cancer seems to be." She pointed at the lurid Bible. "He's kind of looking that way these days."

Blanchard grimaced. If the owner looked that bad, he wouldn't last long. "I've heard of people getting mad at God because they're sick," he said. "I think if it ever comes down to it, I might be one of them."

"What really has him ticked is that he claims he made a deal with God, and he kept his end of the bargain. He says a deal is a deal, and he expects God to hold up His end. But God's not taking any of the boss's calls."

"Is your boss planning on suing the Big Man?"

"If I were him, I'd be getting my mind right and my affairs in order. It's a fair bet that, barring any miraculous recoveries, we may be having a closeout sale soon. If you wait, you might get a better deal."

"Do you sell a lot of Bibles?" Blanchard asked. He wasn't really that interested in how business was going, but he enjoyed talking with Vanny and wanted to keep the conversation going as long as he could.

"Almost none. If you ever want to make a little money, start with a lot of money and go into the Bible business. But the boss didn't seem to mind, back when he was feeling better. He seemed happy to pay me to sit and twiddle my thumbs most of the time. He has more money than he can ever spend, anyway, so losing a little here didn't seem to bother him much. Back in the good old days, porn, diesel fuel, and slum lording made him rich. But now that he's sick again, I guess all bets are off. Like I said, he was looking pretty rough the last time I saw him, and I don't think he'll last long this go-round."

"Sounds like he's the only one sticking to the deal," said Blanchard. He had picked up a nice 1968 Gideon's and was admiring its simple lines and unostentatious demeanor.

"It does, doesn't it? You'd think that if you made a deal with God, you could sort of take that with you to the bank. Maybe the fact that he moved all the porn inventory over to the truck stop and started selling it there instead of getting rid of it counted against him. Maybe if he had just shoveled it all into a pit and burned it, he'd be healthy as a horse right now."

"No one's perfect," Blanchard said. "I've known a few rich guys along the way, and they didn't get to be rich or stay rich by throwing away stuff that they could sell. Anyway, it was probably just good luck that he got better in the first place and bad luck that he got sick again. Why would God go out of His way to cure the porn king of South Carolina?"

"I can think of plenty of folks more deserving," Vanny agreed. "But these things are hard to figure sometimes."

"I'm curious. What does your average Bible outlet customer look like?"

"Oh, I don't know," Vanny replied. "They look a lot like you, I guess. Not you personally. What I meant was, most of the people who come in here look like regular folks."

"Except for the creepy guy?"

"Except for the creepy guy. As a matter of fact, a few of my Bible customers used to be porn customers."

"Well, the Lord moves in mysterious ways," Blanchard said. "You led them down the path to evil thought and impure deed, and now you're bringing them back into the fold. You're kind of like a missionary."

Covey strolled back from the bathroom and joined them. He had a necklace for his wife, a small crucifix on a slender silver chain. Ford Man, who had been checking out refrigerator magnets with Scripture printed on them, took his opportunity to head back toward the facilities. The rest of the boys had drifted to the front and were milling around near Blanchard and Vanny. They all had a small item or two to purchase. It was an unwritten rule in Sawmill Gravy, and in Skyye before that, that if you stopped and used the restroom, you did business with the establishment that housed it. It was the right thing to do. Toilet paper and soap weren't free, and there was always the unspoken hope among the band members that if they paid it forward, then the tip jar might well be overflowing come the following weekend's engagement.

"Are you going to buy a Bible?" Covey asked Blanchard. "We've got a long way to go, and I want to get back on the road."

"If they're just regular Bibles, I guess I don't want one." Blanchard sounded very disappointed. At this rate, he would never find himself basking in the wholesome goodness that was hidden inside Flora North's pants, and that would truly be a shame for him, at least, if not for Flora. "Thanks for your time," he said to Vanny, the only Bible salesman he had ever known.

"It was my pleasure," she replied. "You boys have been the first people through the door today, and I enjoyed the company. Where are you heading?" She stepped to the counter and began to ring up the various purchases.

"Sequoyah, Georgia," Blanchard said. "It's a wide place in the road not too far south of Chattanooga." He had picked out a cigarette lighter with a fish on one side and three crosses on the other. He flicked it to be sure it would function before placing it on the counter. "We played near Spartanburg the last two nights."

"Are you a band?" Vanny asked.

"Yes ma'am," Chicken Raines said. "Have you ever heard of REO Speedwagon?"

"I have!" Vanny said.

"Well, that's not us," he replied with glee.

"How many times are you going to tell that joke?" Tucker asked.

"I love that joke," Chicken replied. "I may never stop telling it."

"Great, Chicken," Covey said. "Stick to what works. It gets better every time."

The boys finished paying, and one by one they filed back out to the bus. As they resumed their seats, Vanny hurried out from the Bible Outlet Sore and knocked on the bus door. Covey opened it, and Vanny handed one of the lurid white pain Bibles to Blanchard.

"You stopped for a Bible," she said, "so I figured I'd give you one on the house. This one is inscribed."

"Jesus signed it?"

"No. I did. You boys drive careful."

Blanchard took the book and held it in his lap. Covey closed the door and backed the bus away from the building. Once they were underway and back on the interstate, Blanchard opened his new Bible and read the inscription.

"What's it say?" Covey asked.

"It says 'Thou Shalt Call Me,' and there's a phone number."

"I think a phone number is better than a misprinted Bible," Covey said. "What do you think?"

"I think the Lord really does work in mysterious ways," Blanchard replied.

"CAN'T GET TO HEAVEN ON A HELLBOUND TRAIN"
(Blanchard Shankles/John Covey)

Can't spread your wings if you're nailed to the ground
Can't play a song 'til you find the right sound
Can't find peace when you're swimming in pain
Can't get to heaven on a hellbound train

Can't love a woman if your heart's been broke
Can't get high if there's nothing to smoke
Can't stay dry dancing out in the rain
Can't get to heaven on a hellbound train

Can't live like a king when you've got no home
Can't stay in one place when you're bound to roam
Can't pull over when you're in the wrong lane
Can't get to heaven on a hellbound train

Can't hold your baby when she wants to let go
Can't keep guessing when you really oughta know
Can't cross the river when you're bound in chain
Can't get to heaven on a hellbound train

Can't see the sun on a cold winter's night
Can't be a man when you're drowning in fright
Can't hold a note when you've lost the refrain
Can't get to heaven on a hellbound train

Can't go up when you're falling straight down
Can't roam the hills when you're living in town
Can't be Abel if your brother was Cain
Can't get to heaven on a hellbound train

Can't glimpse her smile when your eyes won't see
Can't hold her tight if she wants to be free
Can't stand the loss when there's nothing to gain
Can't get to heaven on a hellbound train

Can't spread your wings if you're nailed to the ground
Can't play a song 'til you find the right sound
Can't find peace when you're swimming in pain
Can't get to heaven on a hellbound train

"Old Man"
Neil Young
-1972-

As time went on, Blanchard and Geneva settled into a new routine. She kept the house, and he took care of the yard. She cooked the food, and he washed the dishes. Neither answered the phone or paid for it to be there, and eventually it went permanently silent, as if it had finally given up. Neither had a driver's license, but since Blanchard could drive and wasn't particularly concerned about the legalities of the enterprise, he took over Benton's car and did the driving for the both of them, although he missed the wind in his hair as he piloted his little MG. Geneva continued her daily journey to the high school and pursued her studies while Blanchard removed attending school from his to-do list. He figured that he would at least have to hide from the truant officer or explain himself to the principal, but quitting high school turned out to be one of the easiest things he had ever done. He simply quit going, and no one seemed to care or perhaps even to notice.

"If I had known this, I would have quit years ago. They didn't even send out someone to check on me!" Blanchard had been absent from school for two weeks at this point and had never been more content. He had spent that time driving the roads during the day looking for a full-time job and playing his guitar at night. He and some friends had started a band, and they were as busy as only young musicians could be, smoking a little pot, drinking a few beers, and learning the tunes that they were certain would take them to the stars.

"You sound a little upset," Geneva noted.

"I wanted someone to try to talk me out of it so I could tell them to go away. Other than that, I couldn't be happier!" It wasn't just the administrators down at the school that had failed to follow up, either. It had been almost six weeks since Benton's bad day. His physical remains were now good and cold in the ground while hopefully his life force was tap dancing in hell, and Edna was now very mellow down at the state hospital, coloring, listening to the radio, and having long chats with folks no one else could see. In all that time, no one had come to bother Geneva and Blanchard.

About two months after Benton Shankles's death at the hands of his wife and the Nubian princess, Blanchard found a job working for a local entrepreneur named Dennis Sexton, a traveling auctioneer and antiques dealer. Blanchard hired on as his floor worker and unofficial apprentice. Sexton was sixty-nine when they first met, but they had been hard years—dog years in many senses—and he looked as aged as a weathered shed and claimed that he felt older than he looked. Everyone referred to him as Major. This epithet was a nod to his thirty years in the Army, during which he had risen from the rapidly depleting enlisted ranks on the bloody sands of Omaha Beach to wear a lieutenant's bars on the frigid Pusan Perimeter before finally displaying a major's gold leaves as he walked down the mean streets of Saigon.

"Call me Major," the old man said to Blanchard as he offered his hand to seal the deal.

"Yes sir," Blanchard replied. He would call his new boss whatever the man wanted to be called, provided the work was steady and the paychecks cleared. The money sock at home was nearly empty, and he needed this job.

"You like to work?"

"I like to eat."

Major looked at Blanchard a moment before shaking his head slowly and cracking a toothless smile. He liked a little spirit in the ranks, apparently, provided it didn't get out of hand. Blanchard had been on the payroll for about five minutes by that time, after first outclassing all competition at a hiring event that no one else attended. The word was out among the local young bloods that Major liked to see some sweat for his dollars, and that after all those years in the infantry, he was about as crazy as a rabid preacher on bad cocaine, so all of Blanchard's peers had declined to apply for the position. But Blanchard had more than a passing acquaintance with crazy and didn't think a bit more exposure would hurt, and he really didn't mind hard work, so the job dropped into his pocket like a gold watch at an accountant's retirement party.

Blanchard and Geneva were nearly broke, and this was by far the best offer from the few he had received. He was an underage high school dropout, and potential local employers had not exactly been fighting each other to get their hands on him. Blanchard was weary of having nothing in his wallet but his unlucky condom and the photo that had come with the billfold. Another advantage of this particular job was that Blanchard liked to be left alone, and the rumor was that Major was a hands-off taskmaster provided he was satisfied with the quality and quantity of the work being performed. As for Major's alleged craziness, Blanchard had been the unintended by-product of sexual relations between a pair of totally insane people during a time of unrestricted lunacy in the world, so Major's reputation as an eccentric didn't give him any pause. After a turn at bat with Edna pitching and Benton calling the balls and strikes, everything this side of small mammals nailed to trees looked pretty normal to him.

"Fair enough," Major said. Blanchard fought the strange urge to salute, which for some reason seemed like the thing to do at that moment.

Major was short, knobby, and paunchy with clubbed, yellowed fingers and a chronic cough courtesy of a lifetime of intimate association with a staggering number of Pall Malls. His ears were too large for his bald head, which in turn was oversized for his stooped shoulders. His rheumy eyes were almost useless, but they danced and twinkled like fireflies in the spring night sky. He had a handsome nose, but its placement in the center of his roughshod face appeared to be an error, as if he had been in a hurry that morning and put on someone else's snout by mistake. He had a bad heart, worse knees, weak kidneys, a scarred liver, a prostate the size of a tennis ball, and a digestive system so impaired that all he could eat were bananas, oatmeal, and Maalox.

He worked four and sometimes five auctions per week, fleabitten junk sales held in sheds and back rooms, car sales conducted in parking lots and garages, antique sales brokered in failed shops and decrepit warehouses, livestock sales undertaken in barns, pastures, and farmyards, real estate sales chanted from courthouse steps, and the occasional estate sale, generally held right where the deceased had resided, conducted in the rooms where most of the living and all of the dying had occurred, right there where the departed could float in on a wayward breeze and view the proceedings through the mist separating this world from the next, could witness the squabbling over worthless baubles and forgotten treasures, and could observe the conversion of all their worldly goods into cash for distribution to bickering relatives, overfed lawyers, and other select members of the venal legions of the living.

Major drank good Kentucky bourbon and preferred Maker's Mark when he could get it. He ate Chiquita bananas by the bunch, smoked Pall Mall cigarettes by the carton, drove a white Ford pickup truck with mud flaps that invited passers-by to get their hearts in Dixie or get their asses out, voted a straight Democratic ticket in a state where it was futile to do so, bought Amoco white gas, and watched *Bonanza* reruns whenever he could discover an episode to view and a comfortable chair to sit in.

"Drink the best liquor you can afford, marry the best woman you have the privilege to meet, and burn the best gasoline you can find," he once told Blanchard around a Pall Mall as he carefully poured Maker's Mark from his plaid screw-top thermos bottle into his red plastic coffee cup. "You don't live but one time, and second-best is second-rate, not worth the effort, not worth your time." Blanchard took to heart these words to live by, solemnly delivered by a widowed journeyman who had found his best woman standing destitute in the smoldering ruins of Berlin, who had married and cherished her for over twenty years before subsequently losing her, and who had regularly soaked his grief in sour mash ever since.

On most days and on many nights, Major was sober enough to drive to whatever sale was on the agenda, but seldom was he sufficiently dry to drive home after the auction concluded. Nights were his preferred time for drinking, as if his sobriety were linked to the orb of the sun and followed close behind as it lowered itself in the west. The dark held phantoms for him that he could not confront without fortification, so he drank like a camel at an oasis, drank like he someday hoped to drink the world dry, and this crazy thirst served to founder him, to unman him to such a degree that some nights, he wasn't even conscious when the time arrived for the departure for home.

Thus one of Blanchard's primary duties was that of chauffeur. After each sale concluded, he would assess Major's condition before deciding how best to load him into the truck. Some nights he was ambulatory, mostly, and he would stumble and stagger beside Blanchard as they made their way to the pickup. Other evenings, Blanchard pulled him along in a wagon like he was an inebriated older brother, or rolled him on a hand truck, wheeling him like he was a drunken sack of meal. Occasionally, when Major was just too boneless for wheeled transport to be a practical solution, when he kept flopping out of the wagon or rolling off the hand truck, Blanchard used a fireman's carry. Major was a small man, Blanchard was a big boy, and it wasn't much trouble. Once Major was safely in the truck, Blanchard would take his bearings, draw a deep breath, and begin the slow homeward journey down obscure Georgia and Alabama back roads.

The first time Blanchard drove Major home was after an antique sale in Arab, Alabama. Arab was a small town on Sand Mountain that had nothing to do with the Middle East, regardless of what its name might imply. The local population called it AY-rab, just to avoid any misunderstandings. It was very late, and Blanchard was standing by the truck watching Major smoothly con an old lady out of one of the fried apple pies she had made to sell to the auction goers. The refreshment stand was staffed by good, solid Baptist women who had their minds on the Lord, their eyes on the Bible, and their hands on the pans. Blanchard had already loaded up the furniture and glassware that Major had bought on the sly, and he was waiting with his hands in his pockets for departure time to arrive. Major finally swayed over to the truck, gumming his purloined pie while trying to adjust his truss.

"Damn thing's killin' me," he mumbled. He executed a little half skip as he walked in an attempt to resettle all of his parts into a more comfortable arrangement.

"That pie's going to make you sick," Blanchard observed, pointing at the offending pastry, which did look pretty tasty.

"I can eat pies made by church women."

"I think you have to pay for the pie before Jesus will help you keep it down." Another of Blanchard's duties was to clean up the truck whenever Major ate something that didn't agree with him, which unfortunately was fairly often. He usually did this the morning after the gastronomic mishap, and it was a bad way to start the workday. Often he had to clean the truck twice: once when dealing with Major's digestive woes from the previous evening and again when he lost his own breakfast as a consequence.

"You ready to go?" Major belched loudly, then finished the pie. He had crumbs on his lips and a small dollop of pie filling stuck to his chin.

"We're all loaded up." The lights in the auction house started to go out one by one as the owner hit the switches.

"I don't think I can drive tonight. I'm about three sheets in the wind."

"I know. It might be more like four sheets. Who do you think sold the last three pieces while you were snoring up there on the podium?"

"I thought it got a little hazy there for a minute. But that's the reason I taught you the spiel in the first place. Anyway, you gotta drive."

Major shuffled to the passenger's side of the truck and got in. Blanchard slid in under the wheel. "The truck's got no taillights," he said. "I don't have a license. We're fifty miles from home. It's raining." Blanchard had no issue with any of this, but he was a conscientious employee who liked to keep his boss fully in the decision loop.

"You worry too much. Drive." That first trip home was made without mishap, and from that day forward, Blanchard was officially Plan A whenever Major was in his cups.

One night several months into his career as a professional unlicensed driver, Blanchard was stopped by a constable in Section, Alabama, a town known for its drag strip, for a tough beer joint on Highway 11 called Randall's, and for its relatively high percentage per capita of humorless law enforcement officials. It had been a long day and Blanchard was tired, so he may have weaved a bit as he passed the hidden police car, or it might have just been his turn once again in the cosmic barrel, his time to stand before the forces of darkness and plead his case.

"How old are you, boy?" the policeman asked. All Blanchard could see was the bright glare from the officer's flashlight and a shadow of his right hand as it rested on the butt of his service revolver. Blanchard may not have been legally old enough to drive, but he was sufficiently seasoned to be able to recognize an unwieldy situation when he saw one, and this qualified. He heard a snap as the policeman thumbed the flap on his holster to release it.

"Fifteen, sir." Major had once told him that there were four rules to remember when talking to representatives of the law: keep both hands on the wheel, always tell the truth unless you were certain beyond the merest shadow of a doubt that you could get away with the lie, never volunteer any information, and always say sir. This seemed to be sage advice, and Blanchard intended to follow it to the letter.

"What's wrong with him?" the cop asked, nodding at the passenger seat. Major snored, coughed, mumbled, and snored again.

"He's drunk and passed out, sir. I'm taking him home."

Major frowned at the light trying to encroach upon his dreams. He swatted at the intrusion as if it were a fly buzzing around his head and turned toward the side window.

"Is that your granddaddy?"

"No sir. I just work for him."

"What's your name?"

"Blanchard Shankles."

"Shankles…Shankles. Your name sounds familiar, and you sort of look like someone I might know. What's your daddy's name?"

Given his late father's penchant for straying with all manner of females, Blanchard wasn't entirely certain of the wisdom of claiming direct kinship. He would hate to get shot on the side of the road in Section, Alabama, because of a past dalliance between Benton and the bored wife of small-town police officer, and he considered offering up a substitute name. But he was on the clock, so to speak, and Major's mandate to tell the truth held sway.

"Benton Shankles," Blanchard said, hoping the syllables didn't send the policeman into a blind rage fueled by jealousy and revenge.

His right hand, clearly visible on the steering wheel beside his left, slowly crossed its fingers.

"Ha! Benton Shankles. How is that crazy son of a bitch doing?"

Apparently there was no bad blood here, and Blanchard was not about to be dragged out of the truck and pistol-whipped over the sins of his father. Now if he could just manage to avoid any serious trouble over his own sins, which were paltry when compared to Benton's, he might get home before the sun rose.

"He's dead, sir."

"Dead? What happened to him?"

"My mama killed him."

"Why did she do that?" the officer asked. This was indeed the money question.

"I think she just sort of felt like it. She was kind of crazy. They put her away."

"Did she shoot him?"

"No sir. She beat his head off with a statue."

"You don't say." This last comment didn't seem to require an answer, so per Major's rule number three, Blanchard kept his mouth shut and his eyes straight ahead. The policeman shook his head slowly. "Seems like I might have heard something about that, but I swear I didn't know it was Benton who got laid away. Bad luck."

Blanchard was of the firm opinion that luck one way or the other had not played a big part in his father's demise, but he kept this opinion to himself. "Yes sir," he said.

"Where you comin' from?" the policeman asked.

"Scottsboro, sir. We were at the antique auction over there."

The officer seemed to consider this information carefully. Finally, he spoke again. "Well, you're just doing your job. If you made it up that mountain without runnin' off the side, I guess you can drive good enough to get that old man on home." The highway up the mountain from Guntersville to Section was a narrow, steep road called the Widow Maker, and it had made several since it was first carved into the crumbling face of Sand Mountain by a woebegone chain gang back during the unforgiving, monochrome thirties.

"Yes sir. I know the way."

"And don't let me see you back over here again until you have a license."

"No sir."

"Sorry about your daddy," the lawman said as he switched off his torch.

"Thank you, sir," Blanchard replied. He wasn't sorry in the least, but if the policeman wanted to be, that was his own business. Blanchard dropped the truck in gear and exited the scene before the sympathy factor wore off or Major threw up.

The remainder of the trip was silent. Major was still passed out, and Blanchard was busy with his driving, trying to remember turns and recognize landmarks. Finally they arrived at Major's home, and Blanchard hoisted the old soldier over his shoulder and carried him inside.

He placed Major on top of his bed and pulled up a blanket so the abused old body would not fetch a chill, then left him to his dreams.

In addition to filling a variety of roles when they traveled, Blanchard was also the caretaker of Major's storage building and property. Major had a large warehouse situated on two hundred acres of grass and timber near Sequoyah where he stored items bought by the house—merchandise that Major procured for resale, usually by ignoring legitimate bids from the crowd so he could, as he liked to put it, "buy it right." He also lived in that same cavernous building. His residence was two rooms and a bath tacked on one end of the structure, as if it had been an afterthought, which it had. It contained a bed, a sofa, a chair, a desk, and a TV.

One of Blanchard's duties was to unload and arrange whatever Major purchased so that it could be viewed by potential customers and eventually sold to one of them. The warehouse was a mystical realm, a magic kingdom where mature pieces of furniture and bric-a-brac were made to look young and where new items were carefully aged. Periodically, when Major had acquired enough merchandise, he would have his own auction sale right there in the warehouse. Familiar faces from other auction venues would crowd in, the sellers would become the buyers, and the sale would commence with Major's familiar and distinctive, "Well all RIGHT boys, whaddaya gonna give?" There was a carnival atmosphere at these events. The auction sales lingered through the evenings and often languished on into the wee hours, lubricated by sweat, alcohol, bonhomie, and greed, the Four Horsemen of American business.

Another of Blanchard's responsibilities was that of groundskeeper. He bush hogged, planted, trimmed, dug, graded, and filled as circumstances and Major dictated. One raw day just prior to his sixteenth birthday, Blanchard was bush hogging the front section of the property one final time before winter scratched its wooly head and stumbled across the mountain looking for a meal. As he made another pass, Major flagged him down and slowly climbed aboard the rusty Ford tractor. It wasn't much to look at, but it had been bought right at a farm liquidation sale that Major had conducted, and it had only taken Blanchard eleven hours to drive it from its original home to Major's property. Major reached behind the steel seat and pulled the Three Dog Night eight-track tape from the player that Blanchard had installed. He Frisbee'd the cartridge in the general direction of a rhododendron bush, lit a Pall Mall, and shared a thought.

"I don't see how you can listen to that shit." He hiked his thumb in the direction of the rhododendron.

"Well, I can't now."

"Good. It'll rot your brain. Let's go for a little drive." It was early in the afternoon, a Saturday. Major fumbled at the bib pocket of his overalls and produced a pint of Maker's Mark. As he cracked the seal, the bourbon fumes curled around him like a silk shawl.

They struck out overland, weaving to then fro on the tractor as they avoided jutting stone, swaying pine, yawning gully, and blooming mountain laurel. Major's property sat atop Lookout Mountain and bordered on Little River Canyon. As they plugged along, Major struck up a conversation. This was unusual behavior on his part. He normally talked only when he wanted something and pretty much kept his own counsel the remainder of the time.

"How old are you now?" he asked.

"I'm almost sixteen."

"What grade are you in?"

"I was in the tenth grade, but I quit school."

"Holy Jesus. That's a big mistake. There's a war on. If you're not in school when you turn eighteen, they'll draft you. You don't want to get drafted. You'll end up walking point on a LURP in the Central Highlands." He shifted on the fender and found a more comfortable spot. Then he took another sip of his bourbon.

"I don't think I'll wait to get drafted. I've been thinking I might just go ahead and join up. With all that's gone on, I thought it might be good to get out of town for a while." Blanchard didn't tend to talk much about what had happened to his parents, but Major was aware of Edna's and Benton's statuses as crazy and dead, respectively, and he sometimes shared what could be termed parental advice with his young employee.

Now, though, Major grimaced upon hearing that Blanchard was considering voluntarily doing a hitch in the service. "You listen to me. You don't want anything to do with the military right now."

Blanchard was surprised at the statement, coming as it did from a veteran named Major. Everyone knew he was hard core, a soldier from the old school, a warrior of the first rank. "I don't understand. You were in the Army all those years."

"I was, and it was a good life, mostly. But the Army I was in is gone. Korea shot it at close range on full auto, then Vietnam hit it in the back of the head with a sharpened trenching tool to finish it off. It's all gone now. That's what happens when you send good armies into bad wars. The wars pull the armies down, and what you have left is a lot of killing for no good reason. You take my advice and get back into school. Start thinking about college while you're at it. It'll be my treat. The war can't last forever. As long as you're in school, you're safe."

Blanchard mulled these words. Seldom had he heard Major speak with such urgency.

"I don't know. I'm pretty happy without school. I wasn't learning anything, anyway. If I end up in Vietnam, it's only for a year."

Major sighed and took a long slug of his Maker's Mark. "Listen to what I'm telling you! I have been in three wars. The first one was necessary, I guess, but I might have given you a different answer on the morning of June 6, 1944, when all of those German boys were trying to kill me, and did kill most of my buddies. The other two were shit shows, pure and simple. All Korea accomplished was getting good men killed. No matter what anyone tells you, they didn't die for the greater good. They didn't die protecting democracy, God, country, and their mamas. None of those things were in danger. They just died. They got killed for no good reason at all in a war we wouldn't even call a war, a war we shouldn't have fought that was started by a bunch of rich guys who weren't going to be the ones getting shot at. And compared to Vietnam, Korea was the Crusades. It is a crime what's happening over there. Do you really want to die eleven thousand miles from home in a war we are going to lose? There's not much future in that."

"You think we're going to lose?"

"We already lost. We lost that war the day we walked into the godforsaken place." He took another sip. "Limited warfare my ass," he mumbled, mostly to himself.

They were silent then for a while. Blanchard thought over Major's words as he drove. He had really been considering it, but maybe joining up wasn't the thing to do. He wasn't driven to be a soldier, but he was a firm believer in taking the path of least resistance, and Vietnam had been a distant and ugly fact of his life since before he was old enough to read. It was a reality that must be dealt with in one way or another by the male members of his generation upon reaching manhood, and most of the young men he knew had been there, or were on their way when the time came. And Blanchard knew his time was coming.

"I'll think about what you said," Blanchard told Major. Maybe the old man was right.

"Think hard about it. You're a smart boy. I've loaded too many steel caskets filled with young men just like you onto transport planes for the long flight home."

They drove silent for a while, and eventually they eased up to the edge of that gaping precipice known as Little River Canyon. Major staggered from the venerable tractor and veered toward the canyon rim. Then he caught himself and slanted back toward the trees. He wandered a bit, as if he were looking for a wayward wristwatch or a lost set of keys. Then he came to a sudden halt and stood as erect as he was able, straight as a young elm braving an icy blast from the mysterious northern realms. He waved Blanchard over to where he was standing.

"What do you think?" Major asked.

"About what?" Blanchard had begun to think that Major had started tipping the bottle too early that day, and that as soon as the old man passed out, he would haul him back to his bed and tuck him in for the duration. Then he would get back to mowing. They had had a nice ride and an interesting chat, but he and the boys had a dance to play that night, a paying gig at a local high school, and he wanted to finish up his duties for Major and get on to his night job.

"About here," Major answered. He waved his arm like he was introducing a circus act. "Do you think it's a pretty spot?" They stood in a gently sloping small meadow bordered on one side by the canyon and on the other three by pine trees.

"Well, yeah, I guess."

"This is where I'm going to put the family burial plot. When I say 'I,' that means you."

"I figured." Major was a believer in the imperial use of I.

"When you get it finished, I'm gonna move Alisa here. Right here." He was pointing straight down. "When my time comes, I'll go beside her." His finger moved slightly to the right.

Major's wife, Alisa, was buried at Fort Carson, Colorado, a long way indeed from the love of her life and a longer way still from the ruined Berlin avenues of her youth. She had been in the rare air of the foothills of the Rockies when the Reaper whispered in on the edge of a forbidding wind and cut her down in a single pass, snuffed her as if she had been a candle, ended her with a quick flick of the curved blade during a spare moment in his busy schedule. By the time Major had arrived there from the wilted jungles of Southeast Asia, Alisa was already tucked in under the thin crumbly soil of the High Plains, placed there among tears and lilies by two daughters who needed something to do with their hands lest they lose their minds to sorrow and succumb to the searing knife-stab of loss.

But ever since Blanchard had hired on, he had repeatedly heard Major swear that he was going to bring her home to the mountain, and that they would lay together throughout eternity, man and wife comforting one another there in the long home as the winds whipped up the canyon walls while the lazy river below continued to carve the gorge ever deeper, flowing first to the Chattahoochee, and then to the

Apalachicola, before finally resting from its long journey in the warm waters of the Gulf of Mexico.

"The girls and their husbands can go over there," Major continued. "There's plenty of room for the grandchildren, too, if they've a mind to." He was quiet for a minute, and Blanchard thought that Major had lost the thread of his thought, either due to the general emotion of the moment or as a direct result of the Maker's Mark. Major was overcome, then, and had to console himself with a Pall Mall and a snort from his nearly empty pint bottle. Presently, he recovered, and they spent the next two hours scratching the outline of the family plot in the stubborn mountain sod, laying out the sacred space just so, as was prudent when undertaking a task that would span the ages. As they finished their labor, it began to get cool, the way it does on Lookout Mountain toward sundown, regardless of the time of year. The sun was a red ball on the horizon, and their breath steamed starward as the temperature crept lower. Blanchard loaded Major onto the tractor and drove him back to his apartment at the warehouse.

"I'll start on it tomorrow," Blanchard said. Major just nodded his head and went inside. He had not spoken since they left the plot of ground by the canyon.

Over the next few weeks, Blanchard worked on the project every day that he and Major weren't attending a sale. The tract was sixty feet to the side, gradually sloping toward the canyon's rim, laid out among the trees so that it would be shady and cool. At the four corners and halfway down each side, Blanchard built small cairns of mountain rock, and he looped these together with sections of black iron chain. One of the most interesting and certainly heaviest pieces that Major had acquired during his years of buying and selling was an old cross made of black wrought iron, a monument that Blanchard had heard him represent as The True Cross to at least two prospective buyers, even though it was Blanchard's understanding that the genuine article was made out of wood, was irretrievably lost somewhere along the dusty corridors of history, and was certainly worth more than the three hundred dollars Major was asking. So Blanchard built a large stone pedestal for it, dead center of the graveyard, and it was on this pile of mountain granite that he installed the icon.

It seemed to Blanchard that Major was slowly scaling back on what had been his favorite and only pastime, and that they were going to fewer auctions as the winter season meandered toward spring. But Blanchard shrugged off this behavior, or at least he did until Memorial Day. The yearly Memorial Day antique auction at Doc LeVarn's Furniture Barn in Pisgah, Alabama, was a landmark event, and Major had always gotten there early and stayed long for this sale, but this year, the plan changed. Major said he didn't have time to go.

"Are you kidding?" Blanchard said. "All we have is time! What else do you have to do?" Blanchard liked going to Doc LeVarn's sales, and he liked his daughter, Abby, even more than he did the sales. He didn't want to miss an opportunity to see her just because the boss was fussy and didn't want to go to Pisgah.

"We have to work on the cemetery."

"But it's done."

"Ain't done. Come on." They rode the tractor out to the plot that early May morning. It was not yet summer in high Georgia, and there was still a hint of crispness in the air, a breath of the spring breeze that had until recently strolled the landscape. They arrived at the cemetery, and Blanchard helped Major down from his perch on the fender. The old soldier slowly walked to the spot he had stood upon during their first trip to the area. He looked at the family plot, at the meticulous, respectful work done by Blanchard, and he nodded.

"You've done a good job," he said. "I'm on my way to Fort Carson tomorrow. I'm going to fly out there and get Alisa. While I'm gone, I want you to dig the grave. Right here. Bring me a stick and I'll mark it off." Blanchard did as he was told. Major scratched a rectangle in the mountain grass. Then he stepped a couple of feet to his left and stuck the stick upright in the turf. "Once you get the grave dug, find the prettiest mountain laurel on the property. Then, dig it up and plant it right there." He pointed at the stick. "Mountain laurels were always her favorite."

Blanchard nodded. He had his orders, and they apparently did not include Doc LeVarn or his daughter. So, while Major was gone to retrieve his wife, Blanchard readied her place of repose. He carefully dug the grave by hand, cut the tough sod with a sharp spade, and excavated the red clay one sad shovelful at a time, slowly and with reverence, as befitted the execution of an honorable but somber task. Then he walked that mountain for two endless days, north and west, east and south, until he located the only mountain laurel that would do, the Liriodendron tulipifera that would mark the endless sleep of a woman he had never met but knew quite well, a monument of waxy leaves and delicate purple flowers planted in memory of a life that had been, and of a love that would not pass.

On a clear afternoon under a topaz sky, Major's wife was gently lowered into her final home. Slight gusts from the canyon sighed through the pine needles, tousled at hair, and tugged at hems. Major's youngest daughter sang "Morning Has Broken." Blanchard had tried to talk her into letting him accompany her on guitar, but she sang a cappella, and he had to admit that she did so with such grace and purity that time itself paused, and even the hawks gliding on the eddies over the canyon hung motionless as the notes floated past their wings.

Blanchard's days with Major began to draw to a close that fall. Time crept past, as time will, and Major seemed to lose interest in his business and, to a lesser extent, in Blanchard. Major and Blanchard wandered each his own way like flotsam at the mercy of a ragged surf. Blanchard gravitated toward his band and his music, and toward a montage of memories yet to be made that would include smoky bars and summer street dances, long bus rides and cheap motel rooms, joys and sorrows, each a thread to be woven into the tapestry of his life, each a steppingstone on the paths he would choose to amble.

Major inevitably drifted to the canyon's rim. It drew him like a diviner's rod is drawn by water and faith, called to him with unspoken promises of peace and rest. As the weeks and months passed, he spent more and more time by the mountain laurel, sitting in a lawn chair, drinking Maker's Mark and smoking Pall Malls, quietly chatting with Alisa about all things, and about nothing at all.

And then one day in February, on an underdone and blustery Thursday, the bleakness of the never-ending winter inundated him, and it simply became too much trouble to make the journey back to his rooms. So he stayed.

"SECRETS AND LIES"
(Blanchard Shankles/John Covey)

We met in Biloxi at a bar named Blue Moon
She was hitchin' to Memphis for Beale Street in June
I bought her a Cuervo and a bucket of fries
I told her my secrets and she told me her lies

I told her my secrets and she told me her lies
I should have known better but wasn't that wise
I thought she was mine but to my surprise
I told her my secrets and she told me her lies

We drove up to Graceland, the tomb of the King
I tuned my old guitar but busted a string
She hummed a sad "Hound Dog" with tears in her eyes
She told me her secrets and I told her my lies

I told her my secrets and she told me her lies
I should have known better but wasn't that wise
I thought she was mine but to my surprise
I told her my secrets and she told me her lies

We reached Old Man River, sun low in the west
We climbed the great levee and stood at the crest
I offered my heart which she took as a prize
We both told our secrets, we both told our lies

I told her my secrets and she told me her lies
I should have known better but wasn't that wise
I thought she was mine, but to my surprise
I told her my secrets and she told me her lies

She left the next morning before I arose
With ninety-eight dollars, my car, and my clothes
I promised my all but my love she denies
She left with my secrets, she left with my lies

I told her my secrets and she told me her lies
I should have known better but wasn't that wise
I thought she was mine but to my surprise
I told her my secrets and she told me her lies

"Dream On"
Aerosmith
-Wednesday: Fourth Day-

In the dream, Blanchard was dead, or at least one of him was. He had been having death dreams frequently of late and was growing accustomed to this nocturnal mortality, which was a different matter entirely from enjoying the experience. In the current installment of his recurring nightmare, he floated in an operating room above the draped and intubated version of himself that occupied the table below. The room he viewed was bathed in a clear blue light that strobed from time to time, as if the dream had a short in the wiring or perhaps was lit by a lightbulb that was about to die. The surgical suite was bitterly cold, and oddly, it had the look of a dungeon straight out of a medieval castle, reminiscent of the laboratory from every Frankenstein movie Blanchard had ever seen. There were smoky, burning torches mounted on the walls and vintage machines that whirred and crackled with electricity. Gears and cogs meshed, pistons thumped, and the odor of ozone was heavy in the air. Thick, black chains hung here and there for no real reason. Standing on a stone floor scattered with sand, a group of competent-looking people in surgical scrubs, masks, glasses, and bonnets was working efficiently at the task of trying to revive dead Blanchard, who had flatlined out of sheer stubbornness a few minutes previously, but their efforts appeared to be having no positive effect.

In the background, "Frankenstein" played quietly on a vintage console stereo, but every time Edgar Winter made his way to the synthesizer break, the album skipped and the song began over again. Floating Blanchard didn't know what that meant, but he was certain there was some profound symbolism at play, some hidden meaning he was supposed to understand but didn't, and he was equally sure that the cryptic message was not one he wished to receive. In addition to the Nashville medical personnel he had recently met, the ER doctor from Staunton was there as well. Floating Blanchard supposed that the physician's mom had driven him down for the occasion, or maybe he had ridden the bus. The man hadn't aged a day since he had last seen him, and floating Blanchard wondered if the young doctor had undergone puberty yet. Currently the clinician was busy sweeping up the sand in the floor and taking orders for sandwiches, but he paused in his duties from time to time to pop a nitroglycerin tablet under a random tongue before advising its owner to sit down and refrain from talking.

"He's gone," said the anesthesiologist stationed at the head end of the table. "Call it." His tone was discouraged, and he was shaking his head as if he were unable to comprehend why they had lost dead Blanchard, the heart case that all the doctors had fought over, the one they had all wanted to operate on and save.

"4:47," said Dr. Forrester. He turned to his assistant, who was tall in spite of the pronounced hump on his back.

"A.M. or P.M.?" the anesthesiologist asked.

"Beats me," Dr. Forrester said. "Close him up, please." His assistant nodded and went to work. Floating Blanchard viewed dead Blanchard with detached ambivalence as the members of the surgical team busied themselves with the aftermath of failure. The tubes came out and the clamps came off. Needles were removed and machines were silenced. The incision was closed with broad, rough stitches of what looked like twine. The instruments were counted, and a sheet was unceremoniously pulled up over dead Blanchard's head. A shudder went through floating Blanchard as he watched the blue linen fabric conceal his own face. Dr. Forrester sat down on a rickety wicker chair near the stone wall. Moss grew on the granite blocks beside him, and niter clung to the joints. He stripped off his mask and gloves and began to fill out the death certificate. He looked tired, and maybe a bit dejected at having lost his patient.

"I just hate this part," said Crazy Edna, who had unexpectedly drifted in under the radar and now hovered next to her ectoplasmic son. "It's so sad watching them put down a cause of death. They never get it right, but once it's on there, that's that." Floating Blanchard was startled by the arrival of company, and more so by the identity of his new companion.

"Mama, what are you doing here?" Edna had been dead for many years, but she looked pretty much the same way she always had, wardrobe included. She had died of a broken heart after spending more than two decades at the state hospital she had been unceremoniously remanded to the day following the dispatch of her husband.

"I shouldn't say." Edna didn't answer directly, which was her way, dead or alive. She coasted to the right as a slight breeze caught her. She bumped into and grabbed a weighty chain that hung from the vast and distant ceiling. Once she had steadied herself, she continued her observations concerning death certificates. "On mine they put cardiac infarction. But that was all wrong."

"But you did have a heart attack, Mama. I was there!" Blanchard had gone to Milledgeville on a regular basis to see Edna for all the long years that she had resided there. It had been an unpleasant task—one that he hated, truth be told—but it was the right thing to do in his opinion, and the fact that she didn't seem to care one way or another about his visits didn't diminish their importance in his mind. Ironically, he had been visiting Edna on the Sunday she died. During their time together that day, she had become quite upset about a fellow patient in the day room, one who had looked remarkably like a young Benton Shankles, and after working herself into a high state of agitation, she had dropped dead midway through her attack run on that unfortunate individual. Members of the medical staff tried to revive her, but she was gone when she hit the floor.

"My cause of death was everything that came before it, pure and simple," Edna said, back in the dream. "That's everyone's cause of death. Me, you, your daddy's." Blanchard had never looked at his father's death certificate, although it was somewhere at home in a drawer or up on a shelf, but he had always assumed that the cause of death was *Nubian princess*. "It's our lives that kill us," Edna continued. "Life is a terminal condition." Blanchard had never thought about existence in those terms, but he supposed she could be correct.

"Mama," he repeated once again, "what are you doing here?" He seldom thought of her anymore, and he almost never dreamed of her, yet here she was, waxing philosophical in his death dream like Nietzsche with breasts, hanging from a chain in a dungeon.

"You came to my death, so I thought I would return the favor and come to yours. You look natural down there." She smiled fondly as she looked upon her dead-as-a-mackerel baby boy.

"Are you kidding?" floating Blanchard said. "There's a big hole in my chest, a sheet over my head, and I'm dead." He saw nothing natural about any of it.

"It's a very neat hole, though. Your doctor did a good job. Look at those nice stitches. And you look so peaceful. The undertakers will be fighting over you."

"How do you figure my doctor did a good job? I came in here alive, and now I'm dead. D-E-A-D. Next stop is the morgue, followed by a hole in the ground. I am so screwed. The man killed me after he promised he wouldn't. He said doctors fight over hearts like mine, and he guaranteed that he could fix me up, and he told me I ought to let him do it. So against my better judgment, I did. And then he killed me. I couldn't be any deader down there if he had run over me with his car. I bet you cash money he let a student work on me. That guy over there with the hump is probably him. Son of a bitch! We had a deal!" A cigarette appeared in his hand, and he lit it. "I should have just gotten up out of my bed when I had the chance and had Covey drive me home. I'd be alive right now, drinking a cold one and playing fetch the damn stick with Scrounge."

"Those are bad for you," Crazy Edna said, pointing at the smoke.

"Mama, I'm dead, and this cigarette isn't even real. And neither are you! I can smoke it if I want to." He looked at his mother. "I'll tell you one thing! I'm not paying for any of this. They can send bills from now until doomsday, but they'll be sucking wind. One of the things you can't do when you're dead is write a check to the people who did you in."

"That's telling them, boy," said a voice from behind them. "I didn't pay them when I died, either!" Edna and Blanchard turned, and there, drifting over a steam-powered heart-lung machine that bore great resemblance to a hay baler, was Benton Shankles, bigger than life and as dead as he could be. "Don't take any lip off of them!"

"What the—?" floating Blanchard said. It was like a family reunion, and Blanchard wouldn't have been much surprised if the Nubian princess floated in and started bopping people on the head.

"Don't pay any attention to him," Edna advised. "He's just as full of bull as he ever was. The man doesn't know what he's talking about. Never has."

"It's kind of hard not to pay attention to him," floating Blanchard said. His father looked just as he had the last time he saw him, which wasn't a good thing, and in spite of himself he wondered where the voice had come from, because there was very little head and no mouth on the apparition before him.

"Long time no see, boy," said Benton. The voice seemed to emanate from somewhere within him, like an echo from a canyon.

"Not long enough," floating Blanchard replied. "Not by a long shot." When it came to Blanchard's feelings toward his father, absence had not made the heart grow fonder.

"That was a nice funeral you gave me, by the way. Real nice."

"That was all Geneva's doing. I had nothing to do with it. I was going to roll you into a ditch, pour some gravy on you, and let the dogs out."

"That would have been what he deserved," said Edna. "*Better* than he deserved." Absence had apparently not made her heart grow fonder, either.

"Shut up," said Benton, but quietly, almost to himself. He had learned grudging respect for Edna's tempers the hard way.

Blanchard sensed that he was losing control of his dream and made an attempt to wrest it back from his parents. "Enough, already! Why are *both* of you here?"

"I came to help prepare the body," Edna said. "He came because he didn't do one thing to help me in life, so now he has to help me in death."

"Kind of like in *A Christmas Carol*, huh?" floating Blanchard observed. It had always been one of his favorite tales.

"You see how it is," Benton emanated to his son, his torso turned toward him to emphasize his point. "It's always stacked up against the man, even after he's dead. She cuts me off, goes crazy on me, beats me to death, but *I'm* the one who ends up having to make amends. How is that fair, I ask you?" He held out his hands to augment his question.

"If I could find my hammer and some nails," Edna muttered, "I'd tack him up somewhere out of the way, just to be rid of him." Benton apparently didn't like the sound of that and floated back a few feet, just to be safe.

"You deserved everything you got," floating Blanchard said to Benton. "Next time keep your dick in your pants and be a better husband. Maybe you won't get your head caved in." He then addressed his mother. "What did you mean by prepare the body?" The phrase had an ominous, Old Testament sound to it.

"Do you remember Geneva's cats?" Edna asked.

"Trust me, I will never forget Geneva's cats." He had started to say that he wouldn't forget them if he lived to be one hundred, but it looked like that ship had now left port without him.

"When I finished my work that day, they were prepared properly for a trip to the next world. It's important to leave everything behind when making a journey to the other side."

"You didn't skin *me*," Benton said.

"I wasn't finished. I was resting."

"What are you—?" floating Blanchard began to ask. Then he finally tapped in to the general drift of the conversation. "Wait a minute. You're going to skin him?" He asked this as he pointed at his helpless dead doppelganger on the table below.

"Right down to the muscle and the bone, baby," said Edna. "It's the only way. Do you remember when I died?"

"I do."

"You didn't know any better, so I don't blame you, but I wasn't prepared properly, and now look at me. Stuck in one of your dreams!" She sounded a bit petulant.

"If I had known, I would have had the undertaker fix you up," floating Blanchard said. He wondered if skinning came under the general heading of final arrangements or if there was an extra charge for the service.

"I make the cause of death everything that came before," Dr. Forrester said from below.

"I concur," said the anesthesiologist.

"Well, what do you know," said Edna.

"I'm going to try to wake up now."

"You can't leave yet," said Edna.

"Why?"

"When I died," Edna said, "it was my time to die, and there was no getting out of it."

"Okay. What is your point?"

"Today was your time. You have to stay until it's over and done with. Now move and let us do our job."

"I told you she was crazier than a sack full of shithouse rats," Benton said. "Her dying didn't change that one bit." He took a wicked skinning knife from a scabbard on his belt and descended toward the operating table. "But she's right about this." He snatched the sheet from dead Blanchard and began to inspect him, perhaps looking for a good place to begin his grisly task. In the distance, a cock crowed, and the sound of thunder rumbled.

Blanchard jerked awake from the dream and found himself in his hospital room. "Son. Of. A. Bitch," he said slowly. The drapes were pulled, and it was dark in the room, but he could see a beam of sunlight peeking through the gap where the curtains didn't quite meet. He could smell the odors of a hospital: disinfectant, alcohol, urine, and, oddly enough, peppermint. He could hear the beep, beep, beep of his pulse amplified through the machine he was attached to, and he could hear the bubbling noise from his drainage tubes.

"I must be crazier than a sack full of shithouse rats too," he said quietly. Maybe he was having late onset insanity. Perhaps he had inherited his mama's crazy streak to keep him company in his golden years. He heard a snorting sound from beside him, and he turned his head and saw that Covey was asleep in the recliner. Covey didn't always snore, but when he did, he did so with enthusiasm. "Covey," Blanchard said. "Wake up!"

Covey didn't respond, so Blanchard picked up a magazine from the night table beside the bed and tossed it at him. The periodical landed in his lap with no apparent effect. Blanchard began to cough. Raising his voice had hurt his incision and aggravated his throat, which was still raw from the removal of his breathing tube, and as usual since the surgery, the cough turned into a full-body conniption, a true battle between good and evil with the odds at just about even over which side would ultimately prevail. He fumbled for his bear, and when he found it among the sheets, he grabbed it and held it tight. "Stupid bear," he croaked, then hugged his mute stuffed comrade with all that he had as the coughing fit did its worst. Presently it passed, and Blanchard lay there, sweating, sore, and exhausted. He was thoroughly miserable, and thought he might like to shoot someone with a medical background, anyone at all, just to take his mind off his troubles.

"Hey," Covey said, finally awake. "How are you feeling?"

"If I felt any better, I'd be standing by the side of the road, smiling and waving at strangers. How do you think I'm feeling? I feel like the losing side on the third day of a three-day war. If I felt just a little bit healthier, I'd go ahead and die right now."

"So, a little better, then?" Covey pushed down on the handle on the side of the recliner and moved forward into the upright position. He stood, stretched, took off his hat, and rubbed his head. Then he yawned and replaced his hat.

"Maybe just a little bit," Blanchard replied. He rested from his coughing spell for a few extra moments. "This coughing is killing me though. It's like the insides of my lungs have been spread with peanut butter. Chunky."

"I was talking to one of your nurses about that while you were asleep. She said that'll pass in a couple more days."

"Great. Just two more days." He placed his bear next to him, where he could find it in a hurry. "I had the king of all crazy dreams just now."

"For you, that's saying something. Bad?"

"If you had this dream and told me about it, I'd have you committed."

"That's a pretty bad dream."

"You should have been there. Everyone else was. There was some real weird stuff going on."

"Do you want to tell me about it?"

"I want to run some bleach through my head to get it out of my mind. My mother was in it. Topless of course. And my father. He was topless, too."

"No shirt?"

"No head. Plus, most of the medical people from this joint were there, and the doctor from Staunton, the one who found my heart trouble."

"What happened?"

"I died again."

"That doesn't sound so bad. Well, it does, I guess, but you ought to be getting used to it. You've had dying dreams plenty of times before." Covey opened the curtains. Light flooded the room. "It was too gloomy in here," he said. Blanchard nodded. The light was welcome in spite of the fact that it hurt his eyes. He watched some dust motes for a moment as they scattered in the presence of the sunbeams.

"It was different this time. Like I said, my parents were in it, and they never have been before. And the operating room was like something out of a bad horror movie. Looked like someplace Dracula might live. I was laying down there on the table dead as a bar of iron, and Crazy Edna came to skin me because I was a goner, just like she did to Geneva's cats all those years ago."

"I remember when that happened," Covey said, grimacing slightly at the memory. "That was some pretty creepy stuff, even for her."

"Yeah. You ought to have been out there at the altar at sundown. Anyway, in my dream, Benton came along with Edna to help with the skinning. He looked just like he did the last time I saw him, smashed head and all. Whenever he talked, his voice was like an echo. You couldn't really tell where it was coming from."

"That was one messed-up dream," Covey said. "So, did they skin you?"

"I don't know. It looked like they were about to get started, so I woke up."

"You should have woken up sooner."

"That's what you always say. I was trying to. I knew it was a dream, and I wanted out of it, but I couldn't make myself wake up." He sighed and shifted in the bed. "I may just stay awake from now on. You think they have any speed in this place?"

"I imagine they do, but I bet it's not for the heart patients. If you want my advice, you should forget about the whole thing. You haven't died, and it doesn't look like you're going to, and even if you do, I won't let anyone skin you. That's a promise. So just put it out of your mind. It was only a stupid dream."

"What if you're actually in on it?"

"On what?"

"The skinning."

"I'll make a billfold out of you."

"Thanks. A belt would be better. I've been holding you up for years."

"Hah."

"I wonder what the deal was with Benton? I haven't thought about my old man in years. He was an easy person to forget, and I pretty much have. But there he was. If he'd had a head and brought a condom with him, he probably would have made a run at one of the nurses."

"Your mama would've skinned *him*," Covey said.

"It was a little bit odd that she was in the dream, too. I think about her more than I do him, but still, it's been a while since she even crossed my mind. I feel bad about that sometimes. I really ought to remember her more, out of respect for what she went through and because she was my mama. Most of what ailed her wasn't her fault, and she had a sad life, bless her crazy heart."

"Don't beat yourself up."

"What about you? Do you ever think about your folks?"

"Every now and then, maybe. Look, you're older now than either of your parents were when they died. Life goes on, and we tend to forget about the parts that sucked. It's just the way of things. It's how we survive. My parents have been gone for years. They weren't nearly as screwed up as yours were, and one of them didn't kill the other one, but they had their bad days just like everyone else. Still, I hardly ever think about them. It doesn't mean I didn't love them. It just means that they're dead, and I'm alive, and life is busy."

"I didn't love Benton. That's for sure. More like hate. But her? I wanted to, and I tried my best, but I don't know if I ever really managed it."

"She was a hard woman to love," Covey noted.

"The closest I ever got might have been pity. I did feel sorry for her. She drew some bad cards, and I guess she played them the best she knew how."

"It's easy to feel guilty about the past," Covey said, "especially about people who have passed on. I read somewhere that we feel guilty about dead loved ones because they're dead and we're not. Don't know if that's true, but we all have some guilt we're carrying."

"You're telling me," Blanchard said absently. "Where's Vanny?" She had been there when he went to sleep.

"She had to go. She's having labor troubles."

"I meant to ask her how the business was doing these days, but I kept falling asleep."

"She says she's making piles of money."

"She always has. She's a natural at business."

After her short stint in the outlet Bible industry, Vanny was firmly back in the porn business and doing very well. She called herself the Porn Queen of South Carolina, and her self-appellation might not have been too far from the truth. When the owner of the Bible Outlet Sore finally succumbed to his exotic cancer, Vanny had been surprised to learn that, due to a complete lack of suitable heirs, he had left the business to her. She was amazed and gratified at this serendipitous turn of events, although her feelings of gratitude were dampened considerably when the bank contacted her shortly after the funeral to invite her down to the main branch, where they put the building's outstanding mortgage in her name and established a repayment schedule. Since jobs didn't grow on trees, and because she had always wanted to be an entrepreneur, and in light of the fact that she still had an aversion to working at the glove mill, Vanny had signed on the dotted line, but only after the bank agreed to refinance on better terms with a cash-out option. Vanny had a plan, and she needed a bit of capital to make that dream come alive.

Her first task as a business owner went along the lines of inventory management. Specifically, she had donated every Bible in the Bible Outlet Sore—with the exception of the grisly pain Bibles, which not even the local fundamentalist preachers would take—to various churches in the county with instructions to share them among the faithful as the pastors saw fit. Many of these volumes were subsequently shipped to foreign lands under the auspices of missionary out-reaches, and Vanny always felt a bit proud of the fact that many brand new Christians read their daily dose of Scripture from a Bible provid-ed by the Bible Outlet Sore. She also received a nice tax deduction for her philanthropy, which was an added bonus for bringing the Word to the masses.

After the yellow sheet-metal building on the interstate was emp-tied of its sacred content, Vanny restocked it with an impressive as-sortment of merchandise of a seamier, more secular nature. While it was true that she had experience selling Bibles, she had even more skill selling pornography, and it had always seemed to her that of the two distinctly different product lines, the latter had consistently shown more potential for profit. She was a business owner now, and if her store didn't make money, she didn't get paid. So she went back into the porn business. She began by filling her building with an in-spiring assortment of smut. There were magazines and books. There were videos and books on tape. There were sex toys of all description, from vibrators to blow-up dolls to dildos to whips and restraints to one unnamed object whose purpose and function Vanny never did figure out, but which seemed to sell well, regardless. There were per-sonal lubricants and scented oils and incense. There were condoms of every description: colored, flavored, scented, and the ubiquitous ribbed. There was even a pharmaceutical section of sorts stocked with patent nostrums guaranteed to make users harder, softer, longer, shorter, wetter, drier, or just more prone in general to engage in the sexual act, depending on the specific requirements and limiting fac-tors of any particular carnal situation.

On her grand reopening day, a smattering of confusion stemmed from the independent nature of her local signage contractor, Peanut Howard. Vanny had put in a call to Peanut about two weeks prior to her anticipated reentry into the adult entertainment business, and once she had placed her order to have the current sign on the building replaced with the original Love Shack lettering and the billboard out on the interstate repainted, she had promptly crossed that task from her list and forgotten about it. Unfortunately, so had Peanut. Thus, when the busload of Christian women on the way back from their annual prayer retreat in Asheville decided to stop at what they assumed was still the Bible Outlet Sore to replenish their Bible supply, the revelations they received upon entering the store were both dramatic and life-changing. The reactions from the Christian women all fell into one of two categories: absolute disgust and amazed curiosity. The disgusted group marched back out to the bus to pray for humanity in general, Vanny in specific, and the entire state of South Carolina, each carrying a pain Bible provided free of charge by Vanny as recompense for the outrage. But the curious women browsed a while, and sales to that subgroup as a whole were brisk, considering their demographic. After the bus left the parking lot an hour later, Vanny climbed her stepladder, screwdriver and hammer in hand, to remove the misleading signage. As she worked at Peanut's forgotten task, she reflected on the fact that there were several random Christian husbands and boyfriends somewhere down in the vicinity of Orlando who were perhaps in for an interesting evening, one they might never forget.

Once Vanny got the deceptive name removed and chewed on Peanut until his head ached and his memory improved, the new signs were installed in short order and the Love Shack was reborn. There were no further incidents involving busloads of Christian women, or Christian men for that matter, and for this, Vanny was grateful. Indeed, there were no other hiccups of any description during the transition from the sacred to the profane, with the small but notable exception of that unruly "h," which again fell off soon after its reinstallation. The Love Sack was reincarnated, and, as it had once before, it flourished.

Blanchard was truly glad for her. In fact, if he could, he'd pay a visit to the Love Sack right now. As it was, he had to be content with his recovery, which continued at its slow but steady pace. A phlebotomist visited and conducted his afternoon bloodletting, and a nurse came in to deliver an invigorating shot of heparin directly into his abdomen. The hospital chaplain dropped by to share a few words of comfort around the same time, but it seemed to be a bad moment for spiritual consolation, so he did not stay long. A nutritionist came in the room to discuss lifestyle changes, none of which Blanchard intended to make, but he was politer to her than he had been to the chaplain, most likely because she was cute as a button. After she left, an employee of the rehabilitation unit came by to get him up and walk him, but that plan had to be postponed when the physical therapist discovered that his patient's drainage tubes and urinary catheter had not yet been removed, and that Blanchard was in no mood for a stroll.

"I guess they're running late," he said to Blanchard. "But don't you worry. All that plumbing is scheduled to come out today, plus most of the IV lines. I'll be back in the morning, and we'll go for our walk then." The young man was way too upbeat for a normal human, and certainly too happy for the way Blanchard felt. His badge indicated that his name was Sean, but Blanchard had already dubbed him Skippy in his mind.

"I don't want to walk," he told Skippy. "Ever. I want to lay here, take morphine, and sleep. So leave me alone." Much like the chaplain before him, Skippy was not cute as a button, so Blanchard saw no reason to be civil.

"Let the man do his job, and be nice," Covey said from the other side of the bed. Blanchard held up his hand. When he wanted advice, he would ask for it.

"You know, once you start walking and make it all the way down the hall to the elevators and back, they'll let you go home," Skippy pointed out. "Until you make that milestone, you're stuck right here with me." Blanchard had not been informed of this impediment between him and his release and thought it was a fairly large piece of information for the hospital to be sitting on.

"When you come tomorrow, be here early," Blanchard said. The only thing he wanted more than morphine and sleep was to get out of there. He figured that if he made it as far as the elevator, it would take more than his new friend from the rehab department to keep him from getting on, pushing the button labeled LL, and heading for finer times and greener pastures.

Skippy nodded, made a quick note on Blanchard's chart, and turned to leave. On his way out, he crossed paths with a woman in surgical scrubs. They nodded at one another as they passed. She was an angular woman with wispy blond hair who walked right up to the bed and began to speak.

"Good afternoon Mr. Shankles. My name is Rachel Camp. I am Dr. Forrester's PA."

"What's a PA?" Blanchard asked. In the music business, PA was the acronym for a public address system, the device through which singers' voices traveled on their journey from the microphone to the ears of the crowd.

"It stands for physician's assistant," she said as she snapped on a set of rubber gloves. Blanchard felt a sense of dread. In his limited medical experience, rubber gloves were always the harbinger of trouble. While he was getting himself worked up into a state of high anxiety, she removed her stethoscope from around her neck and listened to his chest, ankles, and wrists. Then she helped him sit up, and she listened to his back an extra-long time, moving the stethoscope from one position to another. She had him breathe, and cough, and she nodded to herself when she finished.

"You can lay back down now," she said.

"What were you listening for?"

"Fluid building up around your lungs."

"And?"

"Your heart sounds very good, and your lungs are clearing up a bit."

"Where's the doctor?"

"He's still in surgery this afternoon."

"He's not coming?"

"He'll be by to see you later today. Are you ready to get those drain tubes out? They have done their job, but I'm sure you won't be sorry to see them go." As she spoke, the tubes gurgled as if in agreement with the sentiment. Apparently it cut both ways, and they wouldn't be unhappy to see the last of Blanchard, either.

"Get them out. I hate these things. This one for sure." He pointed to the one that entered his torso to the left of his sternum, directly beneath his heart. "It hurts all the time. Kind of a deep ache. Even with morphine, it never goes away."

"Probably laying up against a rib," she noted absently. "Sometimes they do that. We'll take care of it for you in just a minute. Then you'll feel much better." As she spoke, without warning, she snatched out the tube. Blanchard was going to turn sixty in a few weeks if the medical establishment didn't kill him first, and in all six of his decades upon the earth, he had never experienced anything quite like the removal of that drain tube. He had fallen from a roof, survived three automobile accidents, and endured a 100 percent blockage of his LAD, but none of those experiences even came close. The pain was profound. It felt like the other end of the neoprene tube had been lashed to his ribcage, and that several ribs had exited his chest along with the tube at the moment of egress. As he heard the PA drop the tube into the drain pan on the floor beside the bed, his breath began to come back, but slowly, as if it were not completely sure that it was wise to do so, and when he was again able to speak, he shared with Rachel Camp his dismay at his recent treatment.

"What the hell's wrong with you?" he gasped. "Are you trying to ki—" At that moment, she snatched out the other tube. An involuntary noise escaped Blanchard, a cross between oof and ugh with perhaps a smidge of argh thrown in for good measure. An upsurge of nausea washed over him, and he barely had time to grab his bear before he leaned over the side of the bed and vomited onto the floor, his PA's athletic shoes, and both of the drain tubes now lurking in the drain pan, no doubt already plotting against their next victim, planning how best to torment another innocent, unsuspecting soul. While his reaction to his abrupt treatment was running its course, Rachel Camp was busy dressing the two fresh holes in his upper abdomen with antibiotic cream, gauze bandages, and tape. Blanchard regained control of his breathing.

"If I had a gun," he said with a shaky voice, "I would shoot you."

"Oh my," she replied. "Good thing we don't allow guns in the hospital." She stepped to the foot of the bed and made a notation on his chart.

"A jack handle, then. If I had a jack handle, I would whack you with it." He took a deeper breath and exhaled slowly. "Covey, go get me a jack handle. A good, long one."

"No," Covey replied. "It's over with now. I never heard the like." He shook his head.

Blanchard glared at his bass player for a moment. Then he gently placed a hand over one of his freshly dressed holes.

"Why didn't you warn me?" he asked Rachel Camp. "I could have prepared myself a little."

"There's really no way to make that pleasant," she replied. "Slower is not better, and warning the patient doesn't help at all. Sometimes it actually makes it worse. So it's best to get it over with. Trust me. I do have to say that you're the only patient I've ever had who threatened to shoot me."

"Sorry about that. I'd 'a gone for a leg. I promise." Blanchard felt a bit sheepish over his threat. He had been caught by surprise, and the words just sort of slipped out.

"Well, that's something, I guess." She looked at the mess in the floor. "I'll send someone in to clean this up. While I'm here, though, I need to remove your urinary catheter."

"Uh-uh," Blanchard said. "You can forget that. No snatching down there. I really will shoot you this time."

"Relax. Removing your catheter is nothing to worry about. It's not like getting the tubes out. It doesn't hurt at all. Besides, you have to urinate on your own before you go home, so it's got to go. And you have to have a bowel movement, too. You want to go home, don't you?"

"Lady, you have no idea. What's the deal with all these rules about what I have to do before I get out of here, anyway? First it was walk to the elevator and back. Now it's taking a leak and...other things. Is there anything else I—"

"There," Rachel Camp said. "Your catheter's out." She made another note on his chart, removed some paper towels from the dispenser on the wall, and wiped her shoes. Then she smiled and gave him a nod. "Have a good day!" she said as she headed for the door.

"It's a little late for that," Blanchard grumbled. "Getting old sucks so bad."

"It surely does," Covey replied. "But they say it beats the alternative."

"I'll get back with you on that."

"CAN'T DIE ON MY KNEES"
(Blanchard Shankles/John Covey)

The clock ticks slowly, the hours chime
Got nothing but memories, this guitar, and some time
Yesterday has vanished like windblown smoke
My dreams are all busted, my heart's been long broke

The days have fallen like leaves from the trees
Drifting along like a hawk on the breeze
Some good, some bad, all better than these
I lived on my feet, can't die on my knees

Sit on the riverbank, stare at the clouds
Remember the spotlights, remember the crowds
Consider the future, forget the dim past
The days of my life all went by too fast

The days have fallen like leaves from the trees
Drifting along like a hawk on the breeze
Some good, some bad, all better than these
I lived on my feet, can't die on my knees

It's three a.m. and the night's too damn long
Need me some sleep but I can't stop this song
Started out young and ended up here
With sadness, heartache, worry, and fear

The days have fallen like leaves from the trees
Drifting along like a hawk on the breeze
Some good, some bad, all better than these
I lived on my feet, can't die on my knees

The days have fallen like leaves from the trees
Drifting along like a hawk on the breeze
Some good, some bad, all better than these
I lived on my feet, can't die on my knees

"Listen to the Music"
The Doobie Brothers
-1972-

Early on, Blanchard realized that one of the unintended consequences of having a really dead father and an institutionalized mother was that, with those two individuals permanently residing elsewhere, the Shankles home became by default the best place for Skyye to practice. This development was no small boon to the band. Skyye had been together about a year by the time Benton's bad morning rolled around, and during that period the group had not been able to secure a permanent place to work out their songs. This lack of a musical home had not been the result of a dearth of effort on the band's part to seek out a proper locale, but no matter where they landed, there was always a compelling reason for them to move on.

Their earliest rehearsals had been at Tucker McFry's house. Tucker's mother, Oleana, was a sweet, calm woman with a substantial hearing impairment who had been willing for them to set up in the living room of her small home, and no matter how loudly they played, she could always be found sitting in her chair, knitting while tapping her toe out of time with the music, happy in the knowledge that her son and his friends were safe and out of mischief. The McFry house seemed perfect for the band's practice needs, but unfortunately, Oleana lived right in the middle of town, just across the street from two churches, and since none of her neighbors shared her auditory loss or her enthusiasm for her son's musical enterprise, the solution had not been a permanent one.

Jimbo Tant's daddy, Scant, was a very small preacher with mighty big ideas about the afterlife and how to avoid the warmer parts of it. He didn't agree with his son's musical aspirations and wasn't so sure about that clutch of longhaired boys he ran with, but he strove heroically to be tolerant even though it wasn't in his nature to do so. He allowed Skyye to practice in the sanctuary of the Little

Hope Baptist Church, and that solution was effective until the Saturday afternoon when he drove out to the church to put the finishing touches on his upcoming sermon, titled "Sin is the Key to Satan's Door." While there, he discovered the boys industriously working on their rendition of "Lola" by the Kinks. He stopped outside the church for a moment to listen, and while he sort of admired the tune, he found that he had grave ecclesiastical issues with the lyrics, as if perhaps they, too, could turn the demonic lock to hell's portal. Thus the boys were banned from practicing at the church, from ever playing that song again, and from drinking cherry colas, just to be certain that they remained on the cool side of Satan's door.

After the group was thrown out of the Little Hope Baptist Church, Chicken Raines's old man, Rooster, gave permission for them to use the old barn that squatted in the back pasture of the family farm, a generous offer not diminished in the least by the fact that the illicit MG roadster parked out there sometimes got in the way. Additionally, there was no electricity in the vicinity of the structure, a condition that Rooster Raines believed added to the appeal of the music his son and his friends were playing. Despite Rooster's opinions on the matter, this lack of electricity and therefore musical volume was an insurmountable problem in Skyye's collective opinion, and since among them they could not scratch up a quarter-mile's worth of extension cords to rectify the matter, they were again forced to search elsewhere.

John Covey's parents had then agreed to a practice session or two in Covey's bedroom, but the Covey family—all seven of them—lived in a mobile home, and when that clan plus all the members of Skyye, including instruments and amplifiers, shared the meager square footage of the dwelling on practice nights, it was a standing room only situation. On top of that, Covey's daddy worked the third shift at the chemical plant in Chattanooga, and even though he wished to be supportive of his children's enthusiasms, the truth of the matter was that he couldn't sleep with all that caterwauling going on—not to mention the fact that Tucker McFry's keyboard was set up at the foot of his bed, and when Tucker sat down, he occasionally sat on the old man's feet—so the band was compelled yet again to seek other avenues.

Simpson Taggart, too, tried to provide a solution by offering the Taggart garage as a practice hall. Unfortunately, the garage was an old one, and the wiring in it was just as ancient, and in the end it was overcome by the overwhelming electrical needs of a struggling rock and roll band. The building caught fire, ironically during a spirited rendition of "Light My Fire" by The Doors, and burned to the ground on a sad and rainy Saturday afternoon. The band escaped harm, as did most of their equipment, although Blanchard lost his Fuzzbuster to the blaze, and Ford Man's cowbell was never quite the same after rising from the ashes.

Ford Man Cooper was more than willing to do his part to help, but he was not able. His family was about as Church of Christ of Pentecostal Holiness as a family could get and didn't even believe in religious music, let alone the devil's tunes that Ford Man and his compatriots played. Because of this firm conviction concerning the salacious nature of music, Ford Man was forced to compound his sin and deceive his parents whenever a practice session came around. He did this by telling them that he was studying at the library, and since his parents did believe in education—provided it did not delve too deeply into evolution, the actual age of the earth, or what revolved around what up in the sky—they approved of Ford Man's supposed scholastic endeavors. However, since the Sequoyah Library was open a mere six hours per week, and never on Thursday or Saturday, which were the two days that Skyye usually tried to practice, Ford Man's deception represented a leap of faith on his part. It was a near impossibility that he would get away with his trickery, but he did, and the fact that he was never caught playing his demon songs was an indication to him that God approved of his duplicity, or at least was willing to let it slide as a small indiscretion that did no harm in a world chock full of pain and sorrow.

During its first year, Skyye had even tried to practice at Blanchard's house despite the fact that a crazy woman lived there. In many ways, the Shankles home was the perfect place for the members of the band to learn songs and enhance their musical abilities. The house had a large upstairs hall, much bigger than any space they had yet tried, and there was room for the equipment there, and places to sit and stand that did not involve someone relocating to the porch if another band member needed to change chords. The twelve-foot ceiling and heart pine walls had good acoustic qualities, and there was plenty of reliable TVA electricity. The home's wiring seemed resistant to spontaneous combustion no matter how raucous the tune, a factor that had become important to the boys after the Taggart garage fire. There were no preachers onsite or just across the street to object to edgy lyrics or pass judgment on rock and roll music in general, and the house was so far from town that, with the possible exception of some tone-deaf cattle, there were no neighbors around to complain if the music got too loud. The only problem was Crazy Edna, and she turned out to be insurmountable.

The last time the band tried to practice at Blanchard's house prior to his parents' relocations, they staged themselves in the upstairs hall, and after tuning up, they found themselves jaunting though a quick rendition of "Proud Mary," just stretching their strings and fingers while warming up the tubes in their amps. Chicken Raines was doing a fine job of singing like John Fogerty, and Blanchard and Jimbo were strumming slow and rich. Covey was intent on his bass plucking; the song was new to him, and his eyes were glued to his fret hand as he committed his finger moves to memory. *Cleaned a lot of plates in Memphis, pumped a lot of 'pane down in New O—* Abruptly, Chicken ceased to sing. The band members all stopped within a note or two of each other, as bands who have played together for a while tend to do when a discordant element pops up to jar the wavelength they all occupy.

"What's wrong, Chicken?" Blanchard asked. The cessation of the song had been so sudden that he had actually jolted forward a bit, as if a tangible physical momentum were disrupted, like an MG bumping into a brick wall or a Nubian princess thumping into a pillow.

"Uh," Chicken said. He swallowed and looked uncomfortable.

"What?"

"We've got company." Chicken nodded toward the other end of the hall. Blanchard looked, and there at the head of the stairs stood Edna, resplendent in her insane glory and very little else. She made an extravagant hand gesture as if blessing them all.

"Dammit," Blanchard said. He meant for it to be a quiet comment, something just for himself, but he had forgotten that he was standing in front of the backup mic, and this was, unfortunately, one of the days when it was freshly soldered, so it was working fine. *Dammit* echoed throughout the upstairs hall and down the stairs.

"Language, baby," Edna said as she strolled up. She was dressed as she usually was in ragged sweat pants, her bare breasts jiggling as she stopped before her son. The members of Skyye—and pretty much everyone else in Sequoyah—were aware of the general nature of Edna's afflictions, but this was the first time any of the boys, except for Blanchard, had seen her with her shirt off. To be fair, it was also the first time any member of Skyye besides Blanchard had seen *any* woman with her shirt off, except in the ubiquitous *Playboy* and *Hustler* photos hidden in their billfolds and under their mattresses, and the reactions there in the upstairs hall were varied but for the most part predictable.

Ford Man carefully placed his sticks on his snare, stood up from his drum stool, and turned around, not out of any sense of judgment, but rather as his way of ameliorating Blanchard's embarrassment, along with his own. Tucker cast his eyes southward and studied his keyboard. Jimbo unplugged and stepped down the hall and out the screen door onto the upstairs porch, guitar, cord, and all, ostensibly to smoke and take a sip from the warm tallboy bottle of Schlitz he had hidden out there. Chicken sighed and punched Blanchard gently on the shoulder, a gesture of solidarity and sympathy. Then he sighed again and sat on the floor. He picked up the copy of *Hit Parader Magazine* he had brought along with him and began to scan for possible songs to learn. Covey just closed his eyes and stood where he was, rigid like a statue. The lone exception to this brotherhood of compassion and support seemed to be Simpson Taggart. He had been leaning against the wall, hands in pockets, listening to the Creedence song when Edna came sauntering into view. At that time, against his will, he had begun to stare.

"Mama, we're trying to practice," Blanchard said. Geneva was gone to a friend's house, and Benton was out roaming, so it had seemed, on paper at least, to be a good time to get the guys together and work out a few tunes. He reached over and flipped his amp to standby. He was frustrated by the interruption, but he was trying hard not to let it show. He had talked to Edna earlier about his friends coming over, and about what they intended to do, and he had elicited from her a promise to stay in her room, listening to the radio until the members of the group went home. He had promised her that if she did this, he would take her to the town's diner after the practice session was over and get her favorite meal, a shrimp plate and a Dr. Pepper. When he proposed this plan earlier, she had nodded, and Blanchard assumed that they had arrived at an arrangement. Apparently, however, the lure of mortifying her son in front of his friends was too strong, and now all bets were off along with her shirt.

"Is Juicy Brucie Braaadley here?" she asked. "I heard one of his songs." She began to sing "Proud Mary," perhaps to jog her son's memory.

"He's not here, Mama." Blanchard shook his head. "You heard the band playing."

"You boys are good," she said, and the normalcy of that simple comment, one that anyone's mother might have made, nearly broke his heart.

"We'd be better if we could practice," he said. Most times he tried to keep it from his mind, but at that moment, Blanchard was heartsick at his bad luck and the cross he had to bear. He wondered for the umpteenth time why he had been cursed with an insane mother. He didn't think he deserved this. It wasn't fair, and some days it wore him to the nub. He wondered what went on in her head, deep in her mind where her ideas queued, way, way down where the light of reason never penetrated the shadows in the dark corners. Did she think that the upstairs hall was a radio station in Boston? Was she hoping to discover her own personal radio personality up there? Or was she even more random than that, and had no hopes at all outside of packing the immediate present with as much chaos as it could hold?

"I was asking him," Edna replied, pointing at Simpson while not looking at him. He was still staring at that which he had always hoped to one day see in the flesh, and which now had appeared before him as if by fine magic. The fact that one of them was painted blue and had slanted eyes drawn on it with a laundry marker didn't bother him in the least and had actually enhanced the experience.

"Are you kidding me, Simpson?" Blanchard asked as he analyzed the dynamics of the situation and realized who was looking at what. "Couldn't get you to quit drooling over my mama's titties, could I?"

"Sorry, man," Simpson said, tearing his eyes away with considerable effort. "I couldn't help myself." The shame of the moment was heavy upon him, like a rusty anchor grabbing the sea floor. "They were just out there, and, you know, I looked." The more he looked at anything else, the stronger the urge became to look back at Edna's torso, to get one more quick peek to tide him over until the next favor of good fortune broke his way.

"That's no excuse," Blanchard said. "You don't see me staring at *your* mama's boobs, do you?" This was the absolute and unvarnished truth, but it was not the apples-to-apples situation that it appeared to be. Simpson's mama, Malinda, was a pious, stern woman who didn't seem to like anyone much, including and perhaps especially her own husband, and since Simpson and his sister were adopted, the odds were at even money around town that *no* one had ever seen her uncovered boobs, or any other parts of her anatomy for that matter, and that this was a condition likely to remain unchanged until sweet Jesus came again, leading the Heavenly Host behind him as he went about the redemption of mankind. If at that time the Son of the Almighty wanted a quick peek, well, perhaps Malinda might relent, but then again, she might not. Still, Blanchard was pissed, and he wanted to make a point about what was and was not done among bandmates.

"I'm really sorry," Simpson repeated. He held out his hands in supplication. "I shouldn't have done it. I feel bad."

"Then why are you still looking?" Blanchard asked. It was true. Simpson's mouth expressed shame and contrition, but his eyes had drifted of their own accord back to the focal point of the current discussion and were again resting peacefully in visual nirvana. "If you think you feel bad now," Blanchard continued, "just think how you're going to feel when I smack you upside the head!" He undid his guitar strap and leaned his instrument against his amp.

"Aw, man. I told you I can't help it!" Simpson was appalled at his own venality even as he was trapped by it. "Please don't stomp me!" He once again dragged his glance away with visible difficulty, as if his head and eyes had become paralyzed. He was a starving man in a doughnut shop, and a pair of crullers was right there. "I just couldn't help it," he said again.

"How about if I can't help kicking your ass? How about if no matter what I try to do, I still end up kicking your ass? That's my mama, for Christ's sake! What's wrong with you? Jesus!"

Chicken Raines dropped his magazine and stood. With his eyes to the floor, he crossed to the disgraced Simpson, took him by the shoulders, and pushed him down the hall and out the screen door to the upstairs porch. Ford Man followed them out. Covey stood in place, eyes still closed. He looked peaceful standing there, as if he were asleep, catching a quick nap between songs. In a moment, voices began to drift in from the porch.

"I ought to toss you over the rail," said Jimbo Tant. "You just don't look at someone's mama's tits."

"I know, I know! But did you see them?" There was a short silence. Then it grew long.

"Yeah, I saw 'em," Jimbo Tant finally, grudgingly, admitted. "But it was an accident, and no one saw me see them."

"They *were* kind of perky," Chicken Raines said in a surprising admission of culpability. *Hit Parader Magazine* had apparently not held his complete interest. Perhaps the current month's selection of songs had not been among his favorites.

"I liked the one with the eyes on it," Simpson said.

"I ought to throw *all* of you off the porch," Ford Man said. "Blanchard is our friend, and that is his mama in there. And she's sick. She can't help herself!" You could take the boy out of the Church of Christ of Pentecostal Holiness, but you could never completely take the Church of Christ of Pentecostal Holiness out of the boy. "Now get back in there and behave like you ought to. If I see any of you looking at something you shouldn't be looking at, Blanchard won't have to whip you. I'll do it for him."

Back in the hallway, Edna was conducting a thorough search of the band equipment, maybe looking for Juicy Brucie Braaadley, or perhaps for her new favorite radio personality, John Records Landecker, whose middle name truly was Records. She looked behind the amps, and in the various guitar cases, and beneath the blanket folded up inside Ford Man's bass drum, and even under Tucker McFry's keyboard. Then she came back to Blanchard.

"I'm hungry."

"We're almost through with practice." Although they had just started, Blanchard no longer felt much like playing. He was mad at his friends, and he was sick of having to run interference between his mother and the rest of the world. He hadn't asked for the job, and he didn't want it. What he wanted was what everyone else seemed to have: normal parents. He wasn't even asking for perfect. He simply wanted a father who wouldn't try to screw every female in the county and a mother who kept her shirt on and didn't try to kill him in his sleep. Was that too much to ask? He realized that way down deep, he probably wasn't even angry enough about the R-rated thoughts of his companions, and that depressed him in a way he couldn't fully understand, never mind explain. It was as if he was wearing out on Edna and did not wish to have to chaperone her any longer.

"Let's go get a shrimp plate," she said.

"Okay, Mama," Blanchard said, defeated and despondent. "You go get dressed and we'll head on down to the diner."

"I'm dressed."

"Dress more," he said. She nodded at this suggestion and wandered to the top of the stairs. Then she began the slow journey down, pausing on each step to look at the walls, the floor, the ceiling, and all that lay beyond as if she had never seen any of it before that moment. As she made her way to her room, she passed a mirror positioned on the wall midway down the stairs. She stopped, and turned slowly to face it. It had her in its spell, Blanchard knew, and it would be disinclined to set her free. Likely she would be in its clutches for a while. Meanwhile, the boys filed back in from the upstairs porch. Blanchard looked at them with a cold gaze.

"There are two kinds of people in the world," he said. "People who look at a guy's mama's tits and people who don't. You guys suck."

"I didn't look," Ford Man said.

"Me neither," said Covey. He opened one eye a bit to make sure the coast was clear. Once he verified that the upstairs hallway was a bosom-free zone once again, he reentered the world of sight.

"I'm clean," said Tucker McFry.

"Ford Man doesn't suck," Blanchard amended. "And neither does Covey or Tucker." Ford Man nodded. He was vindicated. "The rest of you suck."

"Does that mean we can't be in the band anymore?" Jimbo Tant asked.

"It means you suck," Blanchard said, strapping on his guitar and flipping his amp switch. "Come on. 'Proud Mary' won't play itself. Let's get one more run-through done before I have to go to the diner."

"LAST CALL"
(Blanchard Shankles/John Covey)

Playin' back to backs at the Cactus Bar and Grill
Six miles from nowhere near the Arkansas line
Ten days on the road in a blue November chill
Ten more then home to the sweet Georgia pine

Six minutes to midnight, last call for beer
Don't have to go home but you can't stay here

Ridin' that stage at The Last Hard Man
Pilin' those chords like a mountain of snow
Play 'til we can't, then play 'til we can
Play one more then it's time to go

Six minutes to midnight, last call for beer
Don't have to go home but you can't stay here

Spankin' the Strat at the County Line
Standing room only in the Mississippi night
Two hundred drunk bikers all feeling fine
Two hundred drunk bikers all looking to fight

Six minutes to midnight, last call for beer
Don't have to go home but you can't stay here

Play the memories, play the dreams
Turn on the amp and crank it up loud
Rip those tunes 'til the young girls scream
Take no prisoners and own that crowd

Six minutes to midnight, last call for beer
Don't have to go home but you can't stay here

Play the memories, play the dreams
Turn on the amp and crank it up loud
Rip those tunes 'til the young girls scream
Take no prisoners and own that crowd

Six minutes to midnight, last call for beer
Don't have to go home but you can't stay here

"Freebird"
Lynyrd Skynyrd
-Thursday: Fifth Day-

Blanchard's last day in the hospital began with a suicidal redbird and ended with an ill-advised and poorly timed sexual liaison, which is often the case with such things. He awoke early to Covey snoring in the chair, white noise provided by a tired bass player, but there was another sound, as well, a thump...thump...thump coming from just outside his window. He turned his head toward the noise and saw a cardinal—the feathered kind, not a prince of the Roman Catholic Church—trying his best to enter the room through the glass. The bird would back up a few feet, fly in a circle to build momentum, and then aim straight for the glass. The result of every attempt was that he slammed his red head straight into the pane. Then he would shake his head as if he couldn't believe it hadn't worked, regroup, fly back to his starting point, and repeat the process. As the light increased out-side with the rising of the sun, Blanchard saw a brown cardinal, a fe-male, the redbird's wife, perhaps, sitting on a nearby telephone wire in her sensible frock, assumedly watching her flashy, overdressed mate as he attempted to defeat the window through sheer tenacity and misdirected optimism. As he watched, Blanchard could have sworn he saw the brown bird shake her head, as if lamenting that she should have listened to her mama's good advice and been a bit more selective back when she was a young dating bird with her entire life and all the nests of the world before her.

"You married him," Blanchard said to the brown cardinal on the wire. He felt an affinity with her, as if they were kindred souls. "You're all in now, and there's no going back. Just make the best of it." She made a movement that looked remarkably like a shrug while her hardheaded companion continued with his single-minded plan of window domination. She seemed resigned to the likelihood that he would break his neck while pursuing his goal, but her demeanor bore no signs of anxiety or duress. Perhaps there was a sizeable life-insurance policy in play here, Blanchard mused. Maybe after hotshot there beat his own brains out on that unyielding pane of glass, the missus could—after a short but respectful period of mourning—cash the check, gather up the chicks and a few belongings, and start over elsewhere, say in a more southerly locale where the air was always warm, a veritable paradise where every house had a birdbath, the worms and seeds were plentiful, and hawks and cats were against the law.

"Who are you talking to?" Covey asked from his recliner. He stretched and rubbed his close-cropped head and unshaven jaw. When Blanchard had fallen asleep the previous night, Tucker McFry was occupying that chair. Apparently, tending to Blanchard was a team sport, and for some reason the handoffs tended to occur while he was sleeping, a phenomenon no doubt explainable by the fact that sleeping was mostly what he had done since his surgery.

"Those birds out there," Blanchard said, pointing. "That red one is trying to get in." As if to punctuate his sentence, there was a thump from the window. "See? There he goes again. I think the brown one on the wire over there is his old lady. She's watching him screw up." The female raised a wing and pecked at a mite, then flapped a couple of times before settling back in to watch her hardheaded companion perform his strange ritual.

"Well, that's her job," Covey said. "Mine does it all the time." He yawned and stood. "When he finally gives up, she'll give him a few minutes and then casually tell him that she told him so." Blanchard nodded. Bird or man, it was the same old story. Covey knocked on the faux wood of the side table beside the recliner. "I just hope he doesn't get in. My mama always told me that a bird in the house was bad luck. She said it foretold a death."

"That's an old wives' tale," Blanchard said, "and this is not a house. Anyway, it would be bad luck for him, not me. Remember, I'm the son of the woman who used to nail birds to the wall. If he gets in here, I might just have to go all Edna on him. I'm sort of in the mood."

"Fight it off. They have a crazy ward here, up on the top floor, and you don't want to end up there." Covey shuddered in spite of himself. "I remember the first time I ran up on one of your mama's offerings. Scared me." Covey had once looked up while conducting some personal business in the bathroom of the Shankles house, back in the old days when Edna was still in residence and wickedness had ruled, and he had seen a squirrel mounted to the wall who had apparently met his maker the hard way. He had gone a full forty-five years since that day without the need to see something like it again.

"They would tend to do that." Those days were long ago and far away, but Blanchard remembered them clearly. "Especially if you came up on one in an unexpected place. For some reason, those were worse than the ones in the kitchen. I guess we got used to those."

"All I know is, I still keep my eyes to the floor whenever I'm in the john," Covey said.

"Some guys just weren't made for life on the edge."

"Tell you what. If he gets in, I'll catch him in a pillow case and put him back out." Covey offered this alternative to ritual sacrifice as he crossed to the bathroom for his morning visit. "No need to find a hammer."

"I was just about to buzz for the maintenance guy."

"No, really, I'm on this."

While Covey was performing his morning ablutions, the food tray was brought in, placed on the bedside table, and rolled into position. When Covey exited the bathroom, Blanchard was inspecting with suspicion the meal in its vinyl tray. He had been brought a scrambled yellow substance that vaguely resembled eggs but was not, a piece of cold, dry wheat toast, some gluey oatmeal, a cup of fruit, a half pint of skim milk, and a tepid cup of decaffeinated coffee. "Heart healthy," Covey said to Blanchard, gesturing at the meal. "And plenty of it, too! Tuck in."

"Heart healthy means if you can eat it without having a heart attack, your heart must be healthy," Blanchard grumbled. "I can't stand it. They want me to eat this, walk down the hall and back without help, and go to the can before they'll let me out of here."

"No big deal. You've had plenty worse food out on the road. Eat. It's good for you. Just like Mama used to make."

"If you're talking about my mama, unfortunately you're right. Crazy women are lousy cooks." He looked at his friend. "You never know for sure what the secret ingredient is. But if you're talking about your mama, bless your heart. I had always hoped for better for you."

He picked up the bowl of oatmeal, sniffed its contents, and then placed it back on the tray. "Why is it that everything that's supposed to be good for you sucks?" A thump from the window punctuated this observation. These were coming with less frequency, and the thumps were not quite as loud as they had been, indicating either that the redbird was getting the message concerning the feasibility of the task he had set for himself, or he was beginning to suffer from periodic blackouts and really ought to call it a day before the head trauma became fatal and his wife became a free agent.

"It's a federal law, I think," Covey said. "A USDA thing, maybe. Really, though, your breakfast doesn't look so bad. You ought to eat some of it."

"Be my guest," Blanchard said, sliding the tray to the edge of the table, where it balanced precariously. "You better start with those eggs before they harden up. Otherwise you might break a tooth." He gestured with his plastic fork. "To me it looks like something you might find in the dumpster behind the Waffle House. Something the new cook made, the one who just didn't work out."

"Uh-uh. It's tempting, but what kind of friend would I be if I ate a sick man's breakfast? I'm heading to the cafeteria."

"That's more like it. Bring me back two bacon biscuits with extra bacon, a Coke with lots of ice, and a Snickers bar. One of those big ones. That's what I want for breakfast."

"Do you think you ought to?"

"Covey, as soon as I get out of here, I am going to eat what I want, when I want, how I want. Grease, potatoes, salt, booze, sugar. If it's bad for me, I intend to have some. And don't even get me started on how many cigarettes I'll be smoking. There'll be one hanging out each side of my mouth with a third one lit in reserve. So look at this morning as a trial run. If I survive two bacon biscuits, a Coke, and a Snickers bar, we'll know I'm good to go."

"What do you want me to do with this?" Covey asked, nodding at the breakfast tray.

"Break the glass and give it to that stupid bird," Blanchard replied. "He's earned it." The cardinal had finally ceased his efforts altogether and was just sitting on the sill, looking dazed, no doubt formulating Plan B, or maybe just trying to remember his name and the day of the week. His brown companion flew from her perch on the wire over to the sill and landed beside him. She looked at the window and then pecked it gently, as if to show her partner that it continued to be an unyielding surface, and that all his mighty effort had been for naught. Then she took wing and he, with a look of birdly resignation, followed.

While Covey was gone to the cafeteria, Blanchard slowly and carefully got out of bed. He still felt as if he would split in half whenever he moved much, and he tended toward dizziness when he stood. He made his way to the bathroom, moving from handhold to handhold as he shuffled along, stooped like the old man he supposed he was. Finally he arrived, and after resting for a moment from that fifteen-foot journey, he peed and freshened up with a washcloth. He was supposed to eliminate into a plastic jug so that his output could be measured, but that seemed to be too much trouble, especially since he needed both of his hands planted firmly on the walls to keep him in an upright position, so he made an executive decision and skipped the collection phase of the enterprise. After another short rest during which he looked at his emaciated face in the bathroom mirror, fascinated at the strange person he saw there, he was on a slow, unsteady journey to the recliner chair when Dr. Forrester came in.

"Well, now, it's good to see you up," the doctor said. He took Blanchard by the elbow and helped him to his destination.

"It's a lot easier to get around without all those wires and tubes," Blanchard said as he completed his journey and sank gratefully into the recliner, panting. "I feel better just having all that mess gone. I was afraid I'd trip." He took a couple of deep breaths. He was exhausted. "Of course, walking to the bathroom and taking a leak just wore me completely out. I guess the Boston Marathon is out this year."

"You're doing well, and you will continue to feel a little better every day, but I don't want you to rush things. You can expect six to eight weeks of slow recovery. And that's what we want. Slow and steady. Don't be a hero, and don't get impatient. This was a major surgery. Your heart is doing fine. You just had the one blockage, which we already knew, and now you have a brand-new artery bypassing it. Your heart was stopped for four minutes, start to finish. There were no problems with the surgery, and there have been no complications since."

"You do good work. So being worn completely out is normal?"

"It is. Remember, we pretty much had to take you apart to get to your heart. Most of heart surgery is about getting to the area we need to fix. Once we get to it, we do a little plumbing repair, and then we start putting everything back together again. It will take some time for your body to heal from the trauma of the surgery, and you have to let it. I will give you a list of activities you can do, and another one that lists those you should avoid for a while. Pay attention and don't try to do too much." He looked over at the untouched breakfast tray. "How are you eating?"

"I am about to dive into breakfast here in a minute." And he would, just as soon as Covey returned.

"That's good. You have to keep up your strength. You have a lot of healing to do."

"So when can I get out of here, Doc? It's not that I don't enjoy our little talks, and I really appreciate you not killing me, but I'm getting a bad case of cabin fever."

"Have you made it down to the elevators and back?"

"Getting there. Somebody keeps moving them farther away." He had only tried twice, once with Skippy's help and once with Covey's. Both outings had left him so spent that a nap was the only effective remedy.

"And you peed today."

"Just now."

"What about a bowel movement?"

"Not yet but I'm ever hopeful." If those bacon biscuits didn't break everything loose, maybe the Snickers Bar and the Coke would.

"Let's keep you at least one more day," Dr. Forrester said after glancing over Blanchard's chart. "We want to be sure everything's working as it should before we send you home. If you continue to improve today, and if your bowels move, maybe we'll be able to let you go home in the morning." Blanchard was disappointed, but maybe he could stand one more day. He nodded. "Oh, there's another thing," Dr. Forrester said. "You'll see this on the discharge orders, but I like to cover it in person with my patients. You'll start to feel much better soon, but no matter how good you might be feeling, I don't want you to lift more than two or three pounds for a while. A couple of weeks, anyway."

"Whatever you say. What's the deal?"

"Well, you have the thickest breastbone I have ever dealt with. I almost burned up my Dremel getting through it. Now it's all wired back together, but until the bone knits, a strain of any kind might cause the wires to slip. You could end up with a click. It's not a danger, but people who have developed sternum clicks tell me they're extremely annoying."

"If someone hands it to me, can I hold my guitar in my lap and play a bit?" He nodded at the Ovation leaned against the wall. Dr. Forrester picked it up and tested its weight.

"I think that'll be fine, sitting down and resting the weight of it on your legs," he said, handing the guitar to his patient. "But no rough stuff. No, uh, 'Mississippi Queen.'"

"Only slow ballads and church music," Blanchard said. "I swear." He caught a C chord and began to pick out "Dust in the Wind" by Kansas. He started slowly, but he soon became absorbed in his fingerplay and the slow, easy chord progressions, and he slipped gently, without a ripple, out of the hateful hospital room and into the song. He never even noticed when the doctor left, and he was still playing a few minutes later when the door opened. He assumed it was Covey, back from the cafeteria with the illicit breakfast, but when he ceased his playing and turned to welcome decent food, what he saw instead was a pair of orderlies rolling a bed into the room and parking it in the empty space on the other side of his own. A wormy-looking young man with greasy red hair, a scraggly set of whiskers that shouldn't have bothered, and a mouth full of meth teeth looked over from the bed as the orderlies got it parked and locked down. Working efficiently without need for comment, they began the wiring and poking process for the new patient. A young woman stood in attendance, but out of the way. She had a washed-out world-weariness about her that made Blanchard feel bad for her without even knowing her name or her story. He could see that hers had been a path hard to travel, a trail strewn with sharp rocks and lined with brambles. She looked like she belonged with the young man in the bed, like they were a pair of sad peas in a hopeless and diseased pod, and that perhaps she stayed for no other reason than she had no place else to go.

"Dude," said Blanchard's new roommate by way of greeting. He raised his hand, and one of the orderlies took that opportunity to clamp an oxygen sensor onto his finger.

"Kill me," Blanchard muttered, mostly to himself. He shook his head and closed his eyes. With a whisk, one of the orderlies pulled the curtain that hung between the two beds. Blanchard looked out the window and saw that his friend the cardinal had returned to the windowsill. The bird's better half was not to be seen, and Blanchard supposed that she had decided, upon hearing of his plan to return to the window, to find a better deal, perhaps a robin with a law degree or a steady, hardworking dove with a good factory job. It might have been his imagination, but in profile the woebegone bird seemed shorter than before. "This was your doing," Blanchard said to his avian companion while pointing at the pulled curtain and his new roommate beyond. The cardinal tilted his head, but he kept his own counsel at the accusation and held his tongue. "Covey was right. You brought bad luck. When I get out of here, I'm looking you up. We have things to talk about." The bird flapped his wings, pecked at the window halfheartedly, and then flew off. He knew a threat when he heard one, and forewarned was forearmed.

Blanchard listened with dismay to the sounds of settling in from the far side of the curtain. There was murmuring as the patient's protocols were discussed, and beeping as the machines were switched on and calibrated, and clanking as the bed rails were snapped into position, and *ouch* as the needles were inserted. He wished his new roommate no particular ill will, but he was a loner by nature and did not feel like having company, so he hoped that the newcomer slipped into a light, non-lethal coma for the next twenty-four hours or so, at least until Blanchard got out of there, and that his girlfriend was the quiet sort who would read a book, crochet, or simply nap to pass the time. Once he got on his way back to Georgia, Blanchard would have no problem with a full recovery for his new companion and a full and happy life for the young couple.

As Blanchard considered the unfairness of having to deal with a sick stranger, Covey finally arrived back from his breakfast run. He came over to Blanchard's side of the room with a white sack inscribed with a cryptic BAC BISC. There was a large Coke in his other hand and a Snickers bar peeking from his shirt pocket. Blanchard traded his guitar for the sack and the Coke. He removed the lid and took a slow and luxurious sip, unwrapped one of the biscuits with an emotion akin to excitement, and slid a piece of crisp bacon from between its halves. He took a bite, closed his eyes, and chewed slowly.

"How is it?" Covey asked.

"Better than sex."

"Maybe you're not doing it right."

"That's not what all the women say." His eyes were still closed, and the bacon was having its way with him, teasing him to the edge of ecstasy.

"They just want you to give them a free CD. Eat your bacon. I see we have company." He nodded toward the curtain.

"Yeah, they rolled him in a little while ago, just like they owned the place and could do what they wanted to. You were right. That stupid redbird was a bad omen. Now we have a meth head named Dude and his girlfriend sharing the room with us. I hate it, and my advice is, don't touch anything over there. Maybe you should start using the bathroom down the hall." He continued to crunch bacon as he spoke, and when he finished his first piece, he slid another slice from his biscuit, looked at it with reverence, and went to work. "I swear this is the best bacon I've ever had."

"I went out back to the pasture and picked the pig myself."

"Do all bass players have a good eye for pork?"

"Not all of us. I took a correspondence course."

"I like a man who tries to improve himself. You're a good friend." As Blanchard crunched on his bacon, the television on the wall flickered and then blared into life. Covey looked at Blanchard quizzically.

"Looks like Dude has found the remote," Blanchard said. Perhaps because he worked in loud settings, he appreciated quiet when he could get it, and he had never been much of a television watcher on top of that. Back in the dark days before Edna took her one-way ride to central Georgia, she had taken particular exception to all manner of televisions, and the set in the Shankles home had borne the brunt of her ire. Thus it had been difficult to watch any of the four channels they received through all the mystic artwork layered onto the screen, and it had subsequently become impossible to view programs once she got the notion one bleak morning to hurl the Nubian princess through the picture tube. So Blanchard had never really had the opportunity to become addicted to broadcast entertainment. It appeared, however, that the days of his personal enjoyment of a quiet hospital room would now wane like the Tennessee moon. "I didn't think it could get any worse in here," he said to Covey. "Then it got worse."

"I thought you had a private room."

"Nope. What I had was good luck, and it just ran out. My insurance won't pay for a private room. My coverage is so bad that I'm surprised they haven't had me in the lobby or under a tarp out in the parking lot for the past three days." He crunched in silence a moment. "Now that Dude and Misty Lou over there have arrived, Covey, I think it's high time for us to get out of here. Between you and me, they don't look like our sort of folks."

"Five days," Covey said.

"What?"

"You've been in here five days."

"Say what? How did I lose track of two whole days?" Blanchard had misplaced entire days before while navigating the winding road that was his life, but he generally had a good hangover and maybe a dented fender afterwards to tip him off as to what had likely transpired and to remind him not to repeat whatever activity had produced the missing time. In this instance, however, the days were just gone, like his misspent youth, his questionable innocence, and all the hair on his chest.

"You were kind of out of your head on the first day after surgery. Lots of dreams and crazy talk. You sort of reminded me of your mama, except you didn't kill anything. You mostly slept away day two and day three. None of the medical folks around here seemed too upset by any of it. They all acted like nothing special was going on, so I took it as a good sign."

"Five days. No wonder I'm hankering to get out of here." He took a bite of the buttermilk biscuit and let it rest on his tongue.

"This is good. Whoever they have cooking down there knows what they're doing." As Blanchard savored the complex flavor of the biscuit, Dude was busy on the other side of the curtain working his way through the offerings on the television. He established a pattern of changing the channel, increasing the volume a notch or two, watching for a short while, and then saying *nope* before moving on to the next station. For some reason he reminded Blanchard of his recently departed visitor, the redbird at the window. Perhaps it was his single-mindedness and his blind obsession to find a station he liked, one to which he could say *yep*. Blanchard considered betting the guy twenty dollars that he couldn't break the glass and jump through the window, but he was afraid that the thump-thump-thump of Dude trying to earn a sawbuck the easy way would annoy him even more than the mere facts of Dude's existence and his television-viewing habits.

"I saw Dr. Forrester out in the hallway," Covey said as he placed the Snickers bar on the nightstand, positioning it for easy access. "He told me you were doing pretty well and that you might go home tomorrow."

"I might surprise him and go sooner than that."

"What are you talking about?"

"Leaving tomorrow has all these conditions tied to it." Blanchard turned his attention to his second biscuit and began to disassemble it. "And I'm ready to go now." The channel on the television advanced, accompanied by an increase in volume and a *nope*. "Right now."

"What conditions?"

"I still have to walk down the hall, and have a bowel movement, and I'm not allowed to pick up anything heavy, and on top of all that, I have to pee some more, and if they find out I'm eating decent food, all hell will break loose. It's just one thing after another with these people. They're crazy about lining a guy out."

"That's not all that much," Covey said. "None of it should be a problem."

"Maybe not, but I'm sick of the whole business." On the wall, the television station changed again. Blanchard waited for the volume increase and the *nope*, and when he heard them both right on cue, he turned to his friend. "I don't think I can do it, Covey. I've been trying to be nice and play along, but that guy is the final straw. He's going to

watch that TV from now on. Wait and see if he doesn't. He's probably in here for a sleep disorder and plans on watching it all night.
Help me get dressed and let's just go."

"You can't just go."

"Hunker down, hide, and watch me."

"At least wait until you go to the bathroom."

"Oh, now *you're* on the bathroom kick too? I don't *need* to go to
the john, dammit. When I do have to go, I'll go! I hate it that everyone's all up in my personal business!" He worked on his biscuit in silence for a moment. Then he looked at Covey. "Sorry about that. I'm
just edgy." The channel on the television advanced again, accompanied by the usual rise in volume and the ubiquitous *nope*. Blanchard
sighed. "If I don't leave now, Covey, I'm pretty sure I'm going to step
over to the other side of the curtain and beat Dude to death with my
guitar. I can actually see it happening, like I'm having a vision of the
future. I'm telling you, my karma can't take the hit. It's full. When I
die, I don't want to come back as a car salesman or a burro. Plus, all
that swinging and whomping will probably make my breastbone
click."

"Your breastbone?"

"Never mind." The television had stopped on *Wheel of Fortune*,
and the volume had increased again. Apparently Dude was a game
show man, because his search for entertainment lingered here long
past the usual interval, as if it might be at an end. Blanchard and
Covey listened for a few minutes, during which the volume increased
twice. Blanchard turned to Covey. "I take it back about the insomnia.
I think he's in here for his ears. Tell you what. If you look out the
window, you'll see a pawnshop just up the street."

"Okay...."

"I need you to go buy me a pistol. It doesn't have to be anything
fancy. There's some money in my boot. If you don't have enough,
pawn the Ovation."

"I think there's a wait on handguns. You'll be long gone from
here by the time the background check is complete. Especially with
your background. And I'll never get back in here with a rifle."

"You could pretend it was a crutch."

"Uh-uh."

"A baseball bat, then. Get me a bat. It'll be more personal that way." With a start, Blanchard realized that the Nubian princess would be perfect for this situation. She was compact, deadly, quiet, and experienced in the dispatch of annoyance. Looking back over his entire life, though, it seemed that he never had her when he needed her. Bad planning, he supposed.

"It's just one more day," Covey said. "I've got some headphones out in the car. I'll go get them, and we'll fix you up with some music. That'll set you right." A commercial came on at that point, a loud diatribe spoken by an attorney who had huge, Popeye-like arms photoshopped onto his skinny torso. The right arm bore a tattoo of an anchor. He billed himself as the Strong Arm, and, as he struck a muscular pose, this strapping barrister brashly promised to use those strong arms to pummel insurance companies, pharmaceutical firms, and all manner of other evil corporate entities into financial submission as he defended the little man against the inequities of the world.

"You reckon the Strong Arm up there will take my case when I go over and kill my new roommate with a baseball bat?" Blanchard asked conversationally. "That tattoo kind of makes him look like a brawler. I think he could get me off with probation."

"I don't know," Covey replied. "I think he may be more interested in civil law. Something involving a nice, fat check at the end."

"Hey, he paid good money to run that commercial to try and drum up a little business. I'm just thinking about helping him out and throwing some trade his way." In front of their very eyes, the Strong Arm put the beat down on a hapless yet venal insurance adjustor before winding down with a muscular pose and a conspiratorial wink, and he left them with the impression that millions of dollars were stacked in random corporate vaults, just waiting to be claimed by those viewers smart enough to be nailed by a dump truck in a crosswalk before calling the Strong Arm, preferably from the scene of the accident. "See? He's a scrapper. He's my guy."

Wheel of Fortune returned to the hospital room with all of its many decibels in tow. On the television, one of the contestants was buying an unnecessary vowel, because even Blanchard in his mildly agitated and drug-addled state could see that the phrase the contestants were trying to decipher was, ironically, *A Time to Kill.* If possible, the volume seemed even louder than it had been before the commercial. Blanchard made as if to rise, then slumped back in his chair, defeated.

"Don't go kill the new patient," Covey warned.

"Well, then, how about you step over there and tell him to turn the TV off, or at least down?" Blanchard said. "Because if I go over, he's going to have to have the remote surgically removed."

"Leave it be," Covey advised. "No use starting trouble with someone you have to share a room with. Just settle down. You want me to call the nurse to see if you can have something to take the edge off?"

"Some quiet would buff out all my sharp edges. You know what? You suck. I ask for one simple favor from you, one little thing, and what do I get? Attitude."

"Settle down, Blanchard."

"Just never mind. I'll go do it myself." Blanchard took a deep breath and slowly rose from the recliner. Once standing, he weaved to and fro for a moment while establishing his equilibrium. Then he began to shuffle at a measured pace toward the center of the now-divided room, intending to have a word or two with Dude about the realities of cohabitation, the rules of courtesy, and the upper limits of the human auditory system. He ceased his shuffling and poked his head around the curtain. Then, as if he had dipped his forehead into hot oil, he snatched that head back to his own side of the curtain. He slowly eased his head around the edge of the fabric and looked again, just a quick peek, and then he turned with a crooked grin on his face and motioned to Covey. "Come here," he mouthed. "Hurry up."

Curious, Covey crossed the room and arrived next to Blanchard, who held his finger to his lips for silence, and together they eased their heads around the edge of the curtain. There in his bed, Dude was entertaining company. Since he was wired and plumbed and had to somehow overcome the accompanying lack of mobility, he lay on his back while his visitor, the young woman who had been in quiet attendance during the admission process, took care of the more active parts of their encounter. Dude had his eyes closed and exhibited a foolish-looking grin while his companion rode him with a look of concentration generally reserved for entrance examinations to first-tier graduate schools. Blanchard supposed her intense focus on the task at hand was the result of Dude's teeth, which would certainly be off-putting to *him* should he attempt liaison with the man. Or perhaps she was a bit nervous about putting out in the full light of day in a semi-private Tennessee hospital room, with an unlocked door on her right and a flimsy curtain on her left, but was one of those people who had a hard time saying no.

"You have to be kidding me," Covey whispered.

"I wonder why I didn't get one of those," Blanchard whispered.

"It would probably kill you right now."

"No doubt. But it's the principle of the thing, and we all have to die sometime. I'll tell you one thing. I need to get myself a better doctor. That looks like some good cardiovascular exercise to me."

"For *her*, maybe," Covey said. "He's just sort of laying there like a shot buck."

"He's sick. Or maybe she killed him."

"She looks like she could."

"This is the final straw!" Blanchard whispered. "They have me walking to the elevator and hanging around waiting to go to the can, and in the meantime, the new guy is getting laid!" He shook his head, the ignominy of the situation heavy upon him. "I mean, look at him! Would *you* give him any?"

"No."

"Me neither. He's over there mattress dancing, and they wouldn't even let me smoke. It's age discrimination, I tell you. We need to call the Strong Arm."

"Well, you said your insurance sucked," Covey replied sotto voce. "Maybe you should step up to the Gold Plan."

"I wonder what his deductible is."

"Whatever it is, I bet he paid it," Covey said.

"Yeah, I bet they settle up for *that* before, not after."

"That's modern medicine for you. All about the money."

"I can tell you one thing. My physical therapist does not look like that." Blanchard carefully backed away from the curtain, and Covey followed suit. Back on his side of the room again, Blanchard shuffled over to the nightstand and opened the bottom drawer. He had made a decision while critiquing Dude's sexual technique and it was time for action. He removed his street clothes and placed them on the bed.

"Turn around while I get dressed," he said to Covey.

"What are you doing?"

"I've had it with this place. I'm going home. You're driving me." He sat on the bed and removed his hospital gown, which he then wadded and tossed on the floor. He grabbed his shorts and slipped them on. "It feels good to be wearing something that covers my backside," he said.

"Blanchard, you can't go home until they let you."

"Watch me," Blanchard said as he pulled on first one sock and then the other. It was a tricky process without the ability to move his torso much, but he finally managed. "This is not jail, despite what the food tastes like. Edna's baby boy is going over the wall."

"You have to have discharge orders, and medicines, and—"

"Covey, I'm leaving. I've been here five days, and I've had enough of this place. They fixed what I came here to have fixed, and I'm not going to spend the next twenty-four hours watching *Wheel of Fortune* while my new best friend Dude gets his brains screwed out over there by some sweet little thing who must be about as blind as he is deaf." He slowly worked his left leg into his jeans. After steadying himself against the soreness in his chest, he followed with the right leg. Then he gently stood, pulled his pants the rest of the way up, fastened the button and zipped the fly. "I like pants," he said, as if discovering them for the very first time after a lifetime of bare legs and cold knees. "I think they'll catch on." He reached for his shirt.

"What if we leave and you die?" Covey asked.

"What is this? A riddle?"

"I'm serious, Blanchard."

"Don't worry. You'll find another guitar player. Old Dude over there might even play, if you can get his mind off other things. The woods are full of guitar players. Not one as good as me, you understand, but you boys can carry whoever you find along until he gets his feet on the ground." Blanchard had been buttoning his shirt as he spoke, and now he looked down and noticed that he had one button left over. He sighed as he began to undo them. His arms were already tired.

"You know what I mean. How am I supposed to feel if I take you out of here and you keel over on the way home?"

"If I die, it's my time to die. That's some wisdom Edna shared with me recently." He had finished unbuttoning. He took a deep breath, matched up his lowest button with its designated hole, and began the fastening process anew. He was more careful this time to be sure that the count came out correctly.

"What are you talking about? Your mama's been dead for years."

"Not as dead as we all might have thought. While you're standing there, how about helping me with my boots? I can't bend that far, and pulling them on might make me click."

"What is with the clicking you keep talking about?" Covey asked. "I don't even know what that means." Covey picked up a boot, guided Blanchard's foot into it, and slowly pushed the boot home. He repeated the process with the other boot and foot. Blanchard was dressed.

"I already feel better just standing here with my clothes on," Blanchard said. He pocketed his phone, his nitro tablets, his billfold, and the Snickers bar. From beyond the curtain there was a crash as something fell to the floor followed by a loud, satisfied moan from Dude.

"I bet you don't feel better than he does," Covey said.

"Sounds like nobody feels better than he does. I really hate that guy, and I just met him. Are you ready to go? I want to get some gone before any of Dude's buddies show up and they get into the really kinky stuff. It might upset me."

Covey took Blanchard's elbow, and they began the slow journey to the hall. Almost as an afterthought, he grabbed the bear and handed it to Blanchard. Blanchard looked at the stuffed animal, considering, and finally he nodded. "Yeah, the bear can come," he said. Covey then picked up the Ovation, and they headed for the door. As they crossed the boundary to the X-rated side of the room, Blanchard saw that Dude and his companion were snuggled under the thin sheet of the narrow hospital bed, the picture of domesticity and connubial bliss.

"Dude!" said Dude. "You out of here, man?"

"I'm just walking to the elevator," Blanchard said as he shuffled past the foot of the bed. "Anyone comes looking for me, tell them to have a seat. I'll be right back."

"That's cool."

"And keep up the good work," Blanchard added as he entered the room's short entryway. Covey opened the door, and the pair left the room, heading for the elevator, and the parking lot, Georgia-bound and making for home.

"THE MORE THINGS CHANGE"
(Blanchard Shankles/John Covey)

Three score and ten and seven and two
The days drag by since I last talked to you
My world's gone strange, my love's a dead flame
The more things change, the more they're the same.

I woke on a Tuesday to your sad goodbye note
And since that hard day I can't stay afloat
My world's gone strange, my love's a dead flame
The more things change, the more they're the same.

I gave you forever and you pledged me the sun
I sent you my love and you left me with none
My world's gone strange, my love a dead flame
The more things change, the more they're the same.

I called you to tell you my love was still true
Now my words are in voicemail, waiting for you
My world's gone strange, my love a dead flame
The more things change, the more they're the same.

I come by to see you, but I don't find you home
I wanted to settle, but you wanted to roam
My world's gone strange, my love a dead flame
The more things change, the more they're the same.

One upon a time I lived for your touch
I wanted it all, and I wanted too much
My world's gone strange, my love a dead flame
The more things change, the more they're the same.

Three score and ten and seven and two
The days drag by since I last talked to you
My world's gone strange, my love's a dead flame
The more things change, the more they're the same.

"Brown Eyed Girl"
Van Morrison
-1975-

Blanchard Shankles was twenty years of age when he got married. It wasn't his intention to become a husband, and he had been harboring no great aspirations along those lines. In fact, given his experiences with the one married couple he had witnessed up close and personal—his parents—his thoughts concerning lifelong relationships tended toward the observation that the meager dividends they paid did not seem to be worth the abundant trouble they caused. But love is not a neat or convenient emotion, and it seldom bends itself to the weight of facts or the rules of logic, so when he fell for Andrea Joy Hazeltine, it was with the approximate velocity of the proverbial ton of masonry dropping from a cloudless sky on a windless day.

Blanchard met his future bride in the small town of South Pittsburg, Tennessee, at a roller skating rink called Skate. Skate was not an impressive place, as is often the case with roller rinks, and it resembled nothing so much as a massive Quonset hut. Its floor, where the roller skates met the road, so to speak, was concrete rather than the traditional hardwood, and a cinderblock addition on one end housed a snack bar and a selection of pinball machines known throughout South Tennessee for their refusal to pay off. The sign for the establishment sat on a tall pole in the middle of a gravel parking lot. It was canted at a slight angle that changed on occasion due to its proclivity to be struck by vehicles backing out or pulling in. The sign itself was a rusty, neon affair featuring the word "Skate" plus a figure whose arms and legs alternated between the rear and forward positions and were assumedly meant to convey the illusion of skating, but due to the speed at which the lights flickered on and off, the figure actually bore more of a likeness to someone running from great peril, such as from an angry bear.

Skyye had been hired on extremely short notice to play for the weekly Saturday night dance held at that venue, and it was during a smoke break at the event that Blanchard was smitten by the eternal mystery of love. The band that Skyye was replacing—Bonetraffic—had considered Skate to be their regular gig for over a year, but they were summarily dismissed when they attempted to renegotiate their wages by placing their employer in a tight spot. Specifically, they had called the owner of Skate at 11:00 a.m. on a Saturday morning to discuss an immediate increase in salary before they would agree to play at 9:00 p.m. that very night. Albert "Hazy" Hazeltine, owner and operator of Skate, had not responded well to this negotiation technique, both because he thought that the $100 per dance he was paying Bonetraffic was more than sufficient compensation for the noise they produced and because he didn't like anyone trying to jack him up.

Luckily for Skyye, skating rink owners are as clannish as they are cheap, and they tend to talk to one another about the many pressures inherent in the skating industry. Thus, after the firing of Bonetraffic, Hazy was sharing his labor woes with a friend who owned a roller rink over at Albertville, Alabama, one that, ironically, also did business under the name of Skate. During the course of that conversation, Hazy speculated that he might have to cancel his weekly dance that night—which he was loath to do since it was his big money maker—because he didn't have a band, and he doubted if his patrons would willingly pay the $3 cover charge to hear him play Frank Sinatra and Pat Boone records over the PA system. His colleague sympathized with Hazy and passed along to him the contact information for a group of boys known as Skyye, a local band from over at Sequoyah, Georgia, who had always done a good job in Albertville, boys who had their heads on straight and who wouldn't try to jack a man up, regardless of their collective need for a haircut. One phone call later, Skyye was the new house band at Skate. For the sum of $100 per week plus whatever tips they pocketed, they were to play for four hours each Saturday night, help sweep up after the dance, and, should the need arise, make an earnest attempt to subdue Bonetraffic if that group of unemployed musicians came around looking for trouble.

At the dance that night, Skyye's first set was met with great enthusiasm by the patrons of Skate. The skating rink was almost full, a nod both to the slowly expanding reputation of the band and to the lack of entertainment options in South Pittsburg and the surrounding vicinity. The boys played songs from their regular set list plus some new tunes they had learned recently, including "Heart of Gold" by Neil Young, and "Free Ride" by the Edgar Winter Group. After two solid hours of playing, Blanchard and the rest of the band took a break and stepped out back for a smoke and a beer, and it was during that interlude that Blanchard inadvertently met his bride-to-be.

"This is a sweet setup," Covey said as he lit a cherry Tiparillo and twisted the cap from a Schlitz Malt Liquor. "I thought it was pretty slick when they turned on the black light during 'In-A-Gadda-Da-Vida.'" The same lighting arrangements that made roller skating so enjoyable during the rest of the week—except Sundays, of course, when young folks needed to have their minds on the Lord rather than on their feet—seemed to work just fine for the dancers on Saturday nights. Hazy Hazeltine was a visual person and a jackleg electrician on top of that, and over time he had installed black lights, spot lights, strobe lights, sparkle lights, Christmas lights, and a mirrored disco ball for the enjoyment of his rolling customers, and he used these extensively and to great effect on Saturday nights as well.

"You could see who all had lint on their pants," Blanchard noted as he cracked open a can of Pabst Blue Ribbon. This was during the golden age of double-knit, a flexible fabric that liked to wear its wash history for all to see. Blanchard was a blue jean man himself, as were all of his bandmates, but he had nothing against people who wore double-knit and tried not to judge. Still, he wouldn't want his sister marrying one of them, for sure.

"You know what else you can see in black light?" Simpson Taggart asked. Simpson's main duties came before the show during setup and after the show for the load-out, and, in the case of Skate, for the sweep-up once all the revelers had gone home. During the actual show he was free to listen to the music, dance with any girls who would grant him that boon, and drink. Being a conscientious roadie, he took these additional duties as seriously as all his others, and he was pretty much smashed at present.

"What's that, Simpson?" asked Jimbo Tant. He had his pocket-knife out and was crafting a guitar pick from the Clorox jug he kept with his equipment for that purpose. It sat there, forlorn, on the tailgate of the truck, a white plastic vessel riddled with triangle-shaped holes. Being homeschooled on the guitar and a poor boy on top of

that, Jimbo had often found himself without a pick during his forma-
tive guitar years, but he had discovered that the resolution to this
chronic issue was as close as his mama's laundry room. His custom-
made picks were not quite as rigid as the genuine article, and, as a
result, he found that he did not play as well when he used a store-
bought pick.

"You can tell who hasn't brushed their teeth. Anyone with blue
teeth is guilty." Simpson took a sip from the fifth of Boone's Farm
Strawberry Hill he was nursing.

"Seriously, Simpson?" Tucker McFry asked. "You've had all the
babes in the place to yourself for the past two hours. I've had my eye
on you, and you've been working that floor hard. We even played
'Whiter Shade of Pale' to help you out. And now you're going to
stand there and tell me you've been looking at their *teeth*?" He,
Blanchard, and Covey all shook their heads. Sometimes, Simpson just
wasn't right.

"Good dental care is important," he said. No one cared to argue
that notion with Simpson, especially after he pointed out that his respect for proper tooth care came from his sainted mama, a kindly but
toothless woman who knew from personal experience the high price
ultimately paid by those who would not brush and floss on a regular
basis. The unspoken consensus among the group, however, was that
perhaps he was missing the bigger picture when it came to the ladies,
and that each and every one of the females at the dance had a delec-
table variety of better things to look at than teeth, blue or otherwise.

"Are you telling me that if a little sweet thing comes up to you
right now and wants you to go out to her car with her, you're going to
check her teeth?" Blanchard couldn't believe what he was hearing. He
could see that he was going to have to spend a little more time with
Simpson in the future, in hopes of getting him straightened out. The
boy clearly needed guidance.

As the members of Skyye kidded Simpson and otherwise enjoyed
their break, several people had wandered into their vicinity. There was
nothing in the least unusual in this behavior; even early in their career, they had come to realize that folks just liked to hang around the
band, and as far as Skyye was concerned, they were welcome to. Tonight's gathering of extras included a collection of rangy-looking boys

who had arrived as a group but had then spaced themselves casually here and there along the exterior wall of the skating rink. Blanchard's lifelong predisposition to observe people led him to notice that the tallest of the new arrivals had a tendency to squint, which, when combined with his dramatic overbite, lent him a striking resemblance to a squirrel. Blanchard's thoughts were that this was an unfortunate look for the boy, and he was extremely grateful that he himself didn't look like a rodent. Other than that fleeting thought, however, he really didn't give the newcomers much consideration. No one else in the band paid them much heed, either; they had been seeing unfamiliar faces all night, and these newest additions were just six more to add to the barrage of images they would have to categorize and catalog as their time in South Pittsburg expanded. They continued to discuss black lights, Simpson's priorities, and the secret meaning of blue teeth. Then, during a natural break in the conversation, one of the rangy-looking boys, the one Blanchard had checked out and mentally dubbed Squirrel, filled the lull with a question.

"Which one of you jokers is the leader of this outfit?" Squirrel asked this in a belligerent tone, as if his intent were not to elicit information at all. Blanchard looked at him and took a dislike to the boy that overshadowed his initial inclination to cut him some slack because he looked like a tree-climbing varmint. His aversion was understandable, perhaps, given Squirrel's provocative icebreaker. Blanchard tended to dislike people who pushed. They always made him want to push back. It was his way.

"Look, Covey," Blanchard said loudly, as if talking to a crowd of the hard-of-hearing. "A talking asshole." Despite the incendiary nature of his comment, Blanchard wasn't necessarily looking for trouble. He had experienced enough woe during his short life to instill in him a preference for traveling the high road when it was available. But the problem with the high road was that it was, well, *high*, and as such, it was difficult to get up there, and a large portion of the people he had met in his time didn't seem to think the view was worth the effort, and sometimes, frankly, Blanchard didn't think it was, either. Another thing Blanchard had learned along the way was that there are occasions when trouble just seems to seek a body out and won't have it any other way, and given Squirrel's lead-off inquiry, he thought this might be one of those times.

"I thought they were extinct," Covey replied, following Blanchard's lead. He casually placed his malt liquor can on the fender he rested against, freeing up his hands.

"I thought so too, but there you are." Blanchard gestured at Squirrel as if to indicate that no one was more surprised than he was to encounter a chatting sphincter.

"Maybe they're just endangered," Jimbo said. He had folded up his pocketknife and slipped it into his jeans next to his new pick, and he had tucked his curly brown hair behind his ears to get it out of his eyes, and he was now standing shoulder to shoulder with Covey, his bass player, where a good rhythm-guitar player belonged and could always be found, onstage or off. They stood there, backing up their lead player, as was their job and their custom.

"Did you just call me an asshole?" Squirrel asked Blanchard. Two of his buddies stood a bit straighter, as if preparing themselves for action, although they didn't appear enthusiastic about the prospect or optimistic concerning the outcome.

"I did," Blanchard admitted. "But to be fair, Covey did too."

"But you said it first," Covey said in reply, giving credit where it was due while nodding at Blanchard, beside whom Tucker, Ford Man, and Chicken had loosely arranged themselves. He turned and spoke directly to Squirrel. "Blanchard's got good instincts about people. Jimbo and me always just sort of agree with him on general principle."

"He's not too smart, is he?" Blanchard continued his observations to his bandmates, as if Squirrel were a hypothetical construct, a drawing on a chalkboard, perhaps, and not actually standing before them, clenching his fists and looking angry. "And damn sure not too pretty. What is with those teeth? Maybe we ought to take him inside and see if they turn blue. What do you think, Simpson? Blue or white?" Simpson Taggart looked confused, as if he knew the answer to this one, but he needed a minute or two to arrive at the correct response.

"Maybe I ought to kick your ass!" Squirrel said. He had gotten a little louder each time he had spoken, and now he took a step closer to Blanchard. Blanchard could tell that he was getting himself worked up into a fighting state, or at least making the attempt, but he could also tell that Squirrel didn't really want any. He wondered what this was about, anyway. Had Skyye played a song he didn't like? Had Blanchard missed a note or fumbled a chord? Was the pickup truck parked in the guy's reserved spot? Perhaps Blanchard looked like the guy who had run off with Squirrel's wife? Blanchard thought he had better ask before Squirrel got completely out of hand. He had had his fun, but if he kept nudging Squirrel, he'd have to fight him, and if he fought him and broke a knuckle or two on Squirrel's bony head, he'd have a hard time finishing up the second set. If he hurt his left hand, he couldn't grab a chord, and if he damaged his right hand, he couldn't hold a pick. It was a definite problem.

"Okay, I'll bite," Blanchard said. "Before you try to kick my ass, which is standing right here, by the way, if you just can't wait, what's the deal with you guys? What did we do to you? Why are you looking for trouble?"

"Are you deaf?" Squirrel asked. "I asked if you were the leader." Now three of Squirrel's buddies had eased forward until they stood by him. The other two still lounged against the corrugated wall of Skate, and Blanchard got the definite impression that their hearts, at least, weren't in this, which suited him just fine. If whatever was going on came to blows, perhaps those two would quietly head to the snack bar for some popcorn and an Icee.

"I hear just fine. Heard every word you've said. We're a democracy, Ace. We're all the boss. Well, except for Simpson. He's sort of the foreman."

"You sorry son-of-a-bitches took our gig!" There it was. Finally, it dawned on Blanchard who he was talking to, and now the scene playing out around him made a little more sense. Before him stood the members of the infamous Bonetraffic, former house band at Skate.

He took a few moments to retrieve a cigarette from his pack and slowly light it. Then he spoke. "Okay, I get it now. You guys are Bone Head."

"Bonetraffic!" Squirrel took another step toward Blanchard.

"Yeah. That," Blanchard said. He had truly forgotten their name, although to be fair, he hadn't tried all that hard to recollect it. "Not wanting to hurt your feelings or anything, but did anyone ever tell you guys that you have a really stupid name? I'm serious. Boner Traffic? Where did that come from?" He shook his head on behalf of garage bands everywhere, bearing his share of the burden on all of their shoulders. "Maybe after you learn a few more songs, you can do something about that name."

"Said the guy who's in a band called Skyye!" Squirrel said this with disdain.

Blanchard wanted to retort, but he had to admit that the guy had a point. He turned to Covey. "What did I tell you? What the hell did I tell you?" Covey shrugged, as if to convey that perhaps this was not the best of all possible times to discuss the extraneous y and the un-necessary e.

"Anyway," Squirrel said. "You heard what I said just fine! You stole our spot!" He stepped forward again, and as he reached his new line in the gravel, he jabbed at Blanchard's chest with his finger.

"We didn't steal your gig," Blanchard said as he caught Squirrel's hand midair, before his finger had the opportunity to make contact. "And if you want to keep this," he said, "you better put it in your pocket and leave it there. Poke it at me again and you'll be the only one-handed guitar player in Tennessee." Blanchard released the hand, and it dropped to Squirrel's side but did not burrow into his pocket as had been suggested. "I hate to break it to you boys," Blanchard continued, "but you were long gone before Hazy ever thought about call-ing us. We didn't have a thing to do with it. We hadn't even heard of this place until Hazy called and offered us a job. I feel sorry for you, though. I really do. When he called me, Hazy told me how bad you guys suck, and I would truly hate to suck. He told me that he really felt bad about cutting you loose, but he had to do something. You were killing his business. It could be that you're trying too hard. I've seen it happen before. Or maybe you just need to turn the old amps down a little, you know, because louder is not always better. You might work on some easier songs. Have you ever tried 'Secret Agent Man' by Johnny Rivers? It only has about five chords in the whole song! Nothing fancy about any of them. You could probably pick that one right up." He took a final drag from his smoke and casually flipped it. The butt bounced off Squirrel's chest and dropped to the gravel, smoldering.

"Screw you," Squirrel said, brushing an ember from his shirt. "We're a better band than you'll ever be. He fired us because of money. I know he had you lined up before he fired us."

"Oh, he's cheap, for sure," Blanchard said. "$500 a week is not enough for a gig like this. We tried to get $600 out of him, but he just wouldn't budge. We all talked it over, though, and decided we'd go ahead and start low and then work our way up to a decent salary." Covey, Ford Man, and Chicken all nodded their heads. Jimbo grinned and shook his. Simpson looked confused. The last he'd heard, they were working for $100 and had to sweep up after.

"I don't believe you," Squirrel said.

"I don't care," Blanchard replied, and it was the truth. He was tired of Squirrel and was ready to move past him, or over him if that was how it shook out. The choices as he saw them were that Skyye went back to work playing the dance—and it was getting to be about that time—or that Skyye whipped Bonetraffic's ass in its entirety and then went back to work playing the dance. It was time for Squirrel to make the choice. This was his scenario, and, according to the sacred law of the parking lot, it was his call. Blanchard actually preferred the latter option, truth be told, but that was just him. He had enough of Edna in him to make him relish a little dustup when circumstances dictated, but he realized that there were others' feelings on the matter to consider, and he was willing to let the majority rule. It was the American way.

"They really didn't take your job, you know," said an unidentified female voice. Blanchard looked to his left and saw the speaker. He was amazed that he hadn't noticed her before. She was a tall, blond girl, nearly as tall as he was, wearing blue jeans, a denim shirt, and boots. He liked what he saw. "You guys fired yourselves. Hazy didn't find these new boys until after."

"How would you know that?" Squirrel asked.

"I know because he's my daddy, and I was sitting right there writing out the bills when you called him." That bit of news seemed to take the lead right out of Bonetraffic's pencil. The nonspeaking members of the ensemble all looked at Squirrel as if trying to discern their next move, but he seemed momentarily dumbstruck.

"There you go, Slick," Blanchard offered. "I told you we didn't have anything to do with it." Squirrel looked like he might be considering making an additional run at trying to get something started, but his bandmates had not seemed all that intent upon defending the group's honor to begin with, and once it became clear that their current state of employment was self-induced, their interest visibly declined. They sort of sank into themselves, and one after another they began to drift away like tumbleweeds before a light breeze.

"I'll see you after the dance!" Squirrel threatened as he, too, began to slink away.

"I'll be right here," Blanchard assured him. "You can help us load up."

"Asshole," Squirrel offered as a parting thought.

"Pretty much all the time," Blanchard agreed. Covey and Jimbo nodded as well. There was no use in denying an obvious truth. Blanchard turned his attention to the tall young woman standing next to him. Her hair was long, parted in the middle, and braided behind. She wore a pair of eyeglasses that served to magnify the brown eyes behind the lenses. She had nice curves and pretty, white teeth. Her face was scattered with freckles, and Blanchard liked that. He was also fascinated by her nose. It had a bit of an upturn, and he liked upturned noses even more than he liked freckles. He held out his hand to shake hers. "Blanchard Shankles," he said, smiling.

"I'm Andy," she replied, taking his hand.

"That's a cool name for a girl." This wasn't the smoothest banter ever uttered, but Blanchard was a bit tongue-tied at that moment and was doing the best he could.

"Well, actually it's Andrea Joy Hazeltine, but everyone calls me Andy."

"I like it."

"I thought you were going to fight those other boys."

"I thought we were too. Kind of surprised we didn't have to. That one guy who was doing all the talking was pretty mad until you straightened him out. I think he really wanted to scuffle, and I guess he would have had a reason to if we had taken their gig. But we didn't. Is Hazy really your daddy?" Blanchard couldn't see any resemblance at all and figured that Andy must take after her mama.

"All my life." She smiled, and when she did, Blanchard was willing to bet tonight's paycheck that her teeth would not turn blue under a black light.

"These are the boys," he said. "That skinny one there with the long black hair is Ford Man Cooper. He's our drummer." Ford Man smiled, nodded, and twirled one of his sticks. He always had a pair with him, usually stuck in a back pocket, as if he might be called upon to play at unforeseen moments and didn't want to be caught short. "That's Jimbo Tant. He plays guitar." Jimbo shot Andy a quick peace sign. "This is John Covey. He's our bass player." Covey nodded and smiled.

"Call me Covey," he said. He took her hand and shook it.

"This is Chicken Raines. He's our singer and our everything-else guy. If you heard our first set, he played the harmonica on 'Heart of Gold.'" Chicken, always the gentleman, gave her a small bow. "That guy over there with the afro is Tucker McFry. He's our keyboard man." Tucker waved. "That last guy there is Simpson Taggart. He's our sound man and roadie." Simpson had plopped down on the gravel and was trying to roll a joint. The intensity of the preceding several minutes had increased his stress level to a point not manageable by Boone's Farm wine alone, and he was so busy at his task that he did not acknowledge the introduction or the pretty girl it was meant for.

"And you play guitar, too," Andy said to Blanchard. He nodded. She started to speak, then hesitated, then went ahead. "Would you have really fought those boys?"

"Well, that was kind of up to them. I was just trying to have a beer."

"I mean if they had started it."

"Maybe. Probably. Yeah."

"You're what my daddy calls rough boys," she said.

"I don't know about that. But we do come from rough country. Where I come from, when we have a battle of the bands, there are real weapons."

"You're kidding."

"Yeah. I'm just messing around," Blanchard said. He was kidding, but only just. The members of Skyye—sometimes individually and other times as a group—had found themselves rolling around in more than one parking lot during their time together, and Blanchard expected that they would do so again. It seemed to be part of the career path they had chosen. "Do you come to the dance a lot?" he asked Andy.

"I'm here every week," she said. "Heck, I'm usually here every day. Me and my sisters sell tickets and run the snack bar. It's a family business. I've been here tonight since we opened. I saw you set up and heard you play." She pointed at Simpson, still busy with his roll. "I danced with him once, but he kept staring at my teeth, and it sort of creeped me out." Blanchard nodded. He understood the feeling. "I came out here to tell you how much I enjoyed the first half. You guys are really good. Much better than Bonetraffic was, or the band we had before them." Most of the band hung their heads at this compliment. The unexpected praise from a pretty girl in a Tennessee parking lot threatened to overwhelm them. Then the lights in the parking lot switched off and on three times. "That's Daddy's signal," Andy said. "It means it's time to start playing again. He does the same thing at home when I've been on a date and I'm sitting in the driveway in some boy's car." Blanchard noticed that many members of the small crowd they had attracted had stirred themselves and began to ease toward the door. Hazy ran a tight rink, and even the customers came running when summoned.

"Will I see you after the dance?" Blanchard asked.

"During, after, and next week besides. Like I said, I work here."

"Me, too. Maybe you can keep an eye out for Bonetraffic for us."

She looked at him and smiled. Then she leaned in and gave him a kiss. "Bonetraffic is the least of your worries," she said, heading to the snack bar. Blanchard reached up and touched his lips where they had met hers.

"The guitar players always get the women," Ford Man said. "It's like a law or something."

"I'm a guitar player!" Jimbo protested. "When is it my turn?"

"I can't believe I was going to be the one who had to whip Bonetraffic, but you get the girl," Chicken said. "How is that fair?"

"He'll be up all night writing love songs now," Tucker said.

"And I'll have to be up with him, because he can't write one without me," Covey said.

"Anybody got a light?" Simpson asked, holding up his joint.

"Let's go to work," Blanchard said. "We keep standing out here, and Hazy will hire Bonetraffic back. I'd hate to get replaced by those guys."

"DON'T MAKE IT SO"
(Blanchard Shankles/John Covey)

On a sleepy silk night in a long-past June
'Neath the Tennessee stars and the Tennessee moon
When our hands first touched and our lips first met
You said you'd never leave and it ain't never yet

You tell me you're my woman till you're blue in the face
You say you'll stay forever till you leave without a trace
You talk about tomorrow and wrap it pretty with a bow
You tell me that you love me but that don't make it so

We stood before the preacher and we both said that we did
We bought ourselves a house and we had ourselves a kid
We talked about the future and the dreams we planted there
We planned it all so carefully and we didn't have a care

You tell me you're my woman till you're blue in the face
You say you'll stay forever till you leave without a trace
You talk about tomorrow and wrap it pretty with a bow
You tell me that you love me but that don't make it so

It was a bitter March day, snow six inches on the ground
When I lost the life I had and took up the one I found
You told me it was over, and you gave me back your ring
We let it slip away and I don't care about a thing

You tell me you're my woman till you're blue in the face
You say you'll stay forever till you leave without a trace
You talk about tomorrow and wrap it pretty with a bow
You tell me that you love me but that don't make it so

"Our House"
Crosby, Stills, Nash, and Young
-Friday: Sixth Day-

Blanchard sat on his front porch in his favorite of the venerable rockers that had been constants in his life. He rocked slowly as he watched the sky blend from black to gray, on its journey from night to day. Once the sky became light, his birds began to fly in for breakfast. They weren't actually his, but he thought of them as such. He had over the years hung several bird feeders from the lower branches of the old oak tree that grew adjacent to the house, and his flock of regulars had grown sizeable with the passing of time. The first feeder had been hung not long after Edna was hauled away in the back seat of a police cruiser, never to return. He had installed it as his way of making amends for all the birds and other small critters she had sacrificed to the gods of pandemonium. It was an attempt on his part to settle the sizeable karmic debt that his family had incurred, and that he felt needed to be repaid. At first he had had no takers, as if the word had spread among the avian world that the Shankles family was to be avoided unless one wished to learn to fly with a kitchen nailed to one's back. But Blanchard had been patient, and the irresistible tastiness of birdseed combined with the shortness of birds' racial memories had eventually worn down the feathered resistance.

His stuffed bear rested casually in his lap, currently off duty but ever vigilant should the need for assistance arise. Inside on the sofa, Simpson snored gently. He had spent a long night tending to Blanchard's needs, and his fatigue combined with the herbal remedy he had smoked just before lying down promised to keep him sleeping for at least the near future. Beside Blanchard on the porch sat his hound dog, Scrounge. He had acquired Scrounge one night about fifteen years previously from a dumpster behind a tavern in Carrollton, Georgia, that did business under the optimistic but misleading appellation of the Cadillac Club. The name of the establishment implied a top-of-the-line, luxurious quality that the reality of the place did not deliver, but Scrounge had been a pretty good dog nonetheless and could not help what bar he had been abandoned near. Blanchard reached down to scratch his dog between his nicked and floppy ears, and Scrounge growled in his sleep as a gentle reminder that, unlike his owner, he was not an early riser even though he was a loyal hound who knew that his place was beside his master, regardless of his state of wakefulness. In his younger years, Scrounge had sometimes toured with the band and occasionally put in guest appearances up on the platform, where he would flop down center stage with his front paws over his ears while checking the crowd for potential menace. At one point in the band's history, they had added "Hound Dog" by Elvis Presley to the set list, and Covey, who had a way with animals, had taught Scrounge to howl during the chorus, right after the line that went *You ain't never caught a rabbit and you ain't no friend of mine.* It was a crowd-pleaser, for sure, and the high point of the canine's entertainment career, but as the unkind dog years had subsequently stacked upon him like pallets of bricks, Scrounge's world had shrunk to the confines of the porch, the front yard, the food dish, and his bed.

"Wake up, you old, fat dog," Blanchard said quietly, but Scrounge snorted, put one paw over an eye, and settled deeper into his nap. Blanchard shook his head and scratched the dog's ears again. "Man's best friend." Scrounge whimpered. His right leg began to run in its sleep, on the road once again, perhaps, hard on the trail of that elusive mistress, fame.

Blanchard was very tired, and his chest was sore, a condition that arose from the combination of the staples that held it together, the coughing fits that he continued to have, and the strain he had placed on the recently repaired hole in his torso by riding five hours in Covey's car the previous day. But on the bright side, it had been two days since he had experienced any actual heart pain, and he considered that to be a good omen, a sign that perhaps he truly was on the mend. Still, overall, he felt worse this morning than he had the day before his long ride home, and in truth, he felt worse than he had before allegedly being repaired. That seemed wrong to him, somehow. Where he came from, different people had specific functions at which they were supposed to be experts. Thus pilots were skilled at keeping aircraft aloft and passengers alive, musicians such as himself were trained to make people forget their troubles and tap their toes, and doctors were supposed to make their patients feel better. His doctor had made him feel worse, and that seemed counterintuitive to Blanchard, like being thirstier after a drink of cold, clear water than before. Had he been the type of person to second-guess himself, he might have wondered at the wisdom of his decision to leave the hospital before receiving permission to do so. But he wasn't, so he didn't. In his worldview, whatever happened would happen because it was bound to, and there wasn't much to be done about that but survive if he could, and go out with a little bit of class if he couldn't.

He felt like he needed to sleep, was desperate for it in fact, but every time he assumed a horizontal position, he began to cough, and when the hacking began, no matter how tightly he hugged the bear, he still felt as if he were about to split in two. During one particularly dramatic bout of coughing overnight, Blanchard had been unable to locate the bear in the darkness, and once the spell finally passed, he was not particularly surprised to discover that he had developed a definite click in his sternum. He had been warned, after all, about going easy on his breastbone. This was the point at which Simpson had rolled Blanchard a joint, but even that tried-and-true method of pain control had proven ineffective, because every time Blanchard attempted to take a hit, the coughing returned with a vengeance. Finally, Simpson, ever the innovator, had tucked a pinch of dope between Blanchard's cheek and gum, like a discrete dip of snuff.

"Where am I supposed to spit?" Blanchard had asked.

"Don't spit. Swallow." This low-tech approach had finally eased Blanchard's ills to the point where he was able to drift off for a few fitful hours of sleep.

The trip home had been unremarkable. Blanchard was not sure what he had expected, but he was surprised at the lack of resistance to his leaving the hospital; he and Covey had walked out of there without so much as a goodbye from anyone on staff. He supposed he had expected the exercise to resemble an escape of some type, complete with alarms blaring and lights flashing, silenced pistols spitting with nine-millimeter finality, watch caps pulled down low, faces darkened with charcoal, and low-running as they zigzagged down the halls. As it turned out, they more or less just walked out of the place. The only people who had even noticed his departure were his new roommate, Dude, and his amorous unnamed companion, and Blanchard figured they had probably gotten right back to business soon after he and Covey shuffled by and had by now forgotten all about them. In retrospect, Blanchard realized he was being terribly unfair, but he just hadn't taken to Dude, and he secretly hoped that the mean nurse, the one who had relieved him of his backup pack of smokes during his hospital admission, had also taken the time to confiscate Dude's no-doubt impressive supply of condoms. It was the least she could do.

"I need a smoke," Blanchard had said as soon as they completed their journey from his hospital room to Covey's car, a trip that took thirty minutes rather than the ten or so that it would have taken if Blanchard had been hale. During the long shuffle, they had stopped to rest in the hall, at the elevator, and again in the lobby, where Covey left Blanchard slumped in a chair trying not to look like an escaping patient while he went to fetch his car. Blanchard's breathing was fine, but his legs were still recovering from being temporarily dead a few days back, and they did not seem to want to hold him up with their former reliability.

"I don't have any cigarettes," Covey had replied, truthfully. He had suspected that this particular topic might be high on Blanchard's to-do list, and in anticipation of that, while retrieving the car from the parking deck he threw away the pack that had been resting in his shirt pocket all morning. It was his hope to deliver Blanchard to his home alive, and he believed that not allowing him to smoke on the way to their destination might help him achieve that goal, although, since he was dealing with Blanchard Shankles and knew more about him than any living human, that result was neither guaranteed nor likely regardless of what methods he employed to bring it about. Still, since he was involuntarily complicit but complicit nonetheless in Blanchard's bid for independence, he felt that it was his responsibility to seek the most positive outcome.

"What? You always have cigarettes. You were born with them."

"Well, I don't have any now," Covey said defensively.

"Do you need a note from your mama to get some?" Blanchard asked. He was reminded of his high school days, where it had been a rule that a note from home was required before a student was allowed to go up behind the gym to smoke during break time. He had made quite a bit of pocket money in those days due to his ability to forge believable documents of this nature, and he was willing to backslide into his former trade as counterfeiter if that proved necessary. "Stop and get some! I haven't had a smoke in five days, and one of the reasons I just broke out of the hospital was to have a cigarette. Hell, it's the main reason! I'm about to die for one." Blanchard's diatribe winded him, and he had to grab his bear while he coughed awhile and composed himself. "Now look what you did," he croaked.

"You just about died because of bad habits, including cigarettes. Now that you've got five days of clean living under your belt, why don't you just go ahead and quit? They say five days is the magic number, so the worst of it is behind you. The nicotine is out of your system now, and some of this coughing you've been doing is just your lungs saying thank you."

Blanchard looked at Covey as if he were speaking Latin. Noise was coming out of his mouth, but they were just random sounds that didn't make any sense. "Thank you, Dr. Covey," he said. "I want a cigarette. Don't make me have to rough you up."

"You and the bear?"

Thus, at Blanchard's insistent request, Covey had made three stops after they gained access to the car, and none of these side trips lent themselves to the normally accepted conventions of cardiac rehabilitation. The first, in Murfreesboro, Tennessee, had been for cigarettes. Covey still thought this a bad idea in the extreme and had continued resisting the request for the first thirty minutes of their getaway with all the arguments at his disposal, but his guitar player was not to be denied and had nagged at him like a lingering toothache. By this point, Covey had already developed a headache, so he pulled off the interstate at a truck stop and bought a pack.

"Ultra-lights?" Blanchard asked when Covey returned to the car. "You bought me a pack of ultra-lights? I'll have to hold it up and check to see if the end is glowing to know if it's lit." He shook his head, incredulous at Covey's choice. "I'm too old for clean living. It'll kill me!"

"Take it or leave it," Covey had responded. "That's all I'm buying you."

"I'll just go get my own."

"You'll walk home from here if you do."

Blanchard glared at his friend, but he took the cigarettes. He continued to glare as he opened the pack and lit up, and he continued to complain until a coughing spell forced him to hug his bear and hush. "I told you it was a bad idea," Covey said as the car accelerated up the ramp to the interstate.

"Shut...up," Blanchard replied as he regained his breath. Covey thought they might be out of the woods then, and that maybe Blanchard would behave for the remainder of their journey back to Georgia. But he was incorrect. Their next stop was about an hour up the road, when Blanchard decided that nothing went better with an ultra-light cigarette than a sip of good whiskey. Covey would have been the first to acknowledge that a taste of aged bourbon from time to time was one of the subtle pleasures that made life worth living, but he thought it was a bad idea at that particular moment due to Blanchard's circumstances, so again he tried to deflect his friend.

"You remember that list of things you aren't supposed to do for a pretty good while after heart surgery because they might kill you dead on the spot if you do? Bourbon and cigarettes are both on there, you know. Way up near the top, like they're important. So is sex, if that's what you plan on stopping for next." They weren't too far from a truck stop they both knew at which feminine companionship could be rented by the day, by the hour, or even by the half-hour if the driver was behind schedule and on a budget.

"I didn't read it." As far as Blanchard was concerned, if he hadn't read the list, then it didn't apply to him. What he didn't know couldn't hurt him.

"Lucky for you, I did. I read that sucker twice, because I knew you weren't going to and one of us needs to know this stuff. You know you've still got morphine in your system, right? Liquor and morphine don't mix. Each one of them kind of supercharges the oth-er. If I buy you some booze, and you die, how do you think I'll feel?"

"I don't know how you'll feel, but I'll feel great."

"I don't want to live out my life feeling bad because I bought you some whiskey and you killed yourself."

"If I jump out of this car and roll to my death down that embankment over there because you suck, will you feel any better?" Blanchard was being argumentative, but he really wanted a drink. He supposed it was the nicotine talking, or maybe morphine withdrawal. His vices were lonely and wanted company.

"I might," Covey responded, but he knew a lost cause when he saw one, and he was looking at one now. So he again pulled off the interstate, found a liquor store, and purchased a half-pint of Jack Daniels, just a little welcome-home present for the recovering heart patient in his care.

"A half-pint?" Blanchard asked. "Really? All a half-pint will do is piss my alcoholism off." He again shook his head. "I wish one of my *real* friends had busted me out of the hospital. I'd be looking at a fifth right now. Maybe a half-gallon."

"Hand it here if you don't want it," Covey said, reaching for the bottle. "I could use a drink anyway."

"If you want to hang on to that hand, put it on the steering wheel where I can see it and keep it away from my bourbon." Blanchard cracked the seal and took a sniff. "At least you didn't buy ultra-light bourbon. I'll give you that."

Covey sighed. "How about handing me one of those cigarettes?"

"Sorry. I've only got this one pack, and I don't want to run short."

Despite Blanchard's fears that a half-pint wouldn't be enough to achieve the state of inner peace he desired, three small sips produced in him a deep and restful sleep, and Covey found himself driving down I-24 listening to Blanchard's occasional snore, punctuated by an intermittent cough and a random mumble. While he drove, Covey fished his cell phone from his pocket and gave his wife, Anna, a call.

"Hello?"

"Hey, girl. It's me. Just letting you know I'm on my way home."

"I wasn't expecting you until tomorrow or maybe the day after! Did they let Blanchard come home?"

"Not exactly." Covey went on to explain the informal nature of Blanchard's release. When he finished, there was a long pause. Finally, after several silent seconds had dragged by, Anna spoke with a tone she generally reserved for use when she was displeased.

"You broke Blanchard out of the hospital." It wasn't a question.

"Well, yeah, I guess if you want to put it that way."

"And then as sick as he is, you bought him cigarettes and whiskey." Covey was beginning to understand that Anna was not only unhappy with recent developments but mightily so, and that she wasn't fully supportive of the plan currently in motion.

"When you say it like that, it makes it sound—"

"What, John? Makes it sound what? Foolish? Juvenile? Irresponsible? Crazy? Stop me when I hit one you like."

"I don't like any of those. It wasn't like that, Anna. He was leaving whether I helped him or not. He had made up his mind. Once he makes up his mind about something, you know how he is. He's going to do what he's going to do."

"Oh, I know just how he is. And I know how you are too, John Covey. I swear, when the two of you get off together, it's like you're both still seventeen, just two wild boys looking for all the trouble you can find. There's not an ounce of sense between you. Not one ounce! Maybe you should stop at a road house on the way in and see if you can't get into a little brawl."

"Don't be mad." Of all the things that Covey disliked, an old man's list that seemed to grow a bit longer as each year passed, Anna's annoyance was and had always been at the very top. She was quiet again for a moment. Then Covey heard a deep breath come over the phone, all the way from Sequoyah, Georgia.

"Okay. I'm not mad. Not much, anyway, and I'll get over it. If anyone knows that Blanchard Shankles is going to do exactly what he wants to do and nothing else, it's me, I guess."

"I did try to talk him out of it."

"I know you did. To be honest, I'm surprised you kept him there long enough to get the surgery done. He is such a willful man. So stubborn. Well, let me get busy. I need to get some groceries in his house and try to find someone to stay with him for a day or two. Maybe we can keep him from killing himself long enough to heal."

"See if one of the boys is up for it," Covey suggested. "Simpson might be able to stay for a few days. If not, I'll see if I can cover it."

All the members of the band had day jobs of one sort or another, but most of these were flexible. Blanchard dabbled in antiques and junk, a trade he had learned from Major many years back. Covey worked on cars when he wasn't tinkering with the bus, and he was such a good mechanic that there was always another vehicle or two lined up in his driveway waiting for his attention. Ford Man Cooper was a minister of the Gospel. He didn't have a church, per se, but he preached on the side at revivals and such and did so with such fervor that the love offerings were always substantial. Jimbo Tant hauled pulpwood for his brother, $100 per load to pull long logs from all over north Georgia to the paper mill over at Rome. Tucker McFry was an adjunct professor of psychology who taught online courses when he wasn't playing his Leslie. He claimed that being a member of the band had first piqued his interest in the discipline, and that his academic emphasis on abnormal psychology had always been useful when dealing with his bandmates. Chicken Raines was in the poultry business. He had inherited Rooster's three chicken houses when the elder Raines crossed the road, and he had added an additional two houses to his holdings since that time. Simpson Taggart grew and sold marijuana for a living, and in spite of his tendency to smoke up a fair portion of the stock, he still did all right.

"Uh-uh. You've got five cars to work on when you get home. It looks like a car lot out there in the yard, and half the people in town are on foot until you get back and go to work. I might just stay with him myself."

"Blanchard will love that."

"Do I care what Blanchard loves right now? Have I ever?"

"I guess maybe you don't."

"That man can just get over himself. The sun doesn't rise and set on Blanchard Shankles."

"Don't tell him that," Covey said. "What does the band's schedule look like? We got anything lined up?" In addition to being the wife of the greatest living undiscovered Southern bass player, Anna Covey had—since not long after her marriage to Covey—always handled the bookings and the accounting for the various incarnations of the band: first Skyye, then Sawmill Gravy, and finally Murphy's Law. She had a head for details and was a good negotiator, and as such she had been more than a little instrumental in keeping the boys successfully engaged in not losing all their money while playing their songs. Covey liked to kid her that her main appeal was that she worked for room, board, and the occasional romp between the sheets. Her perennial reply to that comment was that *one* of them did, anyway.

"You have next Friday and Saturday at the County Line over near Scottsboro." Of all the many establishments named the County Line that they had played at over the years, the one near Scottsboro was the band's favorite. The beer was painfully cold, the bikers were generally friendly if you didn't poke at them too much, and the proprietor was married to a woman named Carmen who made the best pork barbeque in northern Alabama.

"Maybe we should cancel it," Covey said.

"Why not let Jimbo play lead and put Chicken on rhythm? You'll still have a good, full sound." The County Line was a smallish club with low ceilings, and as such, it was possible to play at lower volumes.

"We could do that, I guess. Blanchard will be pissed if we play without him, but he'll just have to be pissed. It'll be awhile before he can stand up long enough to do a show. I'll bring him a couple of Carmen's barbeques, and maybe he won't fuss too much."

"*Those* will be good for his heart."

"They'll be better for his heart than the fit he'll pitch if I don't bring them."

"You might be right," Anna said. "He does like those barbeques."

"He likes Carmen, too, but I guess I better leave her in Scottsboro."

"I think that's the best plan." Carmen's husband, Knuckles, had been a biker for many rough years before retiring to the marginally more sedate lifestyle afforded him by running a biker bar in rural Alabama. His nickname stemmed from the fact that he had ten huge knuckles, each with the approximate molecular density of mountain granite, and he tended to use eight of them fairly regularly, especially when he spied anyone looking at his wife. "Knuckles would kill him."

"Dead as disco," Covey agreed.

"All right. That's what we'll do, then. You boys shift around a little, we leave Carmen in Scottsboro, and Blanchard can just act like an adult for a change. I'll get word to Jimbo and Chicken and let them know what the plan is. Do you all need to get together to run through the set list with the new lineup?"

"Wouldn't hurt."

"I'll mention that, too. You drive safe. Don't let Blanchard talk you into going skydiving or anything."

"You're not as funny as you think you are."

"Yes I am. Love you." Anna clicked off, and Covey continued to make his way to Georgia.

Blanchard had slept for about an hour, but as they were coming into Chattanooga, he began to rouse. He stretched, and coughed, and yawned, and coughed some more. Then he looked out the side window, chuckled, and spoke in a gravelly voice. "Now there's a guy who is having a really bad day."

"What guy?" Covey asked. Blanchard nodded to their right, and Covey noticed for the first time that he was passing a tow truck pulling what appeared to be a loaded hearse. They could see the casket through the back glass, black, solemn, and flower-draped. The shiny brass handles flashed as they caught the sun as if signaling for roadside assistance. "Yeah, I see what you mean." Covey nodded. "Bad, bad day."

"Maybe the worse day ever," Blanchard said. He was grinning. "You know you have really ticked God off when the hearse breaks down while they're hauling you to the bone yard. This dude must have been a real piece of work. He's probably a Nazi who married his sister or something like that." It really wasn't that funny, but something about being towed to the grave tickled Blanchard. It was one of those situations that sounded made up because it was too implausible to be real.

"Maybe he owned the towing company and made a ton of money with it. Maybe having one of the trucks drag him that last mile was his final wish."

"Nah, Covey. Don't ruin it! I don't want that to be what happened. Work with me, here. I want it to be that the hearse broke down with a dead guy in it. That's what this has to be. We ought to write a song about this! Hold on! The words are coming to me now. Check this verse out: *I was minding my own business just rolling down the road. When the steam shot up and the engine blew. The driver called the shop and they slapped me on the hook. And they dragged me that last mile while the fenders shook.* Huh? What do you think?"

"I think it needs a little work."

"That's where you come in. You're the finishing-touch man in this outfit. You reckon everyone else is already over at the cemetery, wondering where this guy is?" Blanchard chuckled. "You just know his old lady is pissed. I bet she's looking at her watch, and maybe tapping her foot, fussing to her sister or her mama because the guy was late for everything his whole life, and here he goes being late one last time. And the preacher's all like, 'I have a wedding at 2:00.' And the gravediggers are wondering if the boss is going to try to screw them out of overtime. Hey! Fall in behind them, Covey, and let's go to the funeral."

"No. It wouldn't be right."

"You know what your trouble is? You don't know how to have fun."

"Going to a stranger's funeral is not fun. It's disrespectful."

"How can we disrespect someone we don't even know?" Blanchard asked. "Anyway, the funeral's not the fun part. It's the situation." Blanchard fell silent, and Covey thought that perhaps he had fallen back asleep. He eased on past the tow truck and the hearse and began to pull away. After they passed the next exit, Covey could see in the rearview mirror that the combination of sorrow took the exit ramp, on the way to the garage, perhaps, or to the great hereafter, depending on which was closer to the freeway. They drove on a couple of miles before Blanchard spoke again.

"Chili," he said.

"What? Are you cold? I can turn on some heat." He reached for the temperature control.

"No. I want some chili."

"Cigarettes, bourbon, and now chili. Why don't I just shoot you and be done? There's a pistol over there in the glove box. Hand it to me and we'll get this over with."

"Come on, Covey. Just one bowl. It's supposed to be good for you."

"Chili is not good for you."

"Well, I have a taste for it. Those biscuits you bought me this morning made me remember how much I like decent food."

"I promised Anna we wouldn't stop anymore."

"You talked to Anna?" Covey nodded. "Is she happy we're coming home?"

"Happy is not the word."

"All right then! Good old Anna. You've got you a good one there, Covey. You count your blessings, boy. Now how about we celebrate with that chili?"

"Sure," Covey said. They were only an hour from home. He had almost made it. "Why not?" Covey drove past a couple of exits until he spotted a sign for a family-style restaurant that might have chili on its bill of fare. He took the next ramp and navigated through a couple of red lights to get to the diner. They parked, and Blanchard opened his door. "Why don't you let me go in and get it to go?" Covey asked. "You just sit there and rest."

"You can't get it to go because you can't eat chili in the car." Blanchard didn't like to fuss much, but sometimes Covey could be a bit thick. Chili needed a crockery bowl, and a saucer under that, and some oyster crackers stirred up in it, and some cheddar cheese sprinkled over the top, and a dash or two of Louisiana hot sauce to finish it all up. It was much too complicated a dish to eat out of a Styrofoam cup in a vehicle, and a grown man like Covey should have known this. He slowly placed one foot onto the pavement of the parking lot, and then the other. Covey came around to Blanchard's side, helped him stand, and supported him as they made their slow way into the diner. There was plenty of seating available. In fact, the place was empty except for a little girl sitting in a booth, eating French fries while reading a book. Blanchard preferred booths himself, but he wasn't sure he could get in and out of one in his present condition, so they found a table by one of the front windows and sat. They had only been there a moment when a young lady came to their table with menus and a smile.

"I hope you have chili," Blanchard said, waving his away. He looked at their server and smiled in return. He had always believed that one of the finer pleasures in the world was flirting with waitresses. It was a small thing, he knew, but it didn't hurt a soul, and it made him happy, much happier than flirting with nurses, perhaps because he was wearing pants.

"Do we have chili?" she asked. "Between you and me, we have the best chili in town." She looked to be thirty or so, with short black hair and an open, friendly face. Her name pin announced that she was Marianna.

"Is that true, or do they just make you say it?"

"Both. They make me say it, but it is true."

"How do you know?"

"I spend my off days going to other restaurants in town, trying theirs out."

"Is *that* true?"

"No," she admitted. "That's not true. But we do have really good chili."

"That is just what I wanted to hear you say. Bring me a big bowl, with some oyster crackers, and plenty of cheese on top. Oh, and I want a side of Texas toast. Real buttery, and maybe just a little bit burned on one side. And a Coke with lots of ice." Marianna wrote down the order and turned to Covey.

"And for you?"

"I just want a cup of coffee," he said.

She nodded and headed back to the counter. They sat waiting for their orders. Covey gazed out the window at Lookout Mountain in the distance. Low clouds hid the top, as was their habit. The short way home was up that mountain and through those clouds, but that would make for foggy driving at dusk, so he decided to stick to the valley and go the long way around. Blanchard watched the little girl who sat a few booths over from them. She was intent upon her book—a school book, from the looks of the cover—and as she read, she occasionally reached absentmindedly for a French fry. As he watched, he realized that the young scholar was the spitting image of their waitress, Marianna.

In a few minutes, their order arrived. Marianna placed Covey's coffee before him, then served a bowl of the alleged best chili in town plus accoutrements to Blanchard. Covey loaded his mug with sugar, stirred, and took a sip of his coffee as he watched Blanchard dose his steaming bowl of chili with hot sauce, then blend it with his spoon so the cheese melted and the oyster crackers he had scattered over the top were all coated.

"Blow on it so you don't burn your lips," Covey said.

"I know how to eat chili," Blanchard said. He took a small bite and followed it with a sip of his Coke. Then he placed his spoon on the table and looked at Marianna. "Good chili," he said.

She nodded. "I told you," she said.

"I bet that's your little girl," he continued, gesturing toward the booth.

"It is! How did you know?"

"She looks like you. I mean, she looks like you probably looked back when you were a little girl. Is she a good student?"

Marianna smiled. "She makes all As. I'm very proud of her."

"I'm guessing she likes hanging out here with her mama." He took another small bite.

"She likes the French fry part, anyway. I don't get off work until six, so the bus drops her here every day after school. If she gets her homework done, I let her play the jukebox. She likes that part, too."

"That would make me do my homework," Covey said. "If my mama had fed me French fries and let me play the jukebox, there's no telling how far I would have gone."

"Sometimes it gets her to do hers," Marianna responded. "But I have to check, because sometimes she fibs a bit. Especially when it's arithmetic." She picked up tray and headed to greet a group of patrons who had just entered the establishment.

"I like her," Blanchard noted. He tore off a bite of Texas toast and dipped it in his chili. Then he slipped the morsel into his mouth and slowly chewed.

"You like all women," Covey replied. "It's your greatest strength and your biggest weakness."

"I can't help it if most men are shitheads." To his credit, Blanchard harbored few illusions about his own overall worthiness as a member of the gender and included himself in that group of males with whom he did not care to associate.

"I suppose not."

"I'm giving you a pass, by the way. Usually, you're not one."

"You think not?"

"Don't let it go to your head. Did you notice that she's not wearing a ring?"

"Forget it, Blanchard. I'm not driving you two plus the little girl on a date. As soon as you finish your chili, we're going home."

"No. What I meant was that she's a single mother, raising that pretty little girl without any help." Blanchard had decided upon this version of reality early in the ordering process. It was why—unless Marianna for some reason came back from the kitchen with a ski mask over her head and a shotgun in her hand and emptied both barrels into Blanchard and Covey right there where they sat—she was destined for a big tip.

"Blanchard, you don't know anything about her."

"I know she's pretty, and friendly, and a waitress who knows her chili. And I know her old man was a lousy lay, but he managed to get her pregnant in spite of that. Then he married her while he was standing at the business end of her daddy's rifle, and her daddy was secretly hoping that the boy would make a break for it, but he didn't. After they got married, as soon as the bills started coming in regular and times got a little tough, he cut and ran like a coyote stealing a chicken." He shook his head and took another bite of his Texas toast. "He's a sorry bastard, and if I ever run up on him, he's mine."

"Would you listen to yourself? You have no idea if any of that is true. For all you know, she might be married to the greatest guy in the whole world, and her ring is at the jeweler's getting cleaned."

"I know what I know," Blanchard said stubbornly. "Marianna has had a tough run. I can see it in her eyes. How much money do you have?"

"I don't know."

"Well, look!"

Covey sighed, then counted his cash on hand. It came to sixty-seven dollars and some change.

"That's not enough," Blanchard said. "Help me get my boot off."

"What? Why?"

"I've got a $100 bill tucked in there."

"A lot of people keep their money in their billfolds. Or their pockets."

"Are you going to help me or not?"

"Blanchard, why do we need $167 and some change?"

"For the tip!" Blanchard would have thought it was obvious. After he got over this heart business, he supposed he needed to get Covey checked out, in case he was coming down with a light dose of the Old-timer's disease. He just wasn't as sharp as he used to be.

"The tip? Twenty percent of a bowl of chili and a cup of coffee ought to come to about three dollars. Four will kill it dead."

"Cheap bastard. It's guys like you who give eating out a bad name. Help me with my boot." With Covey's aid, Blanchard retrieved the c-note from his footwear. He unfolded it and smoothed it out on the tabletop. Covey went back to his coffee, and Blanchard took one more bite of his chili. Then he pushed the bowl away.

"You don't like it?" Covey asked.

"It's the best in town. I'm just full."

"Your appetite will come back in a few days. Not having much of an appetite for a week or two was also on the list of things you needed to know about heart surgery that you didn't bother to read. We'll get her to bring us a container. It's the least she can do for a $160 tip."

"Nah, that's okay. I've had all I want."

"Your dog might like the rest."

"That dog never leaves my side when I'm home. There's no way he's getting chili."

"Good call. I wasn't thinking." Marianna came up to the table with a coffee pot.

"Would you like a refill?" she asked Covey. He smiled and shook his head. She turned her attention to Blanchard. "Are you finished?" He nodded. "You didn't eat much. Can I get you a to-go cup?"

"No, I'm good."

"Well, I'll just leave this here." She placed the check facedown on the table and headed back to the kitchen. A few more customers had come in, and the place was starting to hop. Blanchard picked up the check and studied the damage.

"How much?" Covey asked.

"Looks like $167 and some change."

Covey nodded. That sounded about right. "I don't know how folks can afford to live in the city," he said as he dropped every penny he had on top of Blanchard's $100 grand gesture.

Blanchard placed both hands on the tabletop and slowly pushed himself to a standing position. "You can't take it with you," he said.

Covey nodded again. "That's what I hear."

"CAN'T NEVER COULD"
(Blanchard Shankles/John Covey)

Can't never could and won't never would
Don't never did and shan't never should
Now I understand what I misunderstood
Can't never could and won't never would

I wanted a lover, you wanted a friend
I wanted to save, you wanted to spend
I wanted to start, you wanted to end
I wanted to keep, you wanted to send

Now I understand what I misunderstood
Can't never could and won't never would

You wanted to travel, I wanted to stay
You wanted to treat, I wanted to pay
You wanted the mountains, I wanted the bay
You wanted to stand, I wanted to lay

Now I understand what I misunderstood
Can't never could and won't never would

I wanted to run, you wanted to walk
I wanted to sing, you wanted to talk
I wanted to ring, you wanted to knock
I wanted to pass, you wanted to block

Can't never could and won't never would
Don't never did and shan't never should
Now I understand what I misunderstood
Can't never could and won't never would

"Hard Luck Woman"
Kiss
-1975-

Blanchard Shankles was an introspective young man, although it would have been difficult to identify this trait just by looking at him; his faded jeans, long hair, and lanky frame belied his inner depth, almost as if he were trying to disguise it. He believed his chronic self-examination to be a peculiarity that he embraced because of his mother, in a meandering sort of way. Edna may have indeed been an introspective person herself, but with all the shorted-out circuits sparking and smoking in her unreliable mind, it was difficult to tell at any given moment whether she was looking within, peering without, or gazing in some other unidentified direction altogether, one that had no name and could not be accessed by normal people via customary routes. So Blanchard did not inherit his proclivity to observe himself from her necessarily, but in acknowledgment of her fate he did like to keep a weather eye on what was going on inside his own head lest he, to employ the vernacular, find himself becoming as crazy as a sack full of shithouse rats, just like his mother before him.

In his reflective moments, he pondered about Edna quite a bit, which was normal, he supposed, given all that had happened to him, to her, and to their family. Whenever he thought about his mother, after the cloud of sadness that always accompanied these musings ascended and he was able to access his thoughts more objectively, he wondered if she could have held off the crazy train if she had seen it barreling down the tracks straight for her, had recognized it for what it was, and had thrown the switch to derail it, or at least to put it on a siding, out of harm's way. Or was her madness a forgone conclusion set at birth, a sentence of doom pronounced at conception that she never had any chance of avoiding? Blanchard just didn't know. If the latter were the case, then he figured that in his own circumstance, he was either screwed or he wasn't, depending on which genes he had inherited from whom. He would either go crazy like his mama had, or he wouldn't; that was all there was to that, and hide those Nubian princesses while you have the opportunity. But if the former scenario were a more accurate representation of how craziness crept upon a soul, then maybe the game wasn't completely rigged against him. Maybe he had a chance, and perhaps he could stave off the encroachment of madness that he so feared. The key, he believed, lay in spotting it promptly, and this was why he was ever vigilant for the early warning signs. He hoped—if his number came up and his turn rolled around to do battle with the demons of the night—that he would at least be able to mount a respectable defense and perhaps prevail, and even if he ultimately lost the conflict, it was his fervent hope to take out a few of the bastards before being clutched in the talons of insanity and dragged bodily to the halls of bedlam, there to live in eternal purgatory among the legions of the demented.

So Blanchard was concerned about his long-term sanity and whether or not his firm grip on reality would weaken as his years on this world rambled by. Thus it was with some trepidation that he set about the wooing of Andrea Joy Hazeltine. He had no doubts about his feelings for her; indeed, he had been enamored of her ever since their first unexpected kiss, and as their relationship blossomed, his love for her grew with each passing week. She was smart, she was funny, and she was the most beautiful person he had ever met, inside and out. And she honestly seemed to like him, a happenstance he couldn't completely understand since he didn't usually like himself that much, but one for which he was extremely grateful nevertheless. And perhaps most important, she filled a chronic vacancy in his world. Due to his fragmented upbringing, he had for his own protection become a loner. This was a fairly common defense mechanism for those who had been harmed by people close to them, and Blanchard had evolved into his solitary existence so slowly that he never really noticed it until Andy stepped into that empty space beside him and filled it. It was only then that he realized he was not only a loner but also lonely, and he did not want to be any longer.

Their courtship was a seamless study in romance, a handholding stroll through a flowered meadow on a mild spring morning, and after dating Andy for only three months, Blanchard realized he had a conundrum to resolve. The issue was a simple one: he wanted to ask her to marry him, and to have her by his side until the oceans boiled and the mountains crashed down from on high. For young men without his peculiar pedigree, admittedly this wouldn't be an issue unless the answer to the time-honored question when popped was in the negative, at which time the bearer of unrequited love could join the Foreign Legion, or perhaps go to sea.

But for Blanchard, the choices were not laid out so cleanly. If he asked for her hand, and she said yes, and they married, what would happen later if he ended up as his mother had, hopelessly insane and on the scout for trouble? This was the issue that gave him great pause, the one that kept him awake at night. It wouldn't be fair to the woman he loved beyond all else to stick her with a crazy man, and he figured there was a better than average chance that he would someday do just that as he walked in those sad and hopeless shoes, his inheritance from his mother, because derangement and the accompanying baggage ran in the family. He puzzled over his enigma for some time, looked at it from this side and that, before deciding that he needed some advice. Deep questions such as the one on Blanchard's mind are often posed to a young man's father, but since his father was an unreliable mentor, and dead to boot, and since the only real father figure in his life, Major, had long since drifted out over the canyon and into eternity, about the only person he could turn to was his best friend and bass player, John Covey.

They were at Blanchard's house, where the band had just finished a practice session. It had been a long one because of Blanchard's insistence that a new song must be practiced until it sounded just like the record, so they had run through "Band on the Run" by Paul McCartney and Wings until it sounded like Paul and Linda were right there in the upstairs hall with them. They had the house to themselves because Blanchard now lived alone. Geneva had moved out the preceding summer to attend college, where she was thoroughly engaged in waiting tables for pocket money, remembering nursing facts and protocols as she slowly navigated toward her chosen career, and forgetting her past just as fast as she was able.

On this particular winter evening, everyone but Covey and Blanchard had already adjourned onto the upstairs porch for a beer and a smoke, either of tobacco or of something a bit more hallucinogenic. This was the usual post-practice protocol for Skyye. Blanchard and Covey were perfectionists when it came to the music, as were the rest of the boys most of the time, and after one practice session a year earlier during which Jimbo Tant had gotten too drunk to rock and roll, or stand, they had all decided—with Jimbo voting *aye* in absentia because he was passed out—that there was a time for all things in the world, and the time for getting messed up at practice was after the songs were learned down to the last note and then played perfectly over and again until the band could do them upside down and asleep, which, ironically, was Jimbo's condition when the necessity for the rule made itself apparent in the first place. So the boys were outside lighting up and swallowing down, and Covey and Blanchard would join them presently for a bit of unwinding themselves, but first Blanchard had something on his mind.

"What do you think of Andy?" he asked Covey.

"Andy? She's a peach. Don't forget that you told me you were going to hook me up with her sister." Covey had met his future wife, Anna, by this point, but they were taking a while to warm up to each other, so the bass player from Skyye was attempting to play the field, an endeavor for which he was not particularly suited, both because he was shy by nature and because the field had proven resistant to his efforts, as if it were fenced with razor wire and patrolled by malicious dogs.

"Yeah, yeah. I remember. I'll take care of it."

"Soon?" Covey placed his bass guitar into the case and snapped it shut.

"Soon. Listen, I want to get your opinion about something."

"Shoot."

"I'm thinking about asking Andy to marry me."

Covey looked surprised at this news. Then he shook his head and grinned. "Hazy will kick your tail all over South Pittsburg."

"Nah," Blanchard said. "Hazy likes me."

"Hazy likes all the money you're making him." It was true. In the three months that Skyye had been the house band at Skate, the average Saturday night crowd had doubled in size, and the weekly dance was a standing room only event, which was how a dance should be. To show his appreciation, Hazy had generously increased Skyye's weekly stipend to a whopping $115, and he had intimated that while he couldn't promise anything, there was plenty more where that came from, and that if the boys from Sequoyah continued to hold up their end of the arrangement, then nothing but the sky was the limit.

"I'll give you that one. Hazy does like the money. But he also likes me."

"He might like you now, but he won't like you if you try to marry Andy. She's only seventeen, and he's kind of crazy when it comes to his girls." Blanchard had to admit that Hazy did seem to be a bit protective of his progeny, so much so that none of the homegrown boys in South Pittsburg were willing to risk his ire for mere love. The general consensus among the local youngbloods was that when it came to romancing any of Hazy's daughters, being single and horny was much preferable to being dead and buried in the field out behind the skating rink. Rumor spoke of two or three unmarked graves out there already—cold, shallow tombs dug hastily in the night.

"Covey, can I get to my question now?" Blanchard asked. He was beginning to think he should have had this heart-to-heart with Chicken, perhaps, or maybe with Ford Man. Covey was his best buddy, as close to him as the brother he never had, but sometimes he just wouldn't shut up.

"Sorry. You caught me by surprise. I didn't have a clue that you were thinking about getting hitched. I think Andy is great. If she'll have you, you'll never do any better. And hey, even if Hazy does thump on you a little, it'll be worth it."

"Will you quit with Hazy already?" Blanchard felt that they had sufficiently covered the topic. Covey held up his hands as if to apologize for the interruption. Blanchard rolled up his cords, unrolled them, and then rolled them up again. Then he continued. "The thing is, I want to get married, but I'm worried about what happened to Edna."

"Okay. You got me there. Back up and tell me what your poor mama has to do with you marrying Andy. Do you think she'll cut up at the wedding?"

"Are you kidding? I guarantee you she would. But that's not what I'm worried about." Inviting Edna to any social event would be like inviting a lion to a sheep convention. Even if the authorities would agree to let her out for the occasion, which they absolutely would not, given the gravity of her initial transgression not to mention some of her recent rather ingenious and quite energetic attacks on staff members at the state hospital, Blanchard would never consider risking it. Too much could go wrong, and he could think of no worse way to begin a life of wedded bliss than by having the topless mother of the groom beat one of the bridesmaids to death with the cake topper during the reception. It would cast a pall over the relationship that might prove difficult to surmount in the years to come, an incident that would always be there between them and true happiness. He was quiet for a long moment. Then he took a little breath and put his concerns out there for the world to see. "I'm worried that someday I might go crazy like she did. And if I do, I might hurt Andy. I might even try to kill her."

Covey looked at him with a frown. He opened his mouth to speak, hesitated, and closed it. Then he put his hands in his jeans pockets and looked up at the ceiling, perhaps hoping to find some wisdom scribbled there. Finally, he looked back at Blanchard and started again. "Where did that come from?"

"It's been on my mind for a while."

"You had a dream, didn't you?"

"Not about this. I just worry that someday I might flip out."

"Blanchard, I don't know too much about crazy, but I don't think it works like that. Do you really believe you're doomed to go nuts one of these days just because your mama did?"

"I don't know. It could happen. People inherit things from their parents all the time. And if I do come down with a dose of the crazy one of these days, it wouldn't be a good idea to be around me. Look at Edna. She's a little woman—what, 130 pounds or so—but you remember what she did to my old man. And it took four of us to get her into the cop car when they came to get her, and we were all big guys, and she beat the living hell out of all of us before we got her in there." Blanchard grimaced at the memory even as he spoke of it.

"You ought to forget about that day. What's done is done. And you ought to forget about this, too. I think you're worried about something that's not even going to happen. Just because one of your folks goes crazy, or has cancer, or dies of a heart attack, that doesn't mean it's going to happen to you."

"I hope not. But it might. Mama's mother was crazy, too, you know. She killed her old man just like Mama did. Well, not just like. She used a knife, but he still ended up dead. Then she hung herself with her wedding dress. If that's not crazy, I don't know what crazy is."

"That's pretty crazy," Covey agreed.

Blanchard shivered slightly as he gave further thought to his ancestry. "I don't know about *her* mother," he said, "my great-grandmother, but I'd be willing to bet she had it, too. It seems like I remember asking Mama about her once when I was a kid, maybe because some other kid was talking about his great-grandmother or something and I wanted one too. You know what happened?" Covey shook his head. "I got shushed," Blanchard said. He looked at Covey as if an eternal truth had been revealed. "They only shush you when something's wrong."

"They only shush you when something's wrong?" Covey repeated. "What does that even mean? What are you, nine?"

"You know it's true."

"I've never been shushed, so I don't know if it's true or not. But even if it is true and every woman in your family since time began has been nuts, you're still safe. You're a guy. I'll tell you who needs to watch out."

"Who?"

"Whoever marries your sister," Covey said. "That's who needs to be keeping a straitjacket out in the shed."

Blanchard nodded. He really hadn't given it serious consideration before now, but he could find no flaw in Covey's logic. Maybe he was safe and it was Geneva who needed to be wary. He shared a thought with Covey. "Whoever marries Geneva needs to watch out even if she doesn't go around the bend," he said. He loved his sister, and they had been through many hard, strange times together, had shared a crucible that forged the normal brother/sister relationship into a bond both stronger than normal and more fragile. She was a survivor, just like he was, tough as sun-dried leather all the way down to the core. He wished her only the good things in life and hoped that her future was not intertwined with Edna's past, but regardless of that, he imagined that if she chose the path of matrimony, she would likely be a hard person to be married to for a variety of reasons. On the bright side, perhaps her theoretical future husband might one day benefit from the chair under the doorknob trick, and if the opportunity ever presented itself, Blanchard would share the information, although only time would tell if it would prove useful.

"Have you had any symptoms?" Covey asked.

"What do you mean?"

"Have you been feeling peculiar? Have you felt any urges to skin a cat or whack anybody with a statue? Do you want to nail a bird to the wall? Do you think little people live inside mirrors? You know, crazy stuff." Covey had lit a cigarette and was using one of Ford Man's inverted cymbals as an ashtray, a transgression that would be unforgiven if discovered.

"No, none of that."

"So what are you worried about? Forget about it. I'll keep an eye on you, and if I see you start to do anything weird, I'll flag you down and we'll get you to a doctor. Maybe some medicine will straighten you out. If not, I'll ship you right off to Milledgeville."

"Thanks," Blanchard said.

"What are buddies for?" Covey asked.

Another unpleasant thought crossed Blanchard's mind. It seemed to be his day for them. "I hadn't even considered how going crazy might affect the band."

"Are you kidding? We can only hope! Every band needs at least one crazy guy. Look at Ozzy, or Alice Cooper, or even Pete Townsend. Those guys are getting rich off of crazy."

"You're not helping."

"Sorry. Okay, here's what I think you should do. Go ahead and ask Andy to marry you, but tell her what you're worried about. Let her decide if she's willing to take the chance."

"I can't do that. I haven't told her about Mama or my old man."

"Maybe you *are* crazy," Covey said. "You can't keep something like that from her. I don't even have a girlfriend, and I know that. You have to tell her."

"I don't know."

"I know," Covey said. "Tell her. And fix me up with her sister."

"Hazy might thump on you, too."

246

"Bring it on."

After giving Covey's advice its due diligence for a couple of days, Blanchard decided that perhaps his friend was correct, and he determined that he would discuss marriage and insanity with Andy come Saturday. He had been feeling dishonest almost since their relationship began about not sharing his sordid family history, but he was afraid he might lose her if he told her the worst of the facts, so he had let the lie by omission linger. But Covey was right. He needed to tell her.

Since he lived a couple of hours from his beloved, Blanchard had taken to driving over to South Pittsburg early each Saturday afternoon to spend the day with Andy. Come evening, the rest of the band would arrive at Skate, and Blanchard joined them there for unloading and setup after his alone time with his sweetheart. Old habits tend to die off slowly, and long after the need for it had passed, he was still living off the grid and didn't have a phone, so these long Saturdays were his only opportunity to speak with Andy and spend time with her, and he always looked forward to them, although this week was trying to make itself an exception to that general rule.

They had agreed the previous week to go on a picnic the next time they saw each other, and when he picked her up at Skate around 2:00, she carried with her a wicker picnic basket and a smile. They kissed when she climbed into the pickup truck, but briefly, due to Hazy's looming presence in the parking lot. He was busy picking up litter. In one hand he wielded a homemade contraption made from a broom handle, some duct tape, and a sixteen-penny nail, and in the other hand he held a large, faded burlap sack. While thus engaged in policing the grounds, he took the opportunity to gaze coolly at Blanchard, as if he were a prime empty beer can or a discarded cigarette wrapper that needed to be stabbed with the stick before being shoved into the sack.

"I need you back by 5:00 to sell tickets," Hazy told his daughter. "Don't be late."

"I'll be here," she replied. Blanchard waved at Hazy, who nodded once in return. Blanchard felt that the fact that he wasn't dead and buried in the field behind the rink was a relatively good sign and reinforced his belief that Hazy liked him, but he didn't want to push his luck on this of all days, so he dropped the truck in gear, and he and Andy left for their picnic.

They were heading for a little park situated close to Nickajack Lake, a dammed-up portion of the Tennessee River not far from South Pittsburg, and after a twenty-minute drive, they arrived and parked near the water. It was a pretty spot, and they had it to themselves, which suited Blanchard. He needed privacy in which to bare his soul, and the presence of a crusty fisherman or an armload of rowdy children would have dampened his determination to lay it all on the table. He and Andy considered the park to be their special place since the night—three weeks into their romance—when they had consummated their relationship right there by the river, under the trees, while a waxing crescent moon discretely looked down upon them.

They set up their picnic lunch on a weathered concrete table that overlooked the wide, gray-green lake. Andy unpacked their lunch, which included bologna and cheese sandwiches, sweet pickles, potato chips, and a couple of snack cakes for dessert. Blanchard was sure that the chips and cakes had come from the snack bar at Skate and was equally certain that no thank-yous to Hazy were necessary, or even wise. For his part, Blanchard had stopped on the way up from Sequoyah and purchased a six-pack of beer, Schlitz tallboys still frosty in the cooler. Andy and Blanchard sat side by side at the table, shoulders touching, eating sandwiches and sipping cold beer, comfortable in each other's presence, as the cool breeze from the moody Tennessee River mussed their hair and tugged at their clothes.

"Nice day," Blanchard said. He had spent most of the past two days memorizing exactly what he was going to say to Andy. He had actually written it all out and committed each word to memory, just like he had done with the Gettysburg Address in Mrs. Ostrander's class back in sixth grade. But he wasn't surprised in the least to discover that—just like back in sixth grade when he had attempted to recite that iconic speech—all those fine and pretty words were now unavailable to him, vanished into the limbo where important phrases often disappear right along with historic speeches. Now he had nothing, and he really hoped that he exited the picnic with a better mark than the C- Mrs. Ostrander had once awarded him.

"It's really nice," Andy replied. She snuggled against him and kissed his cheek.

"I, uh, I need to talk to you about something," he said.

"Okay." Andy looked at him. "Is anything wrong? You sound so serious."

"Well, it's a serious thing. Actually, it's two things. I need to tell you something, and then I need to ask you something." He sighed. "I'm really screwing this up. I'm not sure how to start."

"You're freaking me out, Blanchard," Andy said. She placed her sandwich on the paper plate and took a sip of her beer. "Don't prepare me anymore. I'm prepared. Just tell me."

"Okay. Here it is. My mama is crazy." That didn't seem to convey the extent of the problem sufficiently, so Blanchard tried again. "Really, really crazy. She was committed to the state mental hospital a few years back, and I believe she'll be there for the rest of her life. What got her sent there was, she killed my old man. She killed him while he was sleeping." Blanchard thought some sinking-in might be appropriate at this point, so he stopped speaking and looked at the lake. Way out in the middle, out in the navigation channel, a tug slowly pushed a lash-up of six laden coal barges, mounded high and shiny black in the afternoon sun, riding low in the current as they were guided toward their destination. From beside him, he could feel Andy's gaze as she looked at him. The rest of his life hinged on what she said next. Would she cut and run, or would she stay and hear the rest?

"You were right," she said. "That is a serious thing." She reached around him and hugged him tightly. "I'm so sorry for your family, that you had to go through that. It must have been terrible for you."

Blanchard could smell her hair, and feel her warmth against him. Since she hadn't jumped up and fled from him as if he were a leper, he was tempted to quit while he was ahead for today, go back to his sandwich and his beer, and perhaps present another installment of the life and times of the Shankles family next week, same time, same station. But that wouldn't have been fair to the woman he hoped to marry. She needed the facts and their possible ramifications, and he had already put it off too long.

"That's just part of it," he said, looking at her. "The rest of it is this. Crazy kind of runs in my family. That means that someday, the same thing might happen to me. If it does, and you're close by, it could be a bad day." There. It was out, and Blanchard was relieved. Win, lose, or draw, he had done the right thing.

Andy looked at him with surprise etched on her features, and perhaps a little bit of relief. "I'm glad you told me about your mother," she said. "I know it was hard, and it means a lot to me that you want-ed me to know. But now that you have it out, I don't want you worry-ing about it anymore. Nobody knows what's going to happen in the future, Blanchard. A branch might fall out of this tree and kill us both." She pointed at the tree above them, and in spite of himself, Blanchard looked up. "The dam might break and wash us away. If you want to talk about trouble running in families, bad hearts run in mine. My granddaddy dropped dead of a heart attack when he was fifty-six. He was fine one minute and gone the next. Daddy's already had one heart attack, and if he doesn't calm down some and learn how to take it easy, he's liable to have another one most any time. And he's not even that old. Two of my uncles, Daddy's brothers, have had heart attacks, and one of them died. So I might have heart trou-ble someday too, but I can't spend my life worrying about it. If it happens, it happens, but I hope it doesn't, and I'm not going to fret about it. And you shouldn't worry about this." She smiled at him. "The only thing we have every day is that day. Right now I have you, and our special place, and some cold beer and sandwiches."

"And those chips you lifted from Hazy."

"And those. I don't know that anything could be better than right here, right now. Not for me, anyway. Today is perfect, and to-morrow will take care of itself one way or another. It might be better, or it might be worse. Nobody can say for sure. All I can say is that for me, it'll be different than I thought it would be. It always is."

They both sat there quietly on the gentle Tennessee afternoon and watched as the tug out in the river strained against the current. Several minutes went by before Andy spoke again. "Now what was it that you wanted to ask me?"

"Well, you know how I feel about you." He had prepared some remarks for this portion of the day's activities as well, but they were apparently spending the day with the Gettysburg Address and his comments about insanity on his mama's side of the family and were conspicuous by their absence. He was on his own in uncharted lands, making it up as he went, straining against the current much like a tug out in the mighty Tennessee River.

"I do. I feel the same way about you."

"I was thinking that maybe, you know, since we feel the way we do, that, if you wanted to, we might could get married sometime." Blanchard was mortified by his proposal. He was certain that it had been the worst mishmash of words ever uttered in the combined history of love, marriage, and discourse. He wanted to hang himself from the nearby tree, or perhaps just begin walking forward until the waters of Lake Nickajack covered him up completely, gone from sight and out of mind until that day in the far, far future when his pitiful and inarticulate bones finally made their way to the sea, where all things begin and all things end. While waiting for her response, he found himself fiddling with the bottle cap from his beer, and saw that he was scratching their initials—A.H. + B.S—into the rough cement tabletop. When the silence grew long, he cut his eyes to his left and saw Andy sitting there, smiling and looking at him.

"I think that is a lovely idea," she said. She threw her arms around him and kissed him.

"So you will?" Blanchard asked. Maybe his proposal hadn't been so bad after all.

"Yes, I will. Andrea Joy Shankles. I like the sound of that. Or maybe you could take my name. Blanchard Hazeltine. What do you think?"

"Anything you want. Maybe if I took your name it would keep Hazy from killing me."

"What?"

"Covey thinks your daddy is going to whip my tail over marrying you."

"He'll have a fit, for sure, but he'll get over it."

"When do you want to do it?"

"I don't know yet, but soon. I know that much. We can have the reception at Skate. We'll fix it all up pretty, and my sisters can be in the wedding. My aunt will want to make us a cake." She stopped her planning for a moment and looked at her future husband. "Who do you think we can get to play at the reception?"

"I know some boys who might play."

"Bonetraffic?"

"Well, they need the work."

Blanchard Shankles found himself in the little park beside Lake Nickajack. It was perhaps his favorite place in the world, and he supposed it was natural for him to gravitate here. He sat on the ground facing the water, leaned up against one of the hard benches of the very table at which he had proposed to Andy. That day was now six months in his past, and he remembered her acceptance as one of the finest moments in his twenty-one years. He looked up and noted that the massive tree branch above him had not fallen, taking him with it as it crashed from this world into the next with panache. He found that he was disappointed in this development, and he wondered if he had come to this spot in order to allow the tree one more opportunity at him, one more chance to kill him deader than a highland stone. He shifted his attention from the branch above and cast his gaze upon the mighty Tennessee River as it made its relentless journey past the little park, moving water from here to there, flowing for eternity as it sought the embrace of the sea. He noted that the turgid waters were still within their banks and not rising in the least, which clued him to the fact that the dam had not broken, and that he was not about to drown as the raging waters engulfed him and rolled him far downriver, like a pebble tumbling down a hill during an avalanche. Again, he was disappointed. He lit a cigarette, then took his left wrist into his right hand and checked his pulse. His heartbeat was smooth and steady, as it always was, so the likelihood of him plummeting to the ground at that moment as he succumbed to a fatal heart attack was slim. He was discouraged at the absence of a blinding burst of pain and light to escort him to that everlasting abode out beyond the world of trouble and the ragged boundaries of time. Once, not long ago at this very picnic table, Andy had speculated about all of those fine and thorough ways to die, each one guaranteed to do the job. She had expounded upon how they might one day transpire despite all attempts to avoid them, and how, once that number was called, there was nothing to do but slowly rise and walk toward the light, yet he still lived. It didn't seem fair to Blanchard, but then again, most things didn't.

They had married on a gentle fall evening at Rocky Bottom Baptist Church, the little church in South Pittsburg where Andy's mama, and her grandmother before that, had been wed. The pastor at the ceremony was the same man who had presided over Mrs. Hazeltine's marriage to Hazy, and he was the son of the preacher who had conducted the ceremony when Andy's grandmother walked down the aisle, so he was respected as one who knew his business and did good, solid work. Covey was slated to be the best man at the affair, but when Simpson Taggart learned that he was not to fill that solemn role, his feelings were wounded to such an extent that he was hardly fit for his other duties, such as they were, and Covey felt so bad for him that he relinquished the spot of honor to his friend and roadie. This kindness on Covey's part had a serendipitous effect on his love life when Anna, Simpson's sister, admired this generous gesture regarding her brother and began to look at Covey more as a potential romantic interest and less as an adequate bass player. As a matter of record, their first date had been when she accompanied Covey to the wedding, and along with the remainder of the Sequoyah portion of the wedding party—Geneva, Chicken Raines, Ford Man Cooper, Tucker McFry, and Jimbo Tant—they filled out the pews on the groom's side of the church as best they could.

As for Hazy, he had not been moved to violence over the engagement, nor had he suffered a second heart attack over it. Oddly enough, considering his reputation as a man prone to excitability, with the exception of the occasional extra rumble and growl directed toward his new son-in-law, Hazy seemed to have come to an acceptance of the marital arrangement quite readily, causing the boys in the band to acknowledge that he must have really liked Blanchard after all.

The reception was held at Skate, as Andy had wished, and she and her mama and sisters turned the venerable skating rink into the envy of that year's crop of South Pittsburg brides. Andy's aunt was a baker both by trade and disposition, and she crafted a wedding cake worthy of the occasion, tall and delicate, white, tasteful, and tasty besides. Andy's mama, who was not a baker, either by trade or by disposition, made a groom's cake for Blanchard that was supposed to look like a guitar, but that sort of resembled a run-over cat, or perhaps a raccoon, depending upon lighting and point of view. But it tasted all right, and everyone made a fuss over it regardless of appearance so she wouldn't feel bad about how it had turned out. The music for the event was supplied by Skyye, minus its lead guitar player, who was busy that night cleaving unto the love of his life, and they even went to the trouble to learn "Muskrat Love" for the occasion, although when first asked to do so they had sworn against it, strictly as a matter of pride. But Andy liked the song and wanted it for her first dance with her new husband, so they gritted their teeth, sent Simpson to buy a copy of the song, and put together a decent rendition, all in the name of love. After the reception, the newlyweds motored off to Chattanooga in Blanchard's pickup for a poor kids' honeymoon, a $200 splurge among the bright lights of the big city, funded by Hazy, of all people, that included a night at the venerable Read House hotel and trips to both Ruby Falls and Rock City. Then they had set up housekeeping in Sequoyah, right there in the house Blanchard had inherited from his parents, in a manner of speaking. He carried his young bride over the threshold into a home that desperately needed new, better memories to wash away the old, tarnished ones, and he knew in his heart of hearts that he and Andy together would be able to accomplish that task, and to make that sad domicile into a place of light and laughter.

Blanchard Shankles lit another cigarette as he sat there in the little park by Nickajack Lake. Thinking about his marriage to Andy made him sadder than he could say, but he couldn't stop himself from doing it, so he had learned over the past few days to live with the despair. He slowly arose from his spot on the ground, dusted the seat of his pants, and then sat on the top of the picnic table. He looked down at the concrete and saw the sigil he had carved with the bottle cap from a Schlitz tallboy on the day of his engagement: A.H. + B.S. He was surprised that it had not weathered much, but then he realized that it had only been there a short time. If he came back here in five years, it would be mostly gone. If he visited a decade from now, there would be no trace, as if A.H. + B.S had never existed. He sighed and turned away. He could not look any longer. Out on the river, as usual, a tug pushed barges. From his vantage point on the table, it looked as if, this time, the barges contained dirt. It was mounded high, and the vessels were nearly awash with the weight of it. He wondered about the movement of dirt. Dirt was cheap. Who would pay good money to move it? Why wouldn't they just dig some local dirt wherever it was needed? He supposed he didn't understand the dirt business. He had come to realize quite recently that there were many things under the sun that he didn't understand. As he watched the tug swing wide to clear a channel buoy, the mounds on those barges jogged a recent memory.

It had been a random Tuesday, just another unremarkable day with the potential to bring with it all that the world had to offer, and just as easily to snatch it all away. It was late afternoon, and the band had gathered at Blanchard and Andy's house to put the finishing touches on some new songs they were planning to add to the set list: "Born to Run" by Bruce Springsteen, "Lyin' Eyes" by the Eagles, and "Saturday Night Special" by Lynyrd Skynyrd. Practice had gone well, for the most part, but they were still going to have to do some work on "Born to Run" before they put it into the lineup; Chicken was having trouble with Clarence Clemons's sax solo. They were all gathered on the upstairs porch, relaxing and discussing their upcoming engagements. It was chilly, and as they sat, they passed a pint of Ancient Age for warmth, and for wisdom they shared a fat joint rolled from some decent Columbian that Simpson had recently harvested from a patch in the woods up behind the town's water tower. Ford Man was the sole abstainer, as was his custom, of both the alcohol and the pot, but he had taken to heart the more reasonable parts of the Bible and did not judge his bandmates, lest he be judged and perhaps be found wanting.

"I'll get it," Chicken said, referring to the sax solo. "I just need to work on it some more. That guy's great, you know. He's like the Eric Clapton of the saxophone."

"We could leave it out," said Tucker. "Or I could play it on the keyboard."

"It belongs in the song," Blanchard said, shaking his head. "If we're going to play 'Born to Run,' then it needs to be in there. Chicken will get it. He always does. He just needs a little more time."

Chicken nodded. "Give me a few more days," he said. "I'll get it."

"What is this?" Jimbo Tant asked, nodding at the arrival of one of the two Sequoyah police cars. It was the one without all the dents, the one they usually sent out on serious business. The cruiser pulled up in front of the house, down in the driveway below.

"I don't know," Blanchard said as he stood and opened the screen. "Whatever it is, it can't be good. Duck that doobie, and I'll go find out." Jimbo stubbed out the joint, then popped the roach into his mouth and began to chew.

Blanchard traversed the hall and headed down the stairs. He was shrouded in an invisible cloud of dread, but there was nothing to do but go answer the door. The rest of the band members were quiet there on the porch, sipping harsh bourbon, wondering what was up as they waited for their lead guitar player to rejoin them. In their world, a police car was never good news. If one pulled up during a dance, it generally meant that the dance was over. If one pulled up behind them while they were minding their own business in a car out in the flat woods, that meant it was time to toss the beer and hide the dope. And when one crept up on a Tuesday evening for no clear reason at all—the good police car, no less—then it was time to hunker down. They could hear the low rumble of conversation from under them on the downstairs porch, but they couldn't make out the words. Presently, they heard a car door slam. The police cruiser started, then backed out of the driveway. They waited for Blanchard to come back to the gathering and share his news, and they had saved the final sip of the bourbon for him should he need fortification, but he did not appear. As the minutes continued to pass by, he grew conspicuous by his absence, and finally Covey could stand it no longer and went in to see what was keeping him. He found Blanchard sitting in the floor of the downstairs hallway, leaned against the wall by the open front door, in the same spot he had once occupied when he and Edna had awaited the arrival of the authorities. He was staring straight ahead into the gathering gloom of the downstairs hallway, quietly crying.

"Blanchard, what's wrong?" Covey asked. In all the time he had known Blanchard Shankles, he had never seen him cry. Blanchard looked at him and shook his head. He opened his mouth to speak but found that he could not. Then he put his hands over his face and took a ragged breath. He wiped away his tears, but more immediately took their place. Covey kneeled beside his friend and asked again, quietly and gently, "What is it, Blanchard? What did the cop say?"

Blanchard looked at Covey with eyes that contained all the misery in the world.

"Andy's dead," he said, and then his voice failed him.

"BEST LEFT ALONE"
(Blanchard Shankles/John Covey)

You left on a Tuesday late at night in the fall
Now my life's all in pieces, and I can't find them all
The days are just endless, my heart's made of stone
And my mind runs to places that are best left alone

I knew when I met you we never would part
I gave you my soul and you gave me your heart
I wish I still had you but I'm here on my own
So my mind runs to places that are best left alone

My friends all keep saying I live in the past
The days and the weeks and the months fly by fast
And I know it's all true but the seeds have been sown
Still my mind runs to places that are best left alone

Our time was so short, now the years run too long
And I hope you remember as I write down this song
That yours was the only true love I've been shown
As my mind runs to places that are best left alone

Sometimes late at night I remember your smile
And I dream that we talk and we walk for a while
I know it's not real and I always have known
Yet my mind runs to places that are best left alone

You left on a Tuesday late at night in the fall
Now my life's all in pieces, and I can't find them all
The days are just endless, my heart's made of stone
And my mind runs to places that are best left alone

The days are just endless, my heart's made of stone
And my mind runs to places that are best left alone

The days are just endless, my heart's made of stone
And my mind runs to places that are best left alone

"I Don't Need No Doctor"
Humble Pie
-Monday: Ninth Day-

Blanchard Shankles sat in the doctor's office waiting to be seen. It was seven days since he had undergone heart surgery, and he really couldn't say that he was feeling much better. As a matter of fact, he felt decidedly worse than he had the day before Dr. Forrester had made fast and loose with his coronary arteries, and for the past four days he had seemed to lose a little ground every day. When Covey had sat before him with the first aid kit yesterday to change the bandage over his incision, he had noticed that the skin around the staples seemed puffy and red. Additionally, Blanchard had developed a sharp pain in his left lung, he still had the occasional twinge of angina, he was more tired than he thought possible, and he had no appetite. He had refused to take Covey's advice and go to the emergency room in Rome right then, but he had agreed to a trip to visit Babydoc Miller come Monday morning.

Babydoc Miller was the grandson of Sequoyah's longtime town physician, Doc Miller, and he had traveled a circuitous route on his journey to take over his grandfather's practice after first spending ten years in a thriving surgical partnership in upstate New York. He was an excellent surgeon, but over time he became dissatisfied with his associates and with his specialty. Specifically, he found himself spending more and more of his time fixing the people who could afford to stay alive while gently easing the less fortunate down to the free clinic for an aspirin and a kind word. This was not the kind of care he had spent sixteen years of his life training to provide, so when the call came from his ancient grandfather, already well into his eighties, he was ready to step in. Now he spent his days and nights treating everybody for everything, making not much money doing it, and he felt like the doctor he had always wanted to be.

Blanchard was a walk-in on a slow Monday morning, and there was only one appointment ahead of him, so he was ushered into one of Babydoc's two examining rooms soon after his arrival. Covey was with him, and he sat on the single chair after first helping Blanchard up onto the examining table. Blanchard immediately recognized the room as the same one he and Edna had visited all those years ago, right after she went crazy. The posters on the wall were new, but the same skeleton stood in the corner, smiling at him as if he were an old friend back from a long trip, with photos to share, perhaps, and souvenirs to parcel out. He sat on the same examination table that Edna had, a sturdy, wooden contraption fitted with a thin mattress and a clean, white sheet. He had never met Babydoc before, and he vaguely wondered if he would be like Doc. Those were some big shoes to fill.

"I think you should go ahead and take off your shirt," Covey said from his chair.

"You changed the bandage yesterday."

"I want the doctor to take a look at it. I think it might be getting infected. And he's going to want your shirt off no matter what. Probably your pants, too." Blanchard sighed. Covey was wearing him out, but he meant well. He began to unbutton his shirt. The effort of raising his hands to chest level exhausted him, and he stopped to rest for a moment after undoing only two buttons. Before he could begin again, there was a quiet knock at the door. Then Babydoc entered. Blanchard was bemused. Before him stood a carbon copy of the man he had brought his mother to see. He felt a little disoriented, as if he had traveled back in time. Babydoc smiled at Blanchard and at Covey. Then he shook Blanchard's hand and spoke.

"Good morning, Mr. Shankles. I'm Doctor Miller." He had a firm grip just like Doc had, so maybe he would be all right. Blanchard put great stock in how someone shook his hand.

"Good morning, Doc. I knew your grandfather. He was a good doctor and a good man." Babydoc nodded, and Blanchard continued. "This is my advisor, Covey. If you ask him why he's here, he'll tell you it's so I won't lie too much."

Covey nodded as well. That was indeed pretty much the reason he had tagged along. He knew Babydoc both personally and professionally and had recently seen him about the arthritis that seemed to be stealthily making its way up his spine, one vertebra at a time. "Doc," he said.

"Hey, John. How's your back doing?"

"Some better. Thanks for the pills."

"Remember to eat something when you take them. Now, Mr. Shankles, what seems to be the problem this morning?"

"I'm feeling a little rough, Doc," Blanchard allowed.

Covey looked at Blanchard with disbelief. "That's it?" he asked. "That's what you're going to tell him?"

"I was getting to it," Blanchard said with a weariness in his voice that Covey did not like.

"You work on those buttons. I'll give the doctor your medical history." Covey turned to Babydoc. "Blanchard's around sixty. He smokes like a Mack truck that needs a ring job. Last Monday morning right around this time, he had a single bypass of the LAD artery. The doctor used his mammary artery. A few days after that, he left the hospital without his doctor's permission because, well, he's not too bright. Now he's very tired, he won't eat, his heart still hurts, but not as bad as it did, he has a hard pain in one of his lungs that won't ease up, he coughs all the time, and I think his incision is getting infected." Covey looked at Blanchard. "Did I miss anything?"

"I was circumcised when I was born, and I had the mumps when I was four. Other than that, I think you got it all." Blanchard said this absentmindedly. He had defeated another button and was working on the next.

"Let me help you," Babydoc said as he reached in and finished the job. He slipped off Blanchard's shirt and laid it on the table beside him. Then he pulled on a pair of examination gloves and peeled away a bit of the adhesive tape that was securing the fresh bandage to Blanchard's chest. "You know what comes next," he said. "On three. One—" At that point he snatched the bandage free.

"Son of a *bitch*," Blanchard said between gritted teeth. "You don't happen to know a physician's assistant up in Nashville, do you? She can't count either."

Babydoc was pressing gently on the wound and not paying attention to the commentary. "It doesn't look too bad," he said, mostly to himself.

"I cleaned it with alcohol yesterday and put some antibiotic cream on it," Covey said. "It doesn't look as red as it did then."

Babydoc nodded. "Good. That redness is mostly caused by the staples. They need to come out." He reached in a drawer, pulled out a gizmo that looked like it would be more at home in a carpenter's tool belt than in a doctor's office, and made short work of the staples. Then he cleaned and re-dressed the wound. "I think that will be fine." He looked at Blanchard. "This bandage can come off in two or three days, and you shouldn't need another one. If you come by here, I'll remove it and take another look. After that, just keep your scar clean, and it will heal fine. Now, tell me about the surgery."

"I had a 100 percent blockage of the LAD. A guy in Nashville took care of that for me."

"100 percent? Did you have a heart attack?"

"No," Blanchard and Covey said in unison.

Babydoc took the stethoscope from its draped position around his neck, secured the earpieces, and began to investigate his patient. He listened to Blanchard's heart for a long time. Then he listened to his belly, both wrists, both ankles, his neck, and his chest, front, rear, and side. With the exception of the occasional instruction to Blanchard to breathe, or not to, he was quiet as he listened.

"Where does your lung hurt?" he asked as he tapped Blanchard on the back. Blanchard pointed, and he listened there too. Then he took the blood pressure cuff from its rack on the wall and strapped it onto Blanchard's arm. He checked Blanchard's blood pressure on both arms and again on both ankles. Blanchard watched him closely as he did all of this. Sometimes Babydoc grunted, twice he nodded, and once he frowned, which Blanchard didn't like. Babydoc slipped a thermometer under Blanchard's tongue, then turned to Covey. "Why did he leave the hospital against medical advice?"

"He said the television was too loud," Covey said.

Babydoc nodded as if he heard that one all the time. He removed the thermometer, looked at it, and dropped it into a beaker of alcohol. Then he turned to Blanchard. "Mr. Shankles, I think we need to send you back to the hospital for a day or two."

"I just escaped."

"That's part of the problem. I'm guessing that every single doctor and most of the nurses you saw during the last week told you that you ought to be dead?" Blanchard nodded, and Covey backed him up. "I'll skip that part, then. Your heart sounds okay, but your lungs sound like a pair of washing machines. With the symptoms you have, I believe you might have double pneumonia, which is not a good thing to have a week after heart surgery. I don't know for sure what the sharp pain in your left lung is. It could be part of the pneumonia, but without some tests I can't rule out a pulmonary embolism. We need to do a CT scan to check for that and to confirm the pneumonia."

"So the symptom for one of those embolisms is pain?" Blanchard asked.

"The main symptom for a pulmonary embolism is dropping dead," Babydoc replied. "It's kind of similar to the main symptom for a 100 percent blockage of the LAD in that respect."

"You said you were going to skip that," Blanchard said.

"You're right. I did. Sorry. Anyway, since you are apparently immune to sudden death, we need to get you feeling better so you can enjoy your life again. Right now your temperature is high, which means you could have an infection somewhere in addition to the walking double pneumonia, although I think your incision, at least, is okay. Your blood pressure is low, which means—given your recent surgery—you may have sprung a leak. Or it could just be low. That would also explain your fatigue. Of course, having heart surgery a week ago could also explain that. Or pneumonia. Or an embolism. Or an opportunistic infection. Do you see the problem?"

"Too many different things might be wrong?"

"That's the problem. All of them could be, or some of them, or this could be something else altogether. You are about this close to being the proverbial train wreck. We need to put you in the hospital and rule out these potential conditions one by one while taking care of the issues we find. And we need to do it in the hospital because an awful lot can go wrong with you at this point."

Blanchard thought about what Babydoc had said. He didn't want to go back to the hospital, but if he did, at least he would be in a Georgia hospital. And there was no getting around the fact that he felt really, really bad, and he was weary of feeling that way. Plus, he knew that, Babydoc's expert medical opinion aside, he wasn't immune to death, sudden or otherwise, and that it could indeed happen to him. He sighed.

"Okay," he said. "I'll get Covey to run me home so I can feed my dog and pick up a change of clothes."

"Mr. Shankles, you're not hearing me. I'm calling for an ambulance to take you to Rome right now. Then I'm calling the surgeon in Nashville to have your medical records sent to me here and to the hospital. Hopefully he's not in surgery and I can speak directly to him. Then I'm scheduling you for an EKG, a CT scan, a full blood panel, and a broad spectrum IV antibiotic. All of this will be happening as soon as I can make it happen. In the meantime, Sherry will be in with a shot of blood thinner. I'm more worried about the possible clot than I am about the possible leak. You just sit still. I'll be right back. Don't make any sudden moves."

"I hear that a lot," Blanchard said. Babydoc left at a brisk clip. Covey and Blanchard sat looking at each other. A strong sense of déjà vu pervaded the room. When the silence got too loud, Covey broke it.

"Well, at least you didn't have to take off your pants," he said.

"The rest of it wasn't so good, though. Babydoc is a little more excitable than his granddaddy was. He's going to have to settle down if he wants to live to be old."

"You just never saw Doc when you were train-wrecking. He could get a little bent out of shape when he was in the mood."

"I brought a crazy woman to see him who offered to screw him right here on this table, and he took it in stride, just like that kind of thing happened every day. That's a doctor for you. I don't know about these young boys."

"Babydoc is fifty if he is a day," Covey said.

"Still...."

"Don't worry about Scrounge," Covey said. "I'll call one of the boys to come feed him."

"I'm not worried. You could drop a bomb on him and he would be fine. Nothing can kill that dog. So you're going with me?"

"I guess so. You need someone competent to make important decisions for you."

"That's a fact. Reckon I'll live? I know it doesn't sound reasonable, but I feel sicker than I felt last week."

"You heard the man. You are immune to dying. Your heart can't kill you. Your lungs can't kill you. If you don't walk out in front of a bus, you might just live forever."

They ran out of words to say, so Blanchard just sat quietly until Covey got up to help him get back into his shirt. He was doing up the last of the buttons when Sherry, Babydoc's nurse, came in with a shot and three different pills. Blanchard endured the shot and swallowed his medicine, and Sherry left them alone again.

"Pretty," Blanchard said. He leaned to his right and sort of melted into a prone position on the table.

"Way too young for two old coots like us."

"You're right. Between us, we have every possible thing wrong that can go wrong. I've got most of it, and you've got the rest."

"Old does suck," Covey said. "Young is easier."

"What do you think happens when we die?"

"Blanchard, don't—"

"No, really. I'm not getting all down in the mouth. I just want to know what you think."

"I really don't know. I try not to think about it too much, because there isn't anything I can do about it except to try and avoid it as long as I can. That's good advice for you, too."

"Do you think it's a place?"

"Not like this is a place. I think it's a gathering, maybe, but I don't think there are gates or streets or anything like that."

"Do you think you meet people there you used to know? People you loved?"

"I do believe that, but I can't swear that I don't just believe it simply because I want it to be true. I think everybody does."

"I want it to be true, too," Blanchard said. "My whole adult life, I have hoped that someday I would see Andy again. Dying is really going to suck, but seeing her again would make it worth it."

"You're not going to die."

"Maybe. Maybe not. If I go, you can have Scrounge."

"I don't want Scrounge."

"Give Simpson the Ovation."

265

"Stop."

"You can have the house, too. But you might have to knife-fight Geneva for it."

"I want the house less than I want the dog."

"Come on, Covey. I'm trying to be serious here."

"I'm glad to hear that. Serious means doing what the doctors tell you, and staying where they put you, and letting them get you straightened out no matter what it takes."

"That's serious?"

"That's serious."

"Okay. But if some guy starts getting laid in the next bed, I can't make any promises."

"GEORGIA NIGHT SCHOOL"
(Blanchard Shankles/John Covey)

Take a shower and a shave, a brush and a shine
Buy the beer, load the boys, hit the road by nine
Take a left, hang a right, cross the county line
Turn the dial, tune the songs, let the highway whine

The image in the mirror is immortal and cool
Just a young boy heading to Georgia night school

Park the ride at the dance, pay the entry fee
Check the legs, check the eyes, will she dance with me?
Rowdy boys start a fight, are there two or three?
Sirens wail, blue lights flash, and it's time to flee

The image in the mirror is immortal and cool
Just a young boy heading to Georgia night school

Smoke a joint, run that mouth, set the big drag race
Side by side, engine roars drift away into space
Peeling out, laying rubber is the only trace
Squall in second, bark in third, watch the slow car chase

The image in the mirror is immortal and cool
Just a young boy heading to Georgia night school

Now toward dawn, sober up, head to Dad's Truck Stop
Hash and eggs, burgers too, joke about the slop
Eyes straight, heads burrowed down, don't stare at that cop
Here he comes! Look away! Will the other shoe drop?

The image in the mirror is immortal and cool
Just a young boy heading to Georgia night school

Back at home, stretch on out, have one last cold beer
Busted nose, dented car, never show them fear
With some luck, and some help, you'll survive the year
And if not, what the hell, catch another gear

The image in the mirror is immortal and cool
Just a young boy heading to Georgia night school

"Highway to Hell"
AC/DC
-1975-

When Andy met her demise, Blanchard took it hard, and in addition to that, he took it personally. He supposed it might be possible for some men to become widowers at the age of twenty-one and *not* want to take God to task on general principle, just to sort of remind Him, or Her, or perhaps even It, that these were people down here, fragile and important human beings who in most cases deserved better than they were receiving, but it was not in his nature to be so accepting of the whims of fate, and thus he was not. If other people who found themselves in his position wanted to fall prostrate and make a fuss over Jesus after He ripped their loved ones out of this world and frog-marched them to that divine home beyond the sky, sometimes bound and at gunpoint, without regard for either the departed's wishes or for the devastation left behind for the living to endure, then he supposed that was their business, and anyway it took all kinds to make a world. Blanchard, on the other hand, was not that guy. He had no patience for the purported heavenly plan, and he had no intention of putting a pretty face on the random cruelty of existence. What he wanted was answers. He wanted to know what Andy, the love of his life, had done to deserve her fate. And oh yeah, by the way, while he was searching for explanations, he wanted to know why his father had been such a prick and why his mother was spending the rest of her days down at Central State Hospital, coloring pictures of penises and occasionally trying to kill the odd staff member when the voices told her to do so and the mood struck her to comply. And at the root of all his questions was one fundamental inquiry; he wanted to know what it was about Blanchard Shankles that seemed to instill in the Almighty an apparently uncontrolled desire to take away rather than to provide, and what it was about him that just seemed to piss God off.

The full story of Andrea Joy Hazeltine Shankles's departure from the earthly plane was a short one, almost anticlimactic in its simplicity, and more than one person remarked that if it was indeed time to go, then the general wisdom was that it was best to get it over with quickly, although everyone who knew Blanchard knew better than to make this observation in his presence. Andy was not afflicted with a wasting disease, and had not lingered day after day as the clock counted down her remaining moments until finally there were none. She was not in uniform, defending her country and her flag as she sought to protect her loved ones from the hordes of evil gathered out in the world, awaiting their opportunity to slip in under the wire and wreak havoc. She was not robbing a store, skydiving, or shooting Niagara Falls in a barrel, all demonstrably hazardous activities in which one possible and maybe even probable outcome was swift, violent demise. She was, in fact, minding her own business, and not looking for trouble in any sense of the word. She was not engaged in any shenanigans whatsoever as she drove home to share with her husband the very good report she had received at her morning doctor's appointment.

The news she had to share with Blanchard was that their efforts to become parents had been fruitful as well as enjoyable, and that they were to have a baby. After informing her husband that she was with child, she intended to cook him a nice supper—hamburger hash was his favorite, and no trouble at all to fix—before settling in to a quiet evening, as people who are young and in love with the vastness of a full life before them are prone to do. She was content with her life and what it had brought her thus far as she entered the blind curve on U.S. 27, and when she encountered the ragged vehicle heading straight toward her, all the way over in her lane where it had no business being, she had no time even to be surprised, and then she had no time at all. They met head on, and at the exact moment of impact, Andy ceased to be. She was wearing her seatbelt, as she always did, and she was driving five miles below the speed limit, as was her habit, and she had both hands on the steering wheel, at ten and two just like the manual recommended, because she took her driving seriously indeed. None of this mattered in the least, and none of it saved her.

The information that Blanchard received from his uninvited guest on that Tuesday afternoon was that his wife was dead, and that

Junior Rennert, a local reprobate notorious throughout the county for driving drunk, was the one who had killed her. This tragic report was presented by a lawman who was known to be an antagonistic hardliner, a man who had always wanted to be a policeman because he liked to tell people what to do, and to enforce his wishes when necessary if compliance were not shortly forthcoming, but on that day he reached down deep and did his best to deliver the rock-hard news with compassion and kindness, perhaps because he had a wife of his own at home, and two small boys he looked forward to seeing every day when he got off work, and he would never want to be on the receiving end of facts such as those he was delivering to Blanchard Shankles.

For Blanchard, the days that followed the officer's visit were forever ingrained in his psyche as Hell Week, and it seemed to him that from start to finish, each day during that seven-day period was worse than the day before. On Tuesday, he found out that his wife was dead, and that a chronic drunk driver who had been picked up for DUI more times than anyone could remember had killed her but had himself escaped serious injury. Junior Rennert had been in the final hour of an epic two-day drinking binge and was heading home to sleep it off when he hit Andy. He was now residing in jail with superficial head injuries, a scraped elbow, and a broken toe, and had Covey not been present to hold him back, with a little help from the rest of the band, Blanchard would have gone on down to the jail and taken from him that which Junior had taken from Andy.

"Let me up, Covey. I've got something I need to go see about," Blanchard had said. He was dead serious and quite motivated, and it was all Covey could do to restrain him.

"Not going to do it," Covey replied through gritted teeth. He was holding Blanchard from behind, pinning his arms to his sides, and Ford Man Cooper had his legs. With the exception of Chicken Raines, the rest of the boys stood helpless, wishing there was something they could do, and waiting to enter the fray if called upon. Chicken was out in the yard liberating the distributor cap from Blanchard's truck and relocating it to a safer locale, at least for the next day or two. "I'll grant you, Junior Rennert has needed killing his whole life," Covey said. "His mama should have done us all a favor and fed him to the hogs the day he was born. But right now you've got to let this go. You've got arrangements to make, and a wife to bury."

"I'll kill him."

"He'll keep. He'll still need it after this is all over. You can kill him anytime." Tucker McFry and Simpson Taggart nodded at this wisdom. "Right now you've got to see about Andy." Blanchard struggled a while longer, but he finally relented. Covey was right. He could dispense rough justice to Junior Rennert any time, and he knew that Andy would disapprove of drastic action on his part at this particular moment. It wouldn't be dignified, and she would hate it.

On Wednesday, Blanchard discovered that due to the extent of the injuries she had suffered during the accident, Andy would have to be kept in a closed casket, and that he would not have the opportunity to look upon her one last time and tell her goodbye. After receiving this news, Blanchard had insisted that he wanted to see her regardless of trauma, but the funeral director, Genuine Owen, had taken him aside and, as diplomatically as possible, explained that much of what was in that box over there was not even identifiable as having once been human, and that what was in there was in several pieces and no longer even slightly resembled the woman Blanchard had married, and that no good whatsoever could come of looking at her in that condition.

"She was my wife," Blanchard said.

"I know she was," Genuine replied. "And I know you want to say goodbye. But you know how women are. She wouldn't want you to see her like that. Remember her like she was. Think of her on your wedding day, or the day you first met her. Those are the memories you want to keep. If you look at her now, it will trouble you from now until Jesus comes again. Please trust me on this. I know what I'm talking about."

Blanchard had surrendered then, but the thought of Andy spending eternity mutilated and alone, nestled in silk inside her understated blue casket, haunted him, and he knew that it would do so for the rest of his days. She had loved the light, and she had been more than a bit claustrophobic, and now she was lost in the darkness that did not end.

On Thursday, word filtered to Blanchard that Junior Rennert, the man who had killed his wife, was a free man. Through an astonishing combination of clerical error, incompetence, and just plain bad luck, he had been accidentally released from the county jail. The blunder was discovered within the hour, and at least one head had already rolled in consequence with perhaps more to come, but Junior, who had claimed at the advice of assigned counsel that he did not remember the accident at all, apparently did remember that there was someplace else he needed to be. He quickly took the unexpected opportunity to put the wind at his back and went there and laid low, and all efforts to re-apprehend him had so far proven fruitless.

"You should have let me go kill him when I knew where he was," Blanchard said to Covey when he heard the news, his voice as cold as an iron rail on a winter's day. "It wouldn't have been hard, and he wouldn't be running around right now, probably drunk as a skunk, looking for someone else's wife to run over."

"Maybe I should have just let you go," Covey agreed. "But I didn't, and that's on me. I'm sorry, but what's done is done. He'll get his eventually. You'll see."

"I'm not George Harrison," Blanchard said. "I don't believe in karma the way he does. The world won't somehow make Junior pay for his crimes. As far as Junior Rennert is concerned, I am his karma. The next time I see him is the day he dies."

"I don't think anyone will be seeing him for a while. He's long gone. He's found himself a hidey-hole somewhere, and he's dug in deep."

"He'll come up. He'll get thirsty and come up for a drink. When he does, I'll be standing there waiting for him."

In spite of himself, Covey shivered.

On Friday, the day of the funeral, it rained. When the day began, the skies had been as blue as a robin's egg and the breeze as gentle as a baby's sigh, and it looked like it might be a pretty day for Andy to walk that last mile. But throughout the morning, the clouds gathered and darkened, as if the universe itself were in a mood over this latest in a long series of unhappy developments, and by two o'clock, it looked like the last judgment was about to begin. The skies were as black as anthracite coal, and the wind blew hard, cold rain.

Sheet lightning danced on the horizon, and thunder rumbled ominously. Blanchard had wanted to bury Andy up on the mountain in the burial plot he had constructed for Major. He had taken her to the spot by the canyon once, and she had fallen in love with the wind whispering through the tall, straight pines and with the wispy clouds drifting out over the rocky gorge. But Andy's mama wanted her in South Pittsburg with the rest of her people, close to home where she could be tended to, and Hazy had asked Blanchard, man to man as a personal favor, if he would send Andy back to Tennessee for her final rest.

"She was our pride," Hazy said in a thick voice. There was a tear on each cheek. "And my wife's taking this all real hard. Me, too. You're her husband, and it's your right to put her where you want her, but will you bring Andy home, so her mama can look after her? You know, to keep the weeds pulled and bring her flowers and such?"

Blanchard hesitated at first because he didn't want to be separated from Andy, and South Pittsburg was over fifty miles from Sequoyah as the crow flew, and a lot farther than that by road. But then he had the dual epiphany that it didn't really matter where she went down, because the physical part of her was already gone from him. And by the same token, it didn't matter where she was committed because in his heart she would always be with him, no matter where he might be, right there by his side where she belonged. So Blanchard nodded his head, and arrangements were made to inter Andy in the family plot at Rocky Bottom Baptist Church, where all manner of deceased Hazeltines and various branch kin waited patiently for her to join them under the oaks and under the stars.

On Friday afternoon at two o'clock, the procession slowly made its way from the sanctuary to Andy's final home, one hundred yards distant and a million miles away. As the casket left the church—borne by Jimbo Tant, Ford Man Cooper, Tucker McFry, Simpson Taggart, Chicken Raines, and a random Hazeltine cousin that no one knew— the sky opened, and for the next hour, it seemed that all the water contained in the wide space between heaven and earth fell upon the funeral of Andy Shankles.

"Go ahead," Blanchard said, glaring at the sky. "We didn't want a pretty day, anyway, so bring it. Just pile it on." He and Covey walked at the front of the procession, leading the casket and the mourners to the sad hole in the Tennessee ground. Blanchard continued to berate the Almighty, but these comments directed at the architect of all that is and all that will ever be were heard only by Covey and by the front two pallbearers, Ford Man Cooper and the random Hazeltine cousin, who for the most part absorbed them in silence, although the random Hazeltine cousin visibly flinched at each fresh lightning bolt, lest the next one be directed at him. This rough talk focused at the creator of the universe was hard on Ford Man as well, but he took it in stride as best he could while trying not to drop Andy in the rain. Every time Blanchard railed at that which none living could control, Ford Man whispered a quiet prayer of intercession in which he explained that his lead guitar player was, understandably, just a little bit upset, and that he didn't mean a word of it, so please forgive him, and put a measure of peace on his heart.

On Saturday, the morning after the Psalms were said, the songs were sung, and the flinty, thin Appalachian dirt was tamped over his wife, Blanchard found out that, had things gone otherwise, he would have been a father. It was just after sunrise, and he was sitting on the porch of his house. He was rocking and chain smoking, and taking the occasional sip from the much-diminished quart of Jack Daniels that had kept him company throughout the bleak night, when Doc Miller drove up and parked in front of the house. Doc had been unable to come to the funeral the previous day due to a medical emergency involving an unwary stockman, an angry bull, and a barbed wire fence strung one strand too high for easy escape, so he had come by this morning to see Blanchard and pay his respects. He exited his car and came up on the porch. Blanchard gestured to the empty rocker next to his, and Doc took a seat.

"You're up early, Doc."

"When you doctor for a living, if you're not an early riser when you start out, you get into the habit pretty quick. It seems like folks tend to get sick early in the day or late at night." He had started rocking when he sat and picked up Blanchard's rhythm, so they rocked in unison. "You're up early too."

"I've always been an early riser," Blanchard conceded. "Maybe I'd make a good doctor. But this morning, it's more like I'm a night owl.

Never could get to sleep last night. Sat right here for most of it. Everything just kept going round and round in my head."

Doc nodded. "You have that all-nighter look about you. How are you holding up?"

"Been better." He lit a fresh cigarette from his last, reached for the Jack Daniels, and offered the first sip to Doc, who refused.

"It's a little early for me," Doc said. "It's a little early for you, too."

"It is. But it just seemed like a good day for it."

"You're not going to make that a regular thing, are you?" Doc nodded at the Jack Daniels.

"Are you doctoring on me, Doc?"

"Maybe a little. It's my job."

"Nah. I'm good. Not planning on becoming a drunk."

"I just wanted to come by to tell you how sorry I am about all of this. Andy was a good person, and this old world is a sadder place without her." Doc had said similar words many times over the years, and he had always meant them, and they had always been true.

"Sadder place," Blanchard echoed. He nodded. He was certainly sadder, and it was okay by him if the world joined in his melancholy. There was enough to go around.

"I've seen a lot of good people die during my medical career, and I swear I never can see the rhyme or reason behind any of it. It just happens."

"I know."

"She was so happy the other day when I examined her. And when I gave her the good news, I thought she was going to float right out of the office."

"What good news, Doc?" Blanchard hadn't known that Andy had been to see the doctor. He hoped she hadn't been ill and he hadn't even noticed. It would bother him if that were the case. There was a sustained silence on the porch. Blanchard looked at Doc Miller.

"You don't know, do you?" Doc asked.

"Know what, Doc?"

Doc apparently didn't think it was too early any longer. He reached for the bourbon and took a swallow to fortify himself. Then he handed the bottle back to Blanchard.

"Take another sip. A good one. Then I'll tell you," Doc said.

Blanchard did as he was told. The man was a doctor, after all.

"Okay. What news?"

"On the morning she was killed, Andy came to see me for an examination. She was pregnant." As the realization descended upon Blanchard that he had buried a wife *and* a child the previous day, a two-for-one of the worst sort, a wave of nausea passed over him, and he jumped up and ran out into the yard to vomit. He steadied himself with one hand on the bumper of Doc's car as he retched violently, over and over, until there was nothing left inside but an empty place where a family used to be. Then he stumbled back to the porch and flopped down in the chair next to Doc. He wiped his mouth on his sleeve.

"How far along was she?" He felt lightheaded and heavy at the same time.

"A month or so."

"I was going to be a father," Blanchard said. "A father." He and Andy had talked about having a family. They both wanted children, and Andy had wanted a houseful. Blanchard felt both better and worse after hearing about his wife's impending motherhood: better because Andy had gotten to hear the good news and enjoy the brief moments of happiness it brought her, and worse because his own loss was an order of magnitude greater now that he had been robbed of both a wife and a child.

"Blanchard, I'm sorry I said anything. I thought she had called you from the office. She said she was going to. I thought you knew." He shook his head.

"It's okay, Doc. If you hadn't told me, I guess I wouldn't have ever known." He looked over at his physician and his friend, the man who had tended to him and his, and to almost everyone else he knew, since before he could even remember. "It's a terrible thing to know." He paused, and then continued. "It makes me sad in a way I can't even explain, but it would be worse if I didn't know it. At least now, someone will be here to remember. When I remember him, or her, that makes it real. It would be rotten to be gone before you even got here, to not have a name, or any memories tied to you, and to have no one at all even know you had tried to make the trip." He looked at Doc. "This is mine and only mine."

Doc nodded. He understood.

On Sunday, after the commotion accompanying the death and burial of his family had relegated itself to memory, Blanchard found himself alone, which suited him. He planned to drink himself into profound oblivion as he forgot for just one day the new parameters of his miserable existence. But then Covey dropped by to check on his bereaved lead guitar player, and when he did, he made the decision that it might be in Blanchard's best interest to hang around for a bit. Blanchard had been up for three days, and he was very drunk, extremely sad, and seemed that he might be prone to erratic behavior should the opportunity for such appear. When Covey arrived, he found Blanchard in the last place he would have thought to look, sitting in the floor in Benton's former bedroom, leaned against the wall with his legs splayed before him. Arrayed around him in easy reach was an eclectic collection of objects: Benton Shankles's pistol, a dime bag of dope, a nearly empty fifth of Heaven Hill bourbon, a machete, three open packs of Marlboro 100s and a Zippo lighter, a dog-eared copy of *Tales of Power* by Carlos Castaneda, a bag of pork skins, and a stack of albums that included *Abraxas*, *Band of Gypsys*, *Eat a Peach*, *Led Zeppelin IV*, and *Let It Be*. An impressive pile of cigarette butts littered the floor by Blanchard's right hand.

Sitting between his legs looking straight back at her host was the Nubian princess, her black eyes fixed upon his in all of their silent, malicious glory. Blanchard had replaced the single light bulb in the overhead socket with a black one. There were blackout curtains in the room left over from a time long past when Benton had worked the night shift, and these were pulled, so the room had a dark, eerie glow that Covey found disturbing in the circumstances. The new album by Alice Cooper, *Welcome to My Nightmare*, was playing on the console stereo that Blanchard had apparently pushed in there from the living room. Covey sat down on the floor opposite his friend, and for a while they looked at one another. Then Blanchard spoke.

"Welcome to my nightmare," he said. "I think you're gonna like it."

"Probably not the best album for you to be listening to right now," Covey replied, nodding at the stereo. "Let me put *Abraxas* on. You love to hear Carlos Santana play."

"I do. That man is a living, breathing saint. But today is not about what I love. Today is about what I need. Go upstairs and find *Killer*. I want to hear 'Dead Babies.'"

"You on an Alice Cooper binge?"

"Alice is the man." Blanchard said. Then he cocked his head sideways and chuckled. "That's funny, because Alice is a girl's name."

"I got it."

"So go get *Killer* for me. Next to my album stack is another bottle of booze. I need that too." He fished in one of the cigarette packs and retrieved a smoke. With visible effort, he focused his eyes enough to light it.

"I will if you really want me to. But you don't like that album. And you hate that song."

"I told you. Today is not about what I like. Today is about what I need." Blanchard absentmindedly placed his burning cigarette beside him on the floor, looked confused, and then reached for one of his cigarette packs and slid out another cigarette. He lit it, took an appreciative puff, and then noticed the other one still burning on the floor. He picked it up, looked at both, and then looked at Covey. "I need to cut down," he observed.

"It wouldn't hurt." Covey liberated one of the smokes from Blanchard and took it for his own. "Where's the ashtray?" he asked.

"You're sitting in it. What about *Killer* and my whiskey?"

"Okay. I'll go upstairs in a minute." Covey nodded at the various items arranged around his guitar player and let his gaze linger at last on the blue steel of the .38. "So what's the deal with the pistol?"

"My father left me that, great man that he was, along with his good name and this very, very, very fine house."

"I know whose pistol it is. What I want to know is why is it beside you and not up there in the drawer where it belongs?"

Blanchard looked at Covey, then at the Nubian princess, then left and right over his shoulders, even though there was nothing back there but the wall. Then he placed his hands on the head of the figure, as if he were covering her ears. He gestured with his head for Covey to lean in close.

"I got it out last night when the princess showed up," he whispered. "In case she tries to start something. You know how she gets when there are dead folks around."

Covey looked at Blanchard and nodded slowly as he slid his hand over and gently retrieved the pistol. "I'm here now," he said to Blanchard. "You relax, and I'll keep an eye on her."

"You're not as slick as you think you are. I saw you get my gun. Good thing I still have *this*!" He snatched up the machete, knocking over the princess and nearly gouging out his own eye in the process. He looked at his fallen Nubian nemesis, now horizontal on the floor, staring at his left calf with malevolent intent.

"I was going to ask about that too," Covey said, nodding at the blade. "Why the machete?"

"It's in case the gun misfires," Blanchard whispered. "You can never be too prepared."

"Why don't you let me have it?"

"Don't make me chop your hands off. How are you going to play the bass with no hands?"

It was a good question, and Covey had no answer. "Okay. You keep the machete, and I'll keep both eyes on the princess."

"Don't let your guard down. You have to be careful with her. She's wily. She tried to kill me once. Did you know that?"

"I knew."

"She did kill my old man. Well, I guess you could say she was an…accessory." Blanchard's tongue in its current state had a bit of difficulty with alliteration, and he stumbled before getting the word out. "Course, I'm not judging. She must have thought he needed it. I wasn't there, so I can't say." His eyes wandered for a moment, and then they flickered back into the here and now. He looked at Covey. "What do you suppose her feelings are on the subject of Junior Rennert?" He dropped the machete, then reached down and righted the statuette. She now stared at Covey, and he found that he did not care for the attention.

"Blanchard, let's not worry about all that today. How about I make some coffee while you take a hot shower?"

"Don't want a shower."

"Well, you need one. You smell like you've been drunk for three days."

"I've been drinking for three days. I've only been drunk for two." He waved his arm broadly. "You always exaggerate. Bass players are all alike."

"Sorry. How about that shower and some coffee?"

"Can I have *Killer* and more whiskey after?"

Covey was hoping Blanchard would forget about those two particular items because he needed neither in his present condition, but it seemed that he would not. Good memories were an occupational hazard among guitar players. The upside was that they remembered the intricacies of the songs. The downside was that they remembered everything else.

"Sure. Not a problem."

"Make the coffee first. Then I'll take a shower."

Covey went to the kitchen to percolate the coffee, and he made it extra strong. When he returned after ten minutes or so with a steaming cup for each of them, Blanchard was passed out cold, leaned against the wall with the Nubian princess in the crook of his left arm and the machete gripped tightly in his right hand. He snored loudly, as he was prone to do when he had been drinking. Covey sat in his former spot and slowly sipped and watched. Eventually, both cups were gone, and Blanchard was still asleep, so Covey figured he might be out for a while, and that it would be the best thing for him. He arose, carefully removed the machete from Blanchard's grip, and then took both it and the .38 out to the shed behind the house for safe storage. He took Alice Cooper off the turntable and replaced it with *Eat a Peach*. He cued up side two, "Mountain Jam," and dropped the needle into the groove. He left the actuator up on the stereo so that the long song would play over and over until either Blanchard woke up or until the needle finally just wore itself away. He quietly shifted the detritus from the floor around Blanchard and then gently eased him onto his side with his head resting on a pillow from the closet shelf. Then he left Blanchard to sleep it off, and to perhaps put a little more distance between himself and his unspeakable sorrow.

When Blanchard awoke, it was dark, and for a moment he didn't know where he was. He could hear Duane Allman easing his way through the quiet solo toward the end of "Mountain Jam," and he lay there for a while and listened to the notes as they drifted over him, nudging him back into a world that had become for him a place that was less than it once had been, a cold and empty corridor that he would now walk alone, his footsteps echoing into the night. By the end of the song, his tears flowed freely. Then it became quiet, and in the silence he heard three distinct clicks, and "Mountain Jam" began again. He sat up, fell over, and then sat once more. He tried to stand and found that this was impossible, so he sat where he was and slowly smoked a cigarette to fortify himself. Then he gained his hands and knees and crawled into the hall and down it to the bathroom. The effort made his head pound, and he felt a surge of nausea so intense that it seemed it would carry him away. He made it to the commode and managed to get his head over the lip of the bowl. He held on tightly and vomited until he was dry, and he continued to retch until he thought he might collapse in upon himself. Finally, mercifully, the purge was over, and he slumped in the floor and panted. Then he reached into the shower and turned the handles until the water ran hot. He rolled into the tub. Standing was still out of the question, so he lay there shrouded in steam and misery until the scalding water turned cold.

Later, after he had mostly recovered from his binge and found some dry clothing, four aspirins, and a cold Schlitz Malt Liquor, Blanchard realized he was hungry. He rambled around in the kitchen, but there was no food in the house that caught his interest. It was past midnight but not yet morning, and there were no local eating establishments open. He felt pretty good, all things considered, so he decided to drive to Rome, where there were three or four twenty-four hour eateries to choose from. He walked deliberately to his truck, giving his headache some extra time to get itself under control. Chicken had replaced his distributor cap on the day of Andy's funeral, so the vehicle started right up, and Blanchard began to make his leisurely way toward breakfast.

He listened to the radio as he drove, and between songs the all-night deejay informed him that it was nearly three o'clock a.m., thus

Hell Week had entered its final day. For the first fifteen minutes of his journey, the roads were deserted. He drove with his windows down even though it was a cool night, and the wind blasting in and around him purified him, and prodded him a step closer to whole. Blanchard rounded the last curve at the bottom of Lookout Mountain, and he saw a pair of headlights at the far horizon heading his way. As the twin orbs approached him, they moved from side to side. Blanchard began to slow down. The headlights entered his lane completely and headed straight for him. He braked hard, but he needn't have done so, because the lights left his lane as quickly as they had arrived, crossed the shoulder, and then took flight through the Georgia night sky.

Blanchard arrived at the place where the car had left the road at about the same time that the wayward vehicle ceased tumbling down the long, steep embankment it had chosen to travel. He pulled onto the shoulder and left his truck there with the lights on. He stepped around the vehicle and looked almost straight down thirty or forty feet to the scene of the accident. He slid and scrambled down the bank until he arrived at the spot where the car had come to rest on its top. It was mashed and bent beyond recognition. Only one headlight burned now, shining out past the wreck site into a creek bed at the bottom of the embankment, ten feet beyond. He heard a hissing noise from the remains of the car, and a ticking noise from the heat of the now-inert engine, and the sound of someone coughing. He smelled gasoline, burnt motor oil, and fear.

"Hello!" Blanchard yelled. He heard more coughing. Then he heard a voice.

"Help me!" the voice cried. Blanchard staggered back as if he had been physically attacked. He knew that voice. It was Junior Rennert. A cold rage veiled as an icy calm descended upon him. He stood and looked at the car. There was more coughing. Then Junior Rennert spoke again. "Hello?" he cried. "I need some help! I can't get out. The top's all mashed down, and something's stuck through my leg."

Blanchard's hand shook as he reached in his shirt pocket for a cigarette. He lit up before leaning against a rock. He needed a moment to gather his thoughts, so he smoked and considered. Two big concepts were warring within him, and he had no idea which would emerge victorious. It was as if he were floating above himself, a spectator watching to see which way he would go. On the one hand, there was the innate need for human beings to help other human beings in times of distress. It was true that not all people possessed this trait, but Blanchard did, and the smashed car right in front of him contained someone who could definitely use a little help. But on the other hand, the person before him who so desperately needed that help was Junior Rennert. Junior Fucking Rennert, wife-murderer, baby-killer, drunkard, and fugitive from the law. Blanchard had vowed to kill this man, and he was on record as saying that the next time he saw Junior Rennert would be the day Junior died. So here they were.

"I think I know you," Blanchard said as he smoked. His outward calm fascinated him.

"What?"

"I said I think I know you. You're Junior Rennert."

"That's me. Come on, man. Help me get out of here." Junior's voice cracked. It had a whiney edge to it, and he was slurring his words. Blanchard could hear the panic.

"My name's Blanchard Shankles." He flicked an ash.

"I don't know you, buddy!"

"You met my wife the other day. And my kid."

"What are you talking about?"

"You ran into them last Tuesday, literally, in that blind curve outside of Sequoyah."

There was a long silence from the wreckage as Junior digested this information. Or maybe he had died of his injuries. Blanchard noted with interest that it didn't much matter to him either way. Finally, just as Blanchard was about to conclude that Junior had indeed gone to answer for his many transgressions, he spoke again.

"You got me mixed up with someone else, man. I'm in a real bind here. It hurts so bad!"

"You been drinking tonight, Junior?"

"Nah, man. I don't drink much."

"Let's see," Blanchard said. He stubbed out his cigarette and put the butt in his jeans pocket. He never did that, and he wasn't absolutely certain why he did it now, but he suspected he might soon figure it out. Then he scrambled to the wreck, got down on his belly, and looked in through the shattered glass. It was a moonless night, as dark as the grave down at the bottom of that embankment. Blanchard fetched his Zippo from his pocket, flicked it once, and found himself looking at the battered but recognizable features of Junior Rennert. There was no telling where in the car he had been when he left the road, but now he was mostly compacted into the passenger-side floorboard, except for his right leg, which was impaled by the stick shift, and his left arm, which was mashed into the passenger seat by the collapsed roof. Blanchard also saw several empty beer cans, a couple of wine bottles—one empty, the other full—and a half-gallon of George Dickel lying on its side on the ceiling of the car, which was now the floor. It had drained itself during the devastation, and the odor of bourbon wafted from the wreck.

"Put that out!" Junior screamed. "Don't you smell that gas?"

"I do," Blanchard said. "But I'm pretty sure I can get away if the car catches up."

"What about me?"

"That is the question, isn't it? For a guy who doesn't drink much, there sure is a lot of booze in there."

"That's not mine. It's my brother's."

"If you're going to keep having these bad wrecks, you really need to start wearing a seatbelt."

"Look, man. I'm not who you think I am. Help me! I'm in bad shape in here!"

"You're still in one piece," Blanchard noted. "That's not so bad."

"What are you talking about?" There was an underlayment of dread in Junior's words.

"You're still in one piece. They tell me my wife was in three." Blanchard snapped his lighter shut and rolled to a sitting position, looking downhill at the creek bed. "I don't know that for gospel, you understand, because they wouldn't let me see her after you killed her. They locked her in a box and put her in the ground. My baby was in her belly. He's in the ground now, too."

There was silence from Junior. The car continued to hiss, but more quietly. Blanchard had been in uncharted territory all week, but now he felt as if he had wandered off the edge of the map altogether, into that unmarked section where the monsters dwell. The man who had stolen everything in his life worth having was now completely and utterly under his control. He had the power of life and death over Junior, and he had sworn mortal revenge upon him, but now that he was in a position to deliver upon this oath, he didn't know if he could do it. It was a conundrum, and Blanchard was at a loss. He felt weak, and he wished he had Covey there to talk it over with. Covey always told it straight and would give good advice, but all he had was Junior, and he felt safe in his assumption that Junior Rennert would bring a certain bias to the discussion. Then Junior, who had made one mistake after another in a long and unbroken sequence throughout his entire wasted, sorry life, finally made one too many.

"Oh, Jesus, please forgive me!" he wailed. "Heavenly Father, please wash away my sins and lead me to the paths of righteousness."

Blanchard was surprised at this entreaty. "I wouldn't have taken you for a religious man," he said.

"God has His plan for us all." Junior was crying now, either from the stress of the moment, the gearshift in his leg, or some unknowable combination of both.

"You're drunk, squashed into a car like a sardine in a can, talking to a guy whose wife and baby you just recently killed—a guy who is really thinking hard about killing you, by the way, in case you haven't realized that—and you think you're on some divine plan?"

"Yes! I mean no...."

"Let me tell you what I think. I think I was a happy man, living my life and minding my own affairs, until *your* life with its stupid plan reached over into my life and put me right down here in this ditch with you!" Blanchard's calm was gone now. He panted with emotion.

"Oh, God! I'm so, so sorry! Please give me a chance! Please! Do the right thing!"

While Blanchard took deep breaths and tried to regain his composure, he considered these words carefully. He had always believed in second chances. People were fallible, and needed them. And doing the right thing held a certain moral appeal. But where was the justice for Andy and his baby if he let Junior live? The fact that Junior was drunk, upside down, and trapped in a car in a ditch just a week after killing Blanchard's family meant that he wasn't likely to change his ways. So, if he let Junior live, and the guy inevitably killed some other man's wife and baby, would that be Blanchard's fault because he hadn't stopped the pattern when he could have? Did ultimate responsibility work that way? Finally, after several minutes of consideration, he decided that the questions were just too big for him. He wasn't a learned man, or particularly wise, so, like Junior, he would have to let the Lord sort it all out. He stood and dusted off his jeans. He picked up a grapefruit-sized rock, and with it he broke out the working headlight. Then he dropped the stone and began to make his slow, careful way back up the embankment.

"Good luck with your plan," he said to Junior over his shoulder.

"You can't just leave me here!"

"My plan says it's the only way."

"Oh, God! Please! Do the right thing!"

As Blanchard made his way up the steep embankment, leaving Junior to live or die as per the details of his own personal predestination, he was almost certain that he was, indeed, doing the right thing, and he was willing to live with the bare shadow of a doubt that, just maybe, he was not.

"YOU CAN'T GET THERE FROM HERE"
(Blanchard Shankles/John Covey)

Eye Seven Five is a long flat road
Wetter when it rains, slicker when it's snowed
We can sit in the front or we can sit in the rear
It don't matter though, we can't get there from here

Riding on the bus on a Saturday night
Running awful late so there'll probably be a fight
Might as well relax and maybe have another beer
Wherever we're going, we can't get there from here

We've played in the North and we've played in the South
We've sung till the words just won't come out of our mouth
We've sung when we're sad and we've sung with good cheer
We sing to ourselves when we can't get there from here

Piled up in a rest stop north of Dalton Gee Ay
The bus broke down and we've been here all day
If we don't get it fixed we might be here all year
We'd just go home but we can't get there from here

Life on the road is sometimes rough as a cob
But even so it's better than most any other job
So we take it as it comes and we live without a fear
And make the best of nowhere when we can't get there from here

Eye Seven Five is a long flat road
Wetter when it rains, slicker when it's snowed
We can sit in the front or we can sit in the rear
It don't matter though, we can't get there from here

"Knockin' on Heaven's Door"
Bob Dylan
-Sunday: Last Day-

John Covey sat in Blanchard's favorite chair, rocking slowly as he scratched Scrounge between the ears. It had been a long day, and he was tired. The sun, weary as well, was slipping slowly behind the mountains to the west, relieved to finally have this day over. Soon it would be twilight, and moments after that, darkness would slip in over the valley, soft and quiet like a mother's embrace. To his left on the porch sat Ford Man Cooper, quietly tapping out a drumbeat on the arms of his chair. It sounded to Covey like it might be from "Honky Tonk Women," but he could be wrong about that. Jimbo Tant sat to Covey's right; from time to time, Jimbo sighed. Chicken Raines and Tucker McFry sat on the porch floor, leaned up against the side of the house, quietly watching the sun as it eased out of the day. Simpson had gone inside to put on another pot of coffee. He had been tearful all day, and perhaps he was in there composing himself once again. They could hear him rattling around in the kitchen, talking to himself and slamming cabinet doors.

It had been a sad group that met out at Major's old antique barn that morning. The building was abandoned and had been for years, but no one had come for bargains anyway. All the members of Murphy's Law were there, and their wives, and a few of their grown children. Geneva had come into town for the ceremony, as had Vanny and a few others who made the trip out of respect and comradeship. They waited until nine o'clock to allow enough time for stragglers and local friends, and then they began the slow walk out to the cemetery. It was an unhurried journey led by Covey, who carried in his arms a small box that contained the cremains of Blanchard Shankles, lead guitarist, rowdy boy, and one of a kind. They swapped stories as they walked, and comforted one another with both gentle laughter and silent tears. The sun was high in the sky and the air crisp when, finally, they walked past the cemetery that Blanchard had built in his youth. They stood at the edge of the deepest canyon east of the mountains and west of the sea, and it was there that they set the physical remains of Blanchard adrift to mingle with the hawks and with the stars. The breeze was at their backs, and as Covey upended the box with Blanchard's ashes, the wind took him high and far, two places he had always liked to be.

"Take it slow, and take it easy," Covey said quietly.

"He always liked it here," said Jimbo Tant.

"He's with the Lord now," said Ford Man Cooper.

"I hope," said Chicken Raines.

"There'll not be another one like him," said Tucker McFry.

"I'll miss him," said Simpson Taggart.

The walking double pneumonia hadn't killed Blanchard. Nor had the embolism that was discovered lodged in his pulmonary artery, waiting for its chance to burrow in just a little bit deeper and assassinate its host. It wasn't even the nasty case of MRSA that had set up shop inside his incision—discovered during his blood workup—a fifth column infection intent upon mayhem from within. It seemed that Babydoc Miller had been correct in his assertion that Blanchard was a train wreck just waiting to jump the tracks, but none of the maladies that ought to have done him in did. The pneumonia was beginning to clear itself up with the aid of antibiotics, breathing treatments, and a temporary dearth of Marlboro 100s, the embolism had responded well to medication and was mostly dissolved, and the MRSA was slowly giving up its new home as a result of the gentle attentions of an infectious disease specialist who hated staph with an unholy passion. After two days in the hospital, Blanchard felt better than he had in a year, looked better than he had in two, and there was talk of him going home soon, with permission, no less, if he continued to improve.

On his final day in this world, Blanchard was sitting in his hospital room in yet another uncomfortable recliner. Covey had brought his old Ovation twelve-string from home to help him pass the time, and he was picking out "Going to California" by Led Zeppelin when he missed one note, and then another. He abruptly stopped playing. Covey, who was across the room working a crossword puzzle, spoke quietly to his lifelong friend.

"You're getting sloppy," Covey noted. Then he looked up.

Blanchard was staring at his hands; his right one hung limp over the body of the Ovation and his left one lay on the chair arm. Blanchard slowly turned his head and looked at Covey, and there was anger in his gaze, but not one whit of fear. His eyes cut to the clock on the wall.

"Fuck me," he whispered, and then he died. It was 4:47 on a Wednesday afternoon, just another ordinary day. As his crazy mama, Edna, had once prophesied in a dream, everything that had come before had claimed yet another victim.

Covey had jumped into action at that point, and in a little more than no time at all he had most of the clinical staff on the hospital floor in attendance to his departed guitarist. They beat on Blanchard, and they shocked him, and they stabbed him, and they even talked of cutting him, but in the end they just ceased their efforts and left him be. He was gone, and he apparently liked his new digs just fine. He was Shankles stubborn to the last, and he wasn't coming back.

"ONCE IS ENOUGH"
(John Covey)

You get just one run and that's kind of tough
But if you do it right, once is enough

Started south of nowhere, built yourself a band
Didn't like your cards, so you dealt another hand
Learned to play guitar, taught yourself the songs
Found some boys like you, and brought them all along

You get just one run and that's kind of tough
But if you do it right, once is enough

Drove a million miles, played a thousand bars
Dreamed a million dreams, got a hundred scars
Met a lot of women, loved one or maybe two
Knew a pile of sorrow, but hid the other shoe

You get just one run and that's kind of tough
But if you do it right, once is enough

Never gave up hoping, never walked away
Never gave up saying the words you had to say
Always went the distance, always knew the way
Always did tomorrow what you should have done today

You get just one run and that's kind of tough
But if you do it right, once is enough

Sailing with the hawks out over the pines
Humming all the tunes, singing all the lines
You get just one run and that's kind of tough
But if you do it right, once is enough

You get just one run and that's kind of tough
But if you do it right, once is enough

You get just one run and that's kind of tough
But if you do it right, once is enough

Epilogue

Blanchard Shankles stood on the stage in the largest room he had ever seen, the largest room that ever was, the largest room that ever could be. The back wall was the cloudy, distant horizon, a million light years away, out on the edge of nowhere, out past the beginning of the world. There was a glow there, a blue-white luminescence that he could neither see nor ignore, the soul of forever, the spirit of nothingness. He looked up, and the vast ceiling sparkled with each and every star in the night sky, white, and yellow, and blue, and green, and colors for which there were no names, hues that had never been seen or even imagined that he recognized and knew by heart. It was neither warm nor cold, future nor past, and a gentle breeze that he somehow sensed was the wind of time whispered by, tousling his hair and tickling his whiskers as it made its eternal rounds, blowing from the beginning of everything to the oblivion of the end before pushing on past to an eternity of new beginnings, out where heavens were born and spirits were forged.

He looked down, and there was his old Strat, scraped and dented, yet not, slung just right the way he liked to play it, down low like Jimmy Page played his. It shone like a burning harvest moon, sparkled like a diamond in an ice storm, mirrored like an unseeing white hole in the wispy fabric of the universe. He lit a cigarette and stuck it behind the A string up by the tuning key. Roadies bustled about the stage, tending to this and that, rolling cases, dragging cords, and switching on amps. He looked over his shoulder and saw that he was standing before a solid wall of Marshall amplifiers. He turned and looked up, and no matter how far back he leaned, he could not see the top of the stack. He shifted his head to the left, and then to the right, and the amps stretched for infinity in both directions. He reached into the bag at his feet and pulled out his cord. He plugged one jack into the amps and the other into his guitar. He stuck his hand into his jeans pocket and fished out a pick.

Out past the stage stood Andy, alone among the crowd of wandering souls, looking just as she had the last time he saw her. She held the hands of two small girls who looked a lot like her. She smiled at her husband, then kneeled by the girls and hugged them tight. She whispered to them and pointed at the stage. Then, Blanchard stepped up to the mic and struck a chord. Lightning ripped the firmament, thunder roared like a thousand exploding suns, and the sky burst asunder with eternal fire.

—THE END—

Discography

"19th Nervous Breakdown" (Mick Jagger/ Keith Richards), *Got Live if You Want It!* The Rolling Stones, 1966.

"American Pie" (Don Mclean), *American Pie*, Don McLean, 1971.

"Back Door Man" (Willie Dixon), single, Howlin' Wolf, 1961.

"Badge" (Eric Clapton, George Harrison), *Goodbye*, Cream, 1969.

"Band on the Run" (Paul McCartney), *Band on the Run*, Paul McCartney and Wings, 1973.

"Blackbird" (John Lennon, Paul McCartney), *The Beatles (White Album)*, The Beatles, 1968.

"Black Magic Woman" (Peter Green), *Abraxas*, Santana, 1970.

"Born on the Bayou" (John Fogerty), *Bayou Country*, Creedence Clearwater Revival, 1969.

"Born to Be Wild" (Mars Bonfire), single, Steppenwolf, 1968.

"Born to Run" (Bruce Springsteen), *Born to Run*, Bruce Springsteen and the E Street Band, 1975.

"Brown Eyed Girl" (Van Morrison), single, Van Morrison, 1967.

"Crazy Mama" (J. J. Cale), *Naturally*, J. J. Cale, 1971.

"Danny's Song" (Kenny Loggins), *Sittin' In*, Loggins and Messina, 1971.

"Dead Babies" (Alice Cooper, Glen Buxton, Michael Bruce, Dennis Dunaway, Neil Smith), *Killer*, Alice Cooper, 1971.

"(Don't Fear) The Reaper" (Donald Roeser), *Agents of Fortune*, Blue Öyster Cult, 1976.

"Don't Let the Green Grass Fool You" (Jerry Akines, Victor Drayton, Reginald Turner, Johnnie Bellmon), *Wilson Pickett in Philadelphia*, Wilson Pickett, 1971.

"Do You Believe in Magic" (John Sebastian), *Do You Believe in Magic*, The Lovin' Spoonful, 1965.

"Dream On" (Steven Tyler), *Aerosmith*, Aerosmith, 1973.

"Dust in the Wind" (Kerry Livgren), *Point of Know Return*, Kansas, 1977.

"Easy to Be Hard" (Galt MacDermot, James Rado, Gerome Ragni), *Suitable for Framing*, Three Dog Night, 1969.

"Eli's Coming" (Laura Nyro), *Suitable for Framing*, Three Dog Night, 1969.

"Everything's Coming Our Way" (Carlos Santana), *Santana III*, Santana, 1971.

"Evil Ways" (Clarence "Sonny" Henry), *Santana*, Santana, 1969.

"Frankenstein" (Edgar Winter), *They Only Come Out at Night*, The Edgar Winter Group, 1973.

"Freebird" (Allen Collins/ Ronnie Van Zandt), *(Pronounced 'Lĕh-'nérd 'Skin-'nérd)*, Lynyrd Skynyrd, 1973.

"Free Ride" (Dan Hartman), *They Only Come Out at Night*, The Edgar Winter Group, 1973.

"Going to California" (Jimmy Page, Robert Plant), *Led Zeppelin IV*, Led Zeppelin, 1971.

"Green-eyed Lady" (Jerry Corbetta, J. C. Phillips, Dave Riordan), *Sugarloaf*, Sugarloaf, 1970.

"Hard Luck Woman" (Paul Stanley), *Rock and Roll Over*, Kiss, 1976.

"Have You Ever Seen the Rain?" (John Fogerty), *Pendulum*, Creedence Clearwater Revival, 1971.

"Heartbreaker" (Mark Farner), *On Time*, Grand Funk Railroad, 1969.

"Heart of Glass" (Debby Harry, Chris Stein), *Parallel Lines*, Blondie, 1978.

"Heart of Gold" (Neil Young), *Harvest*, Neil Young, 1972.

"Hey Joe" (Traditional), The Jimi Hendrix Experience, 1966.

"Highway to Hell" (Angus Young, Malcolm Young, Bon Scott), *Highway to Hell*, AC/DC, 1979.

"Honky Tonk Women" (Mick Jagger, Keith Richards), single, The Rolling Stones, 1969.

"Hotel California" (Don Felder, Don Henley, Glenn Frey), *Hotel California*, The Eagles, 1977.

"Hound Dog" (Jerry Leiber, Mike Stoller), *From Memphis to Vegas/From Vegas to Memphis*, Elvis Presley, 1956.

"I Don't Need No Doctor" (Nick Ashford, Valerie Simpson, Jo Armstead), *Performance Rockin' the Fillmore*, Humble Pie, 1971.

"I'm Eighteen" (Alice Cooper, Michael Bruce, Glen Buxton, Dennis Dunaway, Neal Smith), single, Alice Cooper, 1970.

"In-A-Gadda-Da-Vida" (Doug Ingle), *In-A-Gadda-Da-Vida*, Iron Butterfly, 1968.

"Inside Looking Out" (John Lomax, Alan Lomax, Eric Burdon, Chas Chandler), *Grand Funk*, Grand Funk Railroad, 1969.

"Iron Man" (Tony Iommi, Ozzy Osbourne, Geezer Butler, Bill Ward), *Paranoid*, Black Sabbath, 1970.

"Joy to the World" (Hoyt Axton), *Naturally*, Three Dog Night, 1970.

"Knockin' on Heaven's Door" (Bob Dylan), single, Bob Dylan, 1973.

"Light My Fire" (Jim Morrison, Robbie Krieger, John Densmore, Ray Manzarek), *The Doors*, The Doors, 1967.

"Listen to the Music" (Tom Johnston), *Toulouse Street*, The Doobie Brothers, 1972.

"Lola" (Ray Davies), *Lola Versus Powerman and the Moneygoround, Part One*, The Kinks, 1970.

"Long as I Can See the Light" (John Fogerty), *Cosmos Factory*, Creedence Clearwater Revival, 1970.

"Love Her Madly" (Robby Krieger), *L.A. Woman*, The Doors, 1971.

"Lucky Man" (Greg Lake), *Emerson, Lake & Palmer*, Emerson, Lake & Palmer, 1970.

"Lyin' Eyes" (Don Henley, Glenn Frey), *One of These Nights*, The Eagles, 1975.

"Magic Carpet Ride" (Rushton Moreve, John Kay), *The Second*, Steppenwolf, 1968.

"Mississippi Queen" (Leslie West, Corky Laing, Felix Pappalardi, David Rea), *Climbing!* Mountain, 1970.

"Morning Has Broken" (Traditional), *Teaser and the Firecat*, Cat Stevens, 1971.

"Mountain Jam" (The Allman Brothers Band, Donovan), *Eat a Peach*, The Allman Brothers Band, 1972.

"Muskrat Love" (Willis Alan Ramsey), *Hat Trick*, America, 1973.

"Never Been to Spain" (Hoyt Axton), *Harmony*, Three Dog Night, 1971.

"Old Man" (Neil Young), *Harvest*, Neil Young, 1972.

"Our House" (Graham Nash), *Déjà Vu*, Crosby, Stills, Nash, & Young, 1970.

"Proud Mary" (John Fogerty), *Bayou Country*, Creedence Clearwater Revival, 1969.

"Purple Haze" (Jimi Hendrix), single, The Jimi Hendrix Experience, 1967.

"Ramblin' Man" (Dickey Betts), *Brothers and Sisters*, The Allman Brothers Band, 1973.

"Riders on the Storm" (John Densmore, Robby Krieger, Ray Manzarek, Jim Morrison), *L.A. Woman*, The Doors, 1971.

"Samba Pa Ti" (Carlos Santana), *Abraxas*, Santana, 1970.

"Saturday Night Special" (Ed King, Ronnie Van Zant), *Nuthin' Fancy*, Lynyrd Skynyrd, 1975.

"Secret Agent Man" (P. F. Sloan, Steve Barri), single, Johnny Rivers, 1964.

"Smoke on the Water" (Ritchie Blackmore, Ian Gillan, Roger Glover, Jon Lord, Ian Paice), *Machine Head*, Deep Purple, 1972.

"Stairway to Heaven" (Jimmy Page, Robert Plant), *Led Zeppelin IV*, Led Zeppelin, 1971.

"Sweet City Woman" (Rich Dodson), *Against the Grain*, The Stampeders, 1971.

"The Devil Went Down to Georgia" (Charlie Daniels, Tom Crain, "Taz" DiGregorio, Fred Edwards, Charles Hayward, James W. Marshall), *Million Mile Reflections*, The Charlie Daniels Band, 1979.

"The Pusher" (Hoyt Axton), *Steppenwolf*, Steppenwolf, 1968.

"The Weight" (Robbie Robertson), *Music from the Big Pink*, The Band, 1968.

"Third Rate Romance" (Russell Smith), *Stacked Deck*, The Amazing Rhythm Aces, 1975.

"Vehicle" (Jim Peterik), *Vehicle*, The Ides of March, 1970.

"White Room" (Jack Bruce, Pete Brown), *Wheels of Fire*, Cream, 1968.

"Whiter Shade of Pale" (Gary Brooker, Keith Reid, Matthew Fisher), *Procol Harum*, Procol Harum, 1967.

"Young Americans" (David Bowie), *Young Americans*, David Bowie, 1975.

"Your Song" (Elton John, Bernie Taupin), *Your Song*, Elton John, 1970.

The Author

Raymond L. Atkins resides in Rome, Georgia, where he is an instructor of English at Georgia Northwestern Technical College and creative writing instructor at Reinhardt University. He lives on the banks of the Etowah River in an old house with a patient wife and a fat dog. His hobbies include people-watching, reading, and watching movies that have no hope of ever achieving credibility. *Set List* is his sixth book. Learn more about him at www.raymondlatkins.com.